BLINDFOLD
fantasy

A Novel Ménage

By

D.L. Roan

Published by D.L. Roan. First Print edition, June 2014

www.dlroan.com

ISBN-13: 978-1499752366

ISBN-10: 1499752369

Cover Design by D.L. Roan

Interior Book Design by D.L. Roan

Photo contributor Canstock.com

Editing by KMS Freelance Editing Service

DEDICATION

For B. May all your wishes come true.

CONTENTS

CONTENTS CONT...

ACKNOWLEDGMENTS

Immeasurable thanks to my fans. You make every bled word worth it. My street team, Passionistas, I couldn't have done it without your endless support and promotion. My husband, you know you are my rock. Thank you for giving me the opportunity to chase my dreams.

~ ONE ~

Vegas, baby!

"Roxy! I got it!" Jayne's purse strap caught on her front doorknob, almost yanking her flat on her butt in her race to get inside and share the unbelievable news with her best friend. She untangled her arm from the ten pound monstrosity and then dumped her laptop case and her keys on the floor just inside the opened door. "Roxy! You won't believe it!" she shouted as she sprinted towards the kitchen.

The kitchen was empty. Jayne spun on her heels, nearly tripping over the bucket of sudsy water in the middle of the tile floor, the burning scent of bleach assaulting her nose and throat. *Hank.* Apparently Roxy's last date with Hank-the-skank hadn't gone so well. Roxy didn't do tubs of double-fudge brownie ice cream and hours of classic romance movies after a break-up. She bought bleach and rubber gloves and spent the next several days *'cleansing the rat bastard from her life'*. Lately they could have saved doing dishes and just eaten off the floor. *Men are pigs.*

"Roxy!" The closer Jayne got to the stairs the louder the music blared. If you could call what Roxy was listening to *music*. A little of her excitement fizzled as she climbed each step, her hands cupping her ears. Jayne turned down the hall and there was her friend on her hands and knees. Roxy's bare feet were sticking out from the bathroom doorway, her backside swaying from side to side to the rhythm of the song. "I hope to *God* you're scrubbing the floor in there!"

1

"Christ, Jayne! You scared the shit out of me!" Roxy jumped to her feet, pushing a sweaty lock of raven hair behind her ear as she raced to the control panel on the wall and switched off the built-in house speakers. "I thought you said you'd be home late tonight. It's three in the afternoon."

A splash of guilt doused a little of Jayne's excitement when she took in her friend's disheveled and depressed state, but nothing could have stifled the squeal that spilled out like a siren when Jayne opened her mouth to tell her friend the news. "Roxy, I got it! I got the job! They had hundreds of drafts submitted, but the city council chose mine!"

"You got it?" Roxy's mouth dropped open and her eyes widened with a dampened excitement Jayne couldn't quite read. "You really got it?"

Jayne nodded hysterically and handed Roxy the folder containing the details of her new employment contract, the ink on the signature line still fresh. Roxy opened the folder and perused over the first page. Jayne couldn't contain her excitement when she got to the bottom. "Six figures?" Rox asked. "I thought they were subcontracting the firm to handle the build."

"And an apartment downtown next to the building site," Jayne squealed, bouncing on her toes as she pointed to the spot on the contract. "The firm will be underwriting, but the development board wants their own architect on the team. *And*…the project manager picked me! I get complete design control, Rox. I can't believe this is happening!" When the corner of Roxy's mouth curled into a barely-there smile Jayne pulled her into a tight hug, not caring two wits about her sweaty clothes. "Please be happy for me, Rox. I couldn't have done it without your help."

Roxy Stark had been her best friend since the first day of ninth grade when she tripped Keith Farmer on his butt. Roxy was the dark, brooding, misunderstood, punk-rocker new girl who didn't give a hoot about anyone or anything. Everyone saw her coming and stepped out of her way. Jayne was nearly invisible. Invisible to everyone except the hottest guy in school, the one guy she wished on a daily basis couldn't see her.

P-p-plain Jayne Simon. Jayne cringed. After more than ten years she could still hear Keith Farmer's taunting voice inside her head. Yes, she was *that* girl. The gangly, underdeveloped, shy, no sense of style, braces until eleventh grade and spoke with a stutter, girl. Every school year began the same way. The teacher would call her name from the roll sheet and the taunting began. *P-p-p-present! P-p-plain J-J-Jayne Simon is p-p-p-present.* The first day of ninth grade started no differently. When her third period teacher called her name she heard Keith clear his throat for the third time that day.

"Can it, farm boy." Jayne turned just in time to see Roxy kick her leg out and tip Keith's chair the rest of the way over, sending him and his books crashing to the floor. The class erupted into fits of juvenile laughter and cheers, turning on their favorite jock and chanting Roxy's insult. *Farm-boy, farm-boy, farm-boy!* Jayne would never forget the look on Keith's face. Roxy was her new hero. And her new best friend.

Rox was the quintessential lost teenager. Her dad was a no-show and her mom was a drunk. Jayne grew up in sheltered suburbia with manicured lawns, white picket fences and perfect parents who hovered. They were complete opposites, but it worked. Roxy was her sister; her rock.

Jayne's parents had been a little leery of Roxy at first, but it didn't take them long to fall in love with her. She moved in the summer after tenth grade and her mom and dad had all but adopted her by the time she and Rox began their senior year. They would never see either of them graduate. Her parents were both killed in a boating accident while vacationing at their lake house, only weeks before graduation. Jayne's heart still ached each time she thought about that horrible day.

Years had passed, but at times the memories were still raw and fresh. As heartbroken as she had been, she knew Rox was just as devastated. Most people only ever have one family, love them or hate them, but Roxy had lost two. She rarely showed her pain though. In true Roxy fashion, she built another iron wall around her heart and stood fearless against the waves of sorrow and guilt that took years for Jayne to overcome. She was always there when Jayne needed her.

Roxy received an art scholarship to Cornell, which just happened to offer one of the best sustainable architectural design programs in the country. Eighteen and still grieving, they moved from Grand Rapids, Michigan to Ithaca, New York. Her dad would have been disappointed that she hadn't chosen to follow in his footsteps at his alma mater, UM, but she couldn't leave Rox. She wouldn't have survived by herself with Rox three states away.

That was eight years ago. At twenty-six, Jayne was about to face the world one hundred percent alone for the first time in her life and she was scared spitless. She knew it was juvenile, but leaving Roxy behind felt wrong. "Come with me, Rox. I'm sure L.A. has a ton of artistic opportunities. Or even San Francisco. You can open your own gallery."

"Don't be silly, Jayne. I have my own studio here." She watched as Roxy artfully masked her disappointment before she handed the folder back and pulled her into another crushing hug. "I'm so proud of you, though. You deserve this, more than anyone."

"I'm not sure if I can do this on my own, Rox. I've never stopped to think what it would be like to not have you there every day to make me crazy and…and…who else is going to ask me for all the crude details about the shirtless guys on the job site?"

"Oh, I'll still be asking you, Jay. You'll just have to give in to my vulgar tendencies and send me some pictures." Roxy gave her a wink and turned back to the bathroom. "Keep those hot pictures rolling in, babe, and I promise I won't miss you for a single second."

"Liar." *Sass*. Rox always used sass to hide her feelings. "Fine," Jayne shrugged when Rox didn't deny her accusation. Jayne swiped at a stray tear as she leaned against the bathroom doorjamb and watched Rox mop up the last of the water on the floor. "If that's the way you're going to be, I won't send you any pictures. I won't call or even text. Then you'll miss me so much you'll have to move to L.A."

Roxy ignored her stilted attempt at humor, stuffing the rubber gloves and paper towels into a trash bag on the floor. Jayne's chest tightened as she watched her friend snatch up a towel and dry the sink to a polish. "When do you leave?" Rox asked.

"Two weeks from tomorrow." *Two weeks.* That sounded so much more exciting an hour and a half ago when she was finalizing the deal in the comfort of her office. How the heck was she supposed to uproot her entire life, leaving her best friend behind, and be ready for the job of her dreams in *two weeks? In Los Angeles?*

"Good." Roxy gathered up the multitude of cleaning bottles and tossed them below the sink. "That gives us time to celebrate in style."

"Celebrate?" Jayne followed as Roxy raced down the stairs to her bedroom.

"Yeah." Roxy sighed and pulled open her top dresser drawer, picking out a handful of clothes. She tossed them on the bed and turned back to Jayne, pulling her into another hug. "I'm sorry, Jayne. I'm not doing backflips, but I am happy for you. Things will be different, but we'll survive. We always have."

Jayne nodded, fighting back another rush of tears. "I wish I could be as confident as you, Rox. I've always admired you for that."

"Can the tears, Jay." Roxy let her go. "Besides, it's not like we're never going to see each other again. It's a year; two or three at most, right? And for Christ's sake, we're not married or joined at the hip. It's time little Jayne pulls on her big girl panties and leaves the nest. Don't you think?"

"Now you're just being mean." Jayne watched in confusion as Roxy pulled more clothes from her dresser before retrieving a suitcase from her closet.

"Mean is my natural defense mechanism. Now go pack while I make some phone calls."

"Pack? Are you kicking me out tonight?"

Roxy snorted. "No, I'm taking you out to celebrate."

She had to pack for that? "I thought we'd go down to Luna's and grab a martini and a pie." It's what they always did when they had something to celebrate.

"Oh, Jayne, Jayne, Jayne." Roxy cupped her shoulders and steered her to her bedroom. "This is your dream job, babe. This isn't a cheese pizza and vodka moment. This is a Vegas strip and margarita moment. Well, I guess technically you can still have a martini in Vegas, but why not try something new?"

"Vegas? Are you crazy?" She couldn't go to Vegas. "It's Monday, Rox. I have a million things to finalize at the firm. I have to get boxes and hire a moving company and I still have to make a few changes to my final proposal Mr. Kirk's project manager requested. I couldn't poss—"

"So wrap all that up with a nice little bow by Thursday and take Friday off. We'll spend the weekend playing the slots and getting wasted on Tequila and cum."

"Eww!"

"Okay, okay! We'll just play some slots and ogle the pool boys from behind our sunglasses." Jayne cringed as Roxy opened her closet. Lots of secrets were hiding in there. Mainly her sloppy house keeping secrets, but Rox knew all about those.

"Come on, Jayne. You need to live a little before you commit yourself to this new gig. I know you. You'll work sunup to sundown and never once look up from your drafting table until this project is finished. I love that about you, honey, but you're going to wake up at your desk one day with coffee stained teeth from all the late-nights and a Post-it note stuck to your cheek that reads *Do Not Resuscitate*." Roxy patted her cheeks and gave her the signature Roxy pout. "Come on! We haven't had a girl's weekend away in over two years! Not since I opened the gallery."

"Oh, please. Don't remind me." As much as it stung, Roxy was right. Once she sunk her teeth into a project nothing else existed. Sustainable Architecture was her life. She loved that she could take an empty space, a small speck of land on the face of the Earth, and transform it into something that supported the delicate balance between human necessity and natural evolution. The process consumed her every waking thought. "But, Rox. Vegas? It's at least a six hour flight. Wouldn't you rather go back to the beach, or the city? You can get just as drunk there as you can in—"

"Yes, Vegas." Roxie pulled out a black cocktail dress from the back of her closet that hadn't seen the light of day since her sophomore year at Cornell. *Oh no!* "If you don't do it for yourself, then do it for me. For us. It's our last chance for a girl's weekend for awhile. You owe me that much."

She snatched the dress from Roxy's busy hands and tossed it into the bottom of her closet. "That's a cheap shot, Rox. Even from you. Are you seriously going to try to guilt me into this crazy idea?"

"If I have to." Roxy thumbed through the other clothes hanging in her closet and shook her head in disapproval. "And you can add shopping to that to-do list, babe. What *is* this? A *Saved by the Bell* costume rack?" A pile of sweaters fell from the top shelf and fluttered to the floor. Roxy pushed them out of the way and scooped up Jayne's favorite heels. "Honestly, Jayne. You have such great taste in shoes. How can you wear *these*, with *this*?" she asked, holding up one of her no-nonsense power suits next to her favorite strappy platform slingbacks.

"Give me those!" Jayne tossed another handful of her painfully outdated clothes into the closet and slammed the door. Her suits were new-*ish*. Those and her sweatpants were all she wore these days anyways. She didn't need anything else. "Is this about Hank?" *Time for a subject change.* "The moment I walked through the door I knew you'd had another fight. Is he going to Vegas without you and you want to stalk him to see if he's cheating?"

Jayne regretted the words the moment they left her mouth. The look on Roxy's face was nothing less than dejection. "Oh, Rox. I'm sorry. That was unfair."

"No. It wasn't." Roxy walked to the side of Jayne's bed and slumped onto the mattress. "I didn't need to follow him anywhere to know he was cheating. All I had to do was walk into Luna's for lunch to see him dry humping some college bimbo at our table."

"Luna's? That's our place!" *How dare he?* "At our table?" He'd ruined it! They'd never be able to eat at their favorite bistro again. *This!* This was why she didn't date hot guys. They were jerks. It didn't matter that she didn't exactly attract the underwear model types. "What a bucket of slime!"

"Come on, Miss Goodie-Two-Shoes. You can do better than that."

"I'm not a Goodie-Two-Shoes. I have to keep it clean for the office. You know how hard the 'F-word' habit is to break." Roxy rolled her eyes and Jayne laughed. "No, I guess you don't."

"You could at least call him the rat bastard he is," Roxy said with a pout.

"He *is* a rat bastard." Jayne sat on the edge of her bed and threw her arm around her best friend's shoulder. "So what did you do?"

"Let's just say he'll be wearing boxers instead of briefs for a while."

Jayne gasped. "No! You didn't! Did you?"

Roxy sighed and shook her head. "No. He didn't even notice me. Luna did, though. I took the package of fresh sardines she brought out to me and made good use of them. In a couple of days his Mercedes will smell as ripe as that whore's cunt."

Jayne cringed. "Oh, but I do like your evil imagination. Very creative."

"Thank you," Roxy huffed. "At least I have that."

Jayne gave Roxy's shoulders a firm, reassuring squeeze. "I'm so sorry, Rox. I know I didn't give you good odds with him from the get-go, for obvious reasons, but you deserved better than that."

"Sorry enough to let me take you to Vegas for the weekend?"

The million and one things she had to get done before she left for Los Angeles jumped out of their box and started pounding on her skull, reminding her of her lack of time. One look at her friend's fake, bratty pout and Jayne couldn't say no. She knew that look masked a load of hurt and disappointment. "Okay, fine. I'll let you take me to Vegas."

"Yes!" Roxy jumped from the bed and skipped towards the hallway.

"But only to play some slots and relax by the pool! No crazy stuff, Rox. I mean it. I can't get arrested and stuck in some slimy Vegas clink before my first day on the job!"

"Oh, stop with the drama! I wouldn't let you get into that much trouble. Besides, they don't lock you up overnight for misdemeanors. Now, get showered and changed and meet me downstairs in fifteen minutes. I'm taking you shopping for ho-clothes!"

~ TWO ~

"I might need something a little stronger than champagne."

Jayne sat at the end of the crowded bar, a dirty martini in one hand and her cellphone in the other. "Where is she?"

After finalizing her two remaining projects, making not two, but *four* not-so-minor changes to her proposal for the Silverland Industries build and uploading them to her soon-to-be boss' assistant, laying down the ground work to manage moving all of her things *and* shopping with Roxy, Jayne had barely made it home in time to change clothes before they left for the airport. She hadn't slept in the last seventy two hours, except for a couple of cat naps at her office. Her backside was still numb from the six hour flight. And thanks to her two hundred pound suitcase, which was stuffed with more new clothes than she could wear in a year—some so raunchy she wouldn't touch with surgical gloves—she had a huge chip in the fingernail on her middle finger when said suitcase slipped from her hand as she lifted it from the trunk of the smelly cab they'd taken to their hotel.

Roxy took off to God knew where, to do only God knew what the moment they checked in, and now Jayne was sitting alone in a bar with a dozen pairs of eyes staring at her. She'd already refused two offers to buy her another drink and one offer of something she didn't quite understand the meaning of, but was sure was illegal everywhere, even Nevada. Thanks to a threatening nod from the bartender, the grungy looking guy quickly retreated and left through the front door. So far, this was not shaping up to be a very relaxing weekend.

"Sorry about that."

Jayne looked up from her phone to see the bartender's heart-stopping, sex on a stick smile. "What?" A head to toe blush covered her body. "Uh...s-sorry, I was t-texting my friend." Silently cursing her nervous stutter—the other reason she was never seen with men who could melt your panties with their smile—Jayne fumbled with her phone, almost dropping it on the floor before she stuffed it into her purse. *Sexy, Jayne. Real sexy.*

With a lot of concentration and practice, Jayne was able to control, and most of the time, altogether hide her embarrassing stutter. Sexy smiles and flirty men made her nervous. The more nervous she was, the worse her stutter, all equaling one big social fail.

The bartender leaned his elbows onto the bar and winked. "I just wanted to apologize for that guy. I usually catch the pushers before they make it past the door, but it's been a busy afternoon."

"Oh, t-that's okay. Thanks, though." The heat from her blush cranked up a few thousand degrees, her gaze jumping into the deep end of her martini glass before he caught her staring. If she could wish for one thing, aside from a cure for her complete lack of organizational skills, it would be to have Rox's confidence and knack for flirting. Heck, she'd be happy to be able to talk to a gorgeous guy without turning into the Earth's second sun.

She had no problem talking to men at work, no matter how handsome or flirty they were. At work she had the shield of a business suit and professional boundaries which lent her an air of confidence that otherwise deserted her in more casual settings. Outside of work, guys like this throw one look her way and she turned into one big puddle of tongue-tied do-me-goop. Not that they looked very often.

She knew she wasn't mincemeat by any means. She was just...average. She had dirty-blonde hair that held just enough of a wave to be unruly instead of bouncy. Thanks to her braces she had perfect teeth, but her lips weren't pouty. Her nose was straight, but not pert or cute. She didn't have dimples and her eyes were a boring shade of hazel. Hazel; a perfect mixture of brown and green. Yeah, that was just a fancy term for the color of mud. And—*thank you, Grandma Sadie*—her hips would never squeeze into anything smaller than a size seven. Add that to her C-cup and you got average, average and average.

Roxy was the complete antithesis of average. At five-foot-eight with a swimmers body, she was a walking piece of art. Her jet-black hair fell long down her back and she had the most alluring green cat eyes. She and Roxy wore the same bra size, but thanks to Roxy's lean body type you'd never think she wore less than a D-cup. She had no problems slipping her long, toned legs into her size four skinny jeans and she could make a priest beg for mercy with just a flirty wink. Jayne? Not-so-much.

As if her thoughts had conjured her up, Roxy blew through the entrance and strutted her way towards the bar, her five inch heels clicking against the bar's expensive slate floor. Jayne could almost hear the bartender's brain cells screaming for mercy as the blood drained from his skull into his lower extremities.

"Sorry I'm late!" Roxy winked at the bartender as she slipped onto the barstool beside Jayne. "I'll have what she's having." A few second's ticked by before the bartender could process his thoughts and drag himself away to do her bidding. When he turned to grab a bottle from the shelf, Roxy pushed up and leaned over the bar to check out his backside. "Now that's exactly what you need this weekend, Jay. Did you give him your phone number?"

"Roxy!" Jayne nearly choked on her drink, another wave of heat flushing her face when she saw the bartender's lip curl into a knowing grin as he poured the Vodka into a glass. She sat her drink on the bar and scolded her friend in a hushed whisper. "I can't believe you just did that! He heard you!"

"Why not?" Roxy shrugged and handed her a napkin. "When's the last time you got laid, Jayne? And I mean *really* laid. Hard, fast and repeatedly by a man who knows what he's doing."

Jayne wanted to melt into the cracks between the floor tiles when she heard the bartender clear his throat and looked up to see him standing across from them with Roxy's drink in his hand. Thank heavens Roxy didn't follow that question up with an invitation to the obviously amused and interested hunk, taking her drink with another silent wink instead. The smile he gave her was pure sin and temptation. A genuine lust flashed in his eyes before he turned to serve another of the hotel's patrons, sparing a quick glance over his shoulder before he took the other man's order.

"See? He's into you. You should definitely give him your number."

Jayne rolled her eyes. "Don't even try it, Rox. We both know he was looking at you." She wasn't jealous, much. Sure, she could appreciate a hot guy as much as any girl, but if she ever did capture one's full attention she wouldn't know what to do with him. Besides, she wasn't into one night stands. No thanks. She'd take Mr. Nice-N-Steady over Mr. Hot-N-Later any day. Of course, that plan hadn't exactly worked out for her either.

She felt the weight of Roxy's stare and looked up to see her shaking her head. "What?"

"You." Roxy reached out and fingered a strand of her hair. "You still don't see how attractive you are."

"Oh, stop. I'm not—"

"Yes, Jayne, you are, and he was totally checking you out when I got here."

"*Until* you got here. The key word being *until*." She didn't miss the disbelieving look on her friend's face. Or was it hurt? "I didn't say that to be mean, Rox. You're stunning, and men just...gravitate to you. They can't help it. Guys like that weren't meant for a woman like me. And truthfully, after seeing the way most of them treat you, I'm okay with that."

"They're not all bad, Jay. Well, okay. Most of them suck donkey balls, but you're short changing yourself if you think for one second he wouldn't drop his jeans and fuck you right where you stand if you gave him the chance."

This time Jayne did choke on her drink. Vodka burned the lining of her nose and throat. "You know I don't do casual sex, Rox," she said between spurts of coughing and laughter.

"Maybe that's your problem. You're always looking for Mr. Relationship when what you need is Mr. One-Night Rodeo Drive." Roxy held up a staying hand, anticipating Jayne's denial. "I know, you don't do casual sex and one night stands. Just let your hair down for a bit and shop a little, Jayne. That's all I'm saying."

Beyond ready to change the subject, Jayne set her empty martini glass on the bar and looked at her watch. "I barely had enough time to dry my hair when I stepped out of the shower and found your note. You were supposed to be here a half hour ago. Where did you go?" Her internal Roxy alarm went off when she saw the devious look on her friend's face. "What did you do, Rox?"

"Nothing." *Oh, crap.* She knew that guilty look. Roxy was up to something. "I just booked us a few shows and…." Jayne flinched when she whipped out an envelope and shoved it at her.

She opened the envelope and peeked inside, her tense and overworked body nearly melting at the thought of what she saw inside. "A massage!" She had the best friend ever. "A spa day is exactly what I need, Rox. Thank you, thank you, thank you!"

"Congratulations, hon. You deserve it." Roxy smiled. "It's an entire package. The hotel has the most amazing spa. We'll get a massage before dinner, then shower and hit the strip. Tomorrow it's mani's, pedi's, waxing, facials, the works! And they even serve champagne."

"I might need something a little stronger than champagne if we're getting waxed." Jayne shuddered at the thought. "It's been a while since I got my hair cut, too. Maybe I could splurge and visit the salon. I hear they have great stylists in these places."

Roxy fished a pen from her purse and jotted something down on a napkin. She tossed a twenty on top of it and pushed it away before Jayne could see what she wrote. Rox grabbed Jayne's hand and pulled her from her seat. "One step ahead of you, Jay. I booked two appointments at the Cirque de Salon for four o'clock tomorrow."

"Did you sell all your paintings or something?" Something troubling flashed in Roxy's eyes, but was quickly masked by her familiar mischievous expression. Jayne looked back over her shoulder in time to see the bartender scoop up the twenty, a wide smile beaming from his perfectly chiseled face when he saw what was written on the napkin. "Did you just give him my number, Rox?"

She followed Roxy out of the bar, the sounds of slot machines and the smell of tobacco assaulting her senses. "No on both counts, Jay. I have a little saved up for fun and I gave him *my* number."

~ THREE ~

Gigolos and Death by Chocolate.

"What did you just say?" It wasn't that she didn't hear Roxy. The question was more of an instant reflex at the shocking and absurd words that had spilled from her best friend's mouth.

"You heard me," Roxy said as she slipped the last bite of their shared piece of Death by Chocolate cake they'd ordered for dessert and pulled out yet another envelope from her purse.

"No!" Jayne held up her hand and pushed the envelope away. "No way, Rox. That's not going to happen. I'm not…no. Just…no."

Jayne took a nervous sip of her wine then gulped down what was left in the glass as the pieces to her Roxy puzzle fell into place. She knew it. She *knew* Roxy was up to something, but this…this was preposterous. She'd gone too far.

They'd spent the whole day primping. Her entire body had been scrubbed, buffed, waxed and polished. By the time they sat down in the restaurant for dinner she felt like a shiny, new Lexus. Roxy had been relentless. When Jayne asked for a natural nail color, Roxy stepped in and handed the nail technician a blazing shade of red she wouldn't have chosen in a million years. Her girlie parts still tingled every time she crossed her legs, thanks to the *full Brazilian* Roxy had insisted on. She was surprised the pain hadn't lasted beyond lunch. The little bit of irritation was gone, but it was definitely something she wouldn't be repeating in the near future.

Okay, maybe one day. Though next time she'd leave a landing strip. That part hurt like heck!

Instead of her usual bang trim and blow-dry, Roxy had insisted on highlights and an up-do, which she would admit made her neck feel like it was the sexy kind of long and elegant. Especially in the new, black halter dress she was wearing. Roxy had pushed and poked all day until Jayne had no choice but to just shut up and go with it. Now she knew why. Well, it stopped here. She was not going along with this.

"It's your perfect fantasy, Jay. The one you've always talked about. Right down to the very last detail."

"You told them my—?" *Oh.My.God.* "That was p-private, Rox! Something I've never told anyone but you! I c-c-can't believe you would share that with..." She flicked the picture of the...*Oh dear Lord!* She was blushing just looking at the picture of the sun-god Roxy had slipped from the envelope. There was no way she could do *that* with *him*.

"Don't get all worked up. I know exactly what you're thinking, Jayne, but think about this. You'll both be blindfolded. He has no idea what you look like—though looking like you do tonight he'd likely give you a free encore—and he won't be able to see you when you turn ten shades of red. Hopefully, by the time he's done with you, you'll be at least eight shades of—"

"Humiliated," Jayne said, tossing her napkin onto her plate. "I c-can't believe you did this, Roxy. Hiring a male hooker?"

"Escort," Roxy reached out and grabbed her hand as she reached for her purse. "Don't be angry, Jayne. Just hear me out."

Jayne slumped back in her padded seat and hid her face in her hands. She should have never gotten on that plane. She took the provocative business card from her friend and slapped it face down on the table. "You've talked me into a lot of things over the years, Rox, but you're not goading me into this. It's just not me."

"So let it be you. It's only one night. Not even a whole night. Do you have any idea how much they charge?"

"Telling me that is *sooo* not helping you right now. And he's a complete stranger! Who—sleeps—with—women—for—a—living!" Who knew where his...*thing* had been?

Roxy shook her head. "They have certified regular health checks, Jayne. These guys are pros, not street-walking crack whores. Protection is mandatory and none of them have criminal backgrounds. They're students and models and from what I've heard..." Roxy lowered her voice and licked her lips as she leaned closer to Jayne. "They're very skilled at what they do."

Jayne snorted. "Like you have any way of knowing that for a fact." She pointed at the photograph slash calling card. "Do you think *Blake* is even this guy's real name?"

"It doesn't matter what—" Their heated conversation beginning to attract attention, Roxy lowered her voice and leaned over her plate towards Jayne. "Listen, Jayne. I love you. You know that, right?" Jayne nodded, though reluctantly. It was times like these that made her question her own sanity much less her friendship with Roxy.

"Good," Roxy nodded. "Then please believe me when I say you need this. I've watched you turn yourself inside out to get this job. Over the last six months you've barely eaten, you've slept on your sofa at work, *when* you sleep, and you haven't dated anyone since Dale and you—"

"But Dale—"

"Was *boring*! You fell asleep the last time he ate you out!"

"Shhh!" Jayne cringed, heat rising back to her cheeks as the weight of more curious stares crashed over her. "Keep your voice down. I told you it was my fault. I'd been awake for two days straight working on that—!"

"And now you are diving headlong into a new work-induced coma, from which you'll surface in a year or two at least ten years older than you are now if you don't loosen up and let yourself breathe for a change."

"But, what if someone finds out? I can't—"

"No one's going to find out, Jayne. I didn't even give them your real name. Who *does* you in Vegas, *stays* in Vegas."

Uhhh! Roxy could be so infuriating. Jayne flipped the picture over on the linen covered table in front her. Delicious didn't even begin to describe this...*Blake.* She couldn't deny the small hint of curiosity that tickled her insides. *What would it be like to be so daring, for just one night?* Sure, Dale had been nice. And yes, Roxy was right. He'd been snooze-alarm boring. All of her previous boyfriends had been...*nice.* Not one of them had even come close to fulfilling even her most basic fantasies. Not that she had many, but who was counting? Marty had tried a blindfold once, but missionary position was still...well...missionary, even when you couldn't see it.

And none of the guys she'd ever dated looked like this. She ignored the hopeful expression on Roxy's face and picked up the postcard sized photo. This guy probably bled testosterone. Sun-bleached spiky hair, ice-blue eyes and sinfully pouty lips she could almost feel kissing her neck; that spot just below her ear. A slight shudder rolled through her. She crossed and uncrossed her legs, unable to ignore the sweaty tingle that mocked her resolve. She focused on the mural of tattoos that covered his left arm and shoulder, wondering if they were real. She'd never considered tattoos sexy, but if they were wearing blindfolds it wouldn't matter. She ran her fingertip over the picture, wondering what he would feel like beneath her fingertips as she traced all those muscles.

"Admit it. You're thinking about it."

She looked up to see Roxy's all too eager smile. Was she? She shouldn't be, but Roxy was right. She hadn't had sex in over six months. A year if you didn't count Dale sex which, now that she thought about it, she didn't. Who knew when she'd come up for air after she started this next project. The Silverland Industries build was ten times larger than the last project she'd assisted on and she almost never saw the sun during the first six months of that one. A relationship outside of her job would be impossible. A relationship at the office was a big fat *no-no!* She couldn't believe she was actually considering this.

"We'll both be wearing blindfolds? The whole time?" She swallowed hard as she looked at the photo again. "He will never know who I am?"

Roxy squealed and did a little happy dance in her seat before she sobered at Jayne's scolding expression. "His blindfold is in an envelope at the front desk with the keycard to the room. He's been left strict instructions to don the blindfold before he walks through the door."

"Our room? Where will you be?"

Roxy shook her head and raked her finger through the leftover icing on the dessert plate. "I rented you another room, on a completely different floor. You will have him all to yourself."

"You already rented a room?" Was she that predictable?

"Jayne, dear. Believe me. This man, whatever his real name is, wouldn't go to waste. If you didn't grab onto him with both hands and fuck his brains out—"

"Okay! I get the picture."

"So you're going to do him—it?" Roxy ran her tongue over her teeth, her lips pulled into the cockiest of knowing smiles.

"I'm thinking about it." Was she really going to do this? She was never going to have another chance like this. And thanks to all of Roxy's pre-escort primping she would never be this *groomed* again, at least not for a while.

"No! No thinking." Roxy wrote their room number on the check and grabbed Jayne's hand, pulling her to her feet and towards the door before she'd barely had time to grab her purse. "I know you. You'll think your way right out of this. There's no time. The appointment is set for eight o'clock. We have to get you dressed and to the room."

"Dressed? Doesn't that defeat the purpose?" She was *so* going to regret this in the morning.

"Trust me, Jay. A man who knows what he's doing can make you come just by the way he undresses you. You want the whole experience, don't you?"

Oh dear Lord, help me get through this. She was pretty sure that was one prayer that would never quite qualify its way through the pearly gates.

"I can't believe I let you talk me into this." Devin Kirk stood at the bathroom sink swiping away the blood seeping from the fresh nick he'd just given himself shaving. *Damn nightmare is what this is.*

"Why not?" Devin's best friend and soon to be ex-business partner, Blake Travers, laughed from the hallway as he approached the bathroom. "Damn, bro! Warn me next time!"

Devin chuckled after Blake threw his arm over his eyes and pivoted on his heels, sidestepping away from the bathroom door. Blake never could stand the sight of someone else's blood. "Freak."

"You're the one freaking out," Blake shot back from the hallway. "It's just pussy. We both know you know what to do with pussy so stop acting like a damn virgin. You bang the chick hard and leave. It's that simple. I'll meet you at The Palace when I'm done and we'll join a game or something."

Just pussy. Devin shook his head as he stared at his reflection. *There's no such thing.* After ending the latest disaster in a long string of relationship nightmares and closing the biggest deal of his professional life, he was weeks overdue for some real R&R. Vegas was not his idea of fun, but since he had to track down his wayward friend and make sure he was going to hold up his end of the deal he'd just made, he figured he might as well do it in person. Maybe catch a few drinks before he jumped headlong into the fray of another project. He hopped on the company jet in Los Angeles and within no time at all he was in Vegas, knocking on his best friend's door.

He could use a hook-up with a hot chick for the night, but not one who was paying for it. Like any well-adjusted, red-blooded male, he was more than confident in his abilities to please any woman, and had done so on countless occasions. Even in front of an audience. But this? Talk about performance anxiety. How the hell did Blake do it? And when did his friend become so callus about women?

"Tell me why I'm doing this again." Death by acute blood loss averted, Devin tossed the strip of toilet paper into the trash, stole a couple pumps of Blake's cologne and followed him into the kitchen.

"Because you have the planning skills of a dick, that's why." He watched as Blake threw what seemed like random leftovers from his refrigerator into a blender along with a triple shot of Stoli Elit Vodka and then hit the puree button. "If you'd at least called and given me a heads up, I could have made other arrangements. I've got two clients tonight. If we both take one, we can clear my schedule quicker and get on with the weekend."

The blender stopped and Blake grabbed two glasses from the cabinet. Devin hoped to hell Blake didn't expect him to drink that shit. "Why are you doing this, man?" Devin had been at a loss for words when Blake told him about his new 'gig' in Vegas as a professional gigolo. He'd been a player in college, they both were, but hell, that was years ago. He understood Blake's need to put some distance between himself and the shit that went down in LA, but this was so far out there. "You can get all the action you want in California. You're the one with the bottomless trust fund, so I know you don't need the money. I don't get it."

"Are you kidding me?" Blake laughed and handed him a glass of the sludge. He took one whiff and almost puked. "This is the life, bro. The best city in the world; fast cars, faster women. The cards are hot more than they're not. I'm not tied to a desk, or a bed." Blake paused and tilted his head in thought. "Unless you count that one time." His finger tapped his chin then he shook his head. "No. No, that doesn't count. I'll tell you about that one later. Smoking hot piece she was." Blake directed Devin to the bar and he took a seat, setting his untouched glass on the counter. "Anyways, as I was saying. It's high class pussy. You're right, I don't need the money. I love the sex with none of the bullshit. Why would I *not* do this?"

"I don't know." Devin shrugged. He couldn't believe what he was hearing. "Maybe because you're the best damn project manager in the business. I mean, c'mon! An escort? You're pushing north of thirty-something! Don't you want…more?"

"More than this?" Blake shook his head. "You know me, Dev. Commitment gives me heartburn. No one can live with perpetual indigestion."

There was a big difference between heartburn and heartache. He might be able to lie to himself, but Blake wasn't fooling anyone else. "It's been three years, man. You think Daphne would have wanted—."

"Don't," Blake snapped.

"I loved her too, you know."

"Yeah, but you weren't *in* love with her," Blake said, his hand held up to cut him off. "Big difference, so don't go there." It was a completely untrue statement, but Blake's curt warning cut through Devin's tenuous attempt to talk to his friend about what was really going on. "Don't worry. I'll be there to get you through the groundbreaking and get everything moving while you're in Toronto, but I'm not staying. I told you I was out and I meant it."

Devin bit back his need to talk some sense into his friend. He knew better than to push Blake. Having watched him nearly kill himself after his fiancé's funeral, Devin was just glad to see him still breathing after not answering his calls or texts for the last three weeks. There wasn't much else he could do in that moment, but he wasn't done trying. He'd just have to try harder once he got Blake back in L.A. where he belonged. "Alright, fine. Just tell me what I'm supposed to do tonight."

"If you have to ask then maybe I should just cancel."

"Fuck off and give me the details." Devin still couldn't believe he was going to do this. Blake handed him a piece of paper and he skimmed over it. "Simone." *Sexy name.* "Blindfold Fantasy?"

"Yeah," Blake hissed after chugging half of whatever that concoction was he'd made and then wiped his mouth with the back of his hand. "It's simple. The chick doesn't want to know who's fucking her and vice versa. You show up, put on the blindfold, play the ravaging prince who can't get enough of her and leave. A couple of hours, in and out and you're done." *A couple of hours?* That didn't sound so simple.

Ha! "I call bullshit! I know your weaknesses, my friend. You like to watch. That's why I'm getting this gig. You can't get it up if you can't see!"

"Man, shut the hell up." Blake studied the glass in his hand.

Devin wished like hell he and Blake could go back to that place in their lives where everything fit. For a few short years they had everything; the club, jobs they loved and a woman who understood and loved them. One tragic phone call erased it all and royally screwed with his friend's head. He'd been a mess for a while himself, but like everything else in his life he kept his grief under tight control. Having to take over Silverland Industries after his grandfather's passing hadn't leant him much time to grieve, for Daphne or his grandfather.

"That's the nature of the gig, man," Blake said with a heavy sigh. "Just get it done and get out. Oh, and no peeking. I had this one chick that caught me sneaking a peek and made Gavin give her money back. He gets a little testy when his pockets aren't heavy."

"Gavin?"

"Yeah, he coordinates the dates." Devin watched in horror as Blake emptied his glass and slammed it down onto the counter with a loud grunt as he forced the nasty stuff down his throat.

"You mean he's your pimp?" Devin pushed his glass away. *Not going to happen.*

Blake shrugged. "You say pimp, I say we're going to be late. Drink up. We gotta go."

"I'm not drinking that shit. No thanks. And where's the picture of this chick?"

"Suit yourself, but you're going to need something. Enough vitamins in that to jumpstart a horse. *Believe* me. Most of the first timers haven't been laid in years. They're greedy." Blake slid from the barstool and set his glass in the sink before he turned to grab his coat.

"Wait, Blake!" Devin chased him towards his garage. "Where's the damn picture? Don't I even get to see who I'm fucking?"

"No picture, man. It's part of the gig." Blake popped the button on the automatic garage door, hopped into his Cadillac Escalade and closed the door, leaving Devin standing there like the idiot he was.

"You fucker! She's a dog, isn't she?" Devin rounded the front of the SUV and hopped into the passenger seat. "You're taking the hot chick and leaving me with Hooch!"

"She's not a dog. Well, I can't guarantee that, but Gavin knows my type." Casually, Blake backed out of the garage and headed towards the strip. "You don't get photos with blindfold fantasies. It defeats the purpose. She's probably just some arm-candy, trophy wife who needs a little action she can't get from her sugar daddy. It happens all the time. Young chick marries some old geezer for money and then finds creative ways to spend it while he's on his death bed. It's the easiest gig out there. Just go with it."

"So, if it's not a problem then let's switch."

"Can't." Blake popped a breath mint and handed one to Devin. "Charlene's a regular, and a platinum client."

Dammit. "Do I even want to know what a platinum client is?"

Blake laughed as they turned onto the strip. "It means the minute her platinum card number hits Gavin's bank account my pants hit the floor."

Devin swallowed back the knot in his throat that was threatening to cut off his airway as Blake passed the line of waiting taxies and pulled up to the front of a high-class hotel. Where had he lost control of this situation? *In and out.* Piece of cake. He wasn't a virgin. He could do this. Blake grabbed his arm as he was about to slip out of the SUV and slapped a stack of foil packets into his sweaty palm. "Mandatory, my friend. Unless she's giving you head. It's up to her if she wants you to come down her throat."

Devin stared at the condoms in his hand. *What an asshole.* "Nice to know." He stuffed the packets into his pocket and straightened his tie. "Any other parting words of wisdom, *dad?*"

"Nope. Just don't screw this up." Devin slammed the door and began the too-short walk to the hotel lobby. He'd showered no less than an hour and a half ago and he already felt dirty. He was a thirty-one year old C.E.O. for crying out loud, with enough of a life to get his own women. Why the hell did he get the feeling he had just regressed into puberty? *Karma's a bitch, Blake.*

His face felt numb from the adrenaline rushing through his veins as he approached the front desk. It was an absurd reaction. He'd checked into and out of hundreds of hotels.

"Can I help you?"

Devin stepped up to the receptionist. "Yes. You should have an envelope for me. Devin—" He coughed into his hand at the slip-up. "Blake. Blake Travers." *Dammit!* He was never going to pull this off.

The woman sifted through a stack of envelopes and pulled one free. "Yes. Here you are, sir. Anything else I may help you with?"

Devin gave her what he knew was a nervous smile and shook his head, turning to the bank of elevators. One potential catastrophe averted. *On to the next.* Inside the envelope was a large, black blindfold and a keycard with a sticky note attached advising him to go to room four-forty-eight. He pushed his way into the crowded elevator, feeling the desperate need to shed his coat and tie as he waited through two stops before he was expelled onto the fourth floor.

Christ, he was going to pass out. He stopped in the hallway and removed his coat, giving his tie a quick yank to ease the increasing pressure on his windpipe. *Breathe dammit!* The closer he got to the room the faster his pulse galloped. This was a nightmare. He paused at the door, blindfold in hand. What was on the other side of that door? Was he about to be assaulted by some sex-deprived cougar? Normally he might find that idea entertaining. He was being ridiculous. He was a fucking guy! He loved sex; hot, sweaty sex with lots of beautiful women. Hell, between he and Blake they'd probably fucked half the State of California, sometimes at the same time, with the same woman...who he could see! *Okay. Just breathe, man. You can do this.* This was no different than picking up a chick in a bar. He'd done that, plenty of times. Maybe not recently, but he still knew how to handle himself.

He looked at the blindfold. He wasn't a hardcore voyeur, but didn't women know men were visual creatures? He'd just have to wing it. He conjured up an image of his last girlfriend. *Not helping.* Rachel, maybe? No, Rachel was a pompous, power hungry, razor-wired bitch. *Stephanie.* Yeah, Stephanie. She was hot. A total control freak, but she was hot as fire between the sheets. He felt his dick twitch as a few of his favorite memories of Steph played through his mind. He could do this. As long as he didn't call out Stephanie's name when he came he'd be fine. *Simone. Simone. Sexy Simone.*

He pulled the blindfold over his eyes and tightened the strap, folding his coat over his arm before he knocked on the door. *Fuck you, Blake! Simone, Simone, Simone. Her name is Simone.*

~ FOUR ~

"Feel what she's feeling. Live in that moment with me."

Jayne jumped from the bed and checked her lipstick for the fifteenth time in the vanity above the dresser. She scolded herself each time that it didn't matter. If this Blake guy played by the rules and she didn't end up dead in a back-alley dumpster somewhere off the main strip, no one was even going to see her lipstick.

She looked at the clock on the bedside table. *Five minutes.* Her heart pounded against her chest, the black and white pinstriped corset Roxy had stuffed her into making it impossible to get the extra needed air into her lungs that her nerves demanded. *Roxy calls this letting myself breathe?* She was going to suffocate to death before this guy had the chance to lay a hand on her. And if she didn't, she was going to kill Roxy when this was over. Then she was going to dress *her* in this get-up for her viewing and bury her with the suitcase full of all the other raunchy lingerie she'd made her buy. She looked into the mirror one last time, tugging at the top of the corset to give everything one final adjustment. She had to admit, this thing made her boobs look enormous.

Spur of the moment my ass. Roxy had this whole thing planned from the moment she'd said the word *Vegas*. Another minute ticked by. Jayne pulled the blindfold over her eyes and tightened the strap. This was so much scarier than she ever imagined it would be. Fantasies were meant to help you survive reality. What happens when fantasy becomes reality? *You freak the hell out, that's what happens! Breathe.*

Daydreaming about it and doing it were two completely different things. That's why they called them fantasies. They weren't meant to become reality. She had been riding the *what-if* bus for the last hour, her overactive imagination sending her into a near panic with all of the disastrous possible outcomes. Not one involved multiple orgasms and a happy ending.

Deciding she'd better sit down before she passed out, she felt her way to the foot of the bed and sunk carefully onto the mattress. Her vision impaired, the heavy silence began to crush her. *It's too quiet.* She ripped off the mask and rushed over to the cabinet that held the television and flipped it on. *Music! Something with music!* Unfamiliar with the channels, she ran back to the bedside table and scooped up the laminated guide, frantically skimming the numbers for something—anything—that would break the silence. She pointed the remote and punched in a number for one of the music stations and jumped when the wailing sound of an electric guitar blasted through the speakers.

"Fudge!" Her clammy fingers shook as she scrolled through. He would be there any minute! Finally, a soft Jazz tune played through the speakers. Jayne tossed the remote in the general vicinity of the bed and closed the curio doors to block out the light from the video playing on the screen. Not that it would matter since they were both going to be wearing blindfolds.

"The blindfold!" She dove for the floor where she'd dropped her blindfold and picked it up, yanking it back over her eyes. She smoothed the hair away from her face and felt her way to the foot of the bed again, her lungs working double time to breathe. The moment the frilly comforter tickled her bare backside she heard the knock on the door and she bolted from the mattress.

"Hello? Simone?" Jayne fought the overwhelming urge to rip off the blindfold. She'd apologize profusely, and then run straight to the airport. "Anyone here?" She startled at the closeness of his voice, a squeak of panic escaping her throat. "Oh good, I thought maybe they gave me the wrong key. Are you Simone?"

She couldn't believe Roxy had used that name. It was a play on her otherwise—you guessed it—average last name, Simon. The sounds of rustling fabric drew her attention back to the stranger in the room. He was closer now; the masculine, clean scent of his cologne tickling her nose.

"Simone?"

"Y-yes," her voice quaked. *Don't stutter!* "I'm right here." She stretched out her arms, her trembling hands seeking him out. She sucked in a breath when their fingers met and tangled together. A wave of heat rolled over her when he stepped closer, his minty breath mingling with hers.

"Uh, hi. I'm Blake." She could hear the smile in his tone. Her hands moved straight to his face, her fingers searching for the blindfold. He was tall, something she hadn't been able to tell from the photograph. When her fingertips found the silken edge of the mask, relief rushed through her veins. This was real. "You're wearing the b-blindfold." Her teeth clenched in frustration. She would have to concentrate harder to keep her stutter under control.

He nodded. Her fingers played over the dimples in his cheeks and she felt when the corners of his mouth drew up into a grin. "It's, uh, what you wanted. Right?"

Her breath lodged in her throat when his big hands skimmed up her sides, the warmth they held bleeding through the thin material of the tight fitting corset. "Yes, I…" *Oh, God.* Jayne took a step back when his arms constricted around her and tried to pull her closer. This was going way too fast. "I-I-I'm sorry. I…this…"

He let her go, his hands dropping away from her back. She flinched again when his fingers skimmed down her arms and laced with hers. It wasn't a sensual caress. He brought their hands to rest on his chest between them. "Are you nervous?"

Jayne nodded, forgetting for a moment that he couldn't see her. "Yes," she whispered, unable to control the trembling in her voice. "I have to be honest. This wasn't my idea. My friend…she…I've never d-done this before and…well…"

She could feel his relief roll through his tense muscles beneath her palms. His posture relaxed, his breathing steadied. Was it possible that he was nervous, too? Or was he disappointed? "It's okay. Don't be nervous." He placed her hands on his shoulders. "We don't have to do anything until you're ready."

She nodded again. Having to say everything out loud was something she had never considered in any of her daydream versions of this fantasy. Contrary to what most people probably thought, she didn't think with a stutter. "Okay," she whispered past the lump of anxiety in her throat.

He moved her hands from his shoulders back to his face. "Let's get to know each other a bit. Are you okay with that?" She remembered to answer *yes* this time, her fingers nervously twitching against his hair line. "Just feel me," he whispered.

When his hands left her wrists she allowed her fingers to roam his face. His hair was so soft, not at all how she had imagined it would feel. It was spiky in the picture, as if he'd used an entire line of hair care products to get it to keep its style. These slick strands were longer and slid through her fingers like silk. She could feel the muscles in her stomach release a little of their tension as she skimmed over the blindfold and found his nose. Gently, she traced its rigid length until her fingers floated over the tip and landed against his soft lips. He smiled, his lips stretching beneath her fingertips and she couldn't help but smile with him, a small giggle bubbling up through the slowly ebbing nervousness.

The hot, wet tip of his tongue danced lightly against the tips of her fingers and she startled, drawing her hands back with a gasp. He chuckled and the sound vibrated against her breasts, sending a tingling ache through her sensitive nipples. When had she gotten so close to him?

"Sorry, I couldn't help myself." He clasped her hands and pulled them back to his lips. "I'll behave. I promise."

This is torture. Devin was dying by degrees. He wanted to touch her so badly. This was not playing out at all like he'd imagined it. She wasn't some spoiled debutant looking for a quick fuck. She was scared to death. Every ounce of nervous energy left his body at the sound of her trembling voice when she spoke. Her panic was profound. It engulfed his senses and filled the room. He wanted to rip off the blindfold and call off the whole thing, but that would probably get Blake fired. *Not a completely bad idea.* He didn't know what to do next. Letting her touch him seemed like the next logical step, but now he was in his own personal hell as her fingers roamed timidly over his body.

He wasn't sure if it was the effects of the blindfold or the unexpected intimacy of the situation, but his skin was remarkably sensitive to her touch. Everywhere her fingers stroked they left a tingling trail that mapped straight to his groin. He listened to her rapid breaths as they slowed to a normal rhythm, her hands a little more bold as they traced the column of his neck. Natural, lusty impulses fought for command of his body, but he quickly reined them in. His fingers curled into fists at his sides to keep from reaching out and crushing her to him.

"I want to touch you. Is that okay?" Several heartbeats ticked by. Her dancing fingers stilled against his neck. When a whispered '*yes*' floated to his ears, he had to force himself to go slow. She flinched a little when the backs of his curled fingers caressed her cheek. A small whimper trembled in her chest sending a sharp flash of need through his. What was it about that sound that set him off?

Her skin was warm against his hand as he cupped her petite, feminine jaw. He could feel the heat of her blush and he wanted to see it! The ends of her bangs tickled his fingers and he let the fingers of his other hand travel the edge of her hairline. A shudder wracked her body when he traced the shell of her ears and cupped her slender neck, finally threading his fingers into the thick hair at the nape of her neck. He wondered what color her hair would be. A soft blonde or maybe brunette. He wanted more than anything to see it with his own eyes, feel the weight of it in his hands. When his fingers found the clip that held it up, he carefully pinched the clasp, a silken wave spilling over his hands onto her shoulders. *Damn this blindfold!*

Her hands stilled against his chest and he felt her tense beneath his touch. "Just breathe," he whispered in her ear, allowing his fingers to trail over the soft skin on her shoulders. Her warm, sweet sigh washed over his neck when she released the breath she'd been holding. Maybe if he gave her something to do it would distract her from her nerves and lessen some of the tension between them. "Can you take off my tie? I'm uh, getting a little hot."

He sensed a slight tremble in her hands as she worked slowly at the knot, the heat inside his shirt climbing by degrees until she finally slid it free from his collar. A spike of adrenaline hit his bloodstream when she proceeded to unbutton his shirt, emboldening him to take the next step. As she worked her way down, he allowed his hands to roam, soaking in the feel of her smooth skin beneath his fingers. In a general way, he knew a woman's skin was much softer than a man's, but he had never noticed how soft until now.

She flinched when his thumbs grazed the outside of her breasts. Regret mixed with understanding once again tempered his need when she took a step back. "This is crazy," she sighed. "I-I-I'm crazy for thinking I could go through with this."

"No, you're not crazy." He cupped her elbows, keeping her at a comfortable distance but not allowing her to back away. "I'm…it's actually relieving to know you're a little nervous, too."

"You're nervous?" Her rigid posture relaxed. "But I thought you did this…this…kind of thing all the time?"

Oh, shit. Way to go, idiot. "I do. I mean, you know," he shrugged. "It's different with everyone. I never know what to expect." *That's good. Go with that. Note to self: punch Blake straight in the throat at the first available opportunity.* His problems with this set-up went beyond his control issues. This kind of deceit was way outside his comfort zone. He was just about to back out of the entire deal and come clean when the sound of the most innocent giggle he'd ever heard flittered through the nervous energy between them.

"I-I never thought about it that way." She relaxed into his embrace and he knew he needed a little more of her. She was different. He sensed an authenticity in her. Something the high-class, high-maintenance, over-confident and sometimes evil women he was accustomed to dating seemed to lack. He had no idea what she looked like or who she was, but there was something infinitely more real and fragile about her; something special he wanted more of.

Taking advantage of the moment, he captured her hand and placed it on his shoulder. "Your music choice is inspiring." Pulling her into his arms, he slipped one arm around her curvy, delicate waist and held her right hand against his chest as he began a gentle sway to the smooth sounds of a mellow saxophone playing from somewhere across the room. "Dance with me for a bit. If we're not more comfortable after a song or two we'll call it a night. No harm. No foul."

She stiffened in his arms for a moment before she let out another one of those nervous giggles and relaxed into their easy rhythm. Intoxicating scents swirled around him. Something tropical he couldn't quite identify. It seemed natural to bury his nose in her hair and draw her scent deep inside. "Mmm, you smell like perfection. What perfume do you wear?"

"Hmm," she sighed. "It's probably the combination of the hundred or so products they used at the salon today. I-I-I'm not really sure. I'm not used to having all this stuff in my hair."

"Ah, a spa day." His nostrils flared wide as he took another deep breath and wondered what other parts of her smelled like. Damn! His clothes felt too tight and the room spun around him a little.

"Yeah," she nodded, and the silky strands of her hair caressed his lips, making his dick ache. "All part of my friend's grand scheme apparently."

Languid calm washed over him as she relaxed even further into his embrace, the hypnotic flow of the music dictating a more sensual pace. "The same friend who set this up?"

She nodded again, and he found himself desperate to hear her voice. The distance between them had once again disappeared and he soaked in the feel of her against him. This was crazy. How could something that felt so awkward a few minutes before feel so good and familiar now? He cleared the knot of need from his throat. Now on a clear mission of their own, his fingers traced the intricately woven satin ties at the back of her corset. With noticeable effort, he reined in the urge to untie them. "Interesting friend you have."

Her breath puffed out in a huff. "Roxy is…well, her heart is in the right place. I tend to lose track of life when I start a new project at work and she was trying to help."

"Hmm, sounds like you love what you do." He could relate. The sights and sounds of hammers swinging, saws cutting, welders arcing, big trucks and monster machines all working together at his command to build the impossible once consumed him. It was what gave him life. The day-to-day, never ending, behind-the-scenes deal brokering with politicians and lawyers was slowly sucking that life out of him now. He hadn't been on an actual job site since his grandfather passed away six months ago. Add in the impossible women his mother continually force-fed him and he was lucky he could breathe at all. Women who thought, since he was now the CEO of Silverland Industries, he should only make sporadic cameo appearances at the office and spend the rest of his life carrying their purse while they shopped in Greece, with his wallet. Hell, he'd sent his wallet in lieu of going himself a few times and they never even noticed.

Those women didn't understand that he had to prove himself to the board. He had employees who worked hard for his grandfather, but owed him nothing. Shareholders who feared a takeover bid, watching and waiting for him to make one misstep. There was no room for error in judgment or he could lose what his grandfather had spent his lifetime building.

He couldn't fault his mother too much for his lackluster personal life, however, considering his own treacherous choices in women lately. Danielle DeVeaux hadn't been after his wallet. If only. She wanted his whole company. Or at least her father did. She was willing to do whatever it took to please dear old dad, even if it meant going to jail. Shock didn't even come close to describing his reaction when he caught her sending Jack DeVeaux, of DeVeaux Holdings and Development, investment details about Silverland Industries' *supposed* secret talks with the City of Los Angeles to build the first—and only—one hundred percent enviro-friendly skyscraper. He still didn't know how she got her hands on the sensitive documents. Either he had an industrial spy on the inside, or she'd knocked him out and found his encryption passwords.

He should have known better than to mix business with pleasure, but he'd never considered DeVeaux to be an enemy. Their companies had worked so well together in the past. The old man had been good friends with his grandfather. Devin was still a little dazed by the entire fiasco. He wasn't green when it came to business. His grandfather had taught him a lot, but apparently he still had a lot to learn about the darker, cut-throat side of corporate competition. One more thing he hated about his new position. Why couldn't he just build things? Of course he couldn't tell this woman about any of that. Tonight he was Blake, and he was beginning to hate that name.

"What do you do that consumes you so completely that your friend felt the need to take such drastic measures?"

She hesitated for a heartbeat before she spoke. "I'm an architect."

His next step faltered and he scrambled not to step on her toes. "I'm in construction…or I was. I mean…my family is." *Dammit!* The words were out before he could stop them!

"Really? Then why do you do…*this*? I mean, not that I'm judging, but…"

Think! Think! Think! "I like working with my hands." *Oh, for Christ's sake!* Could he get any cheesier? Her adorable giggle trailed off when he let his fingers drift over her shoulders, feeling her slight shiver when he paused to caress the inside of her elbows. Desperate to change the subject, he laced his fingers with hers and gave her palms a tender caress with his thumbs. "Feeling more comfortable yet?"

"Hmmm, a little." He could hear the smile in her tone, but he could also still sense a healthy amount of dread. This was supposed to be a fantasy, not a nightmare. How could he make this good for both of them? He could almost see her spread out beneath him. That's when it hit him. The imagination was a wonderful thing.

"I have an idea. Wait right here."

"Where are you going?"

"Not far," Devin said as he felt his way to the nearest wall. "Don't worry. I'm not peeking." He bit his lip, holding back a curse when his knee found the corner of what must have been a coffee table. "Although, this would be a lot easier if I could get an idea what the room looks like."

"I…I guess…"

"Ah! No need. Just stay put for two more seconds." He felt his way to the other end of the wall, pushing a chair out of the way, until he reached the edge of the curtain and pushed it open. His fingers played over the glass until he found the edge of the window. As he suspected, it spanned the length of the wall as most Vegas hotel room windows did to promote a view of the strip. Perfect for what he had in mind. Hopefully it wouldn't backfire on him.

"Still there?"

"Yes."

"Talk to me. Tell me something else about yourself."

"I…I'm not sure what to say."

He chuckled as he tapped his toe in front of him to make sure he wouldn't trip on anything as he made his way back. "Do you like to be teased?"

"I…well, it rarely happens so I-I-I…I don't know."

She was tensing up again. He'd picked up on her little tell; the way she stuttered when she was nervous. He honed in to her voice, stepping close beside her before he whispered in her ear. "Found you." She startled and another of her sexy whimpers escaped. "This is a fantasy, Simone. It's supposed to feel good. Relax and let me guide you through it."

"O-okay." She relaxed into his arms and he guided her towards the window, counting his own steps back. When he felt the cold pane of glass against his outstretched fingertips he stopped, positioning her to face the window but not close enough for her to know it was there.

"Give me your hands." An erotic euphoria bloomed around them as he stood behind her and covered the backs of her hands, entwining his fingers with hers. He moved her palms over her flesh, slowly seducing her skin with her own touch as he pressed his lips to her ear and began to weave her fantasy around them. "Did you ever play pretend as a kid?" He felt her jerky confirmation against his lips. "Pretend we're looking out a large window at the bright Vegas lights shining against the darkest of night skies. Tell me what you see." Her hands paused beneath his. "Let me guide your hands," he coaxed her to relax, leading their hands into a slow descent to her thighs. "Use your imagination and focus on the vision. Look out the window and tell me what you see."

"Um, lights. I see lots of lights."

"Is that all?" he asked when she didn't offer more. He placed a whispered kiss below her ear. "You're an architect. Surely you have more creativity and vision than just lights." He grinned against her heated skin, feeling the trails of gooseflesh form beneath his lips. "Focus on the details. Do you see palm trees, a waterfall? Is there another hotel in front of us or are we facing the mountains?"

"Uh, both. I...I see both." Her shoulders raised and lowered on several long breaths before she continued. "There's a large tower of rooms beside us on the right, a-and I can see the bright stream of red tail lights on the strip below. It disappears behind another tall building."

"Very good." Their hands floated over her hips and crossed leisurely over her waist. "Let's focus on the closest hotel. Can you pick out any of the individual rooms against the darkness?"

"Yes, some."

"Some rooms have bright lights on, maybe a television or two flickering in the background? Some are unoccupied, dark and void of life?"

"Like dots on a map," she confirmed. Her head nodded and he took advantage, leaning in to take a taste of the delicate skin on her neck. "Mmm, good. Now find a room with a faint light in the background; a muted bedside lamp, or a candle burning in the distance, maybe." Crossing her arms over her chest he moved her fingers to caress her shoulders. "Do you see such a room?"

"Yes."

Her once nervous tone became breathy and weak. A bit of pride swelled inside him. He still had a bit of mojo left. He'd succeeded in relaxing her at least. Now it was time to see if his gamble would distract her enough to embrace her fantasy, or end their night for good.

"Simone?"

Her body responded to his voice, molding to his frame before she answered. "Yes?"

"Can you see the naked couple in the window?" he asked, trying hard not to let his own need seep into his tone.

Her breath hitched in surprise, a few baited moments ticking by before she answered him. "Yes."

Perfect. She was embracing her fantasy. He blended in a little of his own desires, but they were distracting her enough to enjoy herself. He guided her right hand above her head, placing it on the top of his shoulder. "Leave it there," he commanded. Untangling his fingers from hers, he traced his fingertips along the sensitive underside of her arm, guiding her other hand in a sensual caress over her breasts. "What are they doing, Simone?"

Her entire body melted into his, her chest rapidly rising and falling with her labored breaths. "I…"

"Are they watching us with barely controlled passion, waiting for me to undress you, or are her palms pressed against the glass, holding herself up as he pushes deep inside her? Are they fucking or watching us, Simone? Tell me." Her fingers began moving beneath his; mindlessly caressing the soft swells above the top of her corset. Stretched out against him like a lazy feline, she breathed a long throaty sigh. His hands moved over her body, pulling her tighter against his aching groin. "Hmmm, or are they doing both, Simone? Watching us as they fuck?"

"Oh! Yes," she hissed when he nipped the shell of her ear. "B-both."

"Mmm, is he kissing her neck, like this?" Her head lolled to the side as he placed an open-mouth kiss at the base of her neck, twirling his tongue over the pulsing throb running through her veins. Then another below her ear. "Or caressing her breasts like this?" She whimpered when he covered her breasts with his hands, a husky moan clawing its way past her lips. She grabbed his hand with her free one and made him knead her flesh harder.

"Oh, yeah. I like that." He massaged her heated flesh. Her pebbled nipples pressed against his palms from beneath the thin fabric of her corset, making him crazy to see them, to hold them up and show them off to whoever may be watching.

Sensualism, in its most basic form, was hardwired into Devin's DNA. It encompassed a diverse array of hedonistic pleasures, and exhibitionism was one of those pleasures; one of his most favored pleasures. For as long as he could remember, he'd rarely been more aroused than when he knew someone might be watching him. It didn't have to be in public, or even a semi-public place, like most might assume. Just the perception of being watched was enough to make him hard as a rock. Voyeurism was a big part of it too, he guessed, but that was mainly Blake's gig. He'd gotten off as he watched people fuck in the aquarium at the club a few times, but he wasn't driven by it the way Blake was. When he did indulge in a little kink, he preferred to be inside the action looking out. Even though he was with a virtual stranger, it had been a long time since he'd felt this kind of satisfaction. He didn't know if anyone was watching them now or not. Chances were good that someone was and he'd never been more aroused at the thought of putting on a show with this woman.

"Tell me, Simone." The salty tang of perspiration tantalized his hunger for her as he tickled her shoulder with his tongue. "Do you like what you see?" Devin slid his palms over her ribcage and down her torso. His fingers kneaded the soft flesh on the inside of her thighs as he swallowed a groan. She felt so good in his hands. "Do you like what he's doing to her?"

With another timid moan, her head fell back against his shoulder. "Yes," she whispered. The hand he'd placed on his shoulder slid up his neck, her fingers fisting in his hair, sending a rush of power racing down his spine. "Yes, I like it."

Devin swallowed hard against his need. He couldn't remember the last time he felt this kind of chemistry with a woman. *Yes.* Yes he could. Three years had passed in a blink of an eye. He embraced the welcomed memories. He didn't think he would ever feel this kind of sexual euphoria with another woman. Certainly not with a woman he'd never once laid eyes on. As surprised as he was at her reaction, he was well aware that she could chill to him at any moment and back away from the fantasy they'd created. He hoped like hell she wouldn't. He found her free hand and delicately gripped her wrist, bringing her palm to his lips for a tender kiss before he stretched out her arm and placed her palm against the cool glass in front of them. "Then be that woman, Simone. Feel what she's feeling. Live in that moment with me."

He turned his face and tasted her lips, a barely there whisper of a kiss. He stayed there, frozen in time and place, the sound of his heartbeat pounding in his ears as their hot breaths mingled between them and tickled his lips. This was it. She had to make the next move. He wanted her beyond reason but he didn't want to be her regret. He wanted to give her something magical. Those stolen moments felt like days trickling by before she turned her face away. He'd blown it. Cold disappointment swirled through his veins. He should go. He wanted to see her again, to get to know more about her. But it wasn't like he could say, *'Oh by the way. I'm not really an escort and my name isn't Blake. Can I get your number? We should go out sometime.'*

He reached up to remove his blindfold and suddenly she was there again, the heat of her body chasing away the cold and her sweet tropical smell surrounding him like a dream. When she pushed up on her tiptoes and pressed her lips to his, a vacuum was created in his universe. Everything around him, everything he knew was sucked inside like an imploding star deep in outer space. When the very tip of her hot, silky tongue grazed the corner of his mouth, that star exploded.

Arresting need flashed behind his eyelids as he opened his mouth to hers, their tongues sliding slowly together in that first heated caress, then another. Her whimpered moan was answered with a hungry growl. He turned her in his arms, threading his fingers through her hair, cradling her head in his hands while he plundered her soul. Fucking hell, she tasted so good.

Again and again their tongues collided, each deep stroke leading them closer to some undefined edge of insanity. Their chests heaved together, every frantic breath followed with another until it was all he could do not to pass out. Desperate for more of her, he tore his lips from hers and found the delicate skin on her neck. Drunk on their unexpected passion, her head lolled back into his hands. He cradled her there as he feasted on her body, his tongue dancing over her shoulder and down to the swells of her breasts. *More!* He needed so much more.

The small dips and valleys of her collarbone played beneath his lips. When he reached the hollow at the base of her neck he felt her nervous swallow against his tongue. Something about the innocence in that made him chase the fire running through his veins; a fire that had completely overpowered him. He sucked on her fevered flesh, blazing a trail up her neck. His teeth grazed her chin and scraped along her jaw until he found her delicate earlobe, drawing out another desperate moan as he traced the shell of her ear with the tip of his tongue. "Touch me," he pleaded when her hands stilled against him. "I need to feel your hands on me."

~ FIVE ~

Discarded clothes and a deluge of condom wrappers.

Jayne was drowning in pleasure. The vision he weaved surrounded her like a fog of passion, so thick it choked out any and all of her apprehensions. Not even a sliver of doubt survived the onslaught of lust that burned its way through her body and mind. Never in her life had she experienced a moment of such complete abandon as the one she was living in now.

The hard muscles in Blake's chest and abdomen, the really yummy ones she remembered from his photo, rippled beneath her touch as her fingers searched for the unfastened buttons on his shirt. She slipped them through, one by one, as quickly as she could. Before she could push the fabric over his broad shoulders, his hands grasped her backside and pulled her tight against his groin. The air that hissed between his teeth was expelled in a long, agonized sigh that fluttered across her neck, stirring a deep ache low in her belly that rolled down between her thighs.

"I want you." His whisper carried more than words. It was fuel to an already raging fire. "Fuck, I need you." Any response she could have uttered was chased away by the cold glass at her back as he ground his hard length against her pelvis. His lips were on hers again, his kiss fanning the flames even higher as his tongue slid deep inside her mouth then retreated, over and over until she had no choice but to tear herself away.

"Breathe," she gasped, her fingers digging into the thick flesh of his shoulders. "I can't breathe in this thing."

In a blink he spun her around and had the silken ties of her corset loosened enough for her to take a deep ragged breath. The feel of his hands on her skin as they snaked beneath the rigid fabric and peeled it away was like nothing she'd ever experienced before. Everything was so much more real. She had never been so in tune with another person's touch. Was it the blindfold? Was it the thought that someone could be watching? She didn't know. She only wanted more.

"Better?" His breath was hot against the back of her neck, one hand kneading her bare breast as the other slid over the front of her lacy thong.

"Ah. *Yes!*" she hissed as her hot skin was pressed against the cool glass. Her nipples throbbed between his fingers, a sharp bite of pain making her draw in a ragged breath.

"I have to taste you," he growled as he sunk to his knees behind her, pulling her thong down with him. His warm hands caressed her thighs, his thumbs swirling over the backs of her knees as his tongue traced over the dimples at the base of her spine. Her knees nearly buckled beneath her.

"Careful." She could hear the smile in his tone. Heat flushed her cheeks from her usual blush as she braced her arms against the glass and stepped out of her panties. He turned her to face him and another wave of primal lust crashed over her as he pressed an open mouthed kiss to the crease of her hip. She swayed in her heels, catching her balance by leaning against the window. Her hand found the top of his head in front of her, her fingers once again feathering through the silky strands of his hair as he knelt in front of her.

Caught off guard, she startled when he lifted one of her legs and draped it over his shoulder, her hands slapping hard against the glass behind her to catch her balance. A sharp nip to her inner thigh was followed by the warmth of his tongue, soothing away the sting. She wasn't going to survive this. If she didn't lose her balance and break her neck, she would burn alive from the inside out. Roxy was right. This was like nothing she'd ever experienced and she wasn't sure she would ever be the same.

His hands skimmed along the outside of her legs; his fingers clenching her hips, holding her steady as his tongue played along her flesh in a teasing dance towards her already throbbing core. When he reached her naked slit he stilled, sending a brief flash of panic rushing along her spine. It was quickly replace with a shiver of lust when his hot, ragged breaths blew over her sensitive cleft.

"Please tell me I'm not dreaming," he begged as he nuzzled his nose against her slit and took a deep, satisfied breath. "No, don't tell me. If I am, I don't want to wake up."

"Ahhh…" Jayne's heady sigh turned into a moan when his hot silky tongue slipped between her folds and began a slow, sensual glide to her clit. *Oh, God.* An involuntary spasm rocked through her core and her hips flexed erratically, pushing hard against his open mouth. Slowly he drank her in, deliberately teasing his way back and forth as his strong hands kneaded her bare flesh, holding her tighter and pulling her deeper into the storm of passion that raged around them. The room spun around her, as if she had too many martinis, too fast. She was beyond tipsy. She was drunk on this man's touch and it felt so unbelievably good to let go of everything and just…*feel* him.

His hungry hum filled her ears as he pushed his tongue further inside her, his teeth scraping lightly over her clit. Jayne screamed, an overwhelming pulse thrumming through her core as she was caught in the demanding grip of an unexpected and explosive climax. Over and over her body shuddered against him. One full-bodied spasm after another gripped her until she collapsed in blissful satisfaction.

"Bed," he panted against her belly as she slid down the cool window and melted into his lap.

Holy sweet Jesus, what just happened? Her entire existence had just been altered in some strange elemental way. That's what happened. Is *this* what she'd been missing all this time? If so, she had been cheated. Completely swindled by every lazy lover she'd ever had.

"Where's the bed?"

His lips closed over her aching nipple and another earth shattering spasm rocked her body. She knew he was saying something, but her brain had been turned to sludge. It took every ounce of willpower she possessed to focus on the words until his repeated question fell into place. A bed. He wanted to know where the bed was. She tried to think, but she might as well have been trying to stack BB's. Nothing was getting through the euphoric fog that surrounded her.

"I, uh...ahh," she gasped, her fingers fisting in his hair when his lips closed around her other nipple and sucked it hard between his teeth. "I don't know. I can't—oh my God that feels so good." He cradled her in his arms and pushed to his knees, teetering to a halt when she protested. "No, please. Don't stop!" She tried to hold on to him, but her muscles were as useless as her brain had become. Her head fell back with another moan when his tongue tickled the underside of her breast and he gave into her plea, gently laying her on the floor in front of him.

"I can't fuck you on the floor," he panted, the heat of his solid frame hovering above her. She didn't care where they were. Rug burns be dammed, she truly didn't care. His tongue was so hot inside her mouth. Her legs wrapped around his hips and pulled him down between her thighs. An answering growl rumbled in his chest as his hips rolled slowly against hers, moving in a rhythm that had her coming apart at the seams. Again.

"Jesus Christ!" His protest was drowned out by hers when he pulled away, his hands working feverishly at his waist as the blessed sound of his belt buckle being unbuckled floated through the air. Then his zipper. *Oh thank heaven!* She reached up to help him. His fingers wrapped around her wrist and her hand was pressed hard against the long length of his erection. *Holy moly! He is definitely well equipped for his job.*

"Oh, fuck yes! Just like that." Her fingers closed around him and stroked his hot, silky skin. Air hissed between his teeth and he pulled away, his hands fumbling for purchase until he was able to pull her up onto his lap. Their bodies collided, arms and legs tangling together until she settled on his lap, the tip of his penis searing a path between her slick folds. Twin spikes of both delicious pain and need rushed through her as his grip tightened on her hips and rocked her over and over him until he tore his mouth from hers.

"Condom!" Even as he spoke his hips rocked beneath her. "Where's my coat? They're in my coat pocket!"

She unwound her arms from his neck, but couldn't stop her hips from sliding against him as he twisted away in a struggled search for his lost coat. She was so close! Within seconds the garment was pulled between them as he fumbled through the pockets. A flutter of packets rained down between them and he cursed as he scrambled to catch one. Jayne couldn't help the giggle that bubbled up at the thought of what they must look like sprawled on the floor, the carpet littered with discarded clothes and a deluge of condom wrappers. Whoever might be watching was getting an eyeful.

"Ahh…" Her laughter was choked back by another ragged gasp when his hands clamped over her breasts. His hot mouth once again covered her nipple. A wicked chuckle vibrated against her breast just before he stiffened around her. Clutching her hips with an almost desperate grip, he held her still against him.

"Don't move!" he ordered, sucking in a harsh, calming breath. His forehead fell against her chest. His breaths billowed out hot and fast against her sweat dampened skin. "Don't move, please. You're going to make me lose it before I can open a damn condom."

Condom? Oh yes, a condom! How could he make the world disappear so completely? When his mouth was on her he didn't just kiss her. He seemed to transport her to some timeless place where everything moved in slow motion and felt so much more real. She squeezed her eyes shut behind her blindfold and gathered back an ounce of control. Only an ounce. She wasn't ready to let the real world back in. Not yet.

"Let me." She felt around until her fingers grazed the sharp edge of a foil packet and then scooped it up. Her trembling fingers worked until she'd ripped it open and removed the condom. She slid back and reached for him, but his hand clamped over hers and halted her movements.

"Wait," he breathed against her shoulder, his other hand sliding up to rest against her neck. "Give me just a minute." A few labored breaths later he raised his head and pulled her into another searing kiss she felt clear down to her toes by the time he wrenched himself away again. "This is your last chance to change your mind, angel. The second after you roll that condom onto my cock, I *will* be inside you. All the way, no turning back, hard and fast inside you."

Her entire body stilled. A charged silence filled the room and Devin hung there, suspended somewhere between epic need and hopeless anticipation as he held his breath and waited for her to make the next move. Every molecule in his body was primed, teetering on the volatile edge of her decision. He was either about to have the best sex of his life with a complete stranger he would never see, or he was going home with a swollen nutsack and possibly a stroke. Seconds ticked by into what felt like decades of erotic torture before he felt the caress of her palm on his shaft as she deftly rolled the condom over the tip of his cock.

"Ah…ahh—!" Silken flesh padded his primal grip on her hips as he crushed her to him, devouring her panted gasps as the swollen head of his cock was engulfed by her wet heat. Inch by inch she took him in until something inside him snapped and he rolled her beneath him.

"Oh, God help me, angel. You're so…oh hell yes." Her hot channel gripped him hard then flooded with slick heat as he pumped further and deeper inside her.

"Blake, uuhmph—!" He swallowed his friend's name from her lips, his tongue sliding deep alongside hers over and over as his rhythm accelerated. Trails of stimulating pain raced along his spine as her nails dug into his skin, her mewling whimpers serving only to push him further into oblivion. His senses were so honed in to the feel of her beneath him he couldn't believe he was wearing a blindfold. He didn't need to see her. She'd become this existential, life-affirming part of his existence. He could see her with every part of his body. It was unbelievable. He'd never seen so clearly in his life.

"Roll with me," he said as he tucked her against him. When he tried to roll to his back he felt the cold edge of something metal brush against his arm. He reached out and touched the object, rejoicing in his lucky find. "There is a God. Hang on to me."

"What—oh!" She clamped her legs around his hips and he pushed to his feet, sliding her onto the bed. "Aaaah!" Air hissed loudly through her teeth as he hooked her legs over his shoulders and pushed deep inside her, grinding his hips against her with each brutal stroke. His arms shook, his muscles burned, his entire body ached for more than he could possibly reach. The bed chirped in rhythm with her panted moans. The scent of sweat and woman filled his senses with a euphoric stimulation to a point he thought he would go out of his mind with need until the first ripples of her next release hugged his dick.

"Oh yeah," he hissed, releasing her legs and gathering her into his arms. "That's it, angel. You feel so good. Squeeze me." She wrapped herself around him in every way a woman could. His hips jerked and lost their steady stride, bucking wildly as she arched beneath him. "That's it. Oh, hell yes! Come for me. Come with me!" He felt his balls draw up tight as the first tendrils of his own release snaked out and latched onto his spine, sending a wave of electricity racing through his body as she shattered around him.

"Fu—mmm—fuck!" Spasm after spasm washed over him as he held himself deep inside her. She trembled beneath him, gasping for air, the salty-sweet tang of her sweat lacing his tongue as he placed another kiss just below her ear and tried to right the spinning room. *What the hell?* He'd never fucked himself dizzy before.

Conscious of his crushing weight, he pushed up on his elbows. Her legs tightened around his hips, crushing him to her, and her inner walls gripped his spent cock even harder. "Oh, damn!" he hissed, his arms giving out beneath him from the blinding, almost painful pressure. His feet remained on the floor as he lay bent over top of her at the edge of the bed. His knees would buckle soon. He was about to melt into the floor when she suddenly let him go.

"Sorry, I…" She pushed against him and he could hear the disappointment in her voice. "Post climax cuddling and pillow talk probably aren't part of the package, are they?" When he lifted his weight off of her she pulled herself away from him and slid further towards the center of the bed. He followed, unwilling to sever the contact between them. He gathered her into his arms and searched for her sinful lips until he found what he was looking for.

"If you think for one second that I'm leaving this room before I make you cum around me at least three more times, you can just get that thought right out of your pretty little head, angel. We're just getting warmed up."

Devin opened his eyes. Three seconds ticked by before the darkness made sense and he remembered where he was. The warm, naked body he was wrapped around shifted against his morning hard-on and the lust-filled events of the previous night replayed in his mind. *Oh shit!* The air in his lungs, even the blood in his veins froze in place for a brief moment as realization set in. What the heck was he still doing there?

Slowly, and so carefully not to wake her, he reached up and slipped off his blindfold, surprised to find the room lit with morning sun. *What the hell?* They must have dozed off while they recovered from another unbelievable round of what he would call the best sex anyone had ever had in the history of the universe. Well, his universe. Holy hell, he'd never cum so hard in his life.

A few slivers of morning sunlight that had managed to escape through the curtains landed on a lock of her hair that was curled over her cheek. The sparse strands of red that ran through her darker blonde hair lit up like fire against her pale, lightly freckled skin. Her blindfold had come off, too, or at least partially. It was slanted over her forehead, but he could still see her eyes. A thin line of leftover eyeliner sparkled beneath her dark eyelashes and he grinned. Most women called them raccoon eyes, but to him it was sexy as hell on her. He couldn't believe it. He took in the woman who'd given him more than one of the best orgasms of his life. He'd kissed and tasted every delectable inch of her he could find, including that cute little mole right below her ear that was calling to him now.

He held his breath when she moaned in her sleep and turned in his arms, giving him his first full glimpse of her face since he'd stepped into the room the night before. Lost in the dark behind his blindfold, he would be lying if he said he hadn't visualized her completely different. He needed to work on his imaginative skills. He couldn't have been more wrong, or more relieved to be wrong. She was the quintessential girl next door, all natural and fresh. No harsh lines or fake, over-stuffed parts. Her eyebrows weren't painted on, her eyes had little lines at the corners that showed how much she smiled and her lips were perfectly kissable, not puffed up with whatever injection craze women were chasing these days.

Another sexy moan vibrated against his sweat dampened skin and he froze, his eyes squeezing closed in hope that she didn't wake. Blake would kick his ass if he got him fired. He thought about that for a moment. If he got Blake fired then he'd have nothing to come back to after he got his project up and running in L.A. *No.* As tempting as that was he had to play it straight. And, as much as he wanted to know who this amazing chick was, he owed it to her to keep his promise of anonymity. *Damn blindfold fantasy.*

It took a few starts and stops, but he managed to extricate himself from Simone and the bed without waking her. He needed a shower. However, by not being able to take one, her scent would stay with him for at least the taxi ride back to Blake's townhouse. He pulled on his slacks and slipped his sockless feet into his shoes, haphazardly buttoning his shirt. He looked like a slob, but he didn't care. His tie had snaked under the bed and he stooped down to pick it up, pausing when his eyes landed on her thong panties lying there on the floor. His fingers itched to pick them up and stuff them in his pocket. Would she think him a pervert if he took them? Probably, but he scooped them up anyways. He wanted at least a little something to remember her by.

He was about to drape his tie around his neck and slip out of the room when he paused, turning back to take one last look at his blindfold fantasy girl. She was sleeping so peacefully, the sheets tangled around her legs and tucked securely over her breasts. *So modest, even in her sleep.* She'd been so shy and embarrassed to claim her sexual needs. Once she did open up, she'd given him the best night of his life. It was a shame he'd never get the chance to tell her.

Stopping short of giving her a parting kiss, he curled his tie on the pillow beside her. As silently as he could, he backed out of the room and slipped unheard through the door. He stood there for a moment, still debating if he should let the door click closed, forever locking him away from any chance of ever finding her. An infectious smirk pulled at his lips at how silly he sounded in his own head. He had a friend to corral and get to L.A. before he left for a month-long trip to Toronto to negotiate a new project and secure the funding he needed. He also had a corporate spy to catch. He didn't have time for distractions like her. He let the handle go and stepped away from her door, feeling the weight of his inheritance land square on his shoulders as he made his way to the elevator. *Why can't I just build things?*

~ SIX ~

Hell on fire. Save me!

"Fine, Mother. I'll ask Nina Thomason to accompany me to the spring picnic." *Three years from now, if I'm still single, maybe I'll ask her.* Of course he didn't let his mother in on this caveat. Right now he'd say whatever he needed to get Mia Silverland out of his hair and on a plane back to California. Hell, at this point he didn't care what state she ended up in as long as she was out of the city of Toronto. Out of the northern hemisphere would be nice. He shook his head. That was a crap plan. His mother couldn't, or wouldn't tolerate the humidity. He'd never hear the end of it.

"Oh, that's a wonderful idea, Devin dear. I'm so glad you're dating again. Nina's mother will be ecstatic!" Devin closed his eyes and took a deep breath as he ushered his mother into her limousine. Typical. Spend the last two hours shoving the poor girl down his throat—Nina *this* and Nina *that*—then she makes like she'd never thought of it before. And he wasn't dating again, dammit.

He closed the door and tapped on the roof, but the beast of a car didn't move. Instead, the heavily tinted window lowered and his mother reached out her hand. "Give me a kiss, dear."

Devin concealed his agitation with a gritted smile, bending down to kiss his mother's cheek. "See you at dinner, Mother."

She smiled and patted the back of his hand. Just when he thought he was in the clear and would be able to get back to his regularly scheduled chaos, she clasped his hand and pulled him back to the door. "Oh, I almost forgot. Can you please call and check on Mallory? Maybe invite her to dinner? She's been a bit distracted lately."

And there it is. The second reason for his mother's impromptu visit. "Mom, Mallory gets distracted by the sound of her own bark."

"Don't insinuate your sister is a dog, Devin," his mother scolded in a tone she reserved only for him and ill-behaved staff. "It's not polite and I don't like it. You know she's not like you. She needs reassurance and guidance. She needs to find a man who—"

Hell on fire. Save me! "Okay, I'll call her!" Again, whatever it took to get this woman the hell away from him for a few hours. He'd thought he'd be free of her in Toronto. She rarely left California since her father's passing. Now she was stalking him, and dragging his sister along with her.

It wasn't that he didn't like his sister. He loved Mallory, but they were so different. Mallory was irresponsible and her lack of direction went beyond anything a GPS could fix. Until last fall she'd been at UC Berkeley studying everything from making wine to mythology. Five years and she still didn't have a major or a diploma. One of many reasons his grandfather made him the guardian over her inheritance until she married a respectable replacement. The word respectable was so subjective.

"Invite her to dinner?" his mother asked in that tone that told him it wasn't a request but an order. He closed his eyes, counted to three then nodded, consoling himself with the knowledge that the restaurant he had standing dinner reservations with while he was in Toronto had a fully stocked bar. "Perfect! I'll see you at seven." She let go of his hand and the limo pulled away from the curb.

He stood there for a moment and watched as the black beast disappeared into a sea of cars that lined the busy downtown street. No one rode in gas guzzling limousines in the middle of the day for everyday use anymore. No one but his mother. She was an old money, over-privileged aristocrat. If there was one fault his grandfather had, it was spoiling her. And, if it wasn't for the fact that she'd already buried three husbands, he'd say she needed a new man to distract *her* instead of his sister. Matchmaking wasn't his thing, but at this point he'd come out ahead if he paid someone to keep her busy for a while. At such an awkward thought his head fell back and he took in the bright blue, late March sky. Would he ever have another thought that didn't conjure up his blindfold fantasy girl?

Hands in his pockets, he strolled up the steps into the hotel lobby and made his way to the bank of elevators. He couldn't help but remember the nervous mess he'd been as he'd made his way to Simone's room that night. Thinking back on it now, he was almost embarrassed at his hesitancy. He and Blake had done crazier things, many of them illegal in some states. He struggled to rationalize it. True, Danielle had done a real number on his head, but it was more than that. Even now, a week later, he couldn't get Simone out of his thoughts. She was under his skin and he liked her there. He'd like it even more if she were in his bed.

He'd deduced that Simone wasn't her real name. Aside from a few cues she'd inadvertently given him during their night together, the hairstylist at the hotel spa caved in and told him as much, though she wouldn't reveal her real name no matter how much money he threw at her. Blake's pimp was of no use. Blake said he'd try to get him to come off some info, but he wasn't holding his breath.

Once in his room, Devin pulled off his tie and crashed into the leather Queen Anne chair beside one of the windows overlooking Lake Ontario. He reached out and touched the glass, feeling the cold from the early spring day seep into his palm. *Where is she?* Was she hunched over a draft table, lost in the world of creativity she claimed so easily consumed her when she was doing what she loved? Or were her thoughts just as consumed by him as his were of her? He reached into his suit coat pocket and withdrew the scrap of silky lace he had peeled from her hips that night in Vegas. Absently, his thumb played over the fine silk threads as he thought of all the possibilities.

Lost to him, she had become just as much of a distraction as if she were there with him, if not more so. He not only woke up hard as hell from dreaming of her, in the middle of his day he often found himself pages deep into ludicrous internet searches for architects named Simone. Even when he applied gender and employment filters there were still thousands of Simone's on every social media website. It was truly sad that he had even bothered to check. He brought her thong to his nose and drew in a long, ragged breath before cursing himself and stuffing them back into his packet.

The last thing he needed was this sort of distraction. Tossing his tie over the back of his chair, he walked to the in-room bar and poured himself a glass of bourbon. Yeah, it was early, but who cared. By the looks of it, the day was only going to get worse so he might as well get an early start. He pulled a cigarette from the pack he'd picked up from the hotel lobby and ran it beneath his nose, taking a long whiff of the fresh tobacco. He hadn't smoked since college, but stress made him crave a drag or two every once in a while.

He had to get a grip on his new reality or he was going to lose everything. His grandfather had been brokering a build for the Canadian tech giant, Stealth Graphene, when he fell ill. They had long since run out of polite patience and were looking to take their deal elsewhere. Unfortunately, due to unexpected changes in the laws and regulations, some of the original terms were no longer viable and he was having a hell of time moving the pieces around to make the deal work. Add that to several takeover bids his lawyers were working on and the glaring deficiency in his time management skills he'd recently come to appreciate since leaving his very pregnant assistant behind in California, he had zero room for thought-consuming mystery women, meddling mothers or an immature, feckless sister.

Devin's cellphone chirped, alerting him to an incoming call. He pulled it from his front trouser pocket and looked apprehensively at the screen to see who it was. *Blake*.

"Please tell me you have some good news," he said on a long sigh.

"Uh, hello to you too, asshole," Blake grumbled.

Leaving his bourbon on the bar, Devin paced to the window again. "C'mon, man. You know I appreciate you. I'm barely treading water up here. Give me a break." He braced his forearm against the glass and rested his forehead against it as he waited for Blake to drop the other shoe that always seemed to fall these days.

"I'm sitting in my old office looking out at a city I hate. Sucks for me, but I'd say you're batting a thousand on this end."

"About damn time." Devin released a huge sigh of relief. He'd never tell Blake, but he honestly believed there was a fifty-fifty chance he'd be left holding the bag when it came to his friend showing up. "And you don't hate, L.A. You just need to get back in your groove."

"I'm not staying, Dev."

"We'll see." It was on the tip of his tongue to ask Blake if he'd been by the club since he'd arrived in town, but he decided against it. Devin had been in a few times to check out the changes he'd heard about. It had been a solid year since he'd stayed to play. It wasn't the same without Blake or Daphne. "You have everything you need?"

"Yeah, man. I'm only waiting on two permits from the city to get stamped through and then we're golden."

Relieved, for now, Devin retrieved his drink and took a long, rewarding swallow. "Is the team assembled?" he asked with a hiss as the liquid fire burned its way down his throat.

"Yup," Blake said. "The technical director arrived Friday and the architect your board wanted finishes up her orientation on Friday. We have our first meet and greet scheduled for the following Monday and the groundbreaking is two weeks after that."

The board. Most of the SI board members drank their lunch through a straw, stunk up his conference rooms with Aqua Velva and missed his grandfather like mad. They were one hundred percent loyal to his grandfather's legacy. However, there were two members who ran the sustainable development committee who seemed to have made it their mission in life to crush him. Demanding they hire an official project architect as a go-between for SI and the city was not only adding an astronomical cost to the project, which he insisted the city subsidize, but it was asinine. There was no reason he couldn't subcontract the design process like any other project. Throw in the fact he was once again assailed with more memories of his own mystery architect and he was now officially in hell.

"Her name isn't Simone by chance, is it?"

"Who's name?"

"The architect!" Devin pinched the bridge of his nose as he felt a jack hammer set up shop inside his skull. "Have you heard anything I've told you about this woman?"

"Not really."

"Seriously? This is how you treat your best friend?"

Blake snorted, "You need to learn the meaning of meaningless sex, my friend."

And you need to remember what it's like to give a fuck! He was one tenth of a second from blasting his friend with the truth. Project manager or not, he needed a huge wake-up call.

"Blake, I'm warning you, man. I'm on the edge." And he was. He felt like he could so easily walk away from it all. He never thought about doing anything else but following in his grandfather's footsteps and he'd been certain he was ready. He seriously hated his life at the moment and wondered if it was all worth it.

"Good!" Blake chuckled.

"Good?"

"Yeah, good! You hate this corporate stuff as much as I do."

"It's not an option, Blake. You know that."

"Her name is Jayne, or June," Blake said without missing a beat on the subject change. "Something insanely normal. And before you ask, no, Gavin hasn't called me back yet."

Devin felt what he knew to be false hope slipping from his grasp. It was ridiculous but he just couldn't let it go. He hadn't experienced a connection like that since the last time he was with Daphne. Blake had been clueless about his feelings for Daphne from the beginning. Devin was a third; an exciting addition to Blake and Daphne's sex life when Blake felt the need to indulge his voyeuristic tendencies. It worked out great for him because A—Daphne was cute as hell and B—it left him satisfied too. He got to indulge in a little show and tell. He and Blake had shared women in the past so it was no big leap to fucking her on his own in front of his friend or with him at the club.

Daphne was shy and unsure in the beginning, but she understood Blake and wanted to give him what he needed. She was what they called a unicorn because really, how many women would do that for their partner? She was a mythical creature; an enigma. What man wouldn't love her?

As a third Devin wasn't entitled to an emotional connection with Daphne. It wasn't supposed to happen, but it did and before long he wasn't fucking her. He was making love to his best friend's girl. And he wasn't the only one. She'd fallen as equally in love with him as she had Blake. They'd discussed it several times, trying relentlessly to figure out how to make it work and what to tell Blake. In the end it didn't seem worth the potential damage. Nothing they could have said would have made a difference. It wasn't like they could all live happily ever after together. Forcing her to choose was out of the question. He'd never hurt either of them that way. Eventually, he and Daphne had agreed privately to cut all physical ties. The guilt was too much. Anytime Blake suggested a play date they made excuses to postpone it, or called it off at the last minute. Soon after that she was gone, taken from them both.

He hadn't grieved less for Daphne than Blake had. He'd simply grieved in silence, in his own way. He'd become numb where Blake had bled openly from the astounding hurt and loss. Shortly afterwards, his grandfather became ill and he'd been thrown into the deep end head first. Sink or swim situations didn't leave much time for grieving. The first person he'd allowed inside his head since then was Danielle DeVeaux. That had been about as much fun as having his dick sucked by a shark. Just when he least expected it, a shy architect he'd never laid eyes on had rocked his world and he was supposed to just walk away and forget about her? Giving up wasn't in his skill set.

One thing was certain, he wasn't going to find her or figure it all out today. "I've gotta go, man. I've got a thousand phone calls to make before I meet Mother for dinner and one of them is to Mallory."

"Oh, shit," Blake choked. "You didn't tell her I was coming back, did you?"

Devin smiled as he left his friend dangling like a gasping fish on a hook. It was true, his sister's crush on Blake probably crossed into stalker territory on more than one occasion. For whatever reason, he was the only person who had been able to hold his sister's focus longer than a television commercial with puppies. Who was he to take that from her? Blake swore it was all an act, that she was really Satan's gatekeeper. He was being ridiculous. Mallory was harmless. Whatever few brain cells she'd been born with had been mutated by the copious amounts of drugs her father had done before she was conceived. What his mother had seen in that stoner was still a mystery.

"Devin, you're not doing yourself any favors if you sick that woman on me!"

"Relax," he chuckled. "I haven't spoken to her since February." When he had to deal with her latest loser boyfriend. He'd ignored a lot of shit from the guys she dated, but abuse was a solid red line. "The ladies in the office you left hot and bothered when you bailed six months ago are the ones you need to worry about. Mallory greased the gossip wheels and if she hasn't heard yet she will soon enough."

"I'll take my chances with them. Just don't…" Devin could hear the panic in his friend's voice and he laughed. "It's not funny!" Blake shouted, making Devin laugh harder.

"Actually, it's pretty hysterical. Payback is a bitch."

"Whatever you do, man, I'm begging you. Give me a heads up if you know she's on her way here, or back in the state!"

"I can't believe you're still afraid of her," he said, another involuntary chuckle slipping between his words.

"It's not fear. It's survival."

~ SEVEN ~

"Want to see it? It's impressive."

"Hey! You can't leave that there!" Jayne scrambled from behind her drafting table and sprinted to catch the delivery guy who'd just blocked the doorway of her new office with a box the size of a small elephant. "Wait! Come back!"

She stood on her tiptoes to peer over the box and down the hall. In mid-sprint towards the elevator, the guy turned and held up one finger to let her know he'd only be a minute. She didn't have a minute! The meeting of her life began in less than five minutes and now she was trapped inside her office. She still had to get her latest draft off the blueprint printer which, for some confounded reason, was at the other end of the building. "Umph!" She pushed against the mammoth-sized box but it wouldn't budge. All she needed was a couple of inches and she could squeeze through the door and get to that meeting! She sucked in her stomach and stretched her torso, squeezing herself into the few inches between the box and the door jamb. *Rrrrrrip.*

"Ouch!" She pushed herself through the doorway and spilled onto the hall floor, a tattered piece of her sleeve still hanging from the industrial staple sticking out from the corner of the cardboard box. "Really?" She pushed to her feet, thankful that the normally busy hallway was empty and no one had seen this new klutzy move. She'd been there three days and already she'd spilled coffee on her keyboard, burned popcorn in the executive break room microwave and locked up the orientation projector when she tried to help the trainer. She didn't know what kind of cruel demon fate had followed her to California, but she was beyond ready to find an exorcist.

Jayne looked down at her torn sleeve and winced. *Nice first impression.* Until now, she considered herself lucky that her new boss had been MIA. She'd been shuffled through the usual corporate training classes and orientation process just like any new hire. Mr. Kirk's very pregnant assistant, Jeanette, had shown her to her office and advised her where to find any supplies she may need, but she had yet to meet the man himself or the project manager she would be working with. She did manage to dig up a picture of Devin Kirk on the company's Intranet. He was very attractive in a smoldering sophisticated kind of way. He had sexy, dark brown hair and minty hazel eyes, not at all muddy like hers. She'd stared at his mischievous smile for a while. It mesmerized her, like there was a naughty word hiding just on the other side of his upturned lips that he was dying to say. There was nothing of her project manager, Blake Travers. She'd never known anyone named Blake. Ever. All of a sudden she was surrounded by them. How was she supposed to work so closely with someone when just the mention of his name made her hoo-hah do the cha-cha? *Maybe he's hideous.* Yeah, that's it. Beer gut, pock-marks, fat, old geezer hideous.

Regardless of how he looked, apparently she would meet her boss and everyone else on the team wearing a uni-sleeve. She considered ripping the other one to make a matching set, but her attention was snagged away from that fashion statement nightmare by the clock hanging at the end of the hall. She could almost hear the second hand ticking like a time bomb against her eardrums.

"Fffffudge!" Tattered remnants forgotten, Jayne sprinted down the hall, around the corner and swiveled her way through the graphic design department's cube farm to the printer room. She could now add being late to her exploding list of brilliant, first impression faux pas. Out of breath, she snatched the blueprints from the stack atop the printer and whirled back through the busy floor and straight into the elevator.

"Did you hear? Blake is back." Jayne's last breath stuck in her throat and a fresh spike of heat rushed to her cheeks. Dammit, would she ever be able to hear that name again without her entire body twisting into a pretzel? She'd been oddly disappointed when she woke to find her mystery gigolo gone that morning, his tie coiled up beside her on the pillow that still held his scent. Anonymity is what she'd wanted, but now her mind was playing tricks on her, filling in all the blanks with daydreams of special connections and feelings that couldn't be real. She'd told herself a million times in the last week that it had all been an act. He was there to fulfill a fantasy and that's exactly what she got. Still, she couldn't help but wonder what he was doing or where he was, which was ridiculous, because she knew exactly what he was doing.

"Word is he's not staying." Jayne turned a little and caught a glimpse of the women talking behind her. She knew they weren't talking about the same man who had occupied her thoughts day and night since she and Roxy had left Vegas, but that didn't stop her memory of Blake from playing back in Technicolor. Another shiver wracked her body and one of the women smirked and winked at her.

"I see you've met Blake, too." The woman's lips curled into a wicked grin. She licked her lips and closed her eyes as she melted against the back wall of the elevator. "I don't need him to stay. I need him to cum. Over and over and over. One night. That's all I need. One night on that sofa in his office and I'd heal his broken heart."

Her friend snorted. "You'd have to fight me and half of SI for your chance at that fine ass." The elevator stopped and the women rushed out, taking with them any hope that her project manager was a troll. *Damn—Darn! Darn-Darn-Darn!* Who was she kidding? She was one stubbed toe away from cursing out loud. Why bother censoring her thoughts?

The doors closed and Jayne had a sudden need to visit the ladies room to splash some cold water on her face. As the elevator reached the conference room floor she was once again yanked back into reality. Her reality. A reality in which she was painfully aware of her disheveled state and more than fifteen minutes late to the meeting of all meetings. She glanced down at her torn sleeve. *Why? Why today?*

She rushed down the hall, passing the executive offices and the reception desks sitting outside each one, all ominously empty of their occupants. All of whom turned to glare at her the moment she blasted through the conference room door. *Oh, no.* She prayed silently to melt into the new industrial carpeting beneath her shoes.

She stepped into the room and quietly closed the door behind her. "I'm sorry I'm late. I was trapped inside my office by this enormous—"

"Sorry I'm late," a male voice echoed behind her. She turned to see the man rush through the door behind her and lazily adjust his tie. "Security sent the delivery guys to the wrong floor and I had to chase them down to get the new printer set up in my office." Jayne was frozen in place as she watched her greatest sexual experience and her worst nightmare morph into a cataclysmic cruel joke.

"Hi," he said, his lips curling into the same seductive smile she remembered from his calling card photo. "Blake Travers, project manager." When she didn't move to shake his hand, Blake took hers into his warm, firm grip. Electricity singed her spinal column and Jayne jerked her hand back.

"I...I-I-I...I don't believe this."

The air in the room was suddenly sucked away, replaced by a heavy fog of confusion and disbelief. Everyone else in the room faded away as Blake's confused expression shifted into and out of focus. She shook her head. Surely she was inside some stress-induced nightmare. *Wake up!* That had to be it. She was dreaming. She was still in bed, tossing and turning, tangled in her sheets. *Wake the hell up!* It was the only explanation. "You," she laughed at her own silliness and poked at the aberration in front of her. "Are you real?"

"Is she high?" An incredulous voice broke through the murmurs of the others in the room.

"I'm sorry, but did I miss something important?" Blake glanced at the other people in the room and then back to her. "You are Jayne Simon, right? My new architect? From New York?" He was drunk, or at least still hung over. She could smell the faintest hint of alcohol mixed in with the intoxicating cologne she still remembered.

When Jayne still didn't respond, he took the blueprints from her hand and held them up, unrolling them to take a look. "Oh, sweetness. You must have caught the wrong floor on the elevator. This isn't the renovations and restoration department. Are they going to try to save that old firehouse? Bravo!" He rolled the blueprints up and handed them back to her.

Not a sign. The man showed not one single sign that he recognized her. No covert winks, stutters or smirks, nothing that suggested he'd spent an entire night ruining her for every other man on the planet. That of course didn't stop her from blushing until she thought she'd catch fire. Had she really just poked the man? Maybe she was high. Someone must have spiked the coffee in the break room. "Do you have a twin?" That had to be it, or was it possible she simply wasn't that memorable?

Blake chuckled. "The world wouldn't know what to do with two of me." Half the room groaned in protest, the other half snickering as he pointed to her sleeveless arm. "You're uh, bleeding just a bit there. You might want to, uh…"

Jayne looked down at her arm and saw a thin trickle of blood. Mortified, she covered the scratch with her hand, but it was too late. She looked up to see Blake turn three shades of green. His eyelids fluttered as his eyes rolled back, paying a temporary visit to the dark side.

"Whoa!" Someone pulled a chair from the table and helped guide Blake into it. He wasn't hung over. He was passing out drunk!

A man, who introduced himself as the CFO, handed her his handkerchief "I have a first aid kit in my office. I'll be right back."

"I'll get it for you, Mr. Larson." A petite blonde jumped from her seat and hurried from the room.

"This is certainly the most bizarre project meeting I've ever attended," someone from the end of the table said before slamming their leather bound notebook closed and pushing it away in an awkward fit of contempt.

Jayne buried her face in her hands to hide her complete humiliation. If this situation got any more embarrassing she would die. Literally. How could she have screwed her life up any more than this? The job of her dreams and she'd slept with her drunk boss before she'd even began. No. Not just slept with. Roxy *hired* him to have *sex* with her, repeatedly; sheet-soaking, headboard-shattering, mind-blowing-orgasm, not-even-on-the-same-planet-as-boring-Dale sex. *Oh. My. God. I'm ruined!*

"I'm sorry, Mr. Larson. I didn't see the kit in your desk."

"Oh, that's right. I gave it to my grandson to play with when he was visiting last month." He smiled friendly at Jayne and nodded. "He's going to be a doctor, you know."

Jayne nodded and returned the man's affectionate smile. "That's okay. I'll just go down to the onsite clinic."

"Do we need to reschedule, Mr. Travers?" Mr. Kirk's assistant asked him. "You're not looking well yourself. Maybe you should accompany Ms..."

"Simon," Jayne supplied for the woman when she hesitated.

"Yes, I'm sorry. I'm terrible with names these days. It must be all the extra hormones. Maybe you should go with Ms. Simon to the clinic. I can notify Mr. Kirk and update the calendars."

Slouched in the chair, Blake shook his head and waved off her suggestion. "No, I'm fine. I just got a little queasy when I saw the...." He motioned to Jayne's scratch. *What?* Oh, okay, so maybe he wasn't so drunk. He smiled up at Jayne and her heart nearly beat out of her chest. Had he really been the one to do all of those things to her? All of those delicious, mind-blowing, spine-tingling, sinful things? Her shoulders quivered with a shiver and another blush colored her face. "If you'd like to visit the clinic I can fill you in on the important stuff later," he dismissed her with a wave.

Stunned, Jayne gathered the plans she'd dropped while assisting Blake to his chair before he fainted. "I need to go back and get the correct plans for you."

"That's okay. We're just doing introductions and covering the project outline today," Blake assured her without leaving his chair. He nodded towards the people gathered around the conference table. "Team, this is Jayne Simon, our resident architect and designer of The Emerald Dream," he announced to the room.

She forced a professional smile and nodded as he introduced different team leaders. People whose names she'd never remember thanks to the constant state of *how-the-hell-did-this-happen* her brain was stuck in. There had to be a sign, a big fat scarlet letter stamped on her forehead that told everyone in that room she'd paid for sex with the man-god beside her. The way they were looking at her, she just knew there had to be.

"Jayne?"

Her head jerked at the sound of her name and she dropped the rolled blueprints back to the floor. "What?" She bent to scoop them up, tucking them securely under her arm. "Yes? Sorry, you were saying?"

"That I'll come by your office before the end of the day and catch you up on everything." Jayne smiled and nodded. That would be great because she was totally lost.

"Jayne?"

"Mmhmm? Yes?"

"Will you be going to the clinic to have that cut looked at now, or am I going to need to use my tie as a blindfold?"

Jayne's heart lurched to a stop like a ten year old diesel engine. Did that mean he knew? Had he finally remembered her? Mortified, she bolted from the room and scrambled towards the elevator, punching frantically at the floor numbers.

Oh, this was bad. She tried to think her way through the nightmare that was unfolding and engulfing her reality. Okay, it was simple. Her pride may be ripped to shreds if he didn't remember her, but that was something she could cope with. She'd never been memorable or extraordinary. A guy like him wouldn't look twice at her in a normal situation and she would shy away from him if he had. So, no loss there, except a few memories she'd have for the rest of her life of how amazing sex *could* be. *Winner!* There was her silver lining. She could access those memories the next time she was having boring Dale sex. It would of course remind her that she would only have amazing sex with a hot guy if she paid for it but, hey? Not a huge news event in her world.

On the other hand, if he did remember her… She wiped the clammy sweat from her forehead and scrubbed her palms over her skirt. The elevator door opened and she shuffled through the crowd in the lobby to the onsite clinic entrance. She suddenly felt ridiculous going to the clinic for a scratch, but whatever. If he did remember her she was so screwed. She would never be able to look the man in the eyes. Where did that leave her working relationship? Sunk, that's where. At the bottom of the ocean with the rest of her career. Some people could pull off work place romances. She was not one of them. Not that she'd tried. She was just that person, the one who could never get away with anything. The entire population of a small country could be doing something against the rules, for years, and the minute she tried it she'd get caught and punished.

Case in point: sleeping with a professional escort. It was literally the oldest taboo profession! The one time in her life she'd done something reckless and sensational and here she was, sitting in a clinic with a staple scratch given to her by her gigolo's obsession with huge printers and looking at what could possibly be the loss of her dream job before she'd even started it.

She signed the forms the nurse handed her and went through the motions, nodding and signing again when they told her to. She needed to speak to Roxy. This was all her fault. If she'd just stuck to gawking at pool waiters instead of hiring a male escort slash project manager, none of this would be happening.

An alcohol swab and Band Aide later, she stopped by the printer room on her way to hide in her office. She sifted through several sets of blueprints that were stacked in the waiting queue, but the Emerald Dream prints were nowhere to be found. Someone was probably staring at the mock-up wondering why anyone would build an eighty story fire house. Still, she'd have to report the loss to Blake. The missing copy had detailed materials and suppliers lists printed with it. She doubted there was anything malicious about the situation, but any project of this size and nature was always a target for poachers. Someone could make any number of underhanded deals to snatch a project like the Emerald Dream away from SI, including buying out supplies so they couldn't make the bid on time or have to pay double to get them back.

Once in her office, she tried calling Roxy but was forwarded to her voicemail. She looked at her watch as she tried to knead some of the tension from the back of her neck. Time differences were a pain in the you-know-what to adjust to. It was lunchtime in New York, but Roxy probably skipped lunch as she normally did when she was holed away in her studio painting. It wasn't unusual for Rox to leave her phone on silent or not hear it with her music blaring. She had to admit she was beginning to worry about Rox.

Things between them seemed strained before she left. Roxy had been quiet and distant and more than once Jayne found herself at the raw end of her sharp-tongued rebukes over otherwise benign issues. Considering the timing and Rox's inability to deal well with emotionally charged situations, she chalked it up to her leaving for L.A. and figured things would be back to normal by now. Maybe they were, but since she found herself talking more to Rox's voicemail than to Rox, she couldn't help but worry.

Jayne sent her a text asking for her to return her call ASAP then logged into her computer. Focusing on anything but her and Blake was a sporadic impossibility. For the next two hours she stared at her monitor but nothing clicked. This! This was why she couldn't do workplace relationships. She had a job to do and she couldn't do it like this. Multi-tasking was one thing. This kind of distraction was dangerous to more than her career. People were depending on her.

"You okay?" Blake's voice filled her office about two seconds before she heard the raps on her door.

"Ffffudmucker! Could you possibly knock *before* you stick your head in the door and scare the stuffing out of someone?" Jayne stooped down and picked up her pen and phone from the floor where she'd inadvertently dropped them when she looked up to see Blake standing in her doorway, looking every bit as gorgeous and hung over as he did three hours ago.

"Fudmucker?" Blake arched an eyebrow as he strolled into her office. "Stuffing?"

"I…I'm trying…was…I *was* trying to cut back on my cursing."

"You're not trying anymore?" The man hitched his thigh onto the corner of her desk and her eyes darted to the thick muscles defined beneath the charcoal dress slacks. *Eff-eff-eff!* She'd had her hands on those thighs, those very same muscles bunching beneath them as she... Her palms tingled with the remembered feel of his coarse hair beneath them. She tried to speak. What she was going to say was a complete mystery, but it didn't matter. The inside of her mouth had become an arid wasteland of words as she forced herself not to look at his crotch. Not having a chair for him to sit in was no excuse. He had no right to torture her like this.

"Mr. Travers, we…"

"Blake," he said and absently brushed his palm over his trousers. "Me Blake, you Jayne." Jayne raised a brow, the parody catching her off guard and inducing an incredulous snort. Had he really just said that?

"That's better." Blake winked at her and pushed off her desk. "You're going to have to loosen up a little, Jaynie girl. Let's catch up over drinks. It's the least I can do to make up for this afternoon."

"Um." *Catch up?* Did he mean catch up since the night they screwed like rabbits or catch up since the meeting? "Make up for what exactly?" Jayne held her breath as she waited for him to say something about their night in Vegas.

"For trapping you in your office with my *huge* equipment." A sly smile tugged at his lips. "Want to see it? It's impressive."

"No!" *Yes! Oh God!* She closed her eyes when they darted to his groin. What did that mean? Did he remember her or not?

"Fine, but I need a drink. Come with?"

He was a blank slate. And a total jerk. Jayne's shoulders fell, one in relief and the other in disappointment. Either he didn't remember her, or he was making a well-defined point not to acknowledge their time together. She was essentially forgettable. She felt her insecurity bloom to the usual blush in her cheeks. What had she expected, declarations of true love? Hardly. She had been a job to him; one of many she was sure.

It's better this way. She told herself that all the way to the elevator. She could carry the memory of that night with her forever, but she only had this one shot at jumpstarting her career. She could do this. She would shield herself in her business suit like she always did and make herself focus on her job. It's the way things should have been from the start.

Jayne pushed the elevator button and the door opened, astonished at the stark difference between the man in front of her and the man who had been so patient and charming in that hotel room. *What a difference a blindfold makes.*

The elevator doors opened and Blake held out his arm for her to precede him inside. She felt his eyes caress her backside. They lingered unabashedly on her breasts when she turned around, raising a suggestive brow when they rose to her face and he realized he'd been caught gawking. Something, she was sure, he wasn't the least bit embarrassed about.

Before the elevator reached the garage floor, Jayne thumbed the button for the lobby. *What a jerk.* A second later the elevator stopped and the doors opened. "Maybe some other time," she said as she pushed the button to close the doors, stepping through them into the lobby before he could utter his protest. If he didn't remember her, she could just as easily forget about him, eventually.

~ EIGHT ~

The 'C' word.

One and a half weeks. Unfortunately for Blake, that was not a hardcore parody of the soft porn movie sensation. It represented how long he'd gone without a decent night's sleep and the exact amount of time it took for their first not-so-minor crisis to rear its ugly head. "Dammit!" He'd hoped to at least get beyond the official groundbreaking before the assholes started coming out of the woodwork. He dialed Jayne's extension, but she wasn't picking up.

"Magnes!" he called out to his borrowed assistant. Set on his decision not to stay in L.A., hiring a temp would have been a waste of time. "Will you locate Jayne Simon and ask her to come to my office, please?"

Blake scrubbed a hand over his jaw and slumped into his ergonomic office chair, feeling the effects of a string of late nights at the bar. At least his headache had taken a hike. He didn't think he could have handled a day like today with a spike in his skull.

Thanks to a radical group of environmental nut-jobs, he already had to hire a security team to guard the empty construction site from the protest groups. It didn't matter that this was one of the most 'green' projects ever constructed in the country, some people would never be happy. Although not this soon, he'd expected it.

In general, everything was ticking along like clockwork. The team leaders were working well together and the permits were all in hand. He didn't want to know what Devin had to promise to get the Emerald Dream pushed to the front of the usual five year waiting period line, but the Mayor had come through on his promises. It probably had something to do with this project putting the city light-years ahead on their sustainability obligations to the Feds. And it was an election year. Lots of things get done, and done quickly, when there's an election looming. They were actually ahead of schedule and he was about to let himself breathe a sigh of relief when Devin called him from Toronto with the news.

He hated that this first attack came at the expense of their new architect. Jayne was one of the most talented and focused people he'd ever known. She was oblivious to the world around her when she was in design mode. The rest of the time she was a walking disaster. Except when she was negotiating changes to her designs, she was probably the quietest and most shy person he knew. She was soft and prickly all at once, and cute as hell when she blushed, which was pretty much all the time.

She tried hard at the ice queen act around him, but it was bullshit. Her cheeks and neck heated to a beautiful raspberry pink every time he walked into a room or when she caught him looking at her. He'd gotten into a devious habit of winking at her to push her buttons. He loved watching her battle her involuntary reactions to his teasing. It was about the only thing that kept him sane during the day.

More than that, he liked her. Being back in L.A., at Silverland Industries, was like living on the fifth floor of his own personal hell. She had become the refreshing drop of water that quenched his otherwise parched existence. A spontaneous grin pulled at his lips. Judging by the number of times he'd caught her staring at his crotch, she wasn't immune to his physical charms either. He wasn't being vain or narcissistic. He was realistic. He was a good looking guy with a trust fund. The question begged to be asked, however. Why was she running so hot and cold? Did he really want to go to the perilous places he'd probably need to venture into to find out? There were a few places in life he would say were worse than where he was. Exploring his possibilities with Jayne could put him right back in one of those places. He'd spent the last three years crawling out of hell's basement. Suddenly the fifth floor didn't seem so bad.

One word summed up dear, sweet Jayne. Trouble. Not the kind of trouble Devin had her pegged for, but the kind that would have him making room in his closet for her stuff sort of trouble. The *anything less than a commitment meant he was taking advantage* kind of trouble. Absently, Blake rubbed at a dull ache that radiated from somewhere deep inside his chest, his body's instinctive warning response to the 'C' word. *Commitment.* Just thinking the word made him cringe. He reached into his pocket and fished out a couple of antacids, his attention suddenly snagged by a set of perfectly shaped hips defined by a tight, black pencil skirt swaying down the hallway towards his office. Hell or not, the idea of taking advantage of Miss Jaynie girl was looking more and more appealing every day. The only thing better than seeing her coming was watching her go.

Blake cleared his throat and tried to clear his dirty mind as she approached. She was innocent. Not in the virginal sense, but one trip to his and Dev's world of corrupted debauchery and she'd run screaming. It had been a while, not since Daphne, that he'd been in the presence of such shy innocence. To be fair, he could have been surrounded by it and simply never noticed. He hadn't exactly been in the market for the *Little-House-on-the-Prairie-in-fuck-me-heels* type lately. Okay, never, but a guy was allowed to be curious. One thing was certain, she couldn't have been the source of the leak Devin wanted her dismissed for.

"You sent for me?" Blake nodded and stood at his desk to welcome Jayne into his office.

"Please, close the door and have a seat." She hesitated a moment before she moved to close the door, casting a weary glance at him as she took the seat in front of his desk. She caught him watching her and her spine stiffened like wrought iron, her hands nervously clasping and unclasping in her lap. The news had apparently made its way through the office gossip girls.

"The Emerald Dream made front page news today." He tossed a copy of the L.A. Times onto his desk in front of her. He hadn't expected her to pick it up and skim over the story as if she hadn't already seen it.

"That's good, right? The Mayor wanted major publicity on the green initiative the city is taking." She folded the paper and laid it back on his desk. "And this could bring SI more sustainable projects."

She didn't know. Blake watched her for any signs that she was lying, not that he was a human lie detector, but he could usually read people well enough. She wasn't lying. *Shit*. He was going to need a drink when this was over. He needed one now but he'd made some jacked-up deal with himself not to drink at the office. He couldn't wait until Devin was back. He hated firing people, especially people who didn't deserve it. But, if she wasn't lying, then why was she so nervous around him? He flipped the paper back open and pushed it back towards her. "Open it to A4."

She opened the paper to the backstory and immediately bolted from her chair. "How did they get this?" She turned and paced his office as she read the article, genuine shock ruling her expressions. "This could bury us. We could be looking at months of delays."

Devin was an idiot. Forget how long it took for him to find her in the first place, and what it would take to replace her. He wasn't firing this woman. He didn't care what his friend wanted. He did, however, have to ask the pertinent question. "Do you have any idea how they could have gotten their hands on your final blueprints and materials lists?"

"No," she said emphatically, shaking her head. She jolted to a halt, the paper slipping from her fingers as her hand covered her mouth in disbelief. "Yes." She sunk back to the edge of her seat, a look of complete bewilderment and regret coloring her expression. "Someone took them off the printer."

"When?" Blake reached for his phone and dialed a series of numbers. "Yesterday?" Maybe he could get a lead on who the hell leaked the crucial info to the press.

She bit her lip and shook her head. "No, it was last Monday. The same day I scratched my arm and you…almost passed out. I picked up the wrong prints by mistake on my way to that first meeting."

Blake did a mental eye roll at his junior associate move. If he hadn't been so distracted at that meeting he would have caught the possible security breach himself in time to prevent this from happening. He was the one who had opened the blueprints and pointed out the mix-up. He needed to get his shit together. He'd tried to slide back into his job, into his life, but he had only been playing the part. He was miserable. He hated every damn day he was there worse than the last. It was affecting his performance and he owed Devin more than that.

When security answered, Blake summoned the director to his office. "And bring your quickest IT guy with you." Ending the call, he pushed from his chair and rounded to the front of his desk, taking Jayne's hand in his own as he leaned against the edge. The poor girl was mortified.

"It will be fine. Devin and I have already called the suppliers to secure most of the materials we'll need well in advance. Only one reported a buyout. The good news is, it's not something we'll need right away."

"You have to believe me," Jayne pleaded. "I was running late and grabbed the wrong blueprints. When I returned from the clinic to switch them out, the Emerald Dream prints were gone. I figured someone picked them up by mistake just like I had with the renovation set. I meant to tell—"

"Relax, Jayne. Don't beat yourself up. Dev and I are the ones to blame. We knew there was a threat. We should have thought to move you up to this floor and assigned you a designated printer."

"Yes, but I should have told you." Jayne startled when his assistant buzzed him that the security and IT guys had arrived.

"Show them in, Magnes." He bent down and scooped the paper off the floor and handed it back to Jayne as his door opened and the men filed in. Blake scribbled the date Jayne referenced onto the back of one of his business cards and handed it to the security tech. "Run video on the third floor for this date and send me anything you have of anyone carrying blueprints from the shared printer on the east end." He looked at Jayne and she nodded to confirm. "And please have Ms. Simon's clearance codes upgraded and her office moved to this floor by the end of the day." He ignored her look of surprise and walked to his personal blueprint printer on the far side of his office. "I also want all of her devices defaulted to this printer immediately."

"I can start as soon as the move is complete, sir." The IT guy nodded and grabbed a pen from the metal container on Blake's desk. "Jot down your full name, employee and office number and I'll get right on it Ms. Simon."

Jayne took the pen and wrote everything down as he requested then handed it back to him. Just as he was about to dismiss everyone and call it a day, Blake's cellphone beeped, the tone indicating a text from Devin. He waved Jayne and the other occupants from the room as he scrolled through his phone and retrieved the message.

Satan's Gatekeeper incoming!

"Shit!" Didn't take her long. She should write a book; *How to Stalk Your Brother's Best Friend in Ten Days Or Less.* "Jayne, wait!"

Jayne halted in the hall just outside his doorway and Blake grabbed his coat, locking his computer before he rounded his desk and joined her. "Let's finish our talk over lunch, shall we?" He hooked his arm around Jayne's and fast-walked her towards the elevator.

"Mr. Travers, I-I-I don't think—"

"Don't think," he said and punched the elevator button. When the doors didn't open he looked at the floor indicator. *Incoming.* He would bet a year's salary when those doors opened Mallory would be inside that elevator. He eyed the stairwell, Jayne's fuck-me heels, then looked up at the elevator indicator again. He couldn't chance it. He'd have to deal with her eventually, but not today. "Take off your shoes."

"Excuse me?" Jayne looked down at her shoes and then back at him. He'd explain later, but right now he just needed to get the hell out of there.

"Give me your shoes!"

"No!"

"Suit yourself." He threaded his fingers with hers and sprinted towards the stairs.

"Stop, please!" Jayne pulled her hand free from the lunatic that had taken possession of her gigolo and braced her palms against her thighs, repeating her plea with every panted breath. She spotted a park bench and hobbled to it, sliding onto it just as a monster cramp gripped the arch of her right foot. "Owwww!" She kicked off her high heels and grabbed her foot, frantically working at the knot that nearly had her in tears.

"I told you to ditch them." Mr. Travers slid to one knee in front of her and took her foot into his large hands.

"No!" She jerked her foot away. The last thing she needed was for him to touch her again and ruin all the work she'd done to forget what it felt like to have his hands on her.

"Don't be ridiculous, Jaynie. Let me help."

"Don't call me that! I'm not Jaynie girl, or sweetness, or angel—ah! Oh yeah, right there." A pained breath hissed through her teeth when his thumbs dug into the knot in her arch. "You didn't tell me we were going jogging! Why not just tie me to your car bumper next time!" He massaged her foot until she could feel the cramp ease. She slouched against the back of the bench and her head fell back on a long sigh of relief. The cramp finally released its hold and all that was left was the amazing feeling of Blake's hands on her again.

Dammit, it wasn't fair! She'd tried to forget. She tried so frigging hard!

Every day she went through the same ritual; wake up hot and hung over from a night of dreaming about *him*—she refused to think of *him* by his first name despite his brilliant *me Blake, you Jayne* caveman remark. Jerk!—spend a few minutes with her new battery-operated, jerk-free boyfriend, take a hot shower and she was good to go. Until she saw his gorgeous face, bright blue eyes and gigolo smile and remembered how good his hands felt on her. All her hard work went straight to hell—heck—dammit! *Urrrr!* He'd smile at her just like he was smiling now and all her memories of how he could make her feel would come rushing back. She'd walk home defeated, eat a pint of double fudge or a piece of pie and fall back into bed with his tie under her pillow! *I'm such a loser! Dammed colossal loser!*

Blake's hands stopped moving and she opened her eyes to see him staring at her, his brows pulled together, his mouth gaping in what she thought was alarm or confusion. "What?" she asked, pulling her foot from his hands and shoving it back into her high heel.

"You think I'm a colossal loser? Really?"

"Oh, man." Her head landed in her palms with a groan. "I didn't mean to say that out—"

"No," he said and backed a step away from her. "It's too late now. You can't take it back. You're right. I am a loser."

What the hell? "I can take it back if I want to!" She reached for his hand as he turned to walk away. "I'm sorry!" He stopped, his head hanging low, his shoulders dropping. "Look, Mr. Travers."

"Blake," he croaked.

"Fine, Blake! Whatever!" she said and stood behind him, her free hand itching to trace what she knew was a deep valley that ran the length of his back between all the well-defined muscles. "I was saying that about myself, not you." His shoulders began to quake and her face scrunched up in disbelief. Surely he wasn't crying. *Is he bipolar?* She stepped in front of him and pulled his hands from his face to see his mile-wide smile, his shoulders bouncing as he released the loud and very obnoxious laugh he'd been holding back.

"Ugh! You're such a jerk!" She slapped his arm and pushed him out of her way, intending to march her way right back to work and take the rest of the day off. She was officially without an office to work in until they relocated her, so why not?

"Jayne, wait!" That was until he caught her arm and tugged her back to him, the scent of his cologne catching in the light breeze around them and settling over her like a hypnotizing potion. "I'm sorry. I couldn't help it." He held her in place as he wiped away his fake tears. "See? I *am* a jerk. I can't help myself."

"A colossal *loser* jerk," she reminded him. Good lord, he still smelled so good.

Arm in arm with her he nodded his agreement, turning them back in the direction he had originally been dragging her, only this time at a more leisurely pace thank goodness. "Just to be clear, you can't not-*not* take it back, Jayne. Once it's out there, it's out there. When you take it back, it's back. You just make it confusing if you circle back again."

"What?" Confused, she looked up to see him smirking at her, holding back another laugh. She tried to jerk her arm away but he wouldn't let her go, tugging her closer to him as they walked along the busy downtown sidewalk. In that one move he'd completely disarmed her, made her crave to know more about him. She was in so much trouble.

When Roxy finally answered her phone, Jayne told her about Blake. Roxy told her emphatically to lock herself in his office, throw away the key and their clothes and screw him until he was out of her system. After she'd laughed her head off, of course. Demented woman. There was nothing funny about this! Things were different for Roxy. She only answered to herself. Jayne didn't have that luxury. The stolen plans were the perfect example. She'd been too distracted by Blake and had forgotten to tell him about them. The gigolo issue aside, she couldn't handle that kind of distraction and do her job.

She'd tried to shrug him off. He was overconfident and cocky; nothing like the sensual man who'd awakened her to a new world of passion and seduction. Yet there was something oddly vulnerable about him that kept nagging at her, keeping her on the edge of disbelief.

He was brilliant at what he did. Everyone on the team respected him. Despite the fact he was a little bit drunk all the time and knew or cared next to nothing for the green technology aspect of the Emerald Dream, from what she'd seen so far he was indispensable as a team leader. He orchestrated every engineer, designer, developer, supplier, and city employee like a master maestro. Nothing fazed him. Why then did she get the feeling it was all an act? Every once in a while, like now, she'd get a glimpse of something that made her think of a lost puppy, betraying the smug jerk he wanted everyone to see. And then he would make her laugh. She didn't have a way to fight that.

"So, do I get to know why I was dragged down the stairs, through the lobby and out of a non-burning building in the middle of the day?"

"Of course," he chuckled. "Why would I not tell you?"

They walked in silence as she waited for him to continue. When he didn't, she looked up to see him watching her with that smug expression on his face. "Ugh, you're so frustrating!" She pulled her arm from his and gave him a playful shove.

"You're so easy to tease," he laughed as he caught his balance and fell back into step beside her. "Yes, I'll tell you. Right after we order."

He pulled her to a stop then guided her through an open glass door into a nearby smoothie shop. Overwhelmed by the sheer number of menu choices and the names of some of the items, she gave Blake a general flavor preference and let him order for her. Whey grass, soy protein, carb buster cluster-nonfat-energy meal; it was all gibberish to her. She was a simple girl who never got into the whole designer coffee thing. Light and a little sweet did the trick. Why should she have to learn a new dialect to order coffee, or a yogurt smoothie?

Ten minutes later she was sucking down the best blueberry-banana smoothie she'd ever tasted, despite asking for vanilla. "You have to tell me what to ask for because I'm definitely coming back here." Her mind numbed over as he began to rattle off ingredients. She inhaled another straw full as she mimicked a handwriting motion with a flick of her wrist. "Mmm, write it down. I'll never remember all that."

He laughed and nodded, taking a long draw from his own smoothie. As if they had been drawn in by the power of his heavy pull, her eyes were fixated on his puckered lips as they wrapped around his straw. Her nipples beaded to two hard points, a sharp, cold tingle inciting them to riot as she pictured those lips wrapped around each one, knowing exactly how they felt against her flesh. She could feel his hot sigh as the silky, stiff point of his tongue circled and tickled her, tasting and sucking. The scrape of his teeth over her nipple as he pulled away, licking and tickling the oversensitive underside of her breast before circling and swirling his way to the other one for more.

Blake's hand slapped the table, breaking her trance. Breathless, she looked up to find him slack-jawed and staring at her mouth, his own smoothie forgotten. The corner of his mouth curled up, his fist clenching into a white-knuckled grip around the edge of the table. "Dammit, woman! Are you *trying* to kill me?"

Jayne gasped, releasing the sucking grip she'd had on her straw. Her daydream washed away with the heat of a fresh blush that flooded her cheeks and neck. Two seconds later what felt like an icepick splintered her skull and imbedded itself between her eyes. "Ahhhh!" She pushed her smoothie away and palmed her forehead, rocking back in her seat as the force of an avalanche plowed through her head. "Brain freeze!"

~ NINE ~

Have you ever been so aroused you lost the world around you?

Jayne stood at the base and looked up at the tallest building in California, soon to be the second tallest. At eighty stories above ground and a tri-level parking garage below, the Emerald Dream would soon take the crown from this one.

"It's amazing from this angle, isn't it?" Jayne looked over to see Blake, his hands tucked casually in his pockets. He leaned back against the softly lit stair railing at the top of an exterior enclave, staring up the side of the building with her.

Uber-embarrassed, she'd tried to excuse herself from the smoothie shop after her brain unthawed. Hiding in her office until her fiftieth birthday seemed like a rational idea at the time. He'd taken her hand before she could bolt and dragged her off again to a nearby boutique where he bought her a pair of comfortable sneakers.

That was six hours ago. She'd made the mistake of telling him she hadn't yet had the opportunity to sightsee or take in any of the local architecture since she'd arrived in town. He took it personal, appointing himself her architectural tour guide. They had since walked what must have been every square foot of downtown Los Angeles, saving the best for last.

"It's hard to believe it took less than three years to build this," Jayne said, glancing back up at the brightly lit crown at the very top of the tallest skyscraper.

"The development company had a kick-ass boss."

Surprised, Jayne lowered her gaze to Blake's. "You mean...?"

"My old man," Blake confirmed, a flash of self-awareness coloring his expression.

"Your father built this?" she asked, gesturing to the monolith structure beside them. A wobbly smirk crossed Blake's lips, a flash of that lost puppy showing in his expression again. She was impressed by both his revelation and his timid smile. Vulnerable was such a different look for him. She liked it. It made her feel less anxious around him.

"He was a bastard, but he knew how to get it done."

"Was?" Jayne shook her head, regretting her impulsive questioning. "Never mind. That's none of my business."

"No, it's fine," he assured her, sinking down to sit on the top step of the concrete flight of stairs that led up to their small, semi-private patio; one of the upper mezzanine entrances on either side that overlooked the busy streets. "He passed away a long time ago."

Answers to several of her puzzling questions about Blake began to take form. "So, that's why you're not into this."

"Into what?" Blake asked, looking up over his shoulder at her.

"This. The Emerald Dream." Jayne tucked her skirt behind her knees and sank to the step beside him, folding her arms over her kneecaps. "You don't care about this project. I've watched you in the meetings and around the office. You go through the motions, but you're not really there. You don't want to compete with your father's work?"

Blake's sarcastic chuckle puzzled her even more. "Trust me. I have zero problems unseating my father's name from this throne," he said, his hand slapping the step between them to punctuate his claim. "Like I said, he was a grumpy old bastard. He died while I was in college. He was fifty when I was born so there wasn't a lot in common between us by the time I was old enough to appreciate this." His hand swept up as he leaned back on the step behind him and looked back up at the skyscraper.

"Wow. How old was your mom?"

She watched as Blake stared back up at the sky. "She was twenty five."

Blake didn't elaborate any further but she didn't have to be a rocket scientist to figure out that arrangement. Maybe she was the reason he moved to Vegas. "Does she live here in Los Angeles?"

Blake shook his head. "I haven't spoken to her in…five years?" He cocked his head in thought. "No, six. Six years. Don't even know where she is. Probably cruising the Mediterranean."

Wow. She'd do anything to have one more day with her parents. She couldn't imagine them being alive and not seeing them for six years. She didn't want to seem rude or insensitive so she kept that thought to herself.

"Then, why are you here?" It was something that had niggled at her from the beginning. Even though he was good at what he did, it was obvious he didn't want to be there. Why would he leave Las Vegas—another job at which he was equally talented— and take a job he hated?

"Devin is my best friend. This project was lined up well before I decided to leave. I promised Dev I'd be here. So…I'm here."

"Devin Kirk? CEO Devin Kirk?"

Blake nodded. "Yeah, you haven't met him yet, but you will next week. He'll be wrapping things up in Toronto and be back in L.A. in a few days. It was his sister, Mallory, I was running from today."

"Oh? An old girlfriend?" Jayne felt an odd twist of jealousy churn in her stomach.

"Hell, no!" Blake huffed. "She's…disturbed," he said, whistling a 'coo-coo' sound. "In an evil kind of way, ya know? She apparently found out I'm back and Devin sent me a heads up as everyone was leaving my office earlier."

The relief Jayne felt irked her more than the spike of jealousy. It wasn't as if he was interested in her. Knowing he didn't remember her at all, a small twinge of hurt arced in her heart, but she shook it off. He wasn't the jerk he'd tried to make himself out to be, or the one she'd wanted him to be. It would have been a lot easier if he was, but he wasn't, and she still wanted him. Which sucked because it wasn't going to happen. That didn't stop her from wanting to know more about him. Unable to acknowledge that she knew about his gigolo job in Vegas without opening the proverbial can of worms, she couldn't help but ask about what had spawned such a drastic career change. "Why did you leave SI in the first place?"

He was silent for so long Jayne was about to apologize for asking when he finally spoke. "My fiancé was murdered; mugged in the parking lot at her gym. The police never found who was responsible."

"Blake, I'm so sorry." To say she wasn't prepared for that admission would have been an understatement of the century. Instinctively her hand moved to his shoulder to offer some form of comfort. Although different than hers, loss was loss. It was all so senseless. She wanted to share that with him; let him know just how well she understood. Before she could find the words he turned his head and looked at her, offering a small, sad smile.

"No...I'm sorry." He shook his head and pushed to his feet. "I didn't mean to blurt it out like that. I haven't talked about it in a while." He offered her his hand and she took it, letting him pull her to her feet. "I couldn't walk the streets or even get a cup of coffee without wondering if the guy taking my change or the person next to me on the sidewalk was the one who'd killed Daphne. It wasn't healthy for me to stay." She supposed not, but becoming a gigolo? He let go of her hand. Feeling a little embarrassed at her meddling, she wrapped her arms around her waist as an awkward silence expanded between them. Afraid another imposing question would come popping, out she didn't dare open her mouth again.

Clearing his throat, Blake leaned against the stone retaining wall, his elbows propped on the metal railing along the top. Awestruck by his beauty, she was taken back to the moment she first saw his photo. Now that she had gotten to know a little of the man behind the gigolo, he was even more stunning. Normally she would say it was strange to call a man beautiful, but not Blake. His long, muscular legs extended out in front of him and crossed at his ankles. His light blue dress shirt stretched across his chest, the buttons and sleeves straining ever so slightly from the thick muscles that bunched beneath them. His cuffs were rolled up almost to his elbows and she could see a few whispering tendrils of his tattoos peeking out from beneath one of them. She tried to remember what they looked like from his picture but failed. She shook her head. She didn't like tattoos. Or at least she never had before. Right now she'd say she was pretty close to tracing them with her tongue if he'd let her. It was difficult to believe he'd touched her, and not just physically, but in so many intimate ways.

Landscaping lights lent enough of a glow for her to see the kaleidoscope of emotions swirling in his eyes. He was vulnerable. He was lost. He wasn't crushed beyond recognition, but there were definitely a few broken and missing pieces. Contrasting the man in front of her with the man who'd seduced her in that hotel room was impossible. They now seemed like two completely different people. She realized then she wasn't being entirely fair to Blake. He had been playing a part and as hard as she tried not to, she had been judging him against that character instead of who he really was. He was just a normal, talented, broken, sexy man, who was watching her stare at him. He threw her one of those disarming winks that told her she was busted. Again. "So, you've been watching me, huh?"

A deep blush flushed her cheeks. She fished for a response to his blatant flirting, but came up empty handed. The intensity in his eyes stole her breath away along with every word in her head.

"I love it when you blush that way." He reached out and caressed her cheek, another deeper flush blooming beneath his fingertips. Dammit, why did she have to be so shy? She glanced nervously between him and the concrete steps. He was going to kiss her. She shouldn't let him do it, but she was going to. She craved him. She wanted more of him. The real him.

He pushed away from the railing and towered over her, the ambient lighting reflecting in his eyes as he looked down into hers. Heat caressed her cheeks when he cupped them in his large, strong hands. Her breath hitched and she let out a startled whimper when he leaned in, nuzzling her temple instead of moving straight for her lips. A sudden and loud bouquet of laughter echoed off the buildings around them. She turned to see a young couple stumble up the first few steps below them and stop, oblivious to their surroundings as they groped and fondled each other in the midst of their own passion-filled kiss.

Jayne turned and covered her surprised gasp with her hand. Things between the couple below escalated quickly. The guy pushed the girl up against the shoulder-high wall, hitching her leg over his hip as he ground himself against her and deepened their kiss. Jayne shielded her eyes and turned away. "We should leave," she whispered.

Blake pulled her into a dark corner of the patio and turned them back to see the couple. Her blood sang with excitement in response to the feel of his arms around her. "The only way out is down those stairs," he reminded her. Oh, God, he was right. They were stuck. He bent to whisper in her ear. "Look at them, Jayne. Look how lost they are in each other's touch." The slow, seductive tone in his voice was different than she remembered. There was a genuine excitement that crackled in the air around them as he spoke, sending a shiver racing through her body. Her heart galloped in her chest as she suddenly found herself inside a reality version of the fantasy world he'd weaved for her before.

Her breath hitched again in surprise when Blake wrapped his arms around her and pulled her against him, keeping his eyes on the couple below. "Oh yeah, look at that." He rested his chin on her shoulder and gestured to the lovers. The woman fumbled with his belt before she unzipped the man's pants and cupped his erection. Heavy need robbed Jayne of her next breath, the unmistakable feel of Blake's rigid erection pressing hard against her backside.

Her sensible side was screaming for her to stop him. It didn't matter that she didn't want to stop. He was her boss. If she continued, she was playing with fire when it came to her career.

"This is wrong. We shouldn't be here," Jayne panted, but she couldn't turn away from the sight below. Her chest ached with the effort it took to drag in each shallow, ragged breath. Eyes slamming closed, her hands flew to his wrists when his fingers gripped her hips and pulled her even closer. When she opened her eyes all she could see was the couple below. The man dipped his head and suckled the woman's nipple through her shirt. Jayne almost cried out as her own nipples pebbled to painful peaks beneath her shirt.

"Have you ever been so aroused you lost the world around you, Jayne? So much so, no one existed in that world but you and your lover?"

Only with you. Was this really happening? She floated between reality and fantasy, the line between the two blurring beyond recognition. The sound of his voice was like a tether, the only thing that kept her from drifting away into the bliss she'd craved since the morning she woke up alone in Vegas. He dragged in a long breath and hummed against her ear. Uncontrolled shudders rolled through her body when he took her earlobe between his teeth and closed his lips around it in an intimate kiss.

"Yes," she gasped, her head falling back against his chest. Her fingers released their grip on his wrists, sliding down to tangle frantically with his at her hips to anchor herself in his stimulating touch.

"That's where they are, Jaynie, lost in themselves; lost to the passion coursing between their bodies." The woman dropped to her knees in front of the man and Jayne felt Blake's hips jerk against her. His raw, tortured growl raked over her skin as she watched the woman take the man into her mouth, the man's arms bracing against the wall, his head thrown back in a silent cry of ecstasy. Blake's grip on her hips tightened, his erection grinding harder against her. "Do you feel it, Jayne?"

Yes! Yes she felt it! Jayne's eyes slammed shut again, the entrenched image of the lovers below breathing new life into her memories of her night with Blake. She'd lain on the bed, her head lulled back against the edge as he hovered above her, her tongue caressing his long shaft as he pushed into her mouth over and over. Her fingers twitched. She could almost feel his coarse hair beneath her fingertips as she raked them over his thick thighs. Her entire body was coiled so tight. Her legs shook, her stomach twisted into knots. Anymore and she would break. She wanted to taste him again. She needed to feel him. "Feed from their hunger for each other, Jaynie. Let go and get lost in their world."

"Blake, I...I can't—"

"Shhh," he whispered in her ear. "Open your eyes, Jayne."

Afraid if she did she would awaken to find it all just another dream, slowly she raised her eyelids. Her mouth parted on a ragged sigh when she looked up to see Blake's hooded eyes fixed on her lips. Was he as drunk on their passion as she was? He dipped his head, hesitating a fraction of a second before his lips touched hers. A sharp zing of arousal ricocheted through her chest, down to her stomach and raced between her thighs. He felt so good. Hot and provoking, the tip of his tongue danced delicately across her lips. She opened to him immediately, releasing a desperate whimper as his tongue slid long and sure against hers, retreating slowly only to return, over and over again with intense desperation. It was like no other kiss she'd ever had.

The sound of a police siren wailed from the street below. Startled, she jerked away from Blake's embrace to see the couple below scurry away in a fit of squeals and deep male laughter. The cop's bright search light flipped on and swept the patio, landing directly on them. She tucked her face into Blake's chest as he turned away, protecting her from view as he waved to the cop. This was so embarrassing. Nothing. She could get away with *nothing*! Not that they were doing anything more than kissing...yet.

The cop pulled away as they made their way down the stairs and onto the sidewalk. Yep, a few more minutes and it could have been so much worse. More awkward silence fell between them as they hurried back to SI. She glanced over and noticed a look of disbelief in Blake's expression that mirrored her own, his eyes fixed blankly on the sidewalk as their quickened steps ate up the distance back to their offices in a fraction of the time it took them earlier in the day. She couldn't begin to process what he was thinking or doubting. Her own thoughts were screaming so loudly she barely heard the traffic passing by in a blur. One thought. Only one thought was creating all of the almost painful chaos inside her head. Blake was *not* her gigolo.

~ TEN ~

All kinds of general fucked-upness.

Blake sat alone in the back of the busy cigar tavern, his legs stretched out along the booth seat as he stared into the numb end of his sixth shot of scotch. Or seventh. Whatever. This place was a little seedy for his tastes, but tonight that served his need to stay hidden. Distracted by a large party that had rambled in a few minutes earlier, the waitress was running behind schedule on their deal to keep his glass full. He nursed his last sip, enjoying the buzz he'd work so hard to find. Letting it slip away because of a busy waitress would be a travesty he wasn't willing to let happen. Not after the day he'd had.

He flung his feet down and stood, grabbing the edge of the table to steady himself. Maybe he was a little bit drunker than he thought. That would be awesome. He heel-toed it to the bar and slid onto a barstool. Several hours had passed since he'd slipped out of that awful club and escaped Mallory's clutches. He figured it was safe enough to leave the shadows that hid the tables in the back. He was confident she wouldn't step foot inside a place so distasteful, but he wouldn't put it past her to peek through the window looking for him.

The cute bartender gave him an apologetic look as she tipped the bottle of whiskey and refilled his glass. She turned to leave but hesitated when he held out a crisp bill with more than one zero printed on it. With little pomp or circumstance, she set the bottle beside his glass and snatched the money from his grasp. His lazy gaze lingered on her ass as she walked away, tucking the bill into her bra. When images of Jayne transposed over the otherwise perfect view, his dick woke up and stretched…again. He closed his eyes against his need and swallowed against the dryness in his throat. Memories of how his little architect felt against him burned through the alcohol fueled fog in his mind.

He didn't know what the hell had come over him. It must have been his lack of sleep. He hadn't even told his mother about Daphne, but he'd spilled his guts to a woman he barely knew? Not that he ever planned to tell his mother anything about his life. He hadn't lied. He didn't know where his mother was and he didn't care. Oh, he had no doubt he'd hear from her eventually. She'd run out of her inheritance some day and come begging. Still, he had no reason to tell Jayne any of that.

He'd spent the last three years dealing with Daphne's murder. He was over it. He really was. As much as anyone could get over losing the person who made them whole. He would never accept her death as some random act of violence the way Devin and the rest of the world had. The flat tires, hang-ups, broken glass, the spray painted messages on her car and front door; too many things had happened before she died for him to believe it was all some tragic coincidence. The police detective assigned to her case determined the way she died didn't fit the profile of the person who had done all those things. It wasn't 'personal' enough, whatever the hell that meant. She was dead. How much more personal did it get?

The cops were wrong. He was ninety-nine percent sure someone had targeted her from their club. Someone who had seen them together. The first few times she'd gotten a flat they hadn't thought anything of it. He'd changed it, had a new one mounted and told her to pay better attention to the roads and what she drove over. Then the nasty messages began. When he first put things together Blake realized it had all begun the first night they played in the club together. The night after he proposed.

His eyes fell closed as Daphne ghosted back to life in his memories. She'd been glorious. She was so shy when he'd first taken her to the private voyeur club him and Dev had been members of since their early college years. Like Jayne and the horny couple the night before, in the beginning Daphne could barely watch the couples fucking in what they called the aquarium; a glass enclosed stage in the center of the main floor where couples, or even singles, who like to show and tell did just that for those who liked to watch.

As some sort of crazy declaration or silly promise, she'd surprised him the night after he proposed. Dev had been their third for awhile, but they had always played in one of the private or semi-private rooms at the club. Or at Devin's place. That night she'd enlisted Dev to put on a show for him. She wasn't a natural exhibitionist, but she and Dev had a chemistry that put them over the top to watch. It wasn't like watching porn. He could get that anywhere. It was about watching her. She got him, both of them, in a way no one else would. He would never get to feel that again.

None of that changed the fact that she was gone and he'd accepted that. Despite what he'd told Devin, he'd even say he was ready to move on. The idea of finding someone new to share his life with was no longer nauseating. That had to count for something. The question was, why? Why would he want to go through that again? Falling into and crawling out of a new bed every night was a hell of a lot easier than falling in and out of love.

Damn, then he'd overwhelmed Jayne with his voyeuristic general...fucked-upness. The moment that couple showed up he'd been fucked. There was no way he could have resisted the temptation.

His next sip turned into a gulp, then another before he slammed his glass down on the bar. His fingers wrapped around the bottle but he wavered against pouring the next glassful as guilt's familiar chill beat out the fire from the whiskey and settled in his chest. None of it mattered if he couldn't control his desires. It had been nearly two years since he'd let that part of himself loose. Knowing it was his warped sexual needs that most likely put Daphne in the crosshairs of some sick bastard, he had smothered that part of himself until he thought he'd killed enough of it to make the guilt die with it. Fine job he'd done of that.

He briefly considered visiting the club. Maybe taking the edge off every once in a while would help him keep it together while he was in L.A. *No.* He had turned in his membership after Daphne's funeral and never looked back. He didn't plan to now. He'd managed to stay away from the private clubs in Vegas, trying to convince himself that part of him was gone. Apparently his kink was alive and well and thriving on his new architect.

What was it about this woman that made his demons suddenly revolt? Somewhere in the back of his mind he knew he hadn't completely choked them out, but why had they all of a sudden decided to wake up and fuck around with his head? Why now? Why her? Sure, she'd responded like a dream to the couple humping on the stairs. Hell, if the cops hadn't showed up she would have been on her knees sucking him off too. The remembered sounds of her whimpers made his groin tighten and his fingers flexed on the bottle. He'd been seconds away from fingering her to her own climax. Screwing in a dark corner, however, where no one could see you was light-years away from being fucked in public by his best friend while he watched. He could already see them together in his mind, Jayne and Devin. He was a sick bastard and there was no way innocent little Jaynie girl was ever going to understand that part of him. *She ordered a vanilla smoothie for Christ's sake.*

Just as he knew he would never fully purge himself of his demons, he also knew he still wanted Jayne. Kink, vanilla, he didn't care. He wanted her. He knew he would screw her and leave her, but he still wanted her. Not that he had a chance in hell of getting her now. His fingers on his left hand toyed with the cork on the bottle as the fingers on his right traced the rim of his still empty glass. Christ, Mallory Silverland could fuck up divine providence without even trying. She'd been particularly evil today when she'd finally found him. His punishment for ditching her yesterday he was sure.

"Oh goodie, you're here!" she'd said when she slithered into his office just as he was about to log off his computer and go home, her words polluted with an artificial sweetener. Blake hadn't bothered to address her. Instead, he opened his top desk drawer and pushed its contents around in search of the year old antacids he hoped like hell were still there. "You didn't forget our date again, did you?"

"I didn't forget our last date, Mallory." He slammed the drawer closed and slung open another one, continuing what was turning out to be a fruitless search. "Can't forget what never existed."

"Aw, don't be snarky with me," she said with her signature pronounced pout. "I haven't seen you in a year. No reason we can't have a little something to drink and catch up." Mallory tucked her designer hand bag under her arm, hiked her short red skirt up her stocking clad thighs then propped her hip onto his desk with practiced seduction. It would have worked, too, if he had any interest in becoming the heartless shape shifter's mindless concubine. He didn't.

He gave up finding any relief for the burning knot at the base of his throat and slammed the last drawer closed, slumping back into his chair to study one of the few anomalies left in the world. She may not be able to actually change physical form, but Mallory's ability to hide her true maliciousness from the rest of the world showed a near supernatural talent.

Not much had changed since he'd seen her last. Her hair was a little longer, darker maybe, her skirt a little shorter. She was still sporting her two favorite accessories; an acidic smile and a pitchfork. "What do you want, Mallory?"

"I want you to apologize, Blake. It was rude of you to run out on me yesterday." She crossed her legs and unclasped her purse, checking her face in one of those cosmetic mirrors women carry. He wouldn't be shocked to find out she truly didn't have a reflection. "Then you can take me out for a drink to celebrate your return. Maybe a little dancing downtown?"

He could hear the words '*then fuck me*' in her tone like a wicked subliminal message you would get when you play a certain song backwards. He held back a chuckle when the words *Mallory is Satan's spawn* began to play on a loop in a guttural voice inside his head. *Fuck!* This is why he left. This is why he could never stay.

"Not going to happen, Mallory." He didn't give a damn about her damaged pride or hurt feelings. He was done taking her shit.

She shrugged and flicked the mirror back into her purse, that innocent smile she showed the rest of the world blooming on her angelic face. *True evil comes in beautiful packages.* "Apologize to me for running away yesterday and take me out or," she hissed as she pulled out a cigarette and lit it. Acrid smoke billowed from her lips and engulfed him. "You can tell Devin about his little nephew. And believe me, by the time I get done with him your version will seem desperate at best."

Blah-blah-blah. Same threat, different day. He pushed away from his desk and grabbed his coat from the back of his chair. "You came to me for help, Mallory. You had the abortion, not me." It wasn't as if the baby was his.

"Need I remind you—"

"No, Mallory!" *Un-fucking-real.* This was just one more perfect example of how his twisted needs had seriously screwed up his life. "You don't need to remind me." Blake shrugged into his coat and fingered the keys on his keyboard to lock his computer. Damn, how he wished he'd known about her penchant for evil back then. He would have never gone to that stupid party and she would be nothing but a forgotten drunken memory.

"Fine." He paced to his door, not bothering to close it when he flipped off the light switch and walked out of his office, leaving her sitting in the dark. "But don't hold your breath for that apology."

Her gleeful squeal sent a fresh fiery eruption of acid rushing up his throat. He had to swallow it back down to keep from puking. She hopped off of his desk and ran to catch up to him, never once faltering in her five inch heels. "One out of two isn't bad." She wrapped her cold fingers into the crook of his elbow and smiled up at him as he pushed the button for the lobby. "I always take what I can get." *Yeah. And then some.*

Just as the doors were about to close, Jayne walked around the corner from her new office. She'd been trying to talk to him all day, but he kept pushing her off. She wanted to talk about what happened the night before. He didn't. He wanted to quit and catch the first flight back to Vegas, or bend her over his desk and fuck her within an inch of both their lives. Both would be fantastic. As she got closer to the elevator he scrambled for something to say to her. She was the perfect excuse to get out of this nightmare with Devin's sister.

Mallory must have sensed his plan. Hell, she probably read his thoughts with her voodoo witchery. The very moment he reached for the door to hold it open, Mallory pulled him down to her and stuck her forked tongue down his throat. Locked in Mallory's wicked grip, he looked past her to see Jayne standing just a few feet away, confusion and hurt joining the flush of red in her cheeks.

The doors closed, locking him inside a private hell with his personal demon.

Blake looked down at the half empty bottle of whiskey in his hands, the picture of Jayne's red face ghosting over the amber colored courage within. She'd thought he was an asshole. And he probably was, but not because he was fucking around with Mallory after he'd fucked around with her. Bottle in hand, he slid off the barstool and stumbled his way towards the door. He shouldn't have shut her out today. He shouldn't have taken Mallory to that stupid club. He shouldn't have fucking come back to L.A. And he certainly shouldn't be on his way to Jayne's apartment. But he'd done all of that and was definitely going to see his Jaynie girl. She needed to know he wasn't an asshole.

~ ELEVEN ~

Somewhere between hell and death.

Her phone rang again, the familiar ringtone reminding Roxy of yet one more thing she was losing. The newly familiar nausea churned in her stomach when she snatched the phone from the kitchen counter. Jayne's smiling face stared back at her for the tenth time that day. Their favorite song played over the speaker until the call kicked over to her voicemail. Silence filled the room once again, but Roxy couldn't hear it over the clamoring chaos in her mind. All of the doctors' voices blended together into one long, monotonous string of bullshit. And they wouldn't shut up.

We're so sorry, Ms. Stark, but a double mastectomy is your only option if you want to survive.

Rage filled her veins. How could this be happening? She first found the lump a couple of months before Jayne got her new job. Thinking it was probably just a swollen gland from a cold she couldn't seem to shake, she procrastinated; fooling herself into thinking it was nothing. When it didn't go away, she made an appointment with her doctor and they immediately scheduled her for a biopsy and an ultrasound. She got the test results back a week before Jayne came home with the news about her job. Roxy had been numb for days, surviving in a zombie fog. She couldn't process what was happening. It wasn't real. Cancer couldn't happen to her. She was only twenty-six years old!

When the numbness began to wear off the fear settled in like a bitter cold winter. *Cancer.* Fuck! She still couldn't make herself say the word. It felt like if she did, she would immediately drop dead. Without acknowledging it, she felt like she had this silent, alien creature living inside her, killing her from the inside out and no one could hear her scream. She was stuck in this reality somewhere between hell and death. And the only way to kill it was to mutilate herself beyond recognition; to cut away a part of her. A major part. She'd had nightmare after nightmare of some faceless monster eating away at her flesh, of standing in front of a mirror and cutting her breasts off with a kitchen knife.

Telling herself that it was okay, that thousands of women went through this every year was a crock of bull. It was supposed to help, but it did *nothing!* The things she'd seen on the internet were so horrific and terrifying. Night terrors eventually got so bad her body wouldn't allow her sleep. She kept herself awake by cleaning and re-cleaning everything. Normally she could lock herself away in her studio and paint through whatever was bugging her, but even that had been taken from her. She couldn't create shit.

At first going to Las Vegas had been a completely selfish idea. Although Jayne had been right about Hank, she felt guilty for making up that story about him. He hadn't cheated on her. She just couldn't tell him. She couldn't stomach the thought of his rejection, which would have happened eventually. Escaping to Vegas seemed like the perfect plan, at least for a few days. She'd wanted to run away, drown herself in men who didn't matter and booze that would make the numbness come back until she couldn't hear the doctor's voices anymore, telling her she was going to die.

When she saw the excitement on Jayne's face that day, she'd been so angry. All of Jayne's happiness in life was tied up in something that, in the end, would never matter to anyone. It was a fucking job! Jayne had never allowed herself to experience love or lust or passion, or any of the elemental things that made life worth living. Instead, Jayne surrounded herself with deadlines and drafting tables and boring men because it was *safe.* If she did all the right things, said all the right things and dated all the *right* men, then somehow nothing bad could ever happen to her. Dammit, she knew!

Roxy knew, now more than ever, that it was all a lie! No one was guaranteed a single breath no matter how *safe* they were. Nothing was safe. Not board meetings or important titles or even trying to save the whole mother fucking planet. Nothing could have kept this from happening to her. It was all one big fucking lie!

Her fingers tightened into a fist around her phone. When the casing cracked so did something inside her. "Fuck you, Jayne!" Even as she threw the phone across the kitchen she regretted the words. She wasn't angry at Jayne. She loved her. She missed her like crazy, and more than anyone in the world she needed her! The phone bounced off one of the cabinet doors and tumbled onto the floor, still in one piece. *Not good enough.* She wanted it to shatter into a million pieces just like her fucking life! One swipe of her arm and all of the porcelain canisters sitting on the kitchen cabinet that belonged to Jayne's mother crashed to the floor, flour and sugar and cereal scattered on the tiles around her feet. "It's not fair!" She shoved at one of the chairs that sat around the kitchen table but it hardly budged. Roxy's anger flared into a raging fury. She couldn't even make a stupid chair do what she wanted! She let out an enraged scream as she shoved the entire table over onto its side, her socked feet slipping in the flour and sugar before she crumbled to the floor. A sob broke free from the knot of fear and resentment that had been building and building inside her chest. *What am I going to do?*

Tears streamed from her eyes, but she hurriedly wiped them away. "Dammit!" She fisted her hands in her hair. She was so screwed up. She needed to talk to Jayne, but she couldn't tell her. Not now when she was finally letting go and living her life outside her safety zone.

A weary snort bubbled up and out. Still, to that very moment, Roxy couldn't believe Jayne had agreed to her gigolo plan. The escort wasn't part of her original plan to get Jayne to Vegas, but once she was there a new plan took shape. While she desperately did need to escape, she wanted to show Jayne what she was missing by playing it so safe. While her best friend had been tying up the loose ends at her old job before they left for Vegas, Roxy sold all her paintings at auction and put her studio up for lease. She'd spent nearly half her profit on that weekend of pure bliss. Jayne had been in heaven for days after they got back.

Roxy smiled at the memory of Jayne's signature blush as she tried to make herself recount all the sexy details to her. She'd been in shock and Roxy had loved every minute of it. Even though they were the same age, she'd always felt like Jayne's big sister; like her protector. Jayne needed to know that there was more to life than being safe.

Jayne was in L.A. now, living out her dream. The minute Roxy told her about her diagnosis, she would end it all and fly back to New York. Jayne would immediately blame herself for leaving then crawl back into her little safety shell, using Roxy as an excuse to never step outside her comfort zone again. *No.* Roxy shook her head and swiped the rest of her tears away. *No way.* She wouldn't let that happen. If for some reason she didn't survive this, she would at least die knowing she hadn't enabled Jayne to hide from life.

Before she could chicken out, Roxy pushed to her knees and shuffled across the kitchen floor, wading through the layers of flour and sugar to reach for her phone. She wiped her hand over the screen to clean it off. When she swiped her finger over the screen it flickered a bit but lit up eventually and she scrolled through the new list of medical related numbers she'd acquired lately. It was three in the morning, but if she didn't make the call now she never would. She dialed the number to the last specialist she'd seen and cleared the tears from her throat while she waited for the after-hours answering service. Thankful she wasn't connected to one of those lifeless, automated *'press one for English'* services, she smiled at the pert, friendly voice on the other end of the phone call of her life. When the woman ended her greeting Roxy cleared her throat again and forced the words through her trembling lips. "I need to schedule my surgery. Can you please have them call me tomorrow?"

The door buzzer rang just as Jayne's call to Roxy clicked over to her voicemail again. Distracted from her concern, she pulled the phone from her ear as she marched to the door, hanging up without leaving another message. She punched the button on the intercom as she looked at the time on her cellphone. "Yes?" Who could it be at midnight? A broken voice crackled through the speaker on her wall. "What? Who's there?" Her head jerked back and she plugged her ear with her finger when nothing but a loud buzzing sound blared through the speaker. She sprinted to her room and grabbed her robe. Pulling it around her shoulders, she shoved her keys and her phone into the front pocket before she went downstairs to see who was at the door. On the way down she made a mental note to let her super know her intercom was broken. While the apartment building was nice, upscale by most standards, it was still downtown L.A. There was no security at the front door, only an electronic lock requiring a code to enter the building. Someone could just as easily sneak in behind another tenant.

The stairs were closer to her apartment than the elevator so, despite the late hour, she opted for the exercise. The sound of rain beating against the front entrance doors surprised her as she approached the bottom of the last flight of steps. She still wasn't accustomed to L.A. weather, but she was sure such a strong downpour this time of year was a rare occurrence. When she reached the glass front door no one was there. She raised her arm above her head to shield what she could of the rain drops and peeked outside. She didn't see his face but there was no mistaking the dark outline of Blake's bus-broad shoulders and his sun streaked spikes as he walked away. *What is he doing here?*

She'd tried to talk to him all day but he kept brushing her off, asking her to come back later or having his assistant tell her he wasn't available to take her calls. Between him and Roxy she was beginning to think she had the plague. Then she'd seen him with Mr. Kirk's sister in the elevator. Based on how gorgeous she was, and how far down his throat the woman had embedded her tongue, she figured he had finally lost his battle of wills and given into her.

"Blake?" she yelled over the whirring hiss of raindrops that fell like a deluge between them. Blake turned on a dime, a little wobble in his step as he paced the twenty or so feet back to the door.

"I thought maybe you didn't want to see me." He stood outside the open door, soaked and disheveled, a complete and beautiful mess. Jayne looked up into his sleepy looking eyes. Raindrops clinging to his eyelashes reflected the pale light cast from the few surrounding streetlights. Her fingers curled into fists as she fought the urge to wipe them away like tears. Instead she grabbed his hand and pulled him inside. Just because he was a jerk didn't mean she wanted him to catch the flu.

"I couldn't hear you from my apartment. I think the intercom speaker is broken." Good Lord he was beautiful! Even in the dim light of the foyer she could see the paleness of his irises. An almost ghostly blue-gray, they glowed with staggering intent, but something seemed off. His eyes lacked their usual sharpness.

"Are you loaded?" she asked, turning her back to the muted sconce on the wall behind her so she could see his eyes better.

"Immensely," he said with a satirical smirk on his face. "My trust fund—among other things—is enormous."

Her brow arched. Yeah, right. He might be right about the *other* things, but a trust funded gigolo? She couldn't smell any booze on him, but he certainly acted intoxicated. "I meant, are you drunk?"

"Just a little bit." He nodded and swayed a tad, holding up his fingers to indicate as much.

Sounds of the flash storm suddenly stopped. In the quiet she could hear his labored breaths, the swish of fabric as he pulled his hand up and ran his fingers through his sexy, wet hair. His dress shirt clung to his skin, outlining every dip and curve of the well-defined muscles beneath it. The scent of rain and his familiar cologne swirled like an intoxicating potion in the damp air around them. She shivered at the sight of him. A dark shadow passed over his features and his golden brows pinched together. He took a breath as if he were going to speak, but stilled his words before they were spoken, his glance bouncing nervously between her and the wall behind her. She suddenly felt exposed, vulnerable to his ability to reject her again. Mixed with her confusion about who he really was, it didn't seem like a very safe place to be, emotionally. When she wrapped her arms around herself and took a step away, a spark of anger flashed in his eyes.

"Blake, why are—"

One step. A single movement was all it took and she was pinned against the wall at the base of the stairs, his lips opening hers with a crushing kiss. His hot tongue pierced her lips and slid deep inside her mouth. Long fingers grasped her hips. His thick thigh slid between her legs and pressed hard against all the right parts. With that one move she felt destroyed and complete all in the same moment. Despite his aggressiveness, she felt strangely worshiped and craved. Like she was an expensive drug he couldn't get into his veins fast enough.

She raked her fingers through his rain-soaked hair and pulled him closer, greedy for more of his taste. He had definitely been drinking, but suddenly it didn't seem important. Blake indulged her demand, tilting his head and sinking his tongue deeper alongside hers with a fierce growl. His grip on her hips moved lower, the heat of his grasp seeping through her thin pajama bottoms when his fingers clenched her ass. Her toes left the ground when he lifted and pinned her to the wall. Sharp, sensual energy spiked through her stomach and fluttered between her legs when his hips rolled hard against her pelvis. She could feel the swell of his erection pressed hard against her pelvis with each upward thrust as she rode his thick thigh.

Her head fell back against the wall when he broke their kiss to trail his tongue along the length of her neck. "I'm not an asshole, Jaynie." She secretly loved when he called her Jaynie. Even in her confusion and bliss, her heart swelled in her chest at the sound of her nickname on his lips.

"What?"

"Why I came here," he continued, his hot breath puffing against her skin. "I needed you to know I'm not an asshole."

"What do you mean?" She gasped when his teeth scraped the top of her shoulder. *How can he think enough to talk?*

His body stopped moving, leaving a heated void between them. She felt his panted breaths and then a long sigh against her shoulder before he lifted his head. "I'm a fucked up individual, Jayne." She immediately missed her pet name. He stared at her lips as he spoke and they tingled with regret that they weren't touching his. "But I would never string you along and fool around with someone else unless we had an understanding."

An understanding? Is that what he'd come here to gain? "Is that what you came here for? To work out some kind of…of arrangement?" She pushed at his chest and moved her head so that she could see his eyes. He was serious. Her heart plummeted and a burning heat flushed over her body, a heat that burned off her arousal like a lingering fog. This was more embarrassing than getting caught by the police. "I can't do this. I can't—"

One of Blake's hands covered her mouth, cutting off her response. The move sent a sliver of alarm skittering up her spine. With a tilt of her chin he forced her to look at him. "I am only going to say this once so I want to be perfectly clear. Do you understand?" When she shook her head, he removed his hand and rocked his forehead against hers. "I am not, nor will I *ever* be, interested in Mallory Silverland. She only kissed me because of my reaction to you when you walked around that corner." His eyes squeezed shut. She sucked in a nervous breath as he slowly pulled open her robe, his large hands framing her ribcage. "It's like a punch in my gut every damn time I see you and she didn't like it." He lifted his head again, his eyes pleading with her before his words could. "I told you. Mallory is the spawn of Satan and she will do anything to fuck up my life. Please don't let her fuck this up, too."

There was more than a little annoyance in his tone. Jayne sensed a genuine abhorrence for Mr. Kirk's sister. More than that, she realized that he'd come to her apartment in the middle of the night, drunk and in a rain storm to tell her. Did what she thought of him really matter that much? "A punch in the gut?"

He dipped his head and touched his lips to hers. Her breath hitched to a stop, but his panted out in short puffs as the tip of his tongue slid out and bumped along her bottom lip, like he was tasting her for the first time. "Every time."

If she stopped to think, the entire scene would be bizarre; too bizarre. So she didn't. She only knew that he wanted her, and she wanted him to touch her. She wiggled from his grasp and took his hand, leading him up the stairs. When he tugged on her hand she stopped and turned. Standing on the step above him she was nearly eye to eye with him. He swayed slightly. His hands raised and pushed the lapels of her cotton bathrobe back, his eyes fixed almost drunkenly on her breasts. She looked down at the front of her gray tank top, soaked through from his wet dress shirt. Under his ice-blue gaze her nipples hardened, straining for his touch. His eyes darted up to hers, a pained expression on his face that begged her permission. "We should go upstairs."

In another one of those singular, swift movements that betrayed his semi-intoxicated state, Blake dipped his knees and scooped her up, her legs instinctually choking his hips. His hot mouth covered the material of her tank-top. The bite of his hard draw on her nipple ran bone-deep through her entire body. Afraid someone would hear them, her hand slapped over her mouth to stifle her scream. The other one wrapped around his neck to hold him closer when he pushed her back against the stairwell wall. "I want you here."

Jayne's blood ran hot and fast through her veins. She skated along the fine edge of a drug-like euphoria, but not so close that she could ignore the possibility of one of her neighbors seeing them. "Not—oh God—not here," she panted each word.

"Mmm, what floor?" Blake asked with a growl, his lips never leaving her breast. He shifted her in his arms, pinning her more securely against the wall before he hitched her higher and his open mouth landed between her legs.

"Ah—fourth—the fourth floor!"

Overwhelmed by a bizarre combination of desperation and shyness, she wiggled against his hold as he drew in a long breath, breathing her in. He chased her up the stairs, wrapping his long arms around her when she reached her apartment, pulling her into another long kiss that curled her toes inside her socks and sent butterflies to flight inside her stomach. Since their night downtown her thoughts had been twisted in knots. Was he her gigolo? How could so many things feel so right and oddly wrong all at the same time? It didn't matter. Blake was really there and, if he was her gigolo, she was about to have sex with him again. Would he remember her then? "Mmm," she hummed and pulled away. "Let me open the door."

"What is this aversion you have to hallway sex?" Blake asked, pressing himself against her as she fumbled with her key.

Her knees nearly buckled when his lips raked over her ear, his tongue flicking out to toggle her earlobe. "Oh!" Startled and a bit disoriented by the things he was doing to her, she giggled when the lock finally turned. The door swung open and they spilled into her foyer. Lust, pure and simple, gripped her hard the moment the door closed behind her and he pinned her against it. He caged her in, his large frame filling the small space and dwarfing her in his embrace. A shiver wracked her body from the cold dampness seeping into her clothes.

"Your shirt is soaked." She wriggled her hands between them and reached for his buttons but he stopped her, locking his long fingers around her wrists. His forehead fell against hers. She peered up to see him squeezing his eyes closed in an expression laden in agony. "What's wrong?"

A heavy breath spilled from his lips and he rocked his head from side to side before releasing her, his large hands coming up to cradle her face in a desperate embrace. "You."

"Me?" Her stomach dropped, the lust in his eyes betraying the words she was hearing.

"No." He shook his head, his eyes narrowing as his gaze left hers and traveled along her hairline, her jaw, her chin then eventually fell upon her lips. "I meant me. I'm what's wrong. I'm no good for you."

The air around them was charged with a tense expectation. Their chests rose and fell together, their heartbeats pounding rampantly as each of their breaths mingled in the millimeter of space between them. It was on the tip of her tongue to tell him who she was, tell him everything regardless of the consequences, but then he was on her, around her, his tongue filling her mouth with wild abandon. Her skin burned from his touch, her spine bowing against the door as his hands tunneled under her shirt and palmed her breasts with a desperate grip.

"You taste so good." So did he. He tasted so different than she remembered. With the faint aftertaste of alcohol he even tasted different than he had the night before. A stifling inferno blazed under her robe. She tried to shrug it off but her hands were fisted in his hair and refused to let go. What was it about kissing this man that made her need to be naked just to breathe?

"Mmm, off," she said, pushing at his shirt. When he moved his hands from her breasts to her ass, she seized her chance. "I need to feel your skin against mine again." Her hands fumbled through his buttons then she pushed his shirt over his shoulders, baring his hairless chest and mural of black ink, just like in his picture. A picture—no, a feeling—flashed through her memory. She could have sworn he had a thin patch of chest hair…and a happy trail that led— Whatever it was, memory or not, it was gone the minute Blake plunged his hand into the back of her PJ's. His hips canted and rolled against hers, pushing himself into her as his long fingers explored her, delving inside her and almost lifting her to her toes with his powerful thrusts.

"Fuck, you're soaking wet." She moaned when one of his fingers found her clit, circling it in time with the rhythmic thrusts of his hips. "And so hot. I need inside you right now, Jaynie girl, or I will lose my mind."

Like cold water sizzling against a sun-scorched rock, the heavy metal ballad of Roxy's ringtone blared through the thin cotton of her robe pocket. *No—no—no—no—no! Not now!* She couldn't ignore it. She had been trying for days to reach Rox. Oh, my God, but what Blake was doing to her made her forget every reason she needed to speak to Roxy, except one. It was clear now. Roxy was avoiding her and she didn't know why.

She pushed her hand into her pocket and wrapped her fingers around her phone. "I have…to take…this call," she mumbled against his lips between kisses. She swiped her finger across the screen and spoke into the receiving end without even bringing the phone to her ear. "Hold on one sec, Rox and don't you dare hang up." Ignoring his confused expression and puppy dog eyes, Jayne dropped the phone back into her pocket and painfully extricated herself from Blake's hold. "I've been trying for days to get her to call me." She couldn't help it. She pushed up on her tip toes and sucked playfully on Blake's bottom lip which he had stuck out in a mocking pout. "Go get naked and wait for me on the couch. I promise. I will be back here in two minutes."

"Will you be naked?" He fingered the lapel of her robe. A shiver ran through her overheated and deprived body when the backs of his fingers skimmed over her nipple.

"I will once you undress me." She ducked away from him before she changed her mind and gave Rox an unintended phone sex session; something she was sure Rox would twistedly enjoy. "Be right back." Jayne held up a finger as she backed towards her bedroom. She needed to get to the bottom of this thing with Rox and get back to Blake before he changed his mind and she was left alone to make out with his tie again like the loser she was.

~ TWELVE ~

Are you a closet mycologist?

"Why have you been avoiding me?" Jayne paced her cluttered bedroom floor. She may be neurotic about her work, but her personal space was far from tidy. *Oh, no!* Had she really left Blake out there with an empty ice cream bucket and all those candy bar wrappers?

"I'm not avoiding you, Jay," Roxy said. Jayne could picture the eye roll that accompanied her sarcastic tone. "Someone commissioned a new piece from the city gallery and I've been under the weather. It took me—"

"You've been sick?"

"Why are we even having this conversation when you obviously have the gorgeous kind of company?"

Jayne covered her eyes, the tips of her ears burning with a fresh blush. "You heard that?"

"You better get naked and get the hell back to whatever you were doing with whoever's there. Unless it's your neighbor. Things can get weird...no. Scratch that. Fuck your neighbor if you want. You only live once."

"He's not my neighbor!" Jayne said in a frustrated whisper. "Rox, it's him! It's Blake!"

She could hear Roxy's near silent squeal. "You naughty girl! Again, what in hell are you doing talking to me? Go fuck him! Wait! Does he know? How did this happen? Did you tell him that you're the blindfold chick?"

"No!" Dammit, she should. She needed to, desperately. It felt dishonest to sleep with him and not tell him. "I didn't tell him. It's a long story, but we kind of had a misunderstanding earlier today and he, well, he's a little drunk. He came here to tell me he was sorry and that he wasn't really an asshole."

Roxy's glee turned into a growl. "Yeah, because showing up drunk to say you're *not* an asshole isn't an asshole move at all."

"Rox, please!"

"You believe him?"

Jayne's thoughts flashed to the sight of Mallory Silverland wrapped around Blake in that elevator. Blake hadn't been holding her. He wasn't even touching Mallory except where she was excavating his stomach contents with her tongue. There was nothing but cold regret in his eyes when he saw Jayne. "Yes, I believe him." She collapsed onto her bed, her hand sliding beneath her pillow, her fingers instantly searching out the tie he'd left with her in Vegas. "But something seems different, Rox. You wouldn't believe what happened last night."

"Jayne?"

The sudden emotional edge in Roxy's tone had Jayne sitting up in bed. "What is it, Rox? What's wrong?"

Roxy was silent a moment too long. Jayne would be denied any answers. "I told you Jayne. You can't hold it against him if he doesn't remember you. Men live in the *now*. They eat, sleep—no—they eat, fuck *then* sleep. Sometimes *occasionally* they think…if you're lucky. Go tell him about Vegas, Jay, and screw him like you will never get enough of him."

"I don't blame him. Not any—"

"Go, Jayne. I'll call you tomorrow and I want every-single-detail!"

"Rox wait!" Jayne bolted from the bed, a feeling of unexplainable sorrow taking root in the pit of her stomach. "Love you."

She pulled her phone from her ear when there was no reply. The call had ended. Roxy had already hung up. What was she hiding? In all the years she'd known Roxy she had never acted like this. The silence from her living room drew Jayne's attention away from the frustrating riddle that was Roxy. She looked at the tie in her hand and a brazen idea took shape. Maybe she could jog his memory if he was blindfolded.

She threw off her robe and left her cellphone on her nightstand. Muffled snoring sounds could be heard from the living room before she even reached the end of the hall. When she rounded the corner she saw Blake, his long, naked legs stretched out along her couch, his head propped at an odd angle against the arm end. Her steps faltered and stilled. She stood motionless for a moment and admired his perfectly toned and chiseled body.

She couldn't let herself feel disappointed. Having the time to study him, without him knowing she was doing so, felt almost as good as kissing him. She tiptoed further into the room and sank carefully down onto the edge of the long coffee table in front of the couch. His tan skin and thick, black tattoos held a stark contrast to her couch's cream colored upholstery. She traced the intricate woven design with her eyes. Thin and wispy-like, the long strands of razor wire coiled around his right forearm and trailed up his bicep. Darker and thicker, the wire became a tangled nest that capped his entire shoulder then disappeared to places on his back that she couldn't see. A stray strand crept around the front of his neck and trailed off his left shoulder, scrolling down to a small symbol she didn't understand or recognize on the inside of his other bicep. Her imagination toyed with the symbols meaning, coming up with all sorts of ridiculous possibilities. She would definitely have to ask him in the morning.

Her gaze traveled the length of his torso, dipping and swaying to the hollows and slopes of his washboard abs. Her eyes snagged on that signature 'V' that led to his groin; the well-formed muscular monument some men have that eradicates all of a girl's smart brain cells then demands they breed with the leftover stupid ones. Apparently she was no exception to the rule. She forced her gaze beyond the border of no return. *Boxers*. He wore boxer briefs. Judging by the tent they were pitched into, he was dreaming happy dreams. Maybe he was dreaming about her. Maybe not.

A funny sounding snort startled her out of her trance, her eyes immediately darting to his. They were still closed. He was out cold and she was suddenly overcome with exhaustion. She retrieved a quilt from her hall closet and carefully draped it over his large frame. It barely covered his feet but it was the best she had. Her bed was only full-sized so her options were limited.

Too few hours later, her alarm clock woke her to the smell of fresh brewed coffee. Roxy's words filtered through her sleep-fogged thoughts. If he was truly this perfect she would never get enough. She pushed herself out of bed and padded down the hallway expecting to see him dressed in his slacks, his hair a ruffled mess, a blond scruff lining his jaw as he leaned against her counter caffeinating his hangover. Instead, she was greeted with a note taped to her automated coffee maker.

Evidently I am an asshole. Sorry. Let me make it up to you tonight?

Dishes setting in precise rows beside her sink caught her eye. Previously dirty dishes that had been washed, rinsed, and dried. Her hand towels were folded and neatly stacked on the other side of the sink. He cleaned her house? Mild shock staggered her steps on the way into her living room where she found the quilt she'd covered him with neatly folded and draped over the end of the couch. No empty ice cream containers or candy bar wrappers were in sight. They were probably flattened and folded precisely into tiny squares then layered in an exact pattern inside the full plastic garbage bag that was sitting beside her front door in the foyer.

"I'm still asleep." She pinched her arm and winced. *Definitely not a nightmare.* If it wasn't for the more than slightly weird and neurotic quality of his gesture, she might say she was having a good dream. *He really is effed up.*

115

Despite that revelation, she swallowed her mortification and paced back to the kitchen only to cough it back up when she opened her refrigerator and found it bare except for a bowl of fresh cut fruit and another note.

Are you a closet mycologist? I saved what I could. I'll cook. See you at the office, Jaynie girl.

Oddly enough she was impressed he knew what a mycologist did. She could imagine his scolding *tsk-tsk-tsk*, mocking her as he divested her of her moldy cheese while she slept. She smiled, picturing his rolling eyes. He was a sarcastic, self-destructive, health nut, clean freak who moonlights as a gigolo and drank too much. She snatched a peach wedge from the bowl and popped it in her mouth before she closed the refrigerator door and padded back to her room. He was a walking oxymoron and she really, really liked him.

Devin's mouth was drawn into what seemed these days to be a permanent scowl as he sat in his best friend's office trying to make sense of what he was hearing. "What do you mean you didn't fire her?"

"I didn't fire her. What is it about those four words that are so difficult to understand?"

Devin watched Blake's smirk grow until it safely reached a full-on, drunken smile and it finally hit him. "Holy shit! You're into this chick!"

Blake's head tilted in thought. He was twelve seconds too long coming up with an argument. Devin didn't buy the half-hearted one he attempted. "Maybe I'm into pissing you off."

"Bull! You're fucking my corporate spy, and if not she's a complete idiot—"

"She's not a spy." Blake rolled his eyes and paced to the panoramic windows that gave both their offices one of the best views of the San Gabriel mountain peaks. He and Blake had lived in

California all their lives. The sights of the snowcap peaks and how they contrasted with the cityscape of Los Angeles still blew his mind.

"And she's not an idiot. It was my fault she was late the day the plans were lifted. Wait!" Blake turned, pinning Devin to his seat with a pointed stare. "It was actually your fault!"

"My fault?" What the hell was Blake talking about? "I was in Toronto! How could this be—"

Blake pointed to his new printer. Devin immediately knew where Blake was going with his lecture, but he chose not to interrupt him. He watched in silence as his friend ranted on. He couldn't be happier for Blake. It was about damn time. He knew if he could get him back to L.A. he could get him back on his game. That didn't mean he wasn't going to give him some shit.

"Let me get this straight." Devin leaned back, relaxed in his chair, his ankle resting on his knee. "Because I didn't buy a printer before I left for Canada, you get to fuck around with the staff and do whatever the hell you want?"

"I get to fuck around and do whatever the hell I want because you need me. And since when do you care about fucking around with the—" Devin smirked when Blake caught on to him. "Piss off," Blake barked.

Devin's booming laugh filled the spacious office. "It feels good to do that."

"Do what?" Blake asked. "Fuck with my head?"

Devin laughed again. "Hell no! I wouldn't get anywhere near your head with my cock." He sat up and rested his elbows on his knees as he watched his friend re-take his seat at his desk. "It felt good to laugh." Devin couldn't believe the changes he was seeing in Blake. Sure, on the outside he looked the same, if not a bit hung over, but there was a flicker of life in his eyes he hadn't seen there in several years. "It's good to have you back."

"I'm not back." Blake's automated response. Devin was almost accustomed to it. If he had time for immature habits like rolling his eyes, he definitely would have done it then.

"Of course you're not. I forgot." Devin shrugged. "So, tell me about this woman, 'Mr. Gigolo'. Maybe I'll stop by and…introduce myself. I could use a distraction from my hunt for Simone." Not that anyone could actually distract him. She'd bewitched him.

Blake skewered him with a stare that was meant as a fiery warning, but only burned away Devin's remaining doubts. "She's not into that, Dev. She's literally one of the most sheltered, straight-laced women I know. She would never be capable of sabotaging SI."

This time Devin's laugh was more of a snort and saturated in disbelief. "This woman has you tied in knots and you're telling me she's vanilla?"

"Man, fuck off. I'm not getting into this with you."

Devin studied Blake. Something was off. Blake never spared details. Either he was really into this woman or…"Ha! You haven't fucked her!"

"What part of fu—?"

"Oh, you must be Mr. Kirk." Blake's office door opened then clicked closed again.

The floor fell out from beneath Devin's feet. He turned towards the voice that had haunted his dreams for almost a solid month; a voice that belonged to the enigma standing in the doorway of Blake's office not four feet away from him.

"Simone?"

His hand reached out and took her offered one, but he really didn't see it, or even feel it in his palm. His vision had tunneled and all he could see was her clean, smiling face. "Simon," she corrected him. His body felt disconnected from his brain as she shook his hand. "Jayne Simon. It's a common mistake. Blake said you were in Toronto. I wasn't expecting to meet you until next week." She turned to Blake and blushed. "I…um…got your notes. I'll come back a little later?"

"I've looked everywhere for you," Devin thought he said. His pulse was pounding in his ears and he couldn't feel his lips. He was sure it had something to do with the amount of blood filling his dick at an alarming rate.

"Excuse me?" she said.

Before he could process a single reason to stop, he had her in his arms and backed against the closed office door. Her body tensed but then melted against his. Time warped, as if they hadn't spent a single minute apart. Fire ignited between them as they shared an almost brutal kiss. Her familiar taste stoked the flames between them into the unforgettable inferno that had haunted his dreams and plagued his every thought since he'd left her alone in that Vegas hotel room. Everything disappeared. The stress of the mess his grandfather left him, the corporate sabotage, the sleepless nights, the nearly unbearable weight of running a business he hated; it all vanished as he fell under whatever spell was weaved around them when she was in his arms. He soaked her in as her tongue met his deep thrusts, over and over. Her silky hair slid through his fingers just like he remembered; her curvy, soft body pressing against him. All too soon, his body rioted as he was brutally snatched back into reality by the sound of Blake clearing his throat.

Devin felt her tense beneath him and he knew the spell had been broken. For now. Of course he had Blake to thank for that. His fingers reluctantly loosened their grip on her hips and he slowed their kiss, unwilling to end it all together. She felt so good. All those nights he'd woken up hard as hell, his heart beating out of his chest as he realized he'd only been dreaming of her beneath him. Knowing he was screwed because he had no clue who she really was or where on Earth he could find her.

Tempted to scoop her up and lay her out on Blake's desk behind him, he withdrew his mouth from hers but held her pinned against the door as he took in the site of her. He breathed her in. Her chest rose and fell as rapidly as his, her cheeks glowed rosy red, her eyes sparkled with the reflection of the snow-capped mountains behind him and his dick twitched violently with the vision that exploded in his mind. Oh, yeah. He was definitely going to take her against the window in his office one day. "God, woman, I've missed you." Her brows drew together in an innocent, confused way that fractured him.

Blake growled over his shoulder. Her eyes shifted to look at Blake behind him, begging for an explanation. He recognized an intimate familiarity in the look she shared with his best friend. *Oh, hell!*

"Are you kidding me? Jayne is Simone? *Vegas* Simone?" Blake asked.

Jayne. Devin liked it. The classic name fit her so much better.

She gasped at Blake's question, her hand rising to her throat in surprise. Her elegant fingers played with a thin chain there; fingers that had wrapped around his cock and stroked him in tandem with her tongue until he thought he would turn inside out with need. His gaze darted up to her lips as his erotic memory progressed. Her tongue peeked out, but she caught herself, drawing her bottom lip between her teeth. An unpleasant medley of understanding and confusion bloomed in her cheeks. Judging by her blush there was a heavy dose of embarrassment there, too. Did she regret their night together after all? "I've thought about you every day, angel."

"Angel?" Blake asked, his voice pitched high in disbelief. "Ten minutes ago you were pissed because I hadn't fired her!"

Jayne's head snapped back as if she'd just been slapped. Her eyes darted between them in a flurry of confusion. "Fired? You were going t-t-to fire me? What on earth for?"

"That's not going to happen, angel."

"Fuck my life!" Devin looked back to see Blake push from his desk, sending his chair crashing into the wall behind him. "I should have known better than—"

"Sit down," Devin commanded. He held back the sudden rush of jealousy induced violence that pushed him to break Blake's nose. The haze created by his utter shock was finally clearing from his head and the pieces were slowly coming together. Under normal circumstances he would have already thrown a punch, but Blake was his best friend. There obviously wasn't any intention on Blake's part to fuck him over, but that didn't mean he was happy about the situation. He needed just a damn minute to pull himself together and figure this out.

"Don't tell me to sit—"

"Can you two please stop pissing on the furniture and explain what the hell is happening?"

Blake's threat froze on his tongue before he could deliver it. He turned with Devin to see Jayne standing in front of them, her spine steel-rod straight, her shoulders broad with her hands on her skirt-wrapped hips and a cold stare in her eyes that didn't match the blush still staining her cheeks. She looked at Devin, that adorable blush deepening to a bright crimson as she spoke.

"It was you, wasn't it?" she asked, her deep blush suddenly running from her cheeks to leave only a pale shadow across her freckles. "You were in that hotel room. Not Blake."

Devin let out a long sigh and nodded, raising his hand to the back of his neck to knead the knot that had taken up permanent residence in the muscles there. "I came to visit Blake. He wasn't expecting me. He had two clients that night and asked me to—"

"Stop," Jayne said sharply. Devin looked up to see her take in a long, shaky breath. Her closed eyes opened to look directly at him, her voice as unstable as her next breath. "Thank you, but I d-don't need to hear how you drew the short straw."

"It wasn't like that!" Devin ground out from between clenched teeth.

"You know about what I did in Vegas?" Blake asked.

Jayne nodded. "My friend showed me a picture of you after she'd hired you for me." A desolate sounding laugh bubbled up through her wobbly smile. "Wow. That sounds so pathetic." Devin watched her eyes glisten, but she choked back her emotions. "It doesn't matter." She gathered herself together, mentally, physically and emotionally shutting herself away. "It's just…never mind," she said, turning on her classy high heels to rush out of Blake's office.

"Jayne, wait!" Blake called after her, but Devin stepped in front of him and closed the door before he could run through it.

"Let her go, man. We need to talk first."

~ THIRTEEN ~

Kamikaze-esque.

The control Devin depended on, kept a ram-rod, steel-tight grip on, had melted from his clenched fists onto the floor and evaporated into thin air, just like it had the last time he was with Jayne. Gathering even a shred of it back was like trying to claw back a subsidy after the checks had gone out. He forced himself to breathe. Her familiar clean and tropical scent still lingered in the room, filling his lungs, sending another jagged shard of need ripping through him.

"Well, you're right about one thing." Devin looked at Blake, his stomach twisting with jealousy flavored regret as he watched the fire in Blake's eyes slowly fade away. A fire he hadn't seen there since before Daphne died. A fire that burned for the woman Devin already thought of as his. "She's definitely not our spy." He pushed away from the closed door and paced to the window to stare out at the mountains. Miles and miles of mammoth mountains that now seemed dwarfed by the massive gulf between him and Blake. "She doesn't have a dishonest bone in her body."

"No, she doesn't," Blake agreed. "I can't believe this entire time she thought I was you."

Still standing at the window, Devin turned his head to look over his shoulder at Blake. "She never mentioned that night?"

Blake shook his head. "I had no idea," he said as he plopped down into his chair. "She never let on that she recognized…wait…" Blake closed his eyes, throwing his head back in disbelief. "She asked me if I had a twin." Devin's shoulders slumped, his hands resting on his hips as he began to put the pieces together. "I can't believe she didn't say anything."

"Surely you don't blame her?"

"No," Blake sighed. "I don't blame her."

Devin turned back to the mid-spring view, so different than that of his view in Toronto. He had a hundred questions and a million random thoughts, but couldn't get any of them to pass through his lips. Silence reigned the moment and several long moments after that. Eventually he heard Blake stand from his desk and pace towards his door. Devin turned just in time to see him pause with his hand on the door knob. "You're done in Toronto?" he asked.

"Yes," Devin answered him. Once his mother and sister found someone else's time to monopolize everything had fallen into place.

Blake nodded, giving the door handle a twist. "I'll have the team ready to hand over to you by mid-week next week, along with all of the latest reports."

"You'll just leave, then? Go back to Vegas?"

"That was the deal, Dev." Blake opened the door, but paused before he walked away. "Look, man. I get it. I told you, I didn't fuck her. She's all yours."

Not all *mine.* "Shut the door. We're not done."

"I'm done."

"Shut. The. Fucking. Door!" Devin knew the second those challenging words were gritted out from between his clenched teeth he'd crossed the line, but hell! His best friend was honed in on the woman he'd spent the last month laying claim to! At least mentally. He couldn't blame Blake, but being fair wasn't exactly his first reflex to their seriously screwed up situation.

Blake lifted his chin, his posture stiff and challenging. Devin could see the fire and life in his eyes had turned to ice, looking colder and greyer than they ever had. "Great impression of my old man." He pulled hard on the office door sending it crashing into the wall behind it. "I didn't take orders from him and I'm sure as hell not taking them from you."

"Dammit!" Devin growled and kicked over a chair, his hands fisting in his hair. He quickly checked his anger when Blake's assistant, frightened and confused, hurried in to check on him. "I'm fine," he assured her and righted the chairs. "Just fu…fine."

They weren't fine! One night in Vegas and *things* had been either amazingly screwed up or brilliantly frustrating, but *nothing* was even close to *fine!* Fully expecting to find it empty, Devin searched out Jayne's office anyways. Her fresh scent hit him square in the chest as soon as he opened the door, but the room was void of its source. Lacking the view of his and Blake's offices, hers was dim and void of any personal touches. He remembered Blake saying he had just moved her office to the executive floor to be closer to the team. Knowing that, the bare walls and lack of clutter made more sense as he studied her space. The dark, sterile room seemed to fit his mood. The weight of his world felt even heavier as he closed her door and sank down into her leather office chair in front of her drafting table.

A full-color mockup of the Emerald Dream lay in front of him. Devin had studied it, memorized it, lived and breathed it for months before he'd hired Jayne. *Jayne Simon.* Still a bit stunned, he rolled the strange name over and over in his head. Strange, but in a good way. It was a classic name and classy fit her to a tee. As he looked at the beast of a building on the paper in front of him he couldn't help but admire her talent. She was a brilliant architect. He was still skeptical about having to hire her instead of subcontracting the position as he normally did, but now he was glad for the inconvenience.

Inconvenient or not, he'd found her, or she'd found him. There was no way in hell he was letting her go now. She ran from them today, but he wasn't concerned. Now that he knew who she really was he would be able to find her anywhere. No. It wasn't her he was concerned about losing.

He picked up one of the twenty or so pencils laid out in perfect order on Jayne's desk and absently twirled it between his fingers. Blake was surrendering Jayne to him in record time, without so much as a single argument. His best friend had never been a fighter, but the old Blake, the one he knew before Daphne's death, would have at least tried to strike some sort of kinky deal.

That's where his thoughts got a little murky. Devin wanted Jayne more than he wanted his next breath. His best friend needed her more. They had shared in the past, but everything with Daphne had been so one sided. He wouldn't be a third with Jayne and, after what he'd just witnessed, neither could Blake. Curious, he allowed himself to imagine Blake with Jayne. He saw Blake wrapped around her, touching her, kissing her, sliding inside her. A rush of energy exploded inside him when he heard her aching moan in symphony with those images. His cock stirred to life and his hips shifted in the seat. Oh, yeah. He could definitely imagine sharing his angel. He would admit there was a slight sense of possession and jealousy he had rarely, if ever, felt before. Those feelings were benign compared to the angst he felt over losing Blake's friendship, or worse, losing Blake. He stared blankly at the blueprints in front of him, the lines blurring in and out of focus as he pulled and pushed at the puzzle pieces in his mind. How was he going to make this work?

Unconcerned with the tidy order of things, the pencil was tossed back onto Jayne's desk as Devin rose from her office chair. He took a long deep breath, noticing the absence of Jayne's scent, and then let it out slowly as he refastened the button on his suit coat. He would handle this just like he handled everything else that was now his responsibility, just like his grandfather taught him; with an iron will to succeed and a determination that lent no room for argument. The memory of his grandfather's voice made him smile. Amongst the many doubts that beat against his thoughts, one thing was certain. He wouldn't solve anything sitting there alone in the dark.

After going home to change and unpack, Devin hopped in his new Audi and drove out to Blake's father's place. The late evening air felt cool on his freshly shaven skin as he sped along the ten towards Mandeville Canyon. It was a long drive on a hunch, but if Blake wasn't there, he would be eventually. He always went to his father's place to sulk and dry out. After four years of frat parties, Devin knew when his friend was hung over, even if just a little. Add that to the fact Blake had been wearing his back-up suit he kept in his office for those times when he didn't have time to go home and change before work…that thought brought Devin's mental musings to a grinding halt. *Exactly where did Blake spend the night if he hadn't slept with Jayne?*

Forty-five minutes later he pulled into the long, private drive of Blake's father's—now Blake's—estate and parked behind his SUV in the circle gravel drive. Why the hell Blake hadn't sold this place yet was beyond him. With eight bedrooms and five bathrooms it was a monstrosity of a museum. Devin couldn't believe Blake had chosen to sell his flat in Santa Monica instead of this place when he'd moved to Las Vegas. When he found out Blake was keeping this place he knew something was severely twisted upstairs. Blake hated this place.

When he reached the main house, he caught a glimpse of Mallory just as she ducked into what he guessed was her latest vehicular obsession. Gravel flew from her tires as she sped off around the circular drive without so much as a wave and disappeared down the driveway. *What the hell?* Devin bypassed the front door and skirted the east garden hedges until he reached the pool house. He tried the doorknob only to find it locked. Before he could knock, the door opened and Blake stepped aside to let him in. "Fucking Grand Central all of a sudden. How the hell did you know I was here?"

"Please," Devin scoffed as he followed Blake down the hall to the sunroom at the heart of the desert-style villa. "I know you better than you know yourself. What was Mallory doing here?"

"Her usual stalker shit." Blake waved it off but didn't elaborate. Devin didn't push the issue. He wasn't there to discuss his sister's latest antics.

The orange glow from the late setting sun reflected off the water in the large swimming pool and cast strong shadows across the landscape. Devin shielded his eyes and gazed out over the lake behind the main house.

"I'm putting it up for sale," Blake said from somewhere behind him. "I've listed it and the flat in town with a realtor."

"About time," Devin said as he glanced up at the main house. "Anyone even live up there anymore?"

"Nope," Blake said and handed him a cold beer. "Just the estate manager."

"Old man Dreyfus?" Devin remembered the manager as a frail and decrepit old crank ten years ago.

"God, no!" Blake snorted and took a pull from his beer. "He left right after my old man died. I think he went to live with his daughter."

"Dreyfus had a daughter?" Devin cringed at the thought of anyone getting that close to the haggard old man. He'd smelled of turpentine and his skin had been the texture of shoe leather.

"I guess there's someone for everyone," Blake said. Devin glanced over just in time to see the regret on Blake's face. *Too bad.* He wasn't going to ignore his friend's slip. He'd opened the door and Devin was stepping through.

"Sometimes there's more than one person." Devin watched as Blake cloaked himself in an invisible iron curtain. "Don't. Don't do that."

"Don't do what?" Blake turned away and flopped down onto the sofa.

"That!" Devin said, pointing to Blake on the sofa with his beer bottle. "Don't shut me out and pretend you know what I'm talking about and you've heard it all a million times."

"I have heard it a million times." Blake took a long sip of his beer then slipped the bottle between his legs, his arms sprawled out to the sides along the back of the sofa in a *hit me with your best shot because I don't give a damn* posture. "What words are you going to use that are any different than what every therapist I've ever seen has said? Or anything I haven't already told myself a thousand and one times? *I know there will be other women besides Daphne. I've accepted it. I've learned from it. I've moved on. I will find someone else to share my life with.* You think that covers it? I think that covers it. If I missed something, please enlighten me because I am sick and damn tired of having this conversation with you!"

Devin knew by the way Blake looked at Jayne, and the way he talked about her that it was true. He was ready to move on.

"I believe you," Devin said and turned back to watch the sunset as he prepared himself to take the next step in his kamikaze-esque plan that had begun to take shape in his head the minute he left SI that morning.

"Then what the hell are you doing here?" Blake asked. "Why aren't you with Jayne?"

Devin watched the last traces of the sun's fire sink below the tree line while he carefully chose his next words. Should he be blunt and declare his intentions, or should he ease Blake into the idea? He pinched the bridge of his nose, his patience with himself wearing thin. This entire situation was making him crazy. He wasn't one to just let things happen. He made them happen. He made decisions then moved on and he was more than ready to get to the next step. He wanted—he needed—to get this settled and get to Jayne. She'd been in his every waking thought during the day and haunted his dreams at night. Now that he'd found her he craved that connection with her even harder.

"There's something different about Jayne."

Blake snorted. "You can say that again. Your mother is iffy, but your sister will eat her alive. She won't survive two seconds with the piranhas that swim in your world."

"Our world, man." Devin took a long sip on his beer, nearly emptying the bottle before he let the cat out of the bag. "I'm not talking about my family."

Devin watched as the first hammer fell. *That got his attention.* Blake sat up on the edge of the cushion shaking his head. "Not my world anymore, Dev. How many times have I told you? I'm out and I'm staying out. Wait….you're not seriously considering *Jayne*…?"

"Not exactly. You haven't seen her, man. It's all new to her, but she has some kink under all that straight lace."

Blake closed his eyes and let out a sigh before he pushed up and walked back into the kitchen. "You may know her body, Dev, but you don't know her." Devin chugged down the rest of his beer as he followed Blake, narrowing his eyes at him when Blake grabbed himself another beer and didn't offer him a fresh one.

"I know enough," Devin said and reached into the fridge to get his own bottle. He wasn't going to be that easily dissuaded or offended. Casually he walked over and clapped Blake on the shoulder. "I know you want her."

"Have you completely lost your mind?" Blake shrugged off his hand. "What part of a blindfold fantasy did you not understand? It's about getting fucked by a stranger, not putting on a show."

"No way, man." Devin shook his head. "If you know her like you say you do then you know she's different. It's not about that with her. She needed the blindfold to hide behind for courage, not some stranger fantasy."

"Exactly! She's vanilla!" Blake shook his head in denial. "You're out to breakfast, lunch and dinner on this, Devin. She could barely watch two strangers going at it in a dark alley. What the hell makes you think she would want to be fucked in one in front of me?"

"Daphne was shy at first too, but—"

Blake pushed Devin, crowding him against the counter. "This has nothing to do with Daphne, you hear me?"

"This has everything to do with her!" Devin pushed him back, his hands balling into fists. For three years he'd stood back and watched as Blake played judge, jury and executioner to his own sexual proclivities, declaring them the sole root cause of some lunatic's random act of violence while living in complete oblivion to reality.

He turned to leave before he said or did something he couldn't take back, but he couldn't make himself take the steps. Instead he turned back and looked Blake directly in the eyes. "You can't run from who you really are, not anymore and neither can I."

"It's more complicated than that and you know it," Blake said.

"You have no idea how complicated!" He and Blake stared at one another, eye to eye, toe to toe. Devin didn't need an invitation to elaborate. It was time Blake knew the truth. "Do you remember what it was like to watch Daphne with me? Do you remember the chemistry—the fire—that burned between us when we made love that first time on the stage at the club?"

Devin felt Blake's pain and loss as he watched it flash across his face. "How could I forget?"

Anger was suddenly all Devin could feel. It controlled his thoughts and laced itself within his words. "Were you that oblivious, that self-absorbed that you didn't see it?"

"See what?" Blake's brows dipped and his lips snarled with his obvious offense. "What the hell are you talking about, Dev? You were a good third. A great one! Do you really need an accolade for fucking my fiancé?"

"I wasn't just a third!" Years of his own pent-up pain and loss came bursting to the surface and it was more than Devin could control. His fist wrapped around a bronze statue that was sitting on a nearby table and he hurled it through the glass that made up the back wall of the cottage. A blanket of glass shards exploded onto the patio and rushed into the pool. "I was in love with her, too."

"What?" Blake's voice wavered with disbelief. Devin lifted his head to see his gaze demanding answers. Answers he had denied him for far too long.

"I was just as in love with Daphne as you were." He watched Blake's disbelief transform his features, but it was too late to stop. The truth was out and the only thing that could make things right was for him to finish telling it. His heart ached as he thought of Daphne's pixy-like face, the love he saw in her deep brown eyes every time she looked at him. He had been so surprised the first time he saw it there in her gaze, hiding behind a hope that Blake wouldn't see it there, too. Determined to remember Daphne with the love she deserved, Devin looked at his best friend and said the words he knew would change them forever. "And she was in love with me."

~ FOURTEEN ~

One piece of the puzzle at a time.

Devin sat on the balcony outside his Century City penthouse sipping a steaming cup of coffee as he surfed through the morning headlines and watched the sunrise over the mountains. Normally he preferred orange juice, but the thoughts plaguing his mind soured his stomach and he opted for a shot of caffeine instead. The usually energizing effects still left him sluggish and distracted. He'd barely slept the night before and when he did he dreamt of Jayne. He wondered what she was doing. Was she a morning person, or was she all frumpy and disheveled in the mornings until she'd consumed a lion's share of caffeine? He'd wanted more than anything to drive to her apartment after he'd left Blake's. To scoop her up, take her straight to her bed and bury himself inside her. Aside from not knowing where she lived, he'd been far too angry when he'd stormed out of Blake's pool house. He knew if she saw him in that state he would have ruined any chance he'd had of making this work with her, if he hadn't already.

Odd for the early hour, a knock at his door grabbed his attention. He walked through the sunken living room to the foyer and peeked through the peephole. Slightly alarmed, he opened the door to find Blake standing there, a bit scruffy but alert and clear-eyed, holding Devin's door key in his hand. "You here to return that?"

"Do I need to?" Blake asked, brushing past him before he could invite him in.

"You know you don't," Devin said as he followed Blake into his kitchen and watched him pour himself a cup of coffee. Not long after he'd gotten home that night, Devin's anger had turned to guilt. He could see the hurt in Blake's eyes when he'd blurted out the truth he'd held in for so long and that was the last thing he'd wanted. "Look, man. I'm sorry I—"

"I knew."

A fist to the gut, a shove, a '*fuck you*' along with a fist to the gut, Devin expected any and all of the above, but he was certainly not prepared for Blake's acquiescence. "You knew?"

Blake squeezed his eyes shut, his hands balling into fists. "I suspected," he said in a gravelly voice that sounded more like a growl.

"When?" Never once had he *suspected* Blake had caught on. "Why the hell didn't you say something?"

"I didn't see it!" Blake shot back. "Not at first. Not until the end, when she was..." He scrubbed a hand over his tired features, his jaw ticking as he clamped down on whatever it was he was about to say. "I knew something was different, more intense than any of our arrangements in the past. I just...I thought about it after you left last night. There was always some thought, something that told me it was different. I didn't want to think about it so I just shrugged it off. Things snowballed so fast after the first few threats against her then...there wasn't time. I wasn't..."

"I get it, man," Devin said when Blake didn't continue. He wanted more. Blake owed them more! Daphne had made herself sick worrying about his reaction and what would happen to them all if they said anything. All this time he knew? Devin's insides churned with need to rail and curse Blake for making him grieve in silence for three long damn years, but he didn't. They had both suffered enough. There was no sense in making either of them relive that pain. He also fought back the instinct to argue Blake's suspicions of how Daphne died. Her murder had nothing to do with those threats. He had far too many other battles to win before he could think about tackling that one.

Sliding down the face of the cabinet behind him, Blake plopped onto the kitchen floor. His legs pulled up to his chest, he rested his chin on his knee and let out a frustrating sigh. "I have to know, Dev. It's eating me alive. Did you...did the two of you...?"

"No," Devin quickly assured him. Coffee in hand, he slid down onto the slate floor across from Blake and propped himself against the island bar. "We would never do that, man. You know that. We were only together with you." He and Daphne had both been adamant about that. As much as they craved each other, they knew the temptation would have been insurmountable had they ever been alone together. "We only talked." Devin scrubbed a hand down his own face. "Shit, man. We tried to tell you so many times. No matter what we thought of, we couldn't come up with a way to make it work. She was...we were both so afraid of losing you."

"I was afraid of losing her too," Blake sighed, the irony of it all reflecting in his voice. "And losing you. I would have been angry but I wouldn't have—"

"Yeah, you would have," Devin cut him off. "You were different back then. Quick tempered and—"

"A selfish asshole?" Blake finished for him.

"Yeah." The corner of Devin's mouth ticked up into a grin.

Blake's snicker was laced with more than a little sarcasm. "You're right. I would have kicked your ass."

Devin nodded but didn't offer an argument. As helpless as he was against the eventual outcome of his relationship with Daphne, he would have deserved it. He was a third. He should have walked away the second he saw that look in her eyes, but he didn't. He couldn't.

"We were both a little self-serving back then." Devin shook off the memories and took a long sip of his coffee. He looked at Blake and read the doubt in his eyes. "Hey," he nudged Blake's foot with his own. "She loved you just as much."

"I know." Blake toasted the air with his coffee cup. "She had a big heart."

A sad but reassuring grin formed on Blake's lips when Devin clinked his coffee mug against his. "We good, man?" He couldn't help but feel a little guilty. He was getting off light and he knew it.

Blake swallowed hard. His head fell back against the cabinet as his next words were spoken on a long sigh. "Yeah, we're good."

Relief filled Devin's chest after he let out a long-held breath. There was no better time than the present to drop the second shoe. Devin's fingers nervously fiddled with the handle on his coffee mug. He cleared his throat and gave Blake another nudge with his foot. "You want Jayne."

Blake shook his head in denial. "I'm no good for her, man."

"What the hell is that supposed to mean?"

Blake shrugged. "It doesn't matter what I want."

"Of course it matters. You're my best friend, you ass."

Blake stretched his legs out and set his half empty mug beside him on the floor. "You saying you'd give her up?" he smirked. "After all that whining and searching? Just like that?"

"Not on your life," Devin scoffed with an incredulous huff. Blake's confusion was nothing less than priceless. "I do *not*, however, want us to repeat the same mistake we made with Daphne."

"What are you suggesting?"

Devin studied his friend, really looked at him, wondering for a moment if he was making the right decision. He'd already decided he couldn't take her from Blake. He loved Blake like a brother. Nothing would change that. Ever. But he certainly couldn't just walk away from Jayne, either. "I want us to share her."

Blake let out a chuckle. "We've already established that. And as I said it won't—"

"Not as a third. As an equal." Devin sat up straight and held Blake's stare. He wanted Blake to know how perfectly serious he was about every word he was about to say. "I want us to be a triad. Three equals in a single committed relationship."

"Seriously?" Blake's surprise was short lived, quickly masked with something Devin couldn't quite put his finger on. Guilt, maybe? "Aren't you putting the cart before the horse a little bit here? You don't even know this woman. *I* barely know her."

"But you've thought about it?" Devin's heart was pounding a mile a minute. At least he didn't get an outright *no*.

"Of course I have. Once or twice maybe...ever, but—"

"You know Jayne is more than a quick fuck or you would have already fucked her."

"Yeah, but that doesn't—"

"I want this, Blake." Devin made sure his tone left no room for question. "I want this for us. I want her and I want you to have her, too. In the few minutes we had together in your office, the tension was palpable. I saw the way you looked at her. Sure I was jealous, for a minute, but not now. Not after I had time to think it through. I don't want you to be on the outside looking in. Ever. I know too well how that feels. I would rather have you with me— with us—from the beginning."

Blake stared at the floor for a few silent seconds before shaking his head. "Like I said, it doesn't matter," he shrugged. "Jayne will never go for it."

"Maybe not." Devin certainly hadn't the time to come up with a plan to convince her. Blake was right. She was shy, but he'd seen firsthand how hot Jayne got when she thought someone was watching them. She may be a virgin to voyeurism and kink, but there was enough curiosity there for him to work with.

He took a deep breath to quell his excitement. One piece of the puzzle at a time. Blake was the key first piece. They had to form a united front if they had any chance of making this work. In his heart he knew this was the right move for them, even if Jayne wasn't the one. She was, though. He could feel it in his bones. He had the privilege of experiencing their kind of chemistry once. He knew how rare it was.

He nodded to Blake and offered his hand, pulling his friend to his feet. "We will never know unless we ask her."

"I don't know about this, Dev," Blake argued as he washed out his coffee mug and set it back inside the cabinet. "Even if, by some insane chance, she does agree to...*whatever* with both of us, I'm not sure I'm ready for this." He turned and looked at Devin. "I mean, fucking around is one thing. Like you said, Jayne isn't the kind of girl you fuck around with."

Devin laughed at that. "The fact that you know that and you were still interested in her tells me all I need to know, my friend." He tossed his mug in the sink and pulled out his phone. "You are more than ready for this."

"Who are you calling?" Blake asked.

Devin motioned for Blake to stay put while he walked into his master closet and snagged a pair of shoes. "Good morning, Jeanette." Too late he realized what an ass he was for calling his pregnant assistant at such an odd hour, he asked her to retrieve Jayne's contact information anyways as he sat on his sofa and pulled on his leather Testoni's. With a cocky smirk on his lips, Blake walked over and held up his own cellphone displaying Jayne's name and phone number.

"Never mind, Jeanette. Please apologize to Glenn for the early call." The last thing he needed in the midst of the circus that had become his life was to lose Jeanette before her scheduled leave because he had been a thoughtless ass. He still had her for two more weeks and he was going to need her for every overscheduled second of it.

Devin hung up the phone and copied her number into his cell. "I assume you know where she lives?"

Blake nodded. Although it was short-lived, Devin couldn't deny the spike of jealousy that pierced his chest at all the time he'd missed with her. "But she won't be there," Blake said. "She's a workaholic. Sunup to sundown, she's always there before I get in. Yesterday when she stormed out was the first day I've actually seen her leave the building except the day I kidnapped her."

"Kidnapped her? What the—"

"The day your sister found out I was back I took Jayne to lunch and held her hostage for the rest of the day so I wouldn't have to deal with Mallory. That's the night I told you about." He held up his cellphone for Devin to see Mallory's call history. "Eighteen calls since the day before yesterday. She showed up last night because she was 'worried' when I didn't return her calls."

Devin pushed up from the sofa and gathered his coat and tie. "I'll talk to her, man. She's usually not this bad, is she?"

Blake shook his head. "You have no idea, bro. Just try to leave me out of it. Don't tell her I told you."

Devin gave him a nod and scooped his keys from the foyer table. "Does this mean you're in?" He asked Blake. He wasn't convinced Blake understood just how serious he was about Jayne.

"It means I'm not promising anything except that I want to see her punch you in your balls when you tell *her* about this brilliant idea." Blake pocketed his phone and followed Devin down to the garage where he'd parked in Devin's visitor's spot.

"The Ducati, huh?" Devin tossed his tie and coat into the passenger seat. He hadn't seen Blake on his bike in years.

"Yeah," Blake pulled on his helmet and straddled the sleek black beast. "I pulled her out of storage yesterday morning. Thinking about selling her."

"Selling her?" Devin cocked his head at Blake. He loved that bike. "Is something wrong with it?"

"Na, just…not here much. It's not practical to keep it stored away." Since when did Blake worry about practicality? Was he in some kind of trouble? "Meet you at the office?"

Devin nodded and slid into his driver's seat, shrugging off the brief suspicion. His friend was in love, or well on his way. A lot of things had changed since Blake left L.A. A sense of hope lifted some of the oppressive weight from Devin's shoulders. He cranked up the volume on his radio as he pulled out of his parking space and followed Blake out of the garage with a new sense of urgency. He couldn't wait to talk to Jayne.

Once he and Blake arrived at SI they rushed immediately to Jayne's office only to find it empty. "Huh?" Blake shrugged. "I guess I was wrong. Give her bit. She's probably down in the break room getting coffee. We have an eleven-thirty meeting with the city council. She's bound to be here any minute."

"I hope you're right," Devin said and closed her office door. "I'll check my messages and meet you back here in ten?"

Blake nodded and headed in one direction as Devin went another. Devin was almost at his office door when he heard Jeanette call for him from down the hall. "Hey, you. Sorry about the early call this morning." He walked over and gathered the stack of files and Jeanette's briefcase from her arms as she exited the elevator.

"Thank you," she huffed, her stylish bangs dancing on her labored breath. "I swear I'm going to pop any minute."

"Oh, no," Devin said as he escorted her to her office just outside his own. "No popping until you've finished training the temp. Even then I'm not sure I'll survive her." Jeanette swore Lori was the best in the temp pool, but Devin wasn't so sure. After two months the woman still managed to screw up every reservation and just a week ago she doubled an entire day of his appointments. He was already running short on time on a regularly scheduled day.

"She'll be fine." Jeanette smiled as she set her purse on her desk. "However, finding a new architect for the Emerald Dream is something I'm glad I won't be here to witness."

Ice ran through Devin's veins. "What are you talking about?"

Jeanette pulled a piece of paper from her purse and handed it to him. "I got a call from Gloria in HR this morning, right after you called. Seems Ms. Simon has resigned effective immediately."

No. She couldn't. This couldn't be happening. "When? What did she say?"

"I don't know, exactly," Jeanette replied. "Gloria said she seemed deeply regretful. A shame, really. Sweet girl. I liked her a lot. I asked Gloria to hold off on the paperwork to give you a chance to talk with her first."

Devin reached over and laid a hurried kiss on Jeanette's forehead. "This!" He shook the paper at her. "This is why I can never survive without you. Thank you!" He took off towards Blake's office but Blake met him halfway down the long hall.

"We have to stop her," they said in unison as they turned for the elevator.

"Who told you?" "Devin asked as he fell into step beside Blake.

They rushed into the elevator and Blake impatiently pushed the button for the garage. "She left me a message on my voicemail."

~ FIFTEEN ~

Sweet Cherry Pie

"Stupid!" Jayne opened the refrigerator door, pulled out what was left of the cherry pie she'd bought from the farmer's market on her way home the day before, grabbed a slice of cheese that had passed Blake's inspection of her refrigerator and slammed the door closed again. *Stupid! Stupid! Stupid!* She should have said no. Okay, she did say no, repeatedly, but as usual she let Roxy talk her into something she had no business doing. Now look at her life. She'd spent the last hour soaking in her new garden tub, somewhere between livid and devastated, examining every aspect of her latest bad decision and she couldn't see any way out of it. She had to leave.

Her gigolo troubles aside, her new job was a pain. She had worked so hard to get to where she was and now she was drowning in a sea of political poop-storms she had no idea how to navigate. She was good at putting things together on paper, but making them happen and explaining them to countless review boards and contractors was apparently not her strong suit. On one side she was dealing with an army of developers who knew nothing about sustainability. On the other was an elite group of power jockeys who knew the laws and what it took to manipulate federal funding, but didn't have an ounce of common sense or an architectural degree. She knew nothing about politics or babysitting.

I'm so screwed! Knife in hand, she opted for a bigger slice of pie and cut the left over portion in half, scooping out a hefty piece onto a plate and coving it with the cheese. Maybe she could get her old position back in New York. It had only been a couple of weeks. They would probably think she couldn't hack it in the big leagues, and they were right. Now was a terrible time to realize it, but she was in way over her head.

"I don't want to go back." Even if she got a handle on the politics at SI, how could she stay? "Ugh!" She banged her head against the cabinet door in front of her as she waited for her pie to warm in the microwave. She could feel her career slipping through her fingers. *One time!* The one and only time in her life she made an irrational, irresponsible decision to do something outrageously sensational, and it comes back to haunt her in the most horrific way possible. Okay, so it wasn't as bad as that. It wasn't as if she went looking for a gigolo. Technically Roxy had paid Blake, but what was the difference? Maybe she should call Gloria back, rescind her resignation then walk right up to Devin Kirk and beg him to take her again. Why not? If she could have sex against an open window on the Vegas strip surely she could navigate a sexual relationship with her boss. She could just imagine the look on Roxy's face if she'd shared *that* little kernel of debauchery with her. At this point she would share *anything* with her best friend if she would just *answer her phone*! Why couldn't she be more like Roxy? She would have slept with both of them! *Ha! There's a thought.* Her body shivered as her mind inevitably created an image to go along with the random thought.

Devin Kirk's fierce kiss had brought everything rushing back with crystalline clarity. Her body responded to him instinctually as it had that night in Vegas, as if it had somehow been changed in an elemental way to recognize him. Blake's kiss, the way he felt against her, the way he acted around her was so different than she remembered from Vegas. Now she knew why. Blake set her on fire when he touched her, like a white-hot flash, but it was a different kind of flame than the one that burned deep and slow between her and Mr. Kirk.

Maybe it was a good thing she hadn't talked to Rox. She'd made the decision to resign and go home, but nothing seemed real until she could tell Roxy about it. She didn't want this to be real. The microwave beeped. Jayne's mouth watered when the scent of hot pie permeated the air. The empty calories she'd consumed the day before had left her starving when she woke from the barely three hours of sleep she'd manage to get the night before. Her stomach was running on leftover fumes just like her nerves.

Just as she opened the microwave door and picked up the pie plate, her front door rattled with a series of heavy knocks sending Jayne into orbit, the plate flying from her hand and bouncing off the counter. Hot, red cherries and melted cheese splattered down the front of her pink cotton robe and ran onto the floor.

"Ouch!" She heard a muffled curse, followed by another barrage of heavy knocks. Jayne abandoned the mess to answer it, carefully stepping around the sticky splatter as she wondered who could be knocking down her door at seven-thirty in the morning for goodness sake! "One second!" She looked through the peephole to see Mr. Kirk and Blake standing on the other side of her door. "Oh, shi—." She looked down at the red cherry sauce on her robe. *Robe!* She was naked under her bathrobe and her soon to be ex-boss and his sin-for-hire friend was at her door! "Uh, one sec!" She scrambled to her tiny laundry room and threw off the robe, frantically searching through the dryer for her sweats. *Knock-knock-bang-knock-bang-knock!* "I'll be right there!"

"Are you okay, Jayne? We heard glass breaking!" Sweats on, she dug out a white tank top and pulled it over her head then dashed back to the front door.

"Yeah," she said, winded from her frantic sprint as she opened the door. "I just…you startled me when you…uh…knocked and I-I-I dropped my plate."

"Dear God, woman! Are you always this accident prone?" Blake covered his eyes and turned away from her.

"What? What is it?"

Devin rushed in and stooped down to examine her face. "You're bleeding!"

"I am?" She reached up and her fingers landed in a dollop of warm, sticky pie filling. "Oh, no. It's not blood. It's cherry pie."

"I have to sit down." Blake wiped his forehead and started for her couch. Devin elbowed him in the side and Blake responded with a grunt. "Okay, fine! Just give me a minute!"

A pocket of laughter escaped through Jayne's confusion. It was so strange to see a guy like Blake get all woozy from the sight of blood. "How did you manage to get through all those tattoos if you can't stand the sight of blood?" she asked him as she closed her front door.

"I don't know. It's different," Blake barked.

"Jayne, we came to apologize." In her state of confusion and amusement, her brows drew together when Blake elbowed Devin this time. "I! *I* came to apologize." Devin rubbed his side and threw a nasty look back at Blake. "You know, you should be the one apologizing. None of this would be happening if it wasn't for you."

"Excuse me, but do I need to be here for this conversation?" Jayne tried to wipe away any remaining pie filling from her face, but she had a feeling she was only making it worse. She stepped over to the mirror on the wall beside her front door to take a look. "I have a mess to clean up in my kitchen, thanks to *both* of you!" She turned around to find both men standing in a stupor, staring….at her boobs. She looked down at her dark nipples, pebbled and poking through her thin, white tank-top. "Oh!" *Oh My God!* Her hands flew up to cover her breasts and she backed quickly down the hallway towards her bedroom, an instant flush of embarrassment flooding her cheeks. "I wasn't expecting company. L-l-let me go change and I'll be right back."

"No!" Both men shouted at the same time. Before she could turn and leave Devin stepped forward and reached for her wrists, taking her hands in his and lowering them away from her chest. "We've both seen you, angel. There's no need to hide yourself from us."

Devin's eyes softened, the sincere tone of his voice soothing her frayed nerves just as he had that night. Before she knew it she was being enfolded into his familiar embrace. It was like being pulled into another world. He felt so good. Until that very moment, snuggled against his warm, strong body, she hadn't realized just how lonely she was. Her life had changed so much and so quickly. Everything was different. Her job, her home, her friends, even the food she ate; all of it was either strange, unavailable or nonexistent. Moving so far away from everything she knew wasn't nearly as exciting as she dreamed it would be. And she really missed Roxy. It was that last thought that created the knot in her throat and caused her eyes to well with tears.

"Shh, it's okay, angel. Just let it out." A small sob bubbled up from her chest and a few tears fell from her eyes. She tried to hold it back, but she just couldn't contain it all.

"I'm so sorry," Jayne said, and tried to push away. Devin loosened his hold but wouldn't let her go. "I just miss my friend."

"Ah. Roxy, right?"

Stunned, Jayne nodded. "I'm surprised you remembered."

"I remember everything about that night, angel." She closed her eyes as he wiped away the remnants of her stray tears. Then she remembered. It wasn't just her gigolo's shoulder she was crying on. Devin was her boss.

"Um, sorry," She swiped at the small wet spot on Devin's shirt. "That wasn't very professional." Embarrassed by her outburst, she waved his hand away and tried to gather her emotions.

"Jaynie girl, I've got news for you." Jayne's breath caught in her chest when she felt the heat of Blake's body at her back. He didn't touch her, but his breath was hot against her neck when he spoke. "We left professional on the steps downtown the other night." She closed her eyes when Blake's arms wrapped around her waist, his hands sliding between her and Devin to rest on her abdomen.

"And *we* left it in Vegas, angel," Devin said. He backed away a step and stooped down to look into her eyes. It wasn't the first time she noticed his hazel irises. Only they weren't minty like they were in his picture she'd found on the company intranet. Swirling with concern, they were a dark, rich moss and they were melting her from the inside out. He traced his thumb over a spot on her forehead then stuck it in his mouth. "Mmm, you always eat pie for breakfast?"

"No," she snorted. Actually snorted! Her hand flew up to cover her face. How much more awkward could she be?

"No?" Devin asked.

She shook her head, her cheeks turning red. "Blake threw away all my food."

"Food?" Blake released her and walked towards her kitchen. "Mold is not a food group, babe. Holy shit! What the hell happened in here?"

Jayne cringed. "I told you, you scared me when you knocked on my door! I haven't met any of my neighbors yet, and the call box is broken." She turned back to Devin and found him smirking at her. "Speaking of which, how did you get in?"

His smirk turned into a sheepish grin. "I own the building." Devin grabbed her hand and led her to her couch. She turned to sit as Blake appeared in the doorway from the kitchen with a melted yellow glob dripping from the tip of his finger.

"What the hell is this?"

"Um, cheese?" Horrified, Jayne tried to push to her feet but Devin held her on the cushion beside him. "Just leave it, I'll get it later," she insisted.

"You eat cheese on your cherry pie?" Blake asked. "That sounds…awful." He shook his head and disappeared into the kitchen again.

"This is so embarrassing." Not only was her kitchen a mess, her entire apartment was in shambles. Once she'd made her decision to resign and go home she'd pulled out all the boxes from her move to L.A., which she'd still had stacked in a corner in her bedroom, and half-heartedly began to re-pack. Her dry cleaning was strewn over her love seat. Her books had been pulled from her shelves and stacked on the floor in the hallway. Several pictures she'd just hung in the small living area had been taken down and leaned in a stack against the wall beside the front door.

"Forget him," Devin said with a wave of his hand. "He's a clean freak. Now that he's seen it he won't be able to focus on anything else, not until it's cleaned."

She remembered what Blake had done the morning before and cringed at what he must think of her now. She looked around the room and let out an incredulous groan. "Then you should probably get him out of here while you still can."

"We're not going anywhere, angel." Devin's arm slid behind her back, snuggling her closer to him. "Not until we figure this out." His gentle hand caressed Jayne's cheek, his fingers traveling from her ear to her chin before he tenderly turned her face up to look at him. "I really have missed you."

Jayne's chest expanded with air and surprise and an overwhelming sense of elation. It almost hurt to breathe. "You did?"

"I still can't believe you're here." Devin smiled and the pressure in her chest grew to bursting. He was gorgeous. His sense of style was completely different than Blake's. While neither of their wardrobes came from the K-mart collection, Devin's tailored suit, shiny dress shoes and expensive cufflinks clashed with Blake's rolled-up sleeves and tattoos. The look fit him like a tailored leather glove. His lush, brown hair was thick and silky. Her hand reached up to trace the line of his sexy, I-forgot-to-shave-this-morning scruff. It was dark and thin, perfectly trimmed. His face had been smooth in Vegas.

"I like it," she said, pulling her hand from his face when she realized she gotten so familiar with him. He quickly captured her hand and brought it back to his cheek.

"I didn't have one in Vegas," he said, turning his head to place a kiss to her palm. "In case you still had any doubts."

She shook her head. "No, not anymore." That one kiss in Blake's office had cured her of all of those little pesky things. She closed her eyes and relived her time with him in Vegas. Every hour of it passed by in mere seconds. "What I don't get is, why?"

"Why what?"

"Why have you missed me? I mean," she turned in his arms and looked up at him. "Gigolo or not, I'm not exactly your type."

Devin chuckled. "I think I demonstrated in at least a dozen ways that you're exactly my type. And I plan on showing you more."

"I don't…I mean…I'm not anyone's type." That sounded pathetic! "This is not coming out right." She took a deep breath and tried to make the words make sense. "You were paid to do those things, or at least Blake was—which now that we're on the subject, I don't understand why he was posing as an escort to begin with—and even then, he passed me off to you instead. I'm not his type either and you can't say you would have ever noticed me at—at—at a bar or even at work had any of this never happened."

"First of all, neither of us knew what you looked like before he *'passed you off'*," Devin countered. "I don't know how it works, but pictures were not part of the deal." Devin turned, his shoulder propped against the back of the couch as he looked at her. "Second, he didn't *'pass you off'*. Blake had a platinum client scheduled the same night, whatever the hell that is. Apparently it's some kind of V.I.P. thing or something. She requested him specifically."

"Actually, Charlene was my only client," Blake said from the kitchen doorway. "Until you, that is."

"What was all that bullshit about fast cars and fast women?" Devin asked.

Blake crossed his arms over his chest and looked down at his shoes. "Just that; bullshit. I met this guy at a high stakes poker table one night. He invited me to this nightclub where I met Gavin and a bunch of other guys. They talked a good game so I thought, what the hell? A few weeks later I had a portfolio and Charlene. Then you showed up."

"Huh," Devin said with a huff and shook his head in disbelief. "I knew you were posing."

"I wasn't—" Blake censored whatever he was about to say, crossing the room instead and taking a seat on the edge of her coffee table across from them. He rested his elbows on his knees and cupped the outside of Jayne's thighs with his hands. "Look, babe.

He's right. There were no pictures and no *'passing you off'* to anyone. It was just the way things happened."

"I'll admit," Devin began, "under normal circumstances I probably wouldn't have noticed you." He held up his hand when she tried to agree. "Only because you hide yourself away behind all that shyness." Jayne shook her head, but she knew it was true. Devin took her hands and held them to his chest. "Just answer me one question." Jayne nodded before she even thought to argue. "Do you regret what happened that night, anything we did?"

Every molecule of her common sense screamed for her to say yes. He was offering her a way out. One word would silence this entire nightmare. She could go home and pretend none of this had ever happened. The word 'yes' was perched on the tip of her tongue, but her body wasn't fighting a fair battle. A memory of the first orgasm he gave her was lobbed over her southern border like a hand grenade and blew it into alphabet soup. She shook her head. "It was the best night of my life." She'd relived every moment of their night together at least a thousand times. She'd be lying if she said she didn't want to repeat them all.

Devin's smile echoed the same memory, sending a flutter through her stomach as he palmed her cheek. "Mine too." He leaned in and touched his lips to hers. It was a quick kiss that conveyed that same familiarity she felt earlier. Something two people who had only met once shouldn't feel. "So," he said, his eyes roaming her face. "Tell us why you quit SI so we can get that settled and move on to more important things."

Jayne looked up to see Blake zeroing in on her with the same intensity Devin had. Heat from her receding blush fired back to life and flooded her cheeks. She couldn't look him in the eyes long enough to tell what he might be thinking. Only a little more than a day had passed since they had been alone together; since Blake had kissed her witless. She felt like such a jerk now sitting beside Devin and wanting him the same way. "How can I stay? I...I slept with you." She looked up at Devin then slanted a look over to Blake. "I almost slept with you, too. I...I can't..."

"Forget that for a second," Blake said.

"Forget it?" She couldn't forget any of it. She knew because she'd tried!

"We'll get back to it in a minute, believe me." Blake held up one finger as he continued. "But first let's get to the crux of the situation. You don't sleep with your coworkers or bosses, is that it?"

"Well, yeah. I mean, no! I don't. How can I sleep with someone who writes my checks? It's just…wrong."

"Whew," Devin let out a breath. "That's an easy fix, angel. Technically you work for the city of Los Angeles. They subsidize your salary."

"They do?"

"Yes, every penny." Devin rubbed the back of his neck as a regretful expression passed between him and Blake. "I didn't want to hire you, so I made them reimburse your salary. But that was before and…"

Jayne pulled her hand free from his. "So let me get this straight." She pushed to her feet and paced to the other side of the room to put some much needed distance between them. "You didn't want me there before, but now that you know we've slept together—and obviously hope to do so again—you're okay with me working there?"

"Whoa! Wait! Time out," Blake broke in. He walked over and grabbed her hand, pulling her back over to the couch where he loomed over her until she slowly sunk back onto the cushion next to Devin. "We can't afford to get sidetracked here. Devin isn't like that, babe. It's true, he didn't want to hire an architect, but it wasn't personal. Then we had that incident with the leaked supplier lists and he thought you might be a corporate spy, yada-yada-yada, but you're not a spy, he knows that, and now we're here."

"A spy?"

Blake shook his head. "Focus, Jaynie." His eyes darted to her breasts then closed as his Adam's apple bobbed on a forced swallow. "I…we need to stay on track."

"Blake assured me it couldn't be you," Devin said, taking her hand back in his. "And now that I know who you are I believe him. That and the fact that he sings your praises every day."

"You do?" What was there to praise? She'd felt like she'd been fumbling her way through every single meeting and mock-up.

"You're the best damn architect I've ever worked with. And, as I'm sure you know, we know nothing about all this Green Peace stuff."

"Green initiative," Jayne corrected him.

"Whatever," Blake said, his hand reaching out to take her other one. "The bottom line is you can't leave, Jayne. I don't know what Devin's grandfather was thinking taking this on, but we can't build the Emerald Dream without you."

"You see, angel? Your employment with SI has nothing to do with us. We can't fire you no matter what does or doesn't happen between us. And before you even think it, we're not doing this just to keep you on the project either." Devin snagged her gaze and said with a tone that left no room for doubt, "For apparent professional reasons, I will beg you to stay at SI if I must. Whether you stay or go is up to you, but know this. I will not walk away from whatever this is between us."

"We," Blake said.

"What?" Jayne looked over to see him focused on her.

"We," he repeated, his eyes darting nervously between her and Devin before they apprehensively settled on Jayne. "*We* will not walk away."

~ SIXTEEN ~

"It's fucked up, I know."

"I-I-I don't think I can do...*that*. I mean, I-I'm not even sure it's legal!" Blake watched Jayne pace the far side of the room like a nervous cat pacing a cage. Her shoulders were tense, her posture as stiff as a board. On the bright side, they both still had their balls. The minute she figured out what they were suggesting she'd all but freaked and bolted from the sofa again. It seemed Devin's Midas touch wasn't doing them any favors. He dug them deeper and deeper with every word he spoke.

"Jayne, look at me," Devin commanded. Jayne paused by the window, her teeth sunk deep into her bottom lip as she reluctantly gave in to his demand. "For just a minute, forget society's rules and everything that demands you label something wrong or right." Devin pushed from the sofa and met her by the window. "It's not as uncommon as you might think. And since when is dating two people at the same time illegal? People do it all the time."

"Devin, please. I...this is so crazy, I don't even know where to begin."

Blake didn't think it was possible, but her blush deepened to an even more profound shade of red. Devin stepped in closer, his fingers digging into her hips just a little to keep her from turning away from him. He was trying too hard. He couldn't bulldoze his way through this or bend her will to his own. Blake wasn't an expert on triads by any means, but he knew it didn't work this way.

"Hey, Dev. Give her a bit." Blake stood and paced to the window. "This isn't something we take lightly and neither should she. She deserves some time to process." He snagged her hand and guided her towards the hallway he assumed led to her bedroom. He truly had intended to leave and give her some space. *Roads are always paved with good intentions.* The large mirror on the wall just beyond the entryway caught his attention. Instead of guiding her into her bedroom and asking her to get dressed and go to breakfast with them, he led her towards the mirror instead. Before she made any decisions, he needed to make a few things clear. Things Devin neglected to mention. Things he knew would most likely make her decision for her. If he was going to take a chance on something this big, he wanted all the cards on the table.

Blake positioned her in front of the mirror as he stood behind her, his fingers laced with hers at her hips. "Do you remember the couple on the stairs?" She caught his gaze in the mirror and gave a single stoic nod. "Devin and I want you, Jayne. Equally and without question, we want to share you; your time, your body, your affection. We will gladly give you time and space to think about it, but I want you to fully understand something before you decide if you want this, too." His hands released hers and traveled slowly up her arms and over her shoulders. He felt her sharp intake of breath as he simultaneously pressed his hard cock to her lower back and trailed his fingers along the slender column of her neck. "Open your eyes, Jayne," he commanded when he saw them flutter closed. "Look at us in the mirror. Can you see how well we look together?" She didn't answer, but he didn't expect her to. He could see her answer in the way her nipples pebbled beneath her thin shirt. "I like to watch, Jayne. There will be times I will want to watch us in a mirror like this." Her skittish whimper spurred him on as his lips traced the outside edge of her ear. "There will also be times I'll want to watch you with Devin and it won't always be in the privacy of a bedroom."

He watched as she processed what he was saying and he could hear her question before the words were spoken. "What do you mean?" He turned her in his arms and cradled her face in his hands as he looked down into innocent eyes; eyes that begged him for the truth.

"A park bench, a movie theatre, a darkened stairwell in downtown Los Angeles." He paused to watch as his meaning settled in. "It's fucked up, I know, but it's a part of who I am, Jayne. It's what I need." He waited and watched. Watched for the moment when she realized she was too good for him and this was all too twisted to be real. When that look never materialized, he couldn't help himself. His mouth crushed against hers in a kiss he'd long to take since she'd walked into his office the morning before. The fire that had burned between them every time they touched flashed to life. A voice somewhere in the distance warned him to stop. He purposefully ignored it. He would be the first to admit his dick was leading the charge for this woman. He wanted to fuck her in every way possible. He could also envision her with Devin. For that one moment he could almost believe it was possible. He could almost feel what had been missing from his life since he'd lost Daphne. Only there was something different, something richer in the taste and feel of Jayne in his arms. He knew if she agreed to be theirs, his life would be complete in a way he never dreamed it could. And it scared the living hell out of him to hope for it.

Devin cleared his throat and Blake released her. Their chests rose and fell together as the flames between them once again calmed to a rolling smolder. He wanted to bank their fire, wall it up and protect it, but he knew he couldn't. He needed her to want it, to want them. For a brief moment he wished he was normal. He wished he could tell Devin to take a hike and keep her all to himself. His hands released her and he backed away before he could give any more credence to that thought. It wasn't possible so there was no use even entertaining it.

"We postponed the city council meeting until Monday," Devin said, nervously taking a step towards her. "Please, take the weekend to think about coming back to SI. I'll have Human Resources hold your resignation until then." Blake was relieved to see that Jayne didn't flinch when Devin took her chin between his fingers and laid a gentle kiss to her lips. "I meant what I said, angel.

This thing between us isn't going away. We want you on this project, but we need you in our bed."

Jayne gave a hesitant nod. Blake opened her front door while he still had the willpower to leave. "Get some food, Jaynie." He asked her to promise when she didn't respond, but he didn't believe her. He would drop off the Ducati at his apartment in town then do a little grocery shopping before he left town for the weekend. There was no way he was staying in L.A. Not with Mallory lurking around every corner. He thought about asking Devin to ride along, but he needed the space. A lot had changed in his life the last few weeks. If Jayne showed up Monday morning a lot more could change. Like her, he needed his own time to process.

Monday morning rolled in slower than a San Fran fog. Blake popped half a roll of antacids into his mouth and choked them down with a swig of muddy coffee left in his mug from the night before. After his weekend bender it wasn't the worst thing he'd tasted in the last forty-eight hours. He eyed the mug before he ran it under some soapy hot water then dried and put it away. The fact that he'd left it sitting on the counter overnight told him just how mucked up he was.

Palming his car keys and phone, he was on the 101 freeway and headed into town before the day's first light peeked over the mountains. He would be early, but it beat sitting in traffic for an hour. If he was lucky, he'd have time to book his flight back to Las Vegas before their meeting with the city council. Once the weekly project status reports were in from all the divisions, he'd hand everything over to Devin and this hiatus from his self-imposed desolation would finally be over.

He didn't know if he would see Jayne or Devin at the meeting. He hadn't heard a single word from either of them all weekend. To say Devin exploded after they left her apartment on Friday would be an understatement, accusing him of purposefully sabotaging their chances with her. Hell, he was probably right. For all he knew Jayne was sitting at home in New York sipping coffee, eating cheese covered pie and scouring the internet for a way to help her forget all the fucked up things he'd put into her head. Things he still wanted more than he ever thought was possible. He hadn't

156

planned on unloading all his twisted baggage on her like that. He just wanted her to know the truth before they were all in so deep that one of them would drown before they got out. He knew that *one* would be him. He honestly didn't have it in him to go through something like that again. It's why he'd taken Gavin up on the gigolo gig. No strings, no drowning.

It didn't matter. He'd spent all weekend second guessing everything. He started out strong; sure that Devin was overreacting in his control freak sort of way and Jayne would come around. By Saturday night the pendulum had swung. He wanted it over. The feeling that Devin had been right still hung on him like a lead coat when he walked into the conference room at the Council Chamber. All the key players were already seated around the long mahogany table, chatting randomly amongst themselves before the meeting began. All but one. Devin greeted him with a fury in his expression that burned too hot to be just about Jayne's absence.

Blake nodded to Oliver Ryles, the council president, and then took the empty seat next to Devin. "What's up?" he asked in a concealed whisper.

"They want to know what we're going to do about replacing Jayne," Devin grumbled back.

Adrenaline dumped into Blake's veins and flooded his body with profound disbelief. "How do they know she resigned?"

Devin shook head. Blake didn't miss the tick in his jaw as he glanced around the room. "I don't know, unless she called them," he hissed. "This is going to blow the deal before we even—"

The meeting room door suddenly swung open and Blake's stomach leapt into his chest. Or at least he hoped that was what was causing the bursting ache just above his sternum. *Damn, she looks amazing.* Jayne's hair was upswept into a wispy looking clip thing. He didn't know what they called it, but he knew women had some kind of name for that style. Her cheeks were flushed with excitement that quickly turned into her signature blush when her eyes swept the room and snagged on his. She wore a dark purple suit that showed every one of her luscious curves and made her skin glow like the angel Devin called her. And hell if she wasn't two inches taller. He and Devin both leaned back in their seats, craning their necks as she rounded the table to check out the sexiest, kick-ass heels any woman ever wore.

"I'm so sorry I'm late," Jayne said and made her way into the room. "President Ryles," she nodded and gave the council president a confident smile as she passed him on the way to the empty seat on the other side of Devin. "Mr. Kirk. Mr. Travers."

"I was led to believe you resigned from the Emerald Dream project, Ms. Simon," the Chairman of the Sustainability Review Committee declared as he fixed his eyes on Jayne's low-cut blouse. Blake could feel the hair on his arms stand on end. He hated politicians with a passion and he had no problem sending this one back to his district missing his teeth.

"I'm afraid you were misinformed, Mr. Camden. I was merely delayed." Jayne pulled her leather-bound portfolio onto the table, unzipped it and then settled herself into her seat with an exasperated huff. "I can honestly say the traffic in this city is definitely not sustainable. I dare say there's not enough recycle centers on the planet to offset such a huge carbon footprint." She met Mr. Camden's gaze with a calculating smile he'd only seen on the first day he'd met her when she left him standing in that elevator after he invited her out for drinks. "Forgive me. I'm not familiar with all of the city's sustainability efforts, yet. Exactly what was your national carbon impact offset rating last year?"

National what rating? Whatever it was it caught the man's attention. Blake watched as the Chairman's lust-filled eyes snapped up to her face. *About damn time, asshole.* The bastard's lips curled into a conceited smirk as he tapped his pen on his notepad. "Not high enough, Ms. Simon. Not nearly high enough."

"Let's get on with this, shall we?" Oliver Ryles called the meeting to order.

He didn't know about Devin, but shock overruled his possessive streak for the next fifteen minutes of their meeting. He watched in awe, still not believing she showed, as Jayne fielded their questions and outlined her plans for the next phase of the build. She stumbled in a few spots, but quickly covered her slight stutter, her only tell of just how nervous she was. She didn't bullshit or hedge when she didn't have the answers they wanted. She assured them she would look into it and moved on.

Soon it was Blake's turn. He hated this part of his job. If it wasn't for Devin, he would have told them all to go to hell. All he wanted was to get Jayne and Devin out of there, find out if she was back for good and if she'd decided to give them a chance. Instead, he droned on about the latest permit changes needed and told them about a snag he'd run into with the public works director. They made the usual promises to cut through the red tape. Blake resisted the urge to make like he was jacking off under the table as they patted themselves on the back for fixing a problem they created. Devin played the man in charge and dazzled them with financials, giving them a euphoric high that would keep them off their backs until it wore off and they had to do this all over again.

By the time they reached the sunbaked parking lot Blake was about to burst. He pulled Jayne to a stop beside his car and crushed his mouth to hers. He thought she was gone. Until he saw her in that room he had convinced himself it was okay. All he wanted to do was get back to a place where he didn't have to feel anything. She walked into that room and it all changed.

"Wait!" Jayne struggled against him. "Not here."

Blake let her go. He looked over to see Devin approaching, a murderous expression on his face. "What?"

"Where's your car?" he asked Jayne. Blake's brows furrowed at the warning look Devin sent him.

"I don't have one. I took a cab."

Devin froze, his jaw going slack. "You're kidding."

"What?" Jayne shrugged, looking between them. "I don't need one to get to the office. Why contribute to the problem?" Blake didn't know what had Devin's blood boiling, but he fully understood the next look he shot him. They were going car shopping. If she was staying.

"Get in the car," Devin barked. He opened Blake's rear passenger door and ushered Jayne in, climbing in after her. Blake slid into the driver's seat and turned the ignition, cranking up the air conditioner.

"Where to, *boss*?" Obviously not amused with Blake's sarcasm, Devin drilled him with another warning look. "The office it is." Blake swore under his breath as he put the car in drive and navigated onto Main Street.

~ SEVENTEEN ~

All cards on the table.

Jayne stood in front of the panoramic window that dominated Devin's office. Her new office, while larger than the one she had in New York, was nothing more than a glorified cubicle. She was oddly grateful for the stark contrast to this. She didn't know how anyone could get anything done with such a distracting view.

"I got a call from Toronto," Devin said, breaking the silence that had filled the room since they arrived back at SI. "As we left the meeting." Jayne followed his eyes to the stack of papers Blake had tossed on his desk when he'd followed them in. "They're backing out of the deal I closed while I was there, siting a breach of contract for leaking the municipal bond details to the Canadian press."

"I have security pulling email records of every employee that had access to the information," Blake said from across the room. "And phone records from Human Resources. All calls into and out of the building are recorded so we might get a lead on who leaked Jayne's resignation, too."

"I didn't speak to anyone other than Grace," Jayne promised. "I thought maybe you had told Ryles this morning before I arrived. I'm sorry I didn't call you to tell you about my decision to stay, but I hadn't officially decided until this morning."

"Are you staying?" Devin asked. He rose from behind his desk and paced to stand beside her at the window.

Her stomach turned as they stood together in silence, waiting for her to either affirm or deny it. He'd been so upset and short with her. Maybe staying was the wrong decision. "I thought you'd be happy about that."

She flinched when his fingers tangled with hers. "I'm sorry, angel. Of course I'm happy. We're both happy. I'm strung a little thin lately, that's all. I tend to shoot first and think later."

She nodded, giving him the benefit of the situation. The contrite look on his face made it easier to forgive him for being short with her, but it didn't ease the knot in her stomach. She'd made herself crazy all weekend trying to make sense of what they were asking her to be a part of. Her under-sexed libido waged a constant battle with her over-taxed, OCD rattled brain. It turned out that Devin was right. Three people in a single committed relationship wasn't uncommon. It wasn't exactly commonplace either, but it wasn't unheard of. There was a lot of information available, even social media groups and websites devoted to the lifestyle. That didn't make what they wanted any less scary.

She wasn't like Roxy. Although, this was another one of those times she wished she was. What they were suggesting was something Rox would try, or maybe she'd already tried it. Jayne didn't know because Rox had dodged all her calls, *all-weekend*. The only thing she knew for sure was that she couldn't see herself doing what they were suggesting. It wasn't her. She had said those exact words to Roxy when the whole gigolo thing was offered in the first place, and look at where it had landed her. Oh, and just to be fantastically cruel, fate added a side of voyeurism into this mix of crazy. She had been undeniably turned on by the distraction Devin had given her to get over her nervous shyness, but it wasn't real. Well, she was definitely naked and they had definitely done it in front of her hotel window, but it wasn't…real. Was it? Could she be an exhibitionist for him? How far would it go?

All weekend she'd gone back and forth. Over and over Jayne talked herself from the edge of the cliff. Over and over she found herself right back there looking beyond that edge, wondering if she could do it. Hours of trying unsuccessfully to reach Roxy had gotten her no closer to an understanding or a decision. So, she did the only rational thing left to do. She broke out her pen and paper, sat down and wrote a list of pros and cons. Multiple orgasms: pro. Of course that was the first thing on her list. Not one, but two, unimaginably sexy, successful men who wanted to give her multiple orgasms: pro. At the same time: pro. Holy shit, she was screwed. There wasn't a con in existence that could negate even one of those pros. Not even losing her job and never being able to show her face in the corporate world again; ever. A girl could live a long time on the kinds of memories they were promising. She could bag groceries. *Paper or plastic?* How hard could that be?

After two days it all came down to two things. She wanted this job, and she wanted more of them. She craved Blake's fire; the way he got excited when he saw her. She liked Devin, too, but admittedly she didn't know anything about him. They had an unworldly physical connection she'd never experienced with another human being. She liked both of them and liked the idea of hoping for more. She just wasn't sure how, if she could get past the craziness of it, she could keep both them and her job mutually exclusive.

After taking a long, hard look, Jayne knew her problems with her job had nothing to do with her ability to do the job, and everything to do with her preoccupation with Blake. Her success that morning was proof she could handle herself, but she had been so distracted by Blake. Adding Devin into the mix created complete chaos. Her mind and body had been thrown into a whirlwind. Not to mention the professional implications it could have if word ever got out about them. Blake kissing her in the parking lot after the council meeting was just one example. Being taken seriously as a professional wasn't going to happen if the world knew she was sleeping with her boss. She looked up to see both Devin and Blake waiting for her to respond. *Make that sleeping with* both *bosses.*

"I'm back, for now." Her voice came out stronger than she expected. It gave her the courage to keep going. "But, we need to talk."

"Okay," Devin and Blake said in unison as they crowded around her.

"I was hired to do a job," she said. "A job I've dreamt of doing my entire life." Her hands wringing together until she could barely feel her fingers, she paced to the far side of the room, once again putting some much needed space between them. She had practiced what she wanted to say to them a hundred times as she got ready for the meeting that morning. It flowed smoothly when she was alone, talking to herself in the bathroom mirror. With them looming over her, all gorgeous male and brooding, her ability to think straight was unraveling as fast as her career. "This is so unfair," she muttered under her breath. "I've worked so hard to get this job, to get to a place where I can make a difference."

"And we need you to do that job, Jayne. The whole project hinges on you being a part of this team."

"Please," Jayne scoffed. She'd thought about that too after they left her apartment on Friday. She might be simple but she wasn't that gullible. No one was irreplaceable, even in this alternate universe. "There were at least a hundred other applicants for this position."

"No," Devin said. "We've already had too many delays. One more will crush the deal." He shoved his hands into his pockets and blew out an exasperated breath. "Believe what you want, but you're a vital part of this project, Jayne. Nothing that's happened, or will happen between us changes that."

"Easy for you to say!" Why did men not get it? "You're not just *in* construction, Devin. You *are* construction. These things never end well for the person in my shoes. Silverland Industries is one of the largest development conglomerates in the world. What am I supposed to do when this…*thing* between us is over?"

Afraid if she faced him she'd cave on the spot, she turned and paced to the window overlooking the city. Parked cars lined each side of the street, a throng of midday pedestrians and tourists passing through the busy intersection at the corner a few hundred feet away. She closed her eyes and laid her palm on the glass. Immediately she was assailed by the silhouetted image of the couple Devin had painted on an imaginary canvas in her mind. A portrait of passion and pleasure, no matter how hard she tried, she could never make herself forget. How much more difficult would it be when it all ended? "Both of you will always have what you love to go back to. All I will have left are the memories."

She didn't have to open her eyes to know it was Devin's hand that covered hers on the window. The heat from his body rushed over her only seconds before she was enveloped by his embrace. "I have memories too, angel." The knot in her stomach morphed into butterflies when his breath tickled the fine hairs on the side of her neck. "I remember every moment of our night together." He turned her in his arms and placed her hands on his shoulders, gathering her as close as she remembered them ever being as he began a slow dance.

"I remember the first time I heard your voice; that nervous little stutter thing you do. I remember wanting to hold you and tell you it was okay because I was nervous, too." With each step they took her body relaxed into the dance. There was no music; only the sounds of their shifting feet against the carpet and her rapidly increasing heartbeat. "I remember the unique scent of your hair." Her forehead fell against his chest and he buried his nose in her hair as one of his hands traveled to the nape of her neck. Her head fell back when he released her hair from the clip she wore. "I remember how the weight of it felt in my hands. I wondered what color it was, whether it was golden blonde or midnight black."

"Devin, please," she pushed at his chest but he didn't let her go. She was losing her grip on whatever control she may have had over this insane situation. She stood there in front of him, her hands resting on his chest. He was seducing her one memory at a time and she was powerless to stop him.

He reached up and fingered a long lock of her hair, holding it up to the sunlight shining in from the window. "The way the sun ignites the hint of red is something I couldn't have imagined, angel." He let the strand fall and she tipped her head back to look at him. "I've never been so glad to be wrong, Jayne."

She closed her eyes and clasped the lapels of his coat into her fists, her head falling back against the window behind her as his tongue tickled a path along her neck. "I can't fight this."

"Don't fight it." Blake's voice, so close to her ear, startled her; pulling her back into her worries just as she was about to let them go.

"Where do we go from here?" She knew as well as anyone there was no satisfying answer to her question. No one knew what the future held in any relationship, but given what was at stake she couldn't let it go unasked. She needed some perspective before she let her heart follow her body's twisted obsession with these men.

"I won't lie to you, Jayne. We have no idea." An intimacy she'd never felt before surrounded them all as Devin pulled her body between his and Blake's. It certainly felt like more than just sex, but she truly had no experience to make that comparison.

"I only know I want more of you," Blake answered. She turned her head to see a familiar passion in his darkened blue eyes. "More of what I feel when I'm with you."

Yes! More! Her hormones picked up picket signs and marched on her ovaries shouting *more-more-more!* Her heartbeat sped up to a blinding rate. A different kind of knot pushed against her chest as her lungs excitedly pumped the extra oxygen her racing blood demanded. The soft silk shirt she wore seemed irritating and tight, chaffing against her heated skin. Their bodies, on the other hand, felt so good wrapped around her. Was she really going to do this? Every time she was with either of these men she felt more excited, emotionally and physically, than she'd ever felt before. Standing between them was like burning alive! "I want that too," she said before she could chicken out.

Their hot breaths caressed her hair, her neck, her face. She could hear the rapid beat of Devin's heart as she melted against his chest, his hands roaming feverishly over her body until they framed her face and she peered up into his hooded eyes. "I'm dying to kiss you again." She could hear the question in his words, asking her permission.

"Then kiss me," she breathed against Devin's lips, so close she could taste him on hers.

His brows raised in warning, the slight shake of his head telling her it wouldn't be that easy. "It won't end there, angel. All cards on the table? We want it all. No turning back and no holding back if we take that step."

His fingers slid behind her neck, holding her captive as they held themselves perfectly still and waited for her to accept their terms. This was it. She was doing this. They were giving her one last out. She was making a conscious decision that could either be the most erotic, rewarding experience of her life, or her greatest mistake. Most likely both.

"Kiss me," she whispered again, bracing herself for Devin's hard and eager kiss, her heart pounding harder inside her chest with the same desperation to feel him. An unexpected ping of excitement ricocheted through her limbs as his lips feathered across hers, his panted breaths caressing them, coaxing them open with flirting glances of his tongue. Her last breath rushed from her lungs when his mouth crushed over hers. His hot tongue slid deep inside, slowly caressing and tangling with hers before he withdrew and came back for more; this time deeper and more impatient.

"Mmm," she moaned, unable to contain the electrifying waves that spread like heat lightning through her body when he pressed himself against her. This time was different than before. Instead of nervousness and fear of the unknown, she knew exactly what he was capable of doing to her and she wanted it. Just like he said, she wanted it all. Her hands wiggled between them until she found his belt buckle and pulled it open, her fingers fidgeting helplessly with his button and zipper until he released her and unfastened them himself. His suit coat long discarded, she chased his mouth as her hands worked feverishly to loosen his tie.

"Take off your shirt," Devin ordered as he unbuttoned his own. She pulled away only long enough to slip her suit coat off and pull her shirt over her head. Sinful aches gripped her entire body as he pulled down the cups of her bra and bared her breasts to his touch before he crushed her against him again, the heat of his skin scorching her own. His hands delved deep inside her suit pants to push them to the ground, pooling them around her ankles. She kicked them off, her head falling back into his capable hands the instant his mouth landed on hers again. Unable to process the onslaught of sensations he summoned from her body so effortlessly, Jayne was immediately lost in a familiar intoxicating fog of sensual lust.

Like a silk ribbon in the wind, she wobbled in her favorite high heels as Devin turned her around. He lifted her arms, placing her hands behind his neck, offering her up like a sacrifice. Blake stood in front of her, his shirt open, the ends of his belt hanging lose as he unzipped his slacks. He let them fall to the floor then kicked them away, his socks and shoes already gone. She bit her lip against the heavy pulse that vibrated between her thighs. Was there ever a more gorgeous man? How had she missed the allure of tattoos? She still couldn't say she would love them on any other man, but on Blake it was like looking at a breathing canvas of forbidden sins.

"Look at her, Dev," Blake said. "She's about to come apart and we haven't even touched her yet." Her lungs froze when he trailed the backs of his fingers over her nipples. "Breathe, Jaynie." He dropped his hand and puffs of air hissed past her lips, one after another.

"Close your eyes and touch her again," Devin ordered. "Feel how soft she is." Her back arched against Devin's chest as his palms slowly skimmed up her sides and cupped her breasts, holding them out for Blake. She wanted Blake's hands on her. She could almost feel the heat of his lips as they closed around her nipple.

"No way." Blake shook his head. Jayne's eyes followed his hand down to his groin and watched as he pulled himself free of his dark cotton boxers. "I've waited too long for this. I want to watch the two of you." She'd forgotten about him wanting to watch. Right now she was too entranced by what he was doing and what she saw to care. While he and Devin may be close in size, Blake definitely had a little something extra.

"Holy shit, man. When did you get that?" Devin asked as he looked over her shoulder at Blake.

Blake's hand moved up and over the thick bar running through the head of his cock. "A few weeks after I moved to Vegas.

It hits all the right spots." Heat flooded her body when she heard Blake's chuckle and looked up to see him watching her watch him. "Fuck! I love it when you blush like that."

Her breath snagged again when Devin pressed himself hard against her backside, his fingers grasping her hips to hold her against him. "I need inside you, angel. My body has craved you since the morning I left you in Vegas."

She felt Devin work his penis free of his pants then his hands snaked around her hips to the front of her lace panties. When he pulled them to the side she heard a loud hiss. Opening her eyes, she saw Blake's tongue snake out to lick his lips. "Holy shit! You're going to kill me, woman." He waved Devin's hand away, gripping the lace with both hands and ripping it down the seam, revealing her waxed folds. It had been one of her *I can do this, looking over the edge of the cliff* moments when she dared imagine this very moment. Before she could talk herself off the edge, she phone-searched a spa and bee-lined it straight there. Looking at the lust in Blake's eyes made every painful moment worth it.

"Hold up a second, Dev." Jayne's knees buckled when Blake touched her. Devin steadied her in his arms, holding her up. Blake cupped her cheek in his palm as the fingers on his other hand danced along her bare slit, stimulating an exhilarating rush of excitement. "You never cease to amaze me, Jaynie." She tensed in Devin's arms as Blake invaded her body, his fingers mimicking the sure, deep thrusts of his tongue as it slid inside her mouth. In and out, over and over, he penetrated her. Her hips chased Blake's thumb on her clit and then Devin's hard thrusts against her backside. Blake's low hums of approval drew out a long, low moan that drowned out every other sound until she heard herself scream his name as she flew apart in Devin's arms.

Pleasure thrummed through Jayne's body as Blake stroked her down from a high she hadn't felt in weeks. Not since Devin. "That's it, babe. Give me everything you've got." Jayne couldn't hold back as Blake continued to stroke a spot inside her, pulling her farther into her release. Heavy shudders fluttered into tiny spasms as she once again melted into Devin's arms. Blake cupped his hand and brought it to his lips, tasting her before he wrapped his palm around his rigid cock and gave it several long, slow pulls, coating himself in her release.

Devin gathered her up and stood her more steadily on her feet. She kept her balance, but if this was any indication of what she was in for, she was seriously going to have to re-think the practicality of fuck-me heels. "Shoes," she panted. She lifted one foot and kicked off her shoe. Before she knew it Blake was in front of her, supporting her as he lifted her other leg and slid off the other one. "Thank you."

"Don't thank me, baby. We love the shoes, but we don't want you to break your neck." He set her shoes aside but stayed there on his knees, leaning back on his heels. He threw her and Devin a wicked grin and began stroking himself again. "I like this view."

Devin turned her to the window and placed her palms against the glass. "I like this view," Devin said with a haughty laugh. Jayne gasped as she remembered where she was.

"Oh my God!" She looked out at the surrounding buildings, at the traffic below, both vehicles and pedestrians. Anyone and everyone could have been watching them!

"Relax, angel. The glass is mirrored. No one can see inside during the day."

"Are you sure? I mean…what if som—". Jayne's words froze in her chest with her last breath when she felt Devin's hand slide down her back. His fingers trailed down between her cheeks, but he stopped and pressed on a place no one had ever touched before.

Devin bit out another wicked chuckle. "I thought that would distract you." His other hand slid around her hip, his fingers circling her clit. She just had an orgasm with Blake, but there was plenty of pleasure in Devin's touch all the same. Her spine arched against Devin's lips as he feathered his tongue over her skin up to her shoulder. She flenched when she felt him slide between her legs and press the head of his penis to her wet entrance. "I want to remember this moment just like I remember every second of the first time I slid inside you."

"Ah!" Jayne cried out, pushing up on her tiptoes as Devin pushed his way inside her. It was a slow but steady penetration, meant to be felt in the deepest places hidden inside her.

"Just like I'll remember every time I slide inside you." Slower and slower he stroked, in and out, savoring every inch, every movement as if he were memorizing her soul. "Oh, yeah," he hissed as he stilled inside her, his hips pressing hard against her backside. "This is where I want to be. What I've dreamed about for weeks."

They both unleashed a long, low groan when her inner muscles squeezed around him. She couldn't help it. She couldn't tell if it was the end of her first orgasm or the beginning of another. "Please, Devin," she begged. Whatever it was or wasn't, she needed him to move!

"Fuck, that's hot!" Jayne tensed at the sound of Blake's gravelly voice.

Devin took her chin in his fingers and turned her head towards him. "Look at him, Jayne. Look at what you're giving him." As Blake stood with his back against the wall, his legs spread wide, she watched his hand move at a more fevered pace along his shaft. His eyes were shuttered, a glaze of ecstasy coloring his expression. Devin began to mimic Blake's powerful strokes, pulling almost completely out and pushing deeper inside her with more force each time.

Without warning Devin's arm snaked around her waist and her feet left the floor. He turned her to face Blake who pushed away from the wall and crushed himself against her. In a single breath she was sandwiched between them, Devin pushing inside her from behind as Blake's penis stood thick and hard against her belly. Blake's mouth met hers in a tangle of tongues and a clash of teeth. He fumbled for her hand, placing it on his shaft and covering it with his own. They pumped him in time with Devin's strokes, faster and harder until she had to tear her mouth away.

"Fu..fuck me. Oh, fuck." Her voice hitched with each powerful stroke. "I'm coming," she panted as the first wave hit her. "I'm coming again!"

"I can feel you!" Devin cried out, his fingers digging into her ribs as his hips snapped harder and harder against hers. The mingled sounds of their sweaty flesh coming together filled Devin's office. Her head fell back against Devin's shoulder, her entire body arching against him as it shuddered between him and Blake. Blake took advantage and sucked one of her nipples into his mouth and that was all it took. Jayne's orgasm ripped through her body like a Midwestern tornado.

"Fuuuuuck!" Devin stumbled but recovered as he held himself deep inside Jayne, his forehead resting on her back as hers rested on Blake's shoulder. Blake's cock still throbbed in her hand, his seed pulsing out over their fingers as he quelled his strangled groan with an open mouth kiss to the top of her shoulder.

Slowly, they all sank to the floor in a single heap, breaths panting, exhausted muscles quivering beneath sweat covered flesh. Minutes, maybe days passed. Jayne couldn't be sure. She didn't care. She only knew one thing and it meant she was in deep, deep trouble. She wanted more.

~ EIGHTEEN ~

"Questions, Jayne. I want those questions."

Jayne glanced up at Devin with a shy smile as she stepped through the door he held open for her. She cursed the flash of heat that flooded her cheeks when he winked at her. After everything they had done, after what they all did together in his office not six hours ago in front of the entire city of Los Angeles, she still blushed when he looked at her. Admittedly, he was looking at her the same way both men had all afternoon. Like they were going to eat her alive where she stood. Her fears of them being a distraction to her work had been proven to be unfounded. A distraction would mean she was still able to perform her job functions, albeit maybe a little slower than normal. No. They were not a distraction. Devin and Blake were like an atom bomb to her concentration. She considered herself lucky to have even found her office after they peeled themselves off Devin's office floor.

Warm scents of ginger and garlic mingled with other exotic spices and swirled inside the posh restaurant Devin had insisted on for dinner. Her mind was still swimming with a million questions. Mixed with the insanely sexual visions that kept popping into her head at random intervals and she was a walking disaster. Eating was the last thing on her mind.

The dark wood and low lighting contrasted with the bright young hostess who greeted them at the podium. Her friendly grin shifted into a radiant smile when Blake followed them inside.

"Blake!" She squealed and bounced on her toes before launching herself at Blake. He stood stunned for a moment before his arms folded around the beautiful young woman.

"Sydney? What in the world?" Blake set her back on her feet and held her away from him. "What…are you working here?"

Sydney nodded. "Almost a year. I can't believe my luck! Normally I'd be in the back and I would have missed seeing you!"

"In the back?" Blake asked, "Are you the chef here?"

"Close!" she said, casting that same flirty smile at Devin. Jayne was sure she'd caught plenty of guys with that shiny net. "Devin put in a word for me and I've been working my way up to head chef ever since!"

"Don't let her fool you. She practically owns the place now," Devin said. Jayne watched the comfortable byplay between the trio for a moment before Devin made the introductions. "Sydney, I'd like you to meet Jayne Simon. Jayne, this is Sydney DeLucca. She once ran Blake's life at SI as efficient as Jeanette runs mine."

"Oh, how rude of me!" Sydney held out her hand. "I'm usually not so socially inept it's just…," the woman sighed wistfully as she looked back at Blake. "I didn't think I'd ever see you again. I'm so glad you're back."

"I'm not back." The bloom of jealously she was beginning to feel was pinched off at the head with a jolt of uncertainty when she heard Blake re-confirm his plans to leave SI once Devin had things under control. She covered her sudden realization and met Blake's apologetic glance with a weary smile. "I mean. I haven't made it official yet."

Meaning he was still planning to leave. Jayne swallowed her disappointment. She knew the deal. Neither one of them had made her any promises. They'd barely even discussed what it was they were doing. Just because they had sex together didn't mean he would upend his life and move back to California for her. Devin tightened his arm around her, pulling her closer into his side. She couldn't quite make out the meaning behind the look he gave her. Maybe he sensed her regret. Maybe not. Either way his embrace warmed her a little and gave her emotions a soft place to land. She quickly gathered them back before Blake noticed his response had hit a nerve.

"Well, I hope you do so soon, Blake Travers, because this man has gotten way too serious in his new role as C-E-O," she teased, punctuating each letter of Devin's new title with a poke of her finger in Devin's arm. "I never get to see that gorgeous smile—" Sydney paused mid-sentence and stared blankly at Devin, her eyes wide as she studied his face. Jayne glanced up to see him smiling that very same gorgeous smile Sydney was gushing over. The woman looked suspiciously between her and Devin before her mouth dropped open. She slapped a hand up to cover her gasp and Jayne heard the words *'no way'* muffled behind it.

Despite his statement about not staying in Los Angeles, Jayne's insides still fluttered to life when Blake's fingers laced with hers. He and Devin shared another look she didn't quite get. She needed a decoder; one of those 'testosterone for dummies' books. She needed all the help she could get with these two.

After a sharp squeal and another awkward dance, Sydney led them to a private table near the back and rushed off into what Jayne assumed was the kitchen. Devin removed his suit coat and slid in first. Blake ushered her into the circular booth before he removed his own suit coat and slid in after her, sandwiching her between them. "Hell, Dev. How did that happen?" he asked, nodding in the direction Sydney disappeared.

Devin shrugged. "I was having dinner here with Mother and Mallory when she came in to drop off her application. Rafiq, the owner and head chef," he clarified for her benefit she was sure, "shared with me his desire to retire and I knew the minute I saw her walk in she would be a perfect fit."

"She certainly has the talent for it," Blake said. Jayne's mouth went a little dry as she watched him unbutton and roll back his sleeves. Thick veins and muscles rippled beneath his bronzed and tattooed skin. When his hands paused mid-roll she looked up to see that he'd caught her watching him again. "I think I like you watching me as much as I like watching you."

Jayne grabbed her glass and gulped down a few swallows of ice water. "So, Sydney's an executive assistant and a chef?" she asked. She tried to hide her jealously under her embarrassment, but she wasn't sure it worked. "Impressive."

"It is," Blake agreed. He stared after Sydney for a long moment then glanced back at Jayne, a cocky grin dominating his face. "You're jealous!"

Jayne shook her head, but she sucked at lying. Devin chuckled beside her and she turned to see him ginning at Blake. "I'm afraid, if you're not careful, angel, it will be Blake and I who will be battling that big green monster. Although, I've never been opposed to a little girl on girl action. How about you, Blake?"

Blake shook his head. "Na, Syd's like a sister, man. Doesn't quite work for me." Her face burned with embarrassment. The thought that Sydney could be a lesbian never crossed her mind.

"We're teasing, angel," Devin nudged her with a flirty wink. "Sydney's partner, Michelle, is an amazing pastry chef. I'll have to take you by her bakery one morning." He passed her a menu and gave her another playful nudge. "I like that you're already a little possessive of us though."

"Sydney was still in culinary school when she worked for SI," Blake said. "We gained at least twenty pounds apiece the year before Daph...before I left. Didn't we, Dev?"

Jayne didn't miss the slip. Devin threw his arm behind her and gave Blake a shove. Blake threw him a look that said *'piss off'* and Jayne giggled. There was no mistaking that one. Maybe she didn't need that decoder after all.

"What's so funny, angel?" Devin asked, his hand finding its way to the nape of her neck.

She shook her head. "You two. You're like brothers with all your secret looks and shoves. I'm right here, you know."

"Oh, we know, babe," Blake said in a low toned whisper. She jumped when his hand squeezed her thigh and slid all the way up between her legs. "I like this suit, but right now I'd kill to have you in one of those skirts that drive me mad." Although the dining room was dimly lit and they were mostly isolated from view, she was grateful for the long table skirt when his thumb pressed expertly on her clit.

"You…you like my skirts?" When Devin's lips grazed her ear they nearly had to peel her off the ceiling. "Wait!" She pushed at Blake's hand and squirmed away from Devin. "Time out!"

Both Devin and Blake chuckled but thankfully relented. Their waiter greeted them and Devin ordered a bottle of wine. As soon as the waiter left he and Blake turned in the booth, giving her their full attention as Devin began asking her questions. "You moved from New York. Is that where you grew up?"

She shook her head, the mention of New York bringing Roxy to the forefront of her thoughts. "No, Rox and I moved there to attend Cornell. I grew up in Michigan." She told them about Rox and how they eventually became sisters. Knowing Blake was still sensitive about the loss of his fiancé, she tried to stay away from talking about her parents until they asked about them directly. "My father was an architect at a firm in Grand Rapids and my mother was a stay at home mom."

"Was?" She met Blake's gaze and recognized the shadow that ghosted over his expression. It was the same one that still haunted her from time to time. She told them about her parents and the horrible accident that had taken them from her and Rox. Before the inevitable sadness that had crept into their conversation could consume her, their waiter came to their table and began the obnoxious yet distracting process of taking their order. She'd never heard of many of the items on the menu so when Devin insisted he order for her she accepted graciously. There were apparently more than four courses, but everything after the salad was lost in translation.

The food came and went. What she was able to eat she liked. Sydney had commandeered the kitchen and made them all a spectacular meal. Devin and Blake asked more questions. By the time dessert was served she was beginning to feel the events of the day take their toll. She pushed the overly sweet tart around in the fancy sauce that lined her plate as she asked a few questions of her own. She was shocked to learn that Devin's dad passed away from a stroke three months before he was born. He spoke fondly of his mother, but she could tell there was some tension in their relationship.

"I pretty much grew up at my grandfather's estate while she was off marrying husbands three and four," Devin paused for a minute and chuckled. "And five I believe."

"At least she kept in touch," Blake said as he emptied the remaining wine into his glass.

"So you kept your father's last name?"

Devin nodded. "My mother gave me the choice when I was old enough. He was a good man. I wanted to honor him."

"And Mallory?" Saying her name left an unpleasant taste in Jayne's mouth. Remembering her tongue down Blake's throat was about as pleasant as a root canal.

"Mallory is the product of husband number four," Devin sighed as he swallowed his last sip of wine. "She's…different. In all fairness, we have a lot of years between us. I was in grad school when she was getting her learner's permit so I can't blame her completely. We just never clicked."

Blake's cellphone rang, cutting off her next question. Whoever it was he apparently didn't want to talk with them. In the time it took him to silence the call she'd already forgotten the question she was going to ask next, but it didn't matter. It was nice getting to know more about them, but it still felt so strange. On one hand she knew these men better than she'd known any man; at least in the physical sense. Yet, as they answered her mirroring questions, she realized they were little more than strangers. Everything was backwards and upside-down and confusing as hell.

"What's the matter, angel? You don't like the dessert?"

"You want me to order some cheese?" Blake teased.

"Ha-ha." Jayne smiled, but it did nothing to ease the sinking feeling that was beginning to spiral around her. "I just…," she shook her head. She was tired and she was making things way too complicated. It was just sex. Wasn't it?

"Talk to us, Jaynie girl. What are you thinking?" Blake pushed his plate away and turned his full attention back to her. Devin did the same, the sudden focus making it even more difficult to think.

"I think I'm just tired," she offered, hoping they would let it go. They didn't respond. Instead they waited quietly for her to continue. Apparently they weren't going to take no for an answer and when she opened her mouth to ask them for a ride home it all came spilling out.

"Everything feels backwards. I've never had sex with a man before at least knowing where he lived. For all I know you guys live in your offices. And what I do know about you...physically...leaves me with a million more questions I have no idea how to ask. I don't want to seem naïve or-or-or...inexperienced, but I am. I have no idea how to please you or how this is supposed to work. And no matter what you say about this not affecting my job, the two of you within a hundred yards of my office makes it impossible to even *think* about my job."

"Is that all?" Blake asked her, his eyes roaming her face, taking in all of the little tells.

"I don't know." She tossed her napkin on the table. "This is all so screwed up I'm sure I'll find something else eventually."

"Agreed," Devin chimed in. "But let me clear up a few points for you before we move on to any others." Devin invaded the small amount of personal space she'd managed to put between them and crushed his mouth to hers. Her head may be confused, but her body knew exactly what it wanted and molded to Devin's like a second skin. Blake's dick swelled to full mast, his well-tailored suit pants suddenly three sizes too small. He watched as she lost herself in

Devin's caress, their tongues openly tangling together. He could almost taste the raspberry sauce she'd fingered from her plate.

There wasn't a more beautiful look on a woman than the aroused look on Jayne's face when Devin let her come up for air. Except for maybe the rumpled and well sated look she was going to have when she woke up between them in the morning. Before she could protest, Blake tilted her chin and took his time showing her one sure way she could please him with her mouth. Damn! He loved the taste of raspberries.

Leaving nothing to chance, Blake captured her wrists. He placed one of her hands on Devin's cock and cupped his own cock with the other. She gasped and tried to jerk her hands away but he held her hand there, Devin now commanding the other. "This should leave you with absolutely no doubt of how much you please us, Jayne." He rotated his hips beneath her hand. "I want you so bad right now it hurts. I want to take you in every way a man can take a woman. I want you on your knees, sucking me off with your mouth. I want your pussy. I want your ass, Jayne. I want every single goddamn inch of you and if that means answering a few questions then please, just ask them."

Wide-eyed, Jayne blinked back her shock. Blake shifted his glance and saw the same expression on Devin's face. So what if he was acting like a cave man gone wrong. She was driving him insane. Watching her with Devin had set him off in a way nothing ever had. He'd walked around all afternoon with a prick in his pants despite coming in her more than capable hands a few hours before. Naïve? Inexperienced? Natural talent trumped experience every day of the damn week in his book.

He would admit there was a small part of him that thought getting some relief would cure him of his unexpected obsession with this woman. He'd get off, get her out of his system and then her and Devin could live happily ever after. That didn't happen. Instead he was sucked into the same dizzying addiction Devin had been hostage to for the last month. He craved her and he wasn't about to let a few questions stand in his way of having her.

Blake nearly exploded when his phone vibrated next to his junk. *Fuck!* This thing with Mallory was getting out of control. She called him morning, noon and night. The more he ignored her the worse she got. He needed to put an end to her manipulation once and for all. He should have come clean with Devin the night she showed up at the pool house. Devin's confession about Daphne had wiped out all thoughts of her strange visit until she began calling him again the next morning. By then they were on the hunt for Jayne. He certainly wasn't bringing it up now.

"Aren't you going to answer it?" Jayne asked.

His eyes locked on hers, he never even blinked. "Questions, Jayne. I want those questions."

She glanced over to Devin and he gave her an encouraging smile. "There's no judgment here, angel. Ask us anything you want, no matter how strange you think it is."

She pulled her hands free and Blake let her go this time. Hot pink began at the base of her throat and flushed up her neck into her cheeks. "Fine," she said, taking a deep breath before she raised her chin and looked him in the eyes. "Did you share Daphne?"

"Yes," Blake said as Devin said *'No'*. Blake glanced at Devin but returned his focus to Jayne as he clarified. "Devin was a third. He had sex with Daphne sometimes and I would watch, but she was *my* fiancé." He looked at Devin and saw for the first time the pain he'd harbored behind his silence. "I didn't know at the time, but Devin and her..." He swallowed hard, the taste of the words he'd never said aloud leaving a strange taste in his mouth. "Devin was in love with her too, but she died before we ever...we never shared her the way we want to share you." Dammit that was harder than he thought it was going to be. His chest began to fill with a searing pain he was sure no antacid would alleviate, though the appreciation he saw in Devin's eyes helped a little.

The feel of Jayne's hand when it grabbed his and squeezed was like a salve to the scab he'd just ripped open. "So this is a first for you, too?" She turned to Devin then back to him. "And this isn't just about sex."

"Angel, if this was just about sex we wouldn't be here," Devin said before he placed a tender kiss to the back of her hand. "The physical chemistry between us is off the charts, but I don't—I didn't know anything else about you. I want to have dinners and movie nights and walks in the park, too. Tonight was just the beginning. Blake has at least gotten to spend some time with you. I want to know what he knows."

"And I *really* want to know what Devin knows," Blake begged. "So let's have it. One question down, nine hundred and ninety-nine thousand, nine hundred and ninety-nine to go. We can do this." He looked at his watch and Jayne slapped at his arm.

"Funny," she said, and rolled her eyes. Oh, yeah. He liked this woman. "Do you…" She fiddled with the napkin on the table. Blake gave her a nudge with his elbow and pointed to his watch. "Jeez, okay! I mean…will you want to *watch* me with anyone other than Devin?"

"Not a chance in hell," they both said in unison. "This is it, babe," Blake stretched out his arms giving her a glance of his broad chest and shoulders. "Don't even think about asking us to share you with another guy, no matter how hot you think he is, because it's not going to happen."

"Oh my-no!" She wiped her forehead as if she had just dodged a bullet. He could barely grasp the thought of sharing her with Devin. Had she really thought they could turn her out to some stranger? "Trust, me," she gulped down the last bit of wine in her glass. "You will never hear that request coming from these lips."

"Good," Devin said and nodded to Blake. Blake took the cue and slid from the booth, ushering Jayne out ahead of Devin.

"Where are we going?" she asked. Blake loved Sydney like a sister. The food was spectacular and they would have to come back to see her frequently, but he'd never been more glad to be leaving a restaurant in his entire life.

"We're going to prove to you that at least one of us doesn't live in our offices," Devin said before he planted a quick kiss on

Jayne's lips. "We can clear up the rest of those questions of yours at my place."

~ NINETEEN ~

A cry for help.

"She's out cold." Devin followed Blake up the stairs and into his loft study after he clicked his bedroom door closed. Blake walked straight to the bar and poured them both a long finger of scotch, which Devin gratefully accepted. "What a long day."

"Going to be a long night, too," Blake hissed after he threw back his glass and swallowed down the smooth liquid fire.

"It was the right call, man. She was stressing way too hard. We don't want to push her away." The minute they were on the road to Devin's place Jayne had unleashed a long yawn. She tried to play it off. They weren't buying it. She was exhausted. After giving her a quick tour of his place, Blake poured her a hot bath in Devin's Jacuzzi tub and they insisted she lock herself away from them for at least thirty minutes. Those thirty minutes came and went. Blake found her dozing in the bubbles and any thoughts of doing anything other than giving her a soothing massage and tucking her into bed was out of the question for the night.

"I know. I'm just..." He watched as Blake stared up at the glass ceiling that capped off the tower above his study. "This thing we're doing. It's surreal."

"You don't have to explain, man. I hear you. I've been sucking wind since the moment I stepped into that hotel room in Vegas." He sank down into one of the two leather chairs that sat in front of his desk as Blake slid into the other. "What do you think I should do about Toronto?" The last thing Devin wanted to do now that he'd found Jayne was go back to Canada. Not if he couldn't take her with him.

Blake rubbed his tired eyes and leaned up to rest his elbows on his knees. "Honestly?" He cupped the back of his neck and rotated his head back and forth. "I'd let it go. We'll find the leak, but we need all hands on deck for the Emerald Dream."

It was Devin's turn to rub the grit from his eyes. "This is turning out to be a nearly impossible build." They'd had more delays than their last three builds combined and they hadn't even broken ground yet.

Blake remained silent, staring blankly at the bookshelf that lined the wall behind the desk. Devin cleared his throat. "What's up? You're zoning."

"Sorry, man," Blake said and shook himself back into the conversation. "Can I ask you something?" He looked at Devin and Devin nodded. "Why are you doing this?"

"Doing what?"

Blake shrugged. "Silverland Industries, the Emerald, Toronto. Hell, all of it. It's apparent you hate this. You've never been the power jockey your grandfather was. Why not sell out and go back to the basics. You've got DeVeaux over a barrel with that stunt his daughter pulled. Why not just let him have it? At a price well above market value of course. Tell him you'll drop the charges against Danielle in exchange."

He'd like to let DeVeaux have it all right. Despite the revulsion at the mention of his ex, for a second Devin allowed himself to entertain the thought of selling out. He stuffed that thought back into the black hole of family responsibility. "I can't," he sighed regretfully. "This is it for me." He pushed out of the chair and made his way back to the bar. "My grandfather started SI with fifty bucks. It was everything he had—"

"In the bank and your grandmother broke his nose when she found out ya-da, ya-da," Blake finished for him. "Forget all that,

Dev, for just a minute. This is me you're talking to, your best friend, not some reporter from the Times. What about your life? Just because he groomed you to take over doesn't mean your grandfather expected you to do so at all costs. Did you ever tell him you were thinking about branching out on your own?"

Devin shook his head. "It's not an option. Not anymore. I have to do this." He hated it. He hated it with a passion, but he couldn't just kill everything his grandfather worked for without even trying. Trying wasn't an option for him. He either succeeded or he failed and he never failed. That only left one option. He was now Silverland Industries.

Blake relaxed back into the leather chair, apparently satisfied he'd said his peace. "You asked, man. I think you should at least think about it."

Devin gave him a nod before he emptied his glass. "I'm beat," he said and headed towards the steps. "You take the left side, I get the right?" he asked over his shoulder when Blake fell in step behind him.

"Sounds fair to me. She's going to need a change of clothes. Who's making the five A.M. run to her apartment?"

"I will," Devin said and cut the lights before he turned down the hall to his bedroom. "You go in there and we won't see you for a week."

Blake chuckled and blew out a sigh of disbelief. "You should have seen her fridge, man. It was war of the worlds in there."

"I don't get it." Devin paused at the closed door. "Her office is like a study in OCD. It's practically sterile."

"I know. I think it's a cry for help," Blake joked.

Devin chuckled silently. He and Blake were just the ones to help her.

Darkness still dominated Devin's bedroom when Blake woke to the distant sound of the shower running. Heat radiated from the ultimately feminine slumbering body beside him. His body was instantly aware of every soft inch of Jayne pressed against him, his dick no exception. He closed his eyes and breathed her in. She had turned from Devin's embrace and snuggled against him sometime during the night and he'd be damned if he didn't want to stay there and snugglefuck her for the rest of the day. He closed his eyes and let his mind play with that thought for a while.

The shower cut off and a few minutes later a half dressed Devin tiptoed into the room, closing the bathroom door so that only a sliver of light filtered into that side of the bedroom. Blake could barely make out Devin's silent nod towards Jayne. He shook his head, letting him know she was still sound asleep. His brows furrowed when Devin shook his head and pointed to him, then Jayne. What the hell was he saying? Devin made a circle with one hand and pushed his index finger on his other hand through it a couple of times then pointed at him and Jayne again. *Oh!* What the hell? Was he giving him permission or something? Agitated at his friend's rudeness, he waved Devin off. A few minutes later he heard the walk-in closet door click closed, followed shortly by the bedroom door and then the front door.

Minutes ticked by. Jayne shifted in her sleep putting his cock in the most tempting of places. One slip of her leg over his hip and he'd be inside her. She shifted again and Blake took advantage, dipping his hand below the t-shirt Devin had given her to wear. Velvety skin slid beneath the pads of his fingers until he found the soft underside of one breast. She filled his hand perfectly. He closed his eyes and remembered what they looked like offered up to him in Devin's hands. She had naturally beautiful breasts with small pink nipples. Her breasts were soft and plump, not rigid with overinflated implants. He liked that about Jayne. She was soft everywhere, and he couldn't resist the temptation any longer.

The pad of his thumb grazed her beaded nipple and Jayne unleashed a sleepy moan. Her hips rotated and pressed against his cock, exposing her throat to him at the same time. He was a goner.

One quick move and he had her leg draped over his hip as he probed her hot pussy with the head of his cock.

"Mmm," she moaned as his head slipped inside. He squeezed his eyes shut as he forced himself to go slow. Their chemistry seemed to borderline on incendiary. He wanted his first time inside her to be a slow carnal memory that would burn deep and long.

"I want inside you, Jaynie." His hips twitched slightly forward and retreated; quick but shallow thrusts that drove him mad. He hoped it was having the same effect on her.

"Hmm, you're already inside me." Sweat beaded instantly on his skin, the sound of her sleepy voice coupled with a persistent press of her hips against him nearly pushing him over the edge. His fingers dug into her ass to still her tormenting thrusts.

"Condom," he said, gritting through the wave of need that coasted through him as he pulled out of her. He rolled to the bedside table and palmed the foil packet he'd left there in anticipation of this very moment.

"Where's Devin?" she asked, turning to see the empty side of the bed.

"He's gone to get breakfast." Blake snuggled her back to him, feathering kisses over her sleepy eyelids, down the straight ridge of her nose until he reached her lips. Playfully, he scrunched his nose and slid his hand into the small space between their mouths. "And mouthwash."

"Oh my God!" Jayne covered her mouth and turned her head, but he caught her chin and turned it back, giving her another playful kiss on her thin little lips.

"I'm kidding." In the dim light he couldn't see her blush, but he could feel and imagine the hot pink flush. He loved teasing this woman. He moved down her jaw back to her ear and sucked her earlobe between his teeth. "I want you to myself for little bit. Only you and me. Devin is giving us a little time."

"What about your piercing?" Jayne asked as he ripped the corner of the packet with his teeth then rolled on the condom with a deft hand. "Won't it…snag or something?"

"It's more fun without a condom, of course, but no. It's fine. Just like me, they're made for pleasure." Wasting no time, he hitched her leg over his hip and within seconds he was right back where he wanted to be. Almost. "Tell me you want me," he whispered across her collarbone as the tip of his cock teased her entrance. "Tell me you want me inside you."

"Mmm," she nodded, drawing her bottom lip between her teeth as he pushed in a little farther and pulled back again.

"Not good enough, babe. I want you to say the words, Jaynie girl."

"I…ahh…I want you inside me, Blake." Slick heat sheathed his cock as he slid deep inside her. "Oh my God, what was that?"

Blake chuckled wickedly, withdrawing and pulsing forward again, drawing out another moan. "I told you. It hits all the right spots." Getting that piercing was the best bet he'd ever lost. Once he got past the *'oh fuck no'* factor, it wasn't all that bad. Taking a piss burned like hell for a few days, but the sounds coming from Jayne were worth every second.

"Finally," he sighed, sliding in deeper on his next thrust. The heat that surrounded him was possibly the best feeling he could possibly imagine. His fingers bit into the soft flesh of her rounded ass, gripping and pulling her closer to him. "Fuck yeah." Dammit, she felt so fucking good, but it wasn't enough. The more he got of this woman the more he wanted! He rolled, trapping her beneath him. Rising up on his arms, he looked down at where they joined and watched as he slid completely out then slowly pushed back in, feeling her heat surround him at the same time. Every muscle in his body tensed when her fingers crept into view. His head snapped up to see her watching them too, but then she stopped.

"Is…is this okay?" The tentative caress against his shaft continued as he withdrew, sending a vicious spike of need straight through him.

"It's more than okay." He swallowed hard as the first tendrils of his orgasm tickled the base of his spine. *No.* It was way too soon. Lowering himself to capture her lips, he searched for a distraction. Something! Anything! He wanted to feel her fall apart around him and that wasn't going to happen if she kept that up. "Touch...ahh...touch yourself, babe." Her fingers moved up to circle her clit and less than a second later her pussy clenched around his cock in a vice-like grip. His nostrils flared as he sucked in a ragged breath, her entire body pulsing to life beneath him. Gritting through the pain of holding himself in check, he watched her as he slid out, stopping the second the head of his piercing passed over her sweet spot causing her mouth to open in a silent cry. She squeezed him tight and he froze, feeling the pressure build as his balls constricted. After a few ragged breaths, he began his assault, flexing his hips with tight, shallow thrusts, stimulating her right where she needed it most.

"Oh, Blake!" Jayne cried out, her back arching beneath him. His arms burned as he held himself above her but he sucked in the pain; focused all his energy on that place inside her that was driving them both over the edge faster than he could control. "Oh, please...don't stop!"

"Tell me to fuck you," he panted into her ear, his arms shaking with need. "Say it like you said it before, Jayne. Say you want me to fuck you."

"Oh, God yes!" Her head reared back against the pillow. Her mouth opened wide on a silent scream. He didn't want silent. He wanted the world to hear her scream his name.

"Tell me, Jayne. Tell me now!"

"Fuck me!" His hips jutted forward, pushing his cock to the deepest depths of her pussy until he felt the very end of her against his head. "Blake!" She screamed his name as his body recoiled and struck again, and again and again. The feel of her legs around his waist sent him crashing into her, no longer able to hold himself up. Together they rocked until it felt as though she'd swallowed him whole, then she shattered around him, taking him down with her one jagged-edged piece at a time.

His orgasm gripped him like a goliath fist. *So this is what Devin meant by sucking wind.* He fought for every breath, every movement costing him more energy than he had. He couldn't drag his arms up to push his nearly two hundred pounds off her, so he tucked his arms beneath her and rolled instead. She melted over him, her panted breaths cooling the sweat that laced his heated skin. She still gripped his spent cock, sending random, white-hot currents flashing through him with each spasm. "Fuck, you're turning me inside out, Jaynie girl."

She lifted her head a fraction and looked up at him with her sleepy, green eyes. Yep. That was the look; the rumpled, well-sated look. It was the most beautiful look on any woman and on Jayne it looked outstanding. "I think you've ruined me," she said, her head falling back to rest on his chest.

Blake chuckled and tightened his arms around her. "Good. I like you this way." She felt so good in his arms, like she was somehow chiseled away from him a long time ago and now she was back where she belonged. He couldn't help but compare the feeling to how he remembered Daphne. It was different, but the same. It was like comparing two different wines, one red, the other a blush, but each having the same taste and quality despite coming from a different vine. Jayne was his sweet blush, while Daphne had been his robust red.

To his surprise it didn't hurt to think about her with Jayne in his arms. She soothed his scars. It scared the shit out of him to think Devin may be right. That somehow they could make all of this work. Now that she was in his arms, it terrified him more that he could be wrong.

"What time is it?" Jayne bolted up and looked around the darkened room, pulling him from his anxious thoughts.

"It's probably close to six," he reached for his watch on the nightstand when Jayne sat up so quick his spent cock fell from her warmth. "Whoa!" He grabbed her hips and sat up with her, leaving her to straddle his hips.

"I have to go! I have to get to my apartment in time to change and…shower." Her words trailed off into a moan as he captured one of her nipples between his lips.

"Devin's got you covered, babe. He's there now picking you up a change of clothes." Blake twisted until he got his legs beneath him then scooted to the edge of the bed and stood with her wrapped around him. "I've got the shower part handled, too." Still a little drunk from his orgasm, he heel-toed it from the bed to Devin's master bathroom.

"No! No-no-no! Please tell me he's not in my apartment!" Blake set her down and gave her a pat on her ass as he searched the myriad of storage cabinets and drawers for a spare toothbrush or two. "Your secret's out, babe. You're a slob. No big deal." He was dying inside as he tried not to laugh at her gasp of horror. "Dev and I both have a cleaning staff. We'll just have to tip them more from now on." He turned to hand her one of the new brushes he found and literally fell dick over drafting table in love with the lust-tumbled woman standing in front of him, covered with the most beautiful head to toe blush he'd ever seen.

~ TWENTY ~

I'm not delivering any babies today!

"Mother, please." Devin sighed, holding his hand up to ward off anything else she would come to regret saying. "I know exactly how bad this looks, but there's absolutely nothing I can do about it. I'm not going back to Toronto to beg them to change their minds and neither are you!" Christ, the last thing he needed right now was his mother stepping in to 'make it all better'.

"Devin, the board is going to rip you ap—"

"And you hold the controlling one percent, Mother. If you want to do something constructive then why don't you show up to a board meeting every once in a while and vote?" He opened and closed drawer after drawer, the pack of cigarettes he kept in his desk for jacked up days exactly like this were nowhere to be found. It was a foul crutch, one that had thankfully never become a habit, but it beat the hell out of losing his hair.

"Veda Thomason is going to have a field day with this, Devin. She'll never let her daughter—"

"I don't give a damn about Veda Thomason's daughter!" Devin raked his hand across his desk and the files at the end flew across the room. Jayne's name was milliseconds from flying out of his mouth. He bit his lip until blood stained his tongue. The last thing he needed was to drag Jayne into this pointless conversation. "Is that what's bothering you, Mother? What the people at the country club will say?"

"Everyone is whispering! They're going to think we're in trouble, Devin. They don't care about some convoluted corporate spy rumor."

"Do you honestly think any one of those elitist blue bloods you play tennis with care that SI lost one municipal contract?"

His mother rose from her seat and leaned over his desk. The warning he read in her eyes reminded him that she was a decorated veteran of the billionaire society class. "Those elitists are married to investors, Devin. Nearly all of those investors own stock in Silverland Industries and every last one of those investors have their balls clutched firmly in their elitist wives fists!" His eyes darted to the fist she held up in front of him, his knees pulling together in a natural protective reflex at the image she painted. "Do you think I don't know you hate doing this job?" Ice ran though Devin's blood. His mother nodded when she recognized his shock. "I see it. Everyone sees it, Devin." Mia Silverland straightened her stance. She paced to the panoramic window and stared out over the city. *She knew?* Devin had wanted to tell her a million times. Maybe this was his chance to back out; do what he'd always dreamed and start his own construction company. Get out of the huge conglomerate development all together and just build things. If she already knew then surely she would understand.

"Like it or not, Devin, your blood runs just as blue as those *elitists* you're so quick to dismiss." She paced from the window and shouldered her designer bag; the little bit of youth she still owned having faded from her features. "This company is *your* heritage. *Your* responsibility. I will not allow you to run daddy's dream into the ground, Devin. I won't. Even if it means using my vote to insure its stability."

"You wouldn't." His mother had consumed one too many mimosas at brunch if she thought she could threaten him. She'd lose everything if she voted him out.

"Devin!"

His office door flew open and who, but Danielle DeVeaux, blew in despite his assistant's pleas. "I'm sorry, Devin. I tried to stop her!"

"You *will* fix this," his mother said sharply, smiling at Jeanette on her way out of his office as if everything was right in the world.

"Devin, we need to talk!" Danielle pleaded.

"Jeanette, call security!" He didn't dare touch Danielle. Quite honestly he'd probably strangle her. Who knew what she was up to? Jesus Christ, this was the day to fuck all days. He wished more than anything he could hit rewind and never set foot outside of his apartment. He'd returned from Jayne's to find her and Blake in the shower together. He hadn't thought twice before he stripped off his suit and stepped in to join them. Jayne welcomed him with open arms. Her body, soft and pliant, was as responsive as he'd ever seen her. Blake held her in his arms as Devin spread her legs and feasted on her until she was screaming for release. His cock had never been happier to give it to her. She was sitting in an office not fifty feet from where he stood in his own private hell and he'd never needed her more.

"Devin, I'm pregnant!"

Devin froze. Every image of Jayne and Blake and everything good in his life flashed before his very eyes in a flurry of panicked images. Right behind those were the numbers. He'd never done basic math in his head so fast in his life. Rancid bile rose to the top of his throat as he opened his eyes and looked at the lying bitch in front of him. She did an astounding job acting the part of accused innocence. He had to give her that. Her razor-wire persona had certainly lost its edge.

"No you're not." He walked to his open office door and pointed at Jeanette's office. "She's pregnant. You're desperate!"

"You're right!" Danielle shouted. "I am desperate, Devin. You have to drop the charges against me. Surely, after Toronto, you know I didn't have anything to do with leaking that information about your contract with the city."

"What do you know about Toronto?" Hell, the leak was barely twenty-four hours old. He hadn't even informed his board or his staff.

Danielle's head snapped back, disbelief mingling with her desperation. "What do you mean? Everyone knows about Toronto, Devin. You can't keep something like that a secret."

"I hadn't intended to, but—"

"Devin, please. I'm begging you. I've lost almost everything. I've become a pariah in every circle our families travel in. My father is the only one speaking to me and that's only because he's my father and he knows I would never do this! He's losing business for defending me!"

The implications of what she was saying began to filter their way through the rage and fury that had been swirling through Devin from the time his mother had stepped into his office. Danielle had nothing to do with the leak in Toronto. Of that he was positive. But he couldn't dismiss the files she'd sent from his computer to her father. He still couldn't fathom how she got past his security codes.

The elevator doors opened up and two armed security guards were joined by two others from the stairwell as they approached his office. He looked back at Danielle, his thoughts now laced with doubt. Could he be making a mistake? His mother's threat echoed through the confusion. Everything was riding on him and his decisions. He didn't have room for doubts or mistakes.

"Escort her from the building and file a restraining order. I want her arrested if she steps foot on any Silverland Industries property after today."

"Devin, no! You can't do this to me! You have to know I had nothing to do with this!"

Devin turned his back on her and strolled back into his office, not even bothering to close his door. He had a meeting in less than five minutes where he planned to tell the board about the leak, of which they apparently already knew. He was then going to walk to the nearest bar and get drunk, forcing himself to bypass Jayne's office on his way, as per their agreement to try to give her space at work. "This day couldn't get any worse."

"Ohhhh!" Devin rushed through his door and followed Jeanette's painful howl. "Devin!"

"I'm right here, Jeanette. What's wrong?"

"I'm about to have my baby on my office floor! That's what's wrong!" Devin rushed inside her office and immediately noticed the large puddle seeping into the carpet. "Please, call Glenn. Tell him to meet us at the hospital."

He hurried to her side, helping her into her chair. Halfway down, she bolted straight up, her knees locking into place as her face distorted with pain. "Oh, shit! Okay, okay. I'll call him. Don't worry, Jeanette. The ambulance will be here before you know it." He fished for his cellphone in his pocket only to come up empty handed. He didn't bother to search for it, grabbing the handset from her desk phone and dialing 9-1-1.

"What are you doing?" Jeanette panted.

"I want to get the ambulance on their way before I call Glenn."

"Are you crazy? It will take them forever to get through lunchtime traffic. You have to take me, Devin!"

One look at the desperation in her face and his day was completely rescheduled. "Okay," he said with a spastic nod of his head. He hung up and dialed Blake's extension instead.

"Hey, what's up, Jeanette?"

"It's me. Jeanette's in labor. I'm taking her to the hospital. Can you call Glenn and let him know then contact the board and reschedule today's ten-thirty meeting?

"Here! Use my phone." Jeanette pointed to her cell lying on her desk. "He's number two on speed dial."

"Never mind Glenn. Just call the board members."

"Got it," Blake assured him. "Which hospital? I want to send flowers."

"Cal-Med," Jeanette said, the last syllable elongated with a high pitched scream.

Devin didn't even bother to hang up the phone, tossing the handset onto the desk as he scooped Jeanette into his arms and ran for the stairs. It might be a little treacherous to navigate, but the way his day was going there was no way in hell he was taking the chance of the elevator breaking down. *I'm not delivering any babies today!*

Four hours and one healthy, screaming baby girl later, Devin was standing in front of the maternity ward watching as the nurses fussed over the dozen or so infants lined up in their little plastic beds. A strange part of him envied every single one of them. He didn't know the first thing about their families or their futures, other than little Sophia's of course. Jeanette and Glenn were going to be exceptional parents. No matter where these babies were headed, they were starting fresh. No responsibilities, no stress. Every day it seemed as though the weight of his inheritance multiplied by three. He was being a selfish prick. He knew that. He had everything; more money than probably any of these kids would ever see in their lifetime, combined, along with everything that money could buy him. He wasn't raised in an abusive home, at least not physically, and he had a clean bill of health. He had Blake, probably the best friend anyone could possibly have and now he had Jayne. Any one of those things was a good reason to give up on wanting anything more and accept that what he had was enough.

One of the babies let out a high pitched scream. A nurse was at the side of the crib before he could blink, replacing his pacifier and doing whatever nurses do. A picture of Danielle holding his child in her arms flashed through his mind. No matter how he twisted the image, it would never look right. He would not have his children turned into the society robots she and his mother had become.

His children. Time stood still as he allowed himself to process that thought. When had his reaction to the thought of fathering a child changed from one of panic to rational calm accompanied by such a detailed parenting objective?

"There you are!" At the sound of Jayne's voice, Devin turned to see Jayne and Blake at the far end of the hall. "We just left Jeanette's room."

"We've been trying to call you," Blake added as they approached, but he could only see the radiant smile that graced Jayne's pale pink lips. "Glenn told us you lost your phone."

When his eyes met hers he knew. He didn't know how he knew or what would come next in their fresh and still fragile relationship, but he knew. She was the one he wanted to be the mother of his children.

~ TWENTY-ONE ~

"I love it when you talk dirty, angel."

A week had passed since Jeanette's unscheduled departure. As expected, Lori was turning out to be far less efficient than Devin's trusted assistant, although it was unfair to judge. As Blake pointed out, Jeanette was truly the best at what she did. No one was going to fill her shoes, not even Lori. Still, it took her two days to get his new phone, something he should have done himself, but if it was any indication of things to come it was going to be a long three months.

The board had granted Devin a stay of execution about the leak situation, on the promise that he find the spy and extricate them from civil society by month's end. Whatever the hell that meant. He was just glad to be catching a break. He'd decided Blake was right and let the deal with the Canadians go without much of a fight. He still wasn't convinced they weren't the ones who leaked the information to get out of the contract. They probably found a lower bid. Without any proof they could claim whatever they wanted. He would let his PR people deal with it. Postponing any new contracts he had pending until they went through the security logs and figured out what the hell was going on was regrettable, but he didn't have a choice. He couldn't afford any other security lapses.

Other than a few minor snags with the FAA over the helipad approval and some sustainable design changes only Jayne understood, the Emerald Dream was back on track and the groundbreaking had been officially re-scheduled. For the first time in months—no, a year—he had time on his hands and he knew exactly how he wanted to spend it.

"Lori, hold my calls for the rest of the day and make a reservation for three at Mélissena." He stopped in her doorway, his arms halfway through his coat sleeves as an image of Jayne popped into his head. He could barely contain the smile that spread across his face when the image morphed into a brilliant plan. "Nix that, Lori. Reserve the Adélaïde room." They would be requiring the private dining experience tonight.

"Yes, sir." Lori jotted everything down with a nervous tick that made him feel like an ass. Surely he wasn't that daunting.

"You did great this week, by the way." Her head jerked up and her eyes widened to the size of saucers. "Thanks for that errand you ran for me today. The keychain was a nice touch." In his front pocket, his fingers played over the spare key to his apartment he'd had her make for Jayne, along with the key to his Mercedes Hybrid. Jayne needed a car and she absolutely loved his hybrid when they took her out to Hollywood to do the tourist thing. She still needed to get her California driver's license, but he agreed. It would make the perfect car for her.

Lori's deer in the headlights look melted into a timid smile at his compliment. That eased a little of his guilt. "It's my pleasure, Mr. Kirk. I'm just grateful for the opportunity."

"And call me Devin. If we're going to be working together we might as well be comfortable about it."

"Yes, sir-I mean…okay," she stuttered.

"Have a nice weekend," he nodded and turned in the direction of his angel's office with an extra skip in his step. He couldn't wait until he updated Blake on their new dinner plans. They had behaved, well mostly, keeping their hands to themselves at the office. It hadn't been easy, but the nights had been filled with enough fun that it made staying away from her during the day bearable.

The night they left the hospital together, after saying goodbye to Jeanette and Glenn, had probably been the second most erotic night of his life. He had driven Jeanette's car to the hospital. Something about a maternity bag and emergency plans. He didn't know. He was parked at the far end of the garage so it was just easier to take her car. Thinking he had a car, Blake and Jayne had taken a cab which left them without a ride home. He would never balk at using a private car service again. His trousers tightened a bit as he repeated the erotic scene that had unfolded in the backseat of that Lincoln.

Blake had pulled her close and whispered something in her ear. At first she looked a little panicked, but Blake whispered something else and the next thing he knew Jayne's hand was tentatively moving up his thigh towards his crotch. She slanted him a shy glance as she fingered his zipper down and reached inside his slacks. A sharp hiss passed between his teeth when he felt the heat of her hand surround his cock. Holy hell! What was Blake trying to do to him?

She gazed out the front window, only a slight tremor in her hand betraying her nervousness as she stroked the length of his dick with long firm strokes. He glanced over to see Blake's arrogant smirk just before she lowered her head into his lap and took him into her mouth. His hips came off the seat. Her hot, silky tongue swirled around him then tickled that spot right at the tip that drove him mad. He choked on the groan that bubble up from his chest, smiling casually at the driver when he caught his glance in the rearview. He wasn't fooled. There was no way in hell the man couldn't tell what she was doing to him. When her mouth vibrated over him with a long moan of her own, Devin looked over to see Blake's hand move up the back of her skirt, his other stroking his dick through his pants.

The bright city lights streamed by in a blur, the sound of the car's tires against the road lulling Devin into a trance. He closed his eyes and let his head fall back against the headrest. The steady rhythm she found allowed the last tentacles of the madness that had gripped his life to slip away for a bit. Jayne's silky hair slid through his fingers as he concentrated on what she was doing to him. He hadn't felt her mouth on him since their first night together. Two long months had gone by since he'd first experienced her genuine caress. Not just in the way she sucked his cock, but everything she did was somehow more real. Never once had he suspected she was after his wealth or his name. There was absolutely nothing fake or nefarious about her. She was his breath of fresh air, his new everyday high. She made him believe giving up his dreams—his life—was worth it. None of it mattered as long as he had her.

When they reached Devin's building, Blake had hiked her skirt up, ripped off her thong and taken her in a fevered storm of lust against the wall in the elevator on their way up to his penthouse. He wasn't the voyeur Blake was, but there was a certain magic in watching their explosive brand of chemistry. Since that night, they'd shared her body, mind and soul in every way but one. Something he hoped to remedy tonight. Renting the Adélaïde room had been a brilliant last minute addendum to his plans for Jayne. Blake had dodged or ignored every attempt to get him back into the club scene since he'd been back. Another thing he hoped to put an end to tonight. Killing two birds with one stone. Multitasking may be Blake's specialty, but Devin had a few tricks up his sleeve.

Blake's door was closed when Devin arrived at his office. He tried the handle and found it locked. He knocked, but there was no answer. It was odd for Blake not to let him know when he was stepping out. Maybe he had been called away by one of the contractors. When he knocked on Jayne's door he half expected to find him with her, but she was alone, and looking every bit as tempting as she had that morning at breakfast.

"Hi, angel." He resisted the temptation to close her door and kiss her breathless. Her no PDA at the office rule was *killing* him. It was his company. He should be able to kiss her anywhere he wanted to. He respected her enough to play along, but one day he was going to take her on the roof for the whole world to see who she belonged with.

"Hey, have you seen Blake?" she asked. "I have some questions about the new sewage treatment and recycling data he emailed me this morning."

"Mmm, I love it when you talk dirty, angel," he teased. She rolled her eyes and clicked through page after page of blueprints on her computer screen. He wondered for a moment if she and Blake practiced their eye rolling together. "I was hoping I'd find him here with you. He's not in his office."

"Darn! I need the addendum to the environmental impact statement, too. He hasn't been answering his calls all afternoon." She looked so cute when she made that pouty face. She'd gotten better at censoring herself, too, but she wasn't fooling him. She could out-cuss a sailor in a hurricane. Something he witnessed firsthand when she experienced her first minor California tremor a few nights before. He and Blake barely noticed until she jumped from the sofa in a crazed panic and hid under his kitchen table like a paranoid crack addict. He and Blake had never laughed so hard. Of course she didn't find an ounce of humor in any of it.

"We'll wait for a bit, but I have a surprise for you tonight. I came by to take you home now to get ready." He maneuvered past the stacks of boxes beside her desk to stand behind her.

"A surprise?" Jayne glanced nervously at the door, but gave in to his wicked bribery to let him touch her in the form of a serious shoulder massage. In the short time they'd been together he'd learned she couldn't resist a massage in any form. With those sexy as hell shoes she wore, foot massages were her favorite.

"Yes, a surprise. You don't like surprises?"

"It's not that. It's…I need to spend at least one night at my apartment soon. You are paying for it." Devin closed his eyes and took a steadying breath. Was she still stuck on that? Having her rental expenses paid for while engaging in a physical relationship with him had been a major contention between them since day one. He got her point. She felt like a kept woman. Honestly, it was a pointless argument to him, but her tone told him she still wasn't happy about living there. He had the perfect solution.

"So move into my place."

"Devin, I can't just move in."

"It's not the same thing if we're actually dating, Jayne. Couples share apartments all the time."

"I know it's not the same, but how would it look, Devin? I can't let people think I'm sleeping my way to the top."

He was so sick of worrying about what other people thought. "We've ridden to work together every day this week. I say, what's left to say?"

"Devin…" She didn't finish her argument. That was fine with him. There really was no argument.

"I want you there with me, Jayne. If you stayed at your apartment I'd be staying there with you so what's the point?"

"And what about Blake?"

"Blake can move in too." He let his hands wander. Her breathy sigh graced his ears when his fingers trailed down her neck to her delicate collarbone. "There's plenty of room, and we only need one bed."

"Stop that!" Her shoulders shook with laughter and a shiver as she playfully batted his hands away. "You're not going to seduce me into moving in with you."

A lighthearted chuckle rolled off his lips. "Too late, angel. You're hooked. Don't try to deny it." He gave her a playful peck on her cheek and stepped back around to the door. "I'll be back in ten. Can you be ready by then?"

She pushed her mouse away and clicked a few keys on her keyboard to lock her computer. "I can't do anymore today until I get that document from Blake." She grabbed her purse and joined him in the doorway. "Can you at least take me by my apartment so I can grab a few things?"

"Sure can. As long as you promise not to lock me out. It will make us really late for your surprise if I have to call the super."

"You mean you wouldn't just break down the door?"

Devin straightened his tie and fished his keys from his pocket as they approached the elevator. "Na, that's more Blake's style. I work smart, not hard."

~*~**~*~**~*~

"Hey man! Where have you been all day?" Devin asked the second Blake walked into Devin's place.

Blake tossed his keys onto the kitchen counter and his duffle bag onto the floor. "I had some errands to run. And I needed to pick up some of my clothes." Fuck, he was doing it again. He'd told himself all the way to Devin's that he was coming clean tonight. No matter what Devin's reaction was it couldn't be worse than pandering to Mallory's insanity.

He did go by his apartment, but not for clothes. Mallory had been calling him every five minutes since lunch. When he answered she would laugh and hang up. That craziness continued for a couple of hours before he got a call from the super about a reported noise disturbance coming from his downtown flat. He left his office and drove straight there to find the place empty. He hadn't been there in days but as far as he could tell nothing had been touched, or so it seemed. There was a red lipstick print on his pillowcase and what he assumed was a pair of Mallory's panties hanging from the bedpost. He knew she'd been there by the heavy scent of the perfume she always wore. How she got in was a complete mystery.

He couldn't take it any longer. She had never been this crazy before. The woman needed professional help and not telling Devin was only making it worse. The deeper he got in with Jayne the more he realized how much he had to lose. Telling the truth was probably going to jack things up for a bit, but it beat the hell out of losing them all together.

"Hey, Dev. Can I talk to you outside for a minute?" Blake's heart was pounding. It was stupid. College was a long time ago. Things that seemed like huge events in his life meant virtually nothing in comparison when diluted with a few years of time. It didn't take hindsight, however, to know that sleeping with Mallory had been a huge mistake. He knew it the second he touched her. He couldn't explain why he did it. He wasn't drunk or on drugs. It was her eighteenth birthday and he asked her what she had wished for. When she told him she wanted him to kiss her, he did. One thing led to another. After what went down at the frat party two years earlier, he knew she wasn't a virgin. It didn't seem like that big of a deal at the time. After that, they flirted on the down low here or there, but as far he knew she'd never told anyone about that night. Sometimes she would hint that she wanted more, but he was always quick to let her know he didn't do relationships. He never led her on. It wasn't until after Daphne's murder that she started acting out and doing crazy shit, but never as bad as she'd been since he'd returned from Las Vegas. Now she was bordering on psychotic.

"Let's talk in the car," Devin suggested. "I reserved the Adélaïde room at Mélissena's for seven." Devin closed the laptop he'd been working on when Blake walked in and slid it into the drawer beneath the workstation alcove he was sitting at. "Jayne's getting ready. Tonight's the night, man. I can't wait any longer."

"Are you joking?" Blake felt the blood vacate his extremities and rush to his face as his heart began to race. "You're not taking her there." Confusion clouded Devin's expression, reminding Blake he still believed Daphne's murder was a random act. He'd been thinking about his declaration to Jayne, about who he was and what his needs were. Before Daphne he'd been a hardcore voyeur. The more public and taboo the sex, the more he was turned on by watching it. Relationships were irrelevant because he didn't do them. He dialed it back with Daphne. He'd stopped hunting for voyeuristic opportunities, but he still loved watching her with Devin in a public forum like the aquarium at their club. Jayne? Jayne was a different story. The thought of some stranger jacking off while watching her made his stomach turn. He wouldn't put her in a spotlight and risk pinging some lunatic's radar. He sure as hell wasn't going to let Devin expose her to that kind of danger.

"It's a private room, Blake. The only ones in or out are the wait staff."

"No," Blake said, raking his hand through his spiked hair. "I'm not down with this, Dev. I can't ask her to do this. I *won't* do this."

"Did I mention it's a private room? Not the—"

"It's a voyeur club, Devin. We haven't even talked to her about that part of...of...our past."

"Is that what it is, Blake?" Devin asked. "Part of our past?"

"Yes—no—I don't..." He dug the heels of his hands into his eye sockets. "I don't know. I think maybe it is." The muscles in Devin's jaw ticked madly as Blake waited in silence for him to respond. He didn't care if it pissed him off and fucked up his plans. He would not budge on this. Not today.

"What's a part of your past?" Blake turned to see Jayne walking towards him, wearing the sexiest little black dress and a pair of red fuck-me heels that made his blood sing through his veins so fast the hair on the back of his neck stood on end.

"Not budging on this," he growled at Devin through the forced smile he offered Jayne.

"Later," Devin said under his breath after he rolled his tongue back up and popped his eyes back into his head.

~ TWENTY-TWO ~

The Haunting of Mallory Silverland

What are they hiding? A foreboding anxiety had dominated the atmosphere from the moment they left Devin's penthouse. It wasn't the food. The French restaurant they sat in far surpassed anything she'd ever experienced on an opulence level. The sharp remarks and ego jabbing contest Devin and Blake had been engaged in all evening made her edgy. Correction. Made her *more* edgy. She'd felt off all week and couldn't quite put her finger on the source of the sudden uneasiness that occupied her state of mind. *Could it, just* maybe *be the lack of sleep and an overdose of orgasms?* Probably, but it felt like more.

Roxy finally called her, or should she say returned *her* eleven calls, giving Jayne little peace of mind about her sudden withdraw from Jayne's world. Rox had been as open as a virgin book about whatever was going on with her lately. In the end, she gave Jayne the same advice she always gave her about the newest developments between her, Devin and Blake. In addition to being green with envy, she was adamant that Jayne not close any doors and just let things happen between them. Oh, and quote, she was '*absolutely not, under any circumstances, allowed to care if anyone accused her of climbing the corporate ladder six inches at a time*', end quote. Something Jeanette had told her Lori overheard in the weekly staff meeting. If they only knew how grossly underestimated their measurements were. Rox later referring to Blake's piercing as a ladder rung had her in tears from laughing by the time Blake and Devin had gotten back from picking up their take-out dinner. After not hearing from her for a week, Jayne felt relieved and a lot less worried when they said goodbye, but Rox was still hiding something.

Her job, another area of her life that had drastically changed, was becoming a headache again. She thought once all the distractions had been eliminated she'd find a rhythm and be able to enjoy the job she worked so hard to get. Devin and Blake had done what they agreed to do and given her *some* space at work. A lot of help that was. Her mind was still swimming with images and thoughts, well into her lunch hour every day, of those two and whatever insanely orgasmic things they'd done the night before. And she could honestly say her lack of concentration had nothing to do with why she was finding her dream job not so dreamy. The politics took absolutely any reward out of making a difference. She had heard her prior bosses complain about it in the past, but she honestly had no idea how stifling and daunting it all could be. While she was able to navigate the ins and outs better than she had a few weeks ago, making her job technically easier, she found that her creativity and ingenuity had been snuffed out in the process. More than once the thought of disappointing Devin had been the only thing that kept her from wanting to quit.

Devin's offer that afternoon for her to move in with him only added to her overtaxed emotional state. Not to mention playing serious games with all her other concerns and fears fighting for space in her head. She liked staying at Devin's and waking up every morning between him and Blake. She loved falling to sleep between them even more. She loved sitting between them, eating take-out in front of Devin's big screen. Outside of visiting Hollywood and driving Devin's Mercedes on the highway that overlooked the Pacific Ocean, Blake's foot massages and the Mexican food had to be her favorite things about California so far; the earthquakes winning the prize for her least favorite. If she had been alone during what they had called a 'tremor', she would have been on the first flight back to New York. Do not stop. Do not pass go. A tremor? Were they joking? The entire freaking building swayed! It certainly gave her a new appreciation for the rigorous earthquake codes they factored into the Emerald Dream design.

The problem wasn't *living* with Devin and Blake. The sex was certainly no hardship. Her ovaries would shrivel up and die if she ever had to go back to boring Dale sex. Having two sets of hands, two mouths, two of everything touching her, caressing her, filling her was like…she couldn't explain what it was like. The feelings they stirred inside her could never be described in a single human language. And holy smokes, the voyeur stuff was scary. Having a ménage was one thing, but doing it in public? So far the things they'd done were pretty tame; giving Devin a blowjob in the back seat of a car while the driver could see and hear *everything*. She had to admit, that was pretty hot. Blake literally *taking* her in the elevator in Devin's building? Off-the-charts. Holy panty ripper! Who cared if the security guys got a show? Having sex with them in the park at the beach? That had pushed her limits more than a bit. There were so many people; some had their families with them. Devin had assured her that no one would see them and he had been right, but it wasn't something she wanted to do again anytime soon.

Everything was moving so fast. In many ways, too fast. At times she felt like Devin was rushing them; pushing too hard. Other times she sensed Blake was still holding back. While Devin made light of Blake moving in, Blake hadn't actually said he was staying in L.A. For all she knew he was still planning to go back to Las Vegas. Devin on the other hand seemed convinced he was ready to take the next step. Yet, he hadn't actually declared any feelings for her other than infatuation and attraction. The attraction was clearly mutual, but she was afraid she could so easily fall in love with both of these men. Devin had said this thing between them was more than just sex, but so far, love was not on the table with either of them. She knew them well enough to know she wouldn't be able to choose between them, but there was so much more she wanted.

Now, after he was particularly excited about the evening, Devin was in a strange mood and Blake was avoiding eye contact. She had a feeling it had something to do with the surprise Devin had planned for her but mysteriously had to cancel. Anytime she or

Devin mentioned it the two men would exchange heated looks and Blake would try to change the subject.

"How's your soufflé?" Devin asked after a long and awkward silence, pointing to her carafe with his fork.

"Are the lemons too tart?" Blake added. "I can ask them for cheese."

"No," she shook her head and laid down her fork. "I'm full actually."

Another uncomfortable silence filled the void between their questions. Just as she was about to ask for an explanation their focus shifted from her to something in the distance over her shoulder. Devin's brows furrowed into a deep V and nearly all the blood rushed from Blake's face. She pulled her napkin from her lap and blotted her lips before she looked over her shoulder to see Mallory approaching their table.

"What is *she* doing here?" Blake asked with a bitter growl.

Devin slanted him a questioning look and stood to greet his sister. "Hello, Mal. What a nice surprise."

"Hello brother, dearest." Jayne watched as Mallory planted two perfectly executed air kisses on each of Devin's cheeks. "I was on my way out and caught a glimpse of you and your table companions." An obviously regrettable scowl on his face, Blake stood and nodded in Mallory's direction. "Oh no, Blakie-poo. You are not getting away that easily."

Blakie-poo? Jayne's spine stiffened as she watched Mallory skirt around Devin and launch herself at Blake. She may have been on the sidelines watching in bewilderment the last time Devin's sister had her claws hooked into Blake, but a lot had changed since the night she saw them in the elevator together. Mallory's hand wrapped around his neck and she pulled him down to her. She lingered there in a more than friendly yet still socially polite embrace a moment longer than was necessary, as if she was whispering something in his ear. Jayne couldn't be sure since Blake's furious expression was blocking her view. She was about to clear her throat when Blake took her by her shoulders and set her apart from him with a not so subtle shove.

"Let me introduce you to Jayne," he said. Jayne forced a smile and nodded as Mallory blinked away her scowled expression and cast Jayne a mocking smile.

"Oh! I know you. You're that secretary—I'm sorry— *assistant* who was working late the night Blake took me dancing. I'm so sorry we didn't catch the elevator door in time."

Dancing? Her brow arched in question as she glanced up at Blake. A very subtle shake of his head was his only response. That and the *she's crazy—please don't believe a word she says* look on his face.

"Architect, actually." Jayne stood and offered Mallory her hand. "And I'm sure there was no offense taken." She didn't believe for a second there was none intended.

"Jayne Simon, my sister Mallory Silverland."

"Architect? Wow!" Mallory covered her mouth in feigned surprise. She took Devin's seat and immediately plucked a cigarette from her clutch purse and lit it.

"You can't smoke in here, Mal! Put that out!" Devin snapped it from her hands and then tossed it into his wine glass.

"But I'm with you, Dev," she said with a pout and reached into her clutch for another. Devin snagged her purse away and Mallory's pout grew to include a nasally whine. "Not having to follow the rules is one of my favorite perks of being related to you." She engaged Devin in a silent standoff that threatened to end in a cataclysmic eruption before the pouting woman flung off her disappointment in Devin's apparent brutish decree with a brilliant transformation that would make any butterfly envious. *Holy Prozac commercial!* All in less than a second her pout turned into a smile, her eyes lit up and she bounced in her seat with a giddy giggle as she snuggled closer to Jayne. "With an office on the top floor, you must be pretty important."

"She is actually." Devin motioned for their waiter to bring over another chair. "Why don't I order another bottle of wine and I'll tell you about the project she's working on."

As Jayne watched the childish play between Devin and his sister, her heart plummeted through her diaphragm and spilled out onto the floor. The project she was working on? Is that all she was to them? She kept waiting for Devin or Blake to add something, anything, to that statement. Something like, *oh, and she's also our girlfriend,* but it never came. She tried to rationalize it. They never promised her anything; they were in an odd relationship; Mallory was unstable. All of those things seemed like appropriate reasons not to declare their relationship. She could see how it could be difficult to explain something like that to their families. Not everyone was as open as Roxy. Yet, no matter the excuse she gave herself, the aching pressure that had seized her chest was still there.

"Are you okay, June? You look a bit peaked. Did the smoke bother you?" Mallory's overly concerned tone and intentional slight of her name made her stomach turn.

"Jayne," Blake corrected her in a gritty snap. "Her name is Jayne."

"Angel, are you okay?" Devin rushed to her side but she waved him off. She was acting ridiculous.

"Yes, I'm fine. It was just a hot flash or something. Probably from all the sugar in the dessert." She played it off and shouldered her handbag. "I do think I'll visit the ladies' room, though. Then can we go?"

Devin nodded. She made her fake apologies to Mallory and excused herself from the table. Thankfully what appeared to be the only other occupant was walking out of the ladies room as Jayne walked in. She bypassed the large velvet lounge and the smaller private stalls and went straight to the handicapped accessible stall where she could lock herself away and gather her emotions, and what was left of her pride, before she was subjected to the long ride home.

She was shocked at her reaction; at just how deep her feelings for them had become. Rejection wasn't something foreign to her. She simply never expected it to come from them. Not yet, anyways. *This wasn't a rejection.* There couldn't be a rejection if no guarantees or promises were made. She turned on the faucet and grabbed one of the expensive terry cloths from the elegantly arranged basket beside the sink. This was why she didn't do casual sex. One of the reasons. The main reason. She wasn't cut out for the lack of emotional attachment. Rox might be able to handle it, but not her. She wanted the whole package; love, kids, the white picket fence she grew up with. And even if she did get some sort of declaration from them, how could she have those things with two men?

The sound of a door opening and closing followed by the sharp clicking of a pair of high heels on the tile floor broke up Jayne's short-lived bathroom pity party. She rinsed her hands in the cold water and quickly dried them, giving the back of her neck a cold swipe before she threw the towel in the hamper. As much as she wanted to stay in that dimly lit stall and feel sorry for herself, Devin and Blake were waiting for her. She certainly didn't want to give Mallory the satisfaction of believing she had somehow chased her off, even if it was partially true.

"It's a shame, you know, destroying another innocent life." Mallory's resonant voice echoed off the walls and filled the small room. "Those two will stop at nothing to fulfill their wicked appetites for sex and debauchery."

Jayne panicked for a split second, wondering if she should play possum and act like she wasn't there; ignore her or open the door and confront her accusations against Devin and Blake.

"It's all just a sick game to them." Jayne opened the door and found Mallory sitting on the velvet lounge; her legs crossed Indian style as she leaned lazily against the wall behind her and blew out a long puff of smoke from the cigarette that dangled between her fingers. "There you are," Mallory taunted in a sing-song voice. "Nice dress, by the way."

"If Blake is so bad why do you want him for yourself?" The look that flashed in Mallory's eyes gave Jayne the feeling she was playing pull the tail with a crazed dragon. As quick as it appeared the demented look was gone, replaced with a mocking smirk. Mallory's head fell back and her loud cackling laughter boomed inside the intimate space.

"Oh, Jaynie girl," she said in the same sing-song voice that sent chills skittering along Jayne's spine. "That is his little nickname for you, yes?" Jayne didn't act to confirm or deny it. Mallory clicked her tongue in a scolding *tsk-tsk-tsk* as she unfolded her legs and stood in front of Jayne. "Nothing is ever as it appears, *angel*." She walked to the mirror, checked her lipstick, flicked her cigarette into the sink then paced the few short steps to the bathroom door. When she twisted the lock on the door, Jayne stopped breathing. Was she locking them in? She didn't know, but the cold, calm look on Mallory's face did nothing to quiet the sense of alarm that gripped her. Mallory paused with her hand on the door handle and studied Jayne as if she were solving some sort of puzzle. Jayne's lungs screamed for air. Panic squeezed her heart in its race against time. She held her herself together, steeling her expressions to hide her complete shock. Like a mask she pulled on and off with ease, the corner of Mallory's mouth kicked up in the same friendly smile she wore for Devin and Blake at the table earlier, her shoulder lifting in a careless shrug. "At least I tried," she said, giving Jayne a head to toe onceover before she opened the door and breezed out of the room.

The breath Jayne held rushed from her chest. Her hands shook. She reached for the lounge, steadying herself as she sank down onto the plush bench-like seat and stared at the closed door. "Holy shit, what just happened?" Blake said Mallory was evil, but she honestly believed he was being dramatic. One look at that woman with Blake in that elevator and Jayne knew she would never be BFF's with Mallory, but this was beyond a personality quirk. It was beyond psychotic. The ease with which Mallory changed complete personalities, like changing her clothes, was highly alarming and too close to psychopathic. Watching her eyes go from fun and sparkly to cold and calculating and then annoyed and blasé all within a few breaths of time was like watching a possession.

"Jayne?" Blake's muffled voice filtered through the closed door. How long had she been there? Her heart still raced as she bolted from the lounge. A quick check in the mirror confirmed her suspicions. She pinched her cheeks to bring some of her blood back into her complexion before she opened and rushed out the door. "Please take me home," she said with a wobbly sigh.

"What the hell? What's wrong? What happened?" Jayne shook her head at Devin's barrage of questions.

"Nothing. I…" She didn't know where to begin. How did she tell him his sister had just threatened her in the ladies room of a five star restaurant? Did she threaten her? Or did she warn her? Warn her about what exactly? She didn't know what the hell to think. And that was after Devin had chosen not to introduce her as anything other than a coworker, not that Mallory had believed him. "Please, just take me home."

"Okay, Jaynie girl." She didn't resist when Blake pulled her into his arms. Devin had the maître d' request the car from the valet. "We'll take you home."

Fifteen minutes later she was sitting in the back of Devin's Mercedes, cuddled in Devin's arms as Blake eased onto the five. The bright city lights faded into looming shadows behind her closed eyelids. Her heartbeat had slowed, but her mind was still racing with vivid images, replaying the last hour and a half. They hadn't pressed her for more of an explanation, thank goodness, because even now she couldn't find the words. She wondered if she should say anything at all. How could she not? Where did she start?

Everything whipped around in her head like a dizzying blizzard of uncertainty. She craved the small space of her apartment. Somewhere she could crawl up into a ball in a dark room and try to make sense of it all. She would miss waking up with them, and making love… *They're not making love, Jayne.* There it was again; that aching pressure inside her chest. Yes. She absolutely needed to put some space between them. Jayne was lost in her thoughts when the car came to a stop. She opened her eyes to find Blake steering the car into the parking garage at Devin's apartment building. "I thought you were taking me home."

~ TWENTY-THREE ~

"You must have the wrong number."

"I need to get a change of clothes." Devin unfolded her from his arms and opened the car door. "Wait here, I'll be right back."

"Wait here? A change of clothes for what?" she asked, rubbing the haze from her eyes.

"I told you, angel. I want to be where you are. Here, at your apartment, it doesn't matter."

Jayne growled in frustration. Devin staying with her completely negated the purpose of going home *alone*. She caught Blake's fiery blue-eyes in the rear view as he sat silently in the driver's seat. "What about Blake? My bed isn't big enough for the three of us."

"Fuck this," Blake said. Pushing the driver's door open, he got out of the car and slammed it closed again. "Do whatever you want." He tossed Devin's car keys to him and started for the elevators.

"Blake, wait!" Jayne unbuckled her seatbelt and bolted from the car. "What is wrong with the two of you?" When Blake didn't stop she left Devin at the car and ran after him.

"I won't be dragged along like a puppy no one wants to take care of."

"What?" Distracted by Devin's sudden appearance beside her, Jayne crashed into Blake when he stopped at the bank of elevators. "What's that supposed to mean?"

"You know we didn't mean it that way! Of course we want you with us." Devin popped his 'P' key into the control panel and gave it an exaggerated twist. "I told you not to sweat it, man. Why won't you let it go?"

Jayne's confused glance ping-ponged between the two men. "Let what go?

A shrill series of car horn chirps announced someone setting their alarm. A few seconds later that someone nodded as they walked by and stepped into one of the *P-less* elevators. "We'll talk upstairs, in private," Devin ordered.

Silence filled the elevator on the long ride up, and the short hallway to Devin's penthouse, and then Devin's penthouse once inside. Jayne was so confused and tired. She was one second away from calling a cab and leaving these two moody jerks to their brood-fest when Devin finally broke the awkward three-way standoff. "I shouldn't have pushed you."

That cleared things up nicely. "Pushed who?" Jayne asked. "Pushed me?" When no one bothered to answer her questions she dug out her cellphone and dialed the cab company she'd used before she came to depend on shuttle-a-la-Devin. Maybe Mallory was right. Whatever game they were playing she wasn't interested.

"Who are you calling?" Devin asked her, taking an anxious step towards her.

"A cab," Jayne blurted out and turned away from him. "I'm going home."

"Whoa-whoa-whoa, babe!" Blake dropped his brooding act and joined Devin on the panic train they'd formed behind her as she paced. "Don't leave. I didn't mean it."

One of those recorded option messages picked up asking her to press one for English and two for something else. She couldn't get her keypad switched on to press anything! Frustrated, she held the phone to her ear and hoped it would transfer to an operator.

"Jayne, please." She sidestepped Devin when he stopped in front of her. "What happened at the restaurant?"

"Why should I tell you? You haven't told me anything." She ignored the alarm on their faces and paced from the den to the kitchen as she waited for the recording to wind through all twelve *hundred* options; English, Spanish, Creole, website info, directions to their headquarters *in* English, Spanish and Creole. Jeez! "All night I've been kept in the dark by the both of you. I don't even know why I was invited. All you've done since we left is bicker and argue." Their bickering was the least of her concerns, but it was the easiest reason to give them. Jayne still didn't know what to make of Mallory's reenactment of the Exorcist, but her pride still stung from Devin's girlfriend-free version of an introduction.

The computer on the other end of the line finally ran out of options and she was transferred to elevator music. *Brilliant*. From the corner of her eye she caught Blake's stealthy approach, but turned away a second too late. His long arms banded around her from behind and hugged her to his chest.

"It's my fault, Jayne. Please hang up and let me explain."

Turning in Blake's arms she caught a glimpse of his regretful baby blues. *Game over*. She'd be the first to admit her brief struggle had been a ruse anyways. She didn't want him to let her go. When she relaxed he reached for her phone and she let it slid from her hand into his. Devin's heavy sigh of relief floated over her hair as his arms joined Blake's around her ribcage. His warm body pressed against her back, sandwiching her between him and Blake. She was right where she wanted to be. Now, if she could only close her eyes and pretend tonight never happened.

"It's just as much my fault, too, angel." That warm calm Devin created when he held her this way began to seep inside and soothe her heart. "You're right. We've been acting like asses."

Finally, she was getting somewhere. "Why?" Jayne turned in Blake's arms and looked up at Devin. "What happened today that we're not talking about? What are you not telling me?"

Her eyes narrowed at Devin when he shot Blake one of his pesky coded looks. Blake let her go, propping a hip onto the kitchen counter as he let out a long, resolved sigh. "Devin and I belonged to this club." A sheepish expression she'd never seen on him dominated his face. "A sex club," he blurted out, peering at her from beneath his lowered eyelashes.

"A voyeur club," Devin clarified.

Heat infused her cheeks as it did every time they talked about sex stuff. She would have thought she would be over it by now, but apparently she was cursed for life. Blake reached out and traced her cheekbone with a tender caress as he always seemed to do when she blushed.

"We used to go there with Daphne. A lot, actually. It was— still is—one of the hottest clubs in L.A. Draws huge crowds." Devin's arms encircled her waist as she watched Blake slip into his memories. "I like to watch, and couples who like to be watched put on a show. With Daphne, we usually stuck to the private rooms, or *peep-lites* as we called them. They were semi private mostly." Blake's foot tapped nervously against the cabinet as he talked. "In the middle of the club is a huge public set called the Aquarium. It's really just this huge glass box with different levels built in. Each level has its own staged props; beds, bondage equipment, a park bench. Different stuff for different fantasies," he shrugged. "Daphne knew I liked the public stuff so she talked Devin into fu—," Blake swallowed and glanced up at Devin, and then back to her, his eyes closing as he continued. "He made love to her in the Aquarium one night. It was the hottest thing I'd ever seen…at the time. Within a few days Daphne began getting hang-up calls. Then her car was vandalized; flat tires, spray painted messages. One night her car windows were busted out. Whoever it was eventually escalated to vandalizing her home. Then one day it just stopped. Everything. We thought it was over."

"Blake believes someone from the club, someone who saw us that night, targeted Daphne," Devin continued when Blake didn't. "He thinks the same person killed her."

Jayne heard the doubt in Devin's statement. "And you don't believe him?"

Devin shook his head. "I don't know. The police know what they're doing. They never found a shred of evidence to connect the two."

"I don't care what the police think." Blake jumped down from the cabinet. "How many times do I have to tell you? I know what I feel, inside here." His fist pounded against his stomach. "I know it was the same person," he said before he turned away and paced out onto the dark balcony.

Jayne stepped away from Devin and snagged his hand, pulling him onto the balcony with her. The night air was cool, but the lack of humidity made it comfortable as she stood next to Blake in her skimpy dress. Anger rolled off him in heated waves. He didn't flinch or sway away from her touch as her hand came to rest between his shoulder blades. "Did they find something? Did something happen with the case today?" They must have gotten some sort of bad news. It was the only thing she could fathom that would have caused such a rift between him and Devin.

Blake raised his arm and snuggled her to his side. "No," he sighed and placed a lingering kiss to the top of her head. "Nothing like that."

Devin pulled his hand from hers and scrubbed it over his face. "It's my fault, angel. Not his. I made reservations at a club tonight. A different voyeur club."

Jayne turned to ask Devin what that had to do with anything, but the words log-jammed inside her throat. "Wait, what?"

"A private room," Devin went on to explain the ludicrous idea. "We've wanted to try some new things with you, and I wanted to surprise you."

She was surprised alright. A voyeur club? Uh, no. No. No. No. And triple no. Sure, she'd said that about sleeping with a gigolo once, too. A voyeur club? This she could safely, definitively and without question say never and mean it. Okay, maybe *never* was a bit harsh, but…just…no.

"Guys, this whole thing is so new and I'm trying to keep an open mind, but a club? I-I-I can't do that, Devin. Not yet. Maybe not ever." She turned and paced to the far end of the balcony overlooking downtown L.A. The previously comfortable air became cool. She hugged herself against a sudden chill as she stared up at the moon in the dark sky. There wasn't a question. If this was where they were headed, what they needed, she couldn't do it. "Blake, I'm sorry. I've tried to give you what you need, and I've actually enjoyed the few things we've tried, but—"

"Don't be sorry, Jayne. I don't want you to do it," Blake said, rushing to her side and taking her by her sleeveless arms. "I don't want that for you; for us." He folded her into his arms again and held her tight in his embrace. "I won't expose you to that kind of danger."

She turned her head against his chest to see Devin beside them shaking his head, an ironic smirk on his face. "You do, don't you? You want me to do those things with you?" She'd learned that Blake wasn't the only one with a sexual fetish. Devin loved the idea of being watched.

"No," Devin huffed. "I don't necessarily believe the stalking theory, but Blake is right." The hard edge he'd carried all evening was suddenly smoothed away. "I was pushing him because I thought it's what he needed, what he wanted but was too afraid to ask for." His hand came up to frame her face, the corners of his eyes crinkling, his brows furrowing with apology. "I'm so sorry, angel. I want…you. I want this to work so desperately I…I know I push too hard sometimes."

"Sometimes?" Blake snorted.

"Okay," Devin snapped. "I'm an overbearing jerk. I think she gets it."

Actually, she didn't get it. If he wanted it to work, then why couldn't he tell his family about her? She was just about to waylay him with that exact question when he pulled the rug out from under her.

"I'm in love with you, Jayne." He stretched out his arm and clapped Blake on his shoulder. "From what I've seen, Blake is in over his head, too."

Wait. What? "You are?"

"You can't tell?" Blake asked. "Jayne, I can't fucking breathe when I'm with you." His voice shook with a rush of sincerity. "Then I can't breathe when you're gone. Just being down the hall and locked away from me in your office makes me nuts. You're smart, and funny, and a complete mess." Her head fell back and she gazed up into those soulful eyes as he spoke the words that nearly melted her heart. "You eat cheese on your desserts."

"Cherry pie," she giggled, because she was otherwise speechless. "I…I only like cheese on my pie."

"I love the way you twirl your hair between your fingers when you're thinking about something." Devin cut in, snuggling up behind her. "The way you separate the pennies from the rest of your change because they're a different color, but you don't separate your laundry." He'd noticed that? His stubble wrecked her resolve as he nuzzled into the crook of her neck and whispered. "I love the way you blush when Blake looks at you."

Blake's lips touched hers, his tongue snaking out in the barest of glances against the corner of her lips and sending a wave of longing straight to her heart. "I love that you try not to curse, but say the word *fuck* when we're making love to you."

"Ma…m…making love?"

"And that adorable stutter you get when you're shy or nervous," Devin chuckled. "Yes, angel. Making love. Is it so hard to believe we feel this way about you?"

Yes. "No, but…" She twisted from their arms, dodging their seeking hands. She hated the doubt Mallory had planted, but she needed to be sure. Standing there in their arms, with their mouths on her, the only thing she was sure of was that she would soon be saying the 'F' word. Repeatedly. "Why didn't you tell Mallory about us tonight?"

"What do you mean?" Devin asked, but she didn't miss the sour expression splash across Blake's face. She reminded them of how she was introduced to Mallory, feeling like a selfish brat for even bringing it up the minute the words left her mouth. It all sounded so trivial after everything they'd just told her.

"Angel, I'm the one who's been telling you not to worry about what everyone says or thinks. Hell, I'll send the news to my mother in a singing telegram if you want. Whatever you need to make you believe this is real." Devin held out his hand. She looked at it, stared at it in fact. The moment she touched him it would be all over. "As far as telling Mallory, I didn't intend to slight you, Jayne, but I would rather wait. She can be…"

"Unstable?" Blake supplied a broader version of a more specific adjective she would have used.

Devin threw Blake a scowl. "Unpredictable," he corrected Blake.

Jayne caught the subtle shake of Blake's head; the warning in his eyes not to dispute Devin's correction. Did Devin really not see her manipulation?

The Haunting of Mallory Silverland preview—not suitable for all audiences— was interrupted by the sound of Jayne's cellphone ringing. Forgetting she'd let Blake take it from her, she was ready to ignore whoever it was until Blake pulled it from his pocket and handed it to her. She didn't recognize the number, but the area code and prefix told her the call was from Ithaca. *Did Rox get a new number*?

"Hello?"

"Yes, my name is Georgia Sheldon. I'm a case manager for the oncology ICU unit at Cayuga Regional Medical Center. I'm trying to reach Jayne Simon."

ICU? "This is Jayne Simon." Devin and Blake stood motionless in front of her trying to interpret her confusion. "Did you say oncology?" Jayne held up a finger motioning that she wouldn't be long. Whoever it was obviously had the wrong number.

"Yes, Ms. Simon. Roxanne Stark listed you as her emergency contact and next of kin on her registration and I'm calling—"

"Next of kin?" Jayne felt her knees give way. "Wait, what are you saying? You must have the wrong number."

The woman's next however many words and sentences ran together in what seemed like a never-ending orchestra of confusion and what had to be total misinformation. The hospital must have pulled the wrong file. By the time the voice on the other end finished Jayne could barely make out what was being said over the loud ringing in her ears. After a series of one syllable responses and a promise to text the number of a crisis management hotline to her, the line went dead. Blake took the phone from her hand. For the next however long moments the only thing her body was capable of doing was breathing. Her eyes were open, but the only thing she could see was Roxy's beautiful face. Her ears were ringing with the sound of her smart and sassy laugh. Her hands were numb, but she could feel Roxy's warm touch. Was this really happening? How could this be happening?

"Jayne!" Her eyes snapped to Devin's. "Angel, talk to us. What happened? Is it Roxy?"

Roxy. For a split second the thick layer of shock thinned. Her heart squeezed inside her chest until she thought it would surely burst. *Oh, Rox. Why?* Why hadn't she told her? Like a light switch flipping on, everything snapped into focus; played on fast forward. "I have to go." She shot to her feet in a frantic search for her purse. How she made it to the sofa from the balcony she would never know. "My purse. I have to go. I have to go home and-and-and I have to pack. Where is my purse?"

"Jayne!" She fought against arms and hands trying to block her from the front door. "Jayne, look at me." She was stopped in her tracks, held away from the door that would lead her to her apartment and then to the plane that would take her to Rox. She had to get to

Rox. She looked up to see Blake's bright blue eyes zeroed in on hers. "Tell. Me. What. Happened."

Another light flashed and everything slowed to a crawl. The woman on the phone, her words played back like a slow warped recording. She repeated the words the woman said, even though none of them made a bit of sense. "Roxy has breast cancer. She…um…she had surgery and…the woman said she won't wake up."

~ TWENTY-FOUR ~

"Just for a little while, I want to forget."

Small specks of lights littered the ground below like sugar strewn across a black velvet landscape. Jayne's eyelids were heavy with exhaustion and thick from the flood of tears that continued to fall in random torrents. The last four hours had been the longest of her life, the one before those a complete blur.

Once again cocooned in the back seat of Devin's car, Devin made a series of calls while Blake drove them to a private airstrip outside L.A. Without a second's hesitation they shuttled her onto SI's corporate jet and within an hour they were airborne for New York.

The lights below blurred into bright starbursts as Jayne's eyes once again welled with tears. How could she possibly repay them? The long sleeves of the t-shirt Blake gave her to wear were soaked with her tears and cold against her cheek as she wiped away more. Numbness was slowly giving way to fatigue. The cabin air blew cold against her skin. No sooner had a shiver wracked her body, Devin was there with a blanket.

"Hey, angel." His lips felt warm against her cheek. "The pilot says were about an hour outside Ithaca." He draped her in the blanket and lifted her into his lap at the end of the buttery leather sofa. "We'll land at Tomkins Regional. I have a car service waiting to take us to the hospital. It's about fifteen miles outside the city, so it shouldn't take us long to get there once we land."

She closed her eyes and tucked her head against his chest, the sound of his heartbeat strong against her ear. "Thank you," she sighed. She'd said the words a hundred times and would say them a thousand more. It would never be enough.

"It's nothing, babe." Blake appeared from the back of the cabin with a glass half-full of caramel colored liquid. He slid onto the cushion beside her then handed her the glass. "Sydney would fix these for me after Daphne passed away. Drink a little if you can. It will help calm your nerves a bit before we get there."

She took a sip. The warm, honey-flavored alcohol soothed her scratchy throat and immediately set to work warming her insides. Blake pulled her calves over his thighs and pushed up the legs of the sweatpants Devin lent her, his thumbs caressing her muscles in comforting circles. She felt like a dwarf in giant's clothing. Her only clean clothes were at her apartment and Devin hadn't wanted to waste the time to drive her there or the time to pack. He and Blake assured her they would take care of whatever she needed once they were in New York and she had been allowed to see Rox. She could add that to the long and ever growing list of things she owed them for.

"I spoke to my great uncle," Devin said with the calming timbre in his voice she'd come to depend on. "He's on several charity review boards at different hospitals around the country. He's contacting the directors at Cayuga."

"Contacting them for what?"

"We'll get her into a private room and find out who's working on her case," Blake said. "Hell, we'll transfer her to the best cancer center in the world if we have to." A tender gleam sparkled in his eyes as he reached out and palmed her cheek, his thumb swiping away a stray tear. "We'll get her the best care possible, Jayne. I promise."

"You would do that?" They'd never even met Roxy.

Devin and Blake exchanged one of their signature looks before Devin nudged her around until he could look into her eyes. "Why wouldn't we, Jayne?" Jayne studied him for several long seconds. He was serious. "Wanting the best is what you do for someone you love."

Was it possible they really did love her? Did she love them back? Could she love both men?

Blake slid to the floor at her feet and took her hands in his own. "There is a lot to figure out here, Jaynie. We know that, but Dev is right. We do the best by those we love." Jayne felt an extra hot rush of heat make her cheeks glow as she looked down into Blake's sincere ice-blue eyes. "I don't need you to say it back. Not yet, but—"

"It's not that..." Jayne shook her head. It might be that. "I mean, I don't know...I..." She worried her bottom lip between her teeth. "I don't know how I'm *supposed* to feel about you helping Rox like this. I've spent my whole life avoiding guys like you. I mean, not exactly like you, but..." Watching Rox get her heart ripped out by every good looking New York jerk in a power suit didn't exactly endear her to the rich and morally challenged. "I've always been the invisible girl. I was happy being invisible...until now."

"Men like us?" Blake questioned her meaning.

She blushed again. She hadn't meant it to sound so accusing. "You know. Handsome, tattooed, vulture capitalist-sex gods who sweat hundred dollar bills and join the witness protection program at the first sign of anything serious between them and one of the half-dozen women they're dating."

Devin laughed. "Oh! Men like us. I see now."

"But..." Jayne held up her palm. "Then I met—"

"Wait. Back up," Blake interrupted. "Can you say that one more time?"

"Which part?"

Blake's lips pulled into a cocky smirk. "The sex god part."

Jayne nudged his shoulder when he cast her a *walked right into that one* look. "But…then, I met you guys."

"Wait. So, you don't think we're sex gods?" Jayne raised an eyebrow and Devin cleared his throat. "Okay," Blake held up his hands in mock defeat. "I'm only trying to make sure I'm clear on what you're trying to say." Jayne appreciated the way Blake was trying to lighten the mood. It was working for the moment.

"I'm *saying*…you're beautiful and strong and-and-and good. And now you're offering something I couldn't possibly repay. You're perfect—" She regretted those last two words the minute they rolled off her tongue and Blake's face lit up like a million watt spotlight. "*Not* perfect but…"

"Perfect for you," Devin said with a hopeful note in his tone.

Jayne nodded, shrugged. "Maybe. I want you to be." Rough stubble prickled against her palm when she cradled Blake's lean, handsome face in her hands. She wanted to love them. Mallory's bizarre warning ghosted through her thoughts and she pushed it away. She wanted to trust them. Blake was so rugged looking with a five A.M. day old scruff. One of them always at her side, neither man had slept. Butterflies took flight in her core when Blake closed his eyes and turned his face. His hand blanketed hers, holding it to his lips as he kissed her palm.

"You don't need to know now, angel." In turn, Devin's hand cupped her face and he planted a soft kiss to her cheek. "All you need to know is that we're here for you. And no more *paying us back* talk. Roxy is important to you, therefore she is important to us. Right, Blake?"

"If it weren't for her we would have never met you." Blake nodded.

"Good point," Devin agreed.

"Let's just get you there," Blake said as she retook the seat beside her, gifting her with one of his distracting winks. "We have plenty of time to sort out the rest."

The next hour felt like days as she was shuttled from plane to car to waiting room after waiting room. As soon as they arrived Devin disappeared to hunt down whoever was in charge while Blake stayed behind and placated her with stale coffee and his strong shoulder to cry on. Somewhere in the back of her mind she knew the guys were doing their best, but enough was enough. She was beyond caring if she got arrested for trespassing or disorderly conduct by the time a nurse came into the small ICU waiting room and called her name.

"That's me." Jayne pushed up from Blake's lap and rushed to where the nurse stood just inside the door.

"Sorry we took so long, Ms. Simon," the nurse said. "But she woke up about an hour ago."

"She woke up?" All of the air in Jayne's chest came gushing out in heavy sobs of relief. Blake held her as she cried and tried desperately to pull herself together so that she could hear more of what the nurse was saying. Something about having to wait for the specialist to remove her breathing tube.

"We'll let you know as soon as she's stable and we'll get you back there to see her." The nurse gave her an understanding nod and left them to wait. More waiting. Waiting suddenly became a blessing and a curse inflicted all at once. She would wait forever if it meant Roxy would be okay.

An hour after the nurse left, Devin found her and Blake huddled together on a small love seat at the back of the otherwise empty family waiting area. Blake had dimmed the lights, but she could easily see Devin's usually well-kept hair was disheveled and hand-raked with frustration. His meticulously groomed beard was two days longer and his suit coat was rumpled. She stood when he approached and he gathered her into his arms the second he reached her.

"I heard the good news," he said on a sigh.

"Did you find out anything else? Anything at all?" No one had given them any news since the nurse advised her Rox had woken up and Jayne was starving for information. Her chest heaved with each anxious breath as Devin shook his head.

"All they would tell me was what they've already told you, but I was able to track down the director. He's scheduled some time to meet with us later this morning about Roxy's care. As long as you have something that gives him permission to talk to us, either her verbal or written consent, he should have more news."

Jayne fished her keys from her purse. "I have something like that, a-a-a form I think, in our safety deposit box at the bank."

Devin cupped her shoulder before she could make her way to the door. "Whoa, angel. It's five in the morning. Nothing is open yet. You're running on empty and so are we. Let's go get something to eat and find a hotel to check into."

Jayne shook her head, but Blake sandwiched her in between him and Devin, taking away every ounce of her will to fight them with each spoken word. "After we've freshened up a bit, babe, we'll come back here and see if there's any news before we meet with the doctors. I promise. We won't be long, but you have to take care of you if you're going to help Roxy." Blake's cellphone rang. He released her long enough to pull it from his pocket then shove it back in after he silenced the ringer.

"We're only a few minutes from our house." She handed her keys to Devin. "You can stay there if you like, but I'm not leaving until I see Rox or unless we're going to the bank."

"Ms. Simon?"

"Yes." Jayne stepped around Devin and paced to the door where another nurse was waiting to greet her. "Is she okay? What happened?"

"Everything is fine," the nurse assured her. "The tube is out, she's breathing on her own now, but the meds will keep her asleep for a few hours."

"Oh, thank God!" Jayne hugged the nurse. "Thank you so much. Can I go back to see her?"

The nurse nodded. "For a little while, but only you." Jayne nodded. The nurse lifted an appreciative eyebrow when Devin and Blake both gave her a swift, soft kiss and told her to take her time. Jayne ducked her head to hide her blush and followed the nurse down the long hall towards her best friend and sister.

~*~ **~ *~ **~ *~

Staring after Jayne, Blake reached into his pocket and silenced the constant buzz from Mallory's endless texts and calls, turning his phone off all together. The only two people he cared to hear from were in the building with him.

"We good?" Hands in his pockets, Devin leaned lazily against the wall beside Blake.

Blake felt rooted to the spot where he stood, staring down a now empty hallway. "You're doing it again."

"Doing what?" Devin asked.

"Pushing too hard." Blake broke his trance and looked over at his best friend. "It's been a week, Dev. Seven days and you're declaring your undying love? And mine?"

"You're telling me you're not in love with her?" Devin argued. "Because I'll call bullshit if you try to push that lie. Hell, I saw it on your face the first time you told me about her, before I knew who she was!"

"That doesn't mean I need you broadcasting it to her or the rest of the world," Blake snapped back, pulling one of the small bottles he lifted from the plane out of his pocket and giving the cap a twist. "There are three people in this little *arrangement*, Dev. And like it or not, we all have our own needs that have nothing to do with you or how desperate you are for this to work." He took a swig of the cheap vodka, letting the entire bottle drain and wishing it was scotch as it burned its way into his veins. "Next thing you know you'll be asking her to move in." The truth of those words ghosted across Devin's face. "Christ. You asked her to move in."

"What's wrong with wanting this to work?" Devin pushed off the wall and dug into his suit coat pocket, pulling out a pack of cigarettes. Blake hadn't seen him smoke in years. "I know you want this, too."

Blake nodded. "I want it." He walked beside Devin as they made their way to the garage and the car waiting for them. "We all want it, but how fast we get there isn't up to you." He stopped at the elevators, cupping Devin on his shoulder. "These things need to be a group decision, Devin, and you need to slow the hell down." He pushed the button on the wall a few times. "Look, I don't get it. This goes beyond control. Why are you pushing this so hard, so fast?"

"I don't know."

"Bull! Why?" Blake demanded.

Devin stepped back to let the elevator clear before Blake followed him in. The doors closed and they rode to the garage level in silence. Once at the car, Devin lit up a cigarette and leaned against the fender. "I don't want to lose it."

"Lose what?"

"Lose this! Lose us! Damn it! We wasted so much time with Daphne." He took a long draw, sucking down the smoke like a fiend on a crack hit before he blew it out in a long, satisfied breath. "I don't want to wait and have someone or some*thing* take it all away."

Like your sadistic sister? Blake palmed his cellphone, flipping it over and over inside his pocket. He was up against a wall with Mallory. He needed to come clean with Devin, but now was definitely not the time. Given how quickly she was spiraling out of control, he was out of time. The skeletons in his closet were about to wage war to get out. He had no doubt her version of events would leave him sucking wind. Getting Jayne out of his system wasn't going to happen, so leaving everything behind like he did before was no longer an option. He would have to set Mallory straight when they got back to L.A, because there was one thing of which he was completely certain. "This thing with Jayne is different than what we had with Daph. I'm not saying I loved her any less, but Jayne? She's fucked me up. You talk about wanting it?" He took what was left of

Devin's cigarette, hot-boxed one last draw then flicked it to the garage floor. "Now you get why I don't want her in those clubs?"

Devin nodded. "Yeah, man. I get it." He nudged Blake's shoulder with his. "We good?"

Blake clapped him on his shoulder and motioned him into the car. "We're solid. No one is going to take this away from us, Dev." *Not again.* He wouldn't survive it. "Let's go get our girl some decent food."

Jayne closed her eyes and took a deep breath. Impossible. That's how she would have described the task of preparing herself to see Roxy in that hospital bed again. A little over twelve hours had crawled by since she was first allowed in for a short visit while Rox slept. She was no more ready to see her now than she was then. Every step closer to Rox's new room sent her blood singing an octave higher through her veins.

After standing in front of her closed door for however long before she worked up enough nerve to walk through it, the last thing she expected to see was Rox's pain-laced smile.

"Took you long enough," Roxy croaked, her voice scratchy from the breathing tube as the nurse had warned it would be. "I thought you'd stand out there all day."

I love you. I'm so glad you're okay. I've missed you so much. You can't ever leave me. Why didn't you tell me? Of all the things she'd wanted to say to her best friend and sister from the moment she received that phone call, her next words were not on the list. They were, however, some of the closest to the truth. "I'm so fucking mad at you right now."

Roxy stared blankly at her, her glassy eyes betraying the pain she was trying so hard to hide. "I'm impressed," she said with a chuckle, then gasped in pain.

Jayne rushed to her side, all her anger giving way to fear. "I'm sorry," Jayne said. Her tears returned and joined Roxy's, falling alongside them when Jayne leaned over her best friend and sobbed against her hair. "I'm so, so sorry, Rox."

"Stop," Rox barked, turning her head away. "I don't want…" Her eyes rose to the opened window on the far side of the room. A moment later a small, sad smile formed behind her tears and she looked back at Jayne. "I can't go there, Jay." The strength it took to swallow back the fear Jayne saw flash in Roxy's eyes left Jayne in awe. Her own tears fell unchecked before she nodded and began swiping them away. "Did the doctors tell you everything?"

Jayne swallowed back a sob. "No," she said, her movements as stilted as her words when she reached for the chair at the foot of Roxy's bed, pulling it closer beside Rox.

Roxy closed her eyes, her face twisting in a grimace as she tried to reposition herself against the stacked pillows behind her back. The sheet covering her chest fell to her waist, revealing the thick layers of gauze and bandages wrapped tightly around her chest. Jayne's hand flew to her mouth to cover her gasp. She quickly choked it back, coughing into her hand to try to cover. Rox didn't buy it. "They couldn't do immediate reconstruction on the left one," Roxy said with breathy puffs as she settled into a comfortable spot and pulled the sheet back up. "I'll have to go back under for that one." One final huff and she opened her eyes, giving another of her forced smiles that made Jayne want to scream. "That should be fun."

"How can you be like that?" Jayne's hands clenched into fists. She knew the odds. She knew there was nothing and no one she could blame, but she was so angry that Roxy was having to go through this at all, much less alone. She wanted to hit something, scream at someone and make them take it all away.

"Like what?"

"Like this! Smiling and-and joking! I-I-I'm so angry with you. For you! How—"

"Oh, believe me," Rox interrupted her rant. "I've had my moments. Mom's canisters are in a million little shards inside a bag in the kitchen."

"Mom's canisters?"

"Yeah," Roxy closed her eyes and took a deep breath. "My last '*moment*'."

"Why didn't you tell me, Rox?"

She was spared from answering as a nurse came in, or so Jayne thought. "How is being the cream filling in a cock sandwich working out for you?"

"Rox!" Jayne blushed, her eyes darting to the nurse who appeared more than amused as she rifled through a few cabinets then left the room again.

"I see I'm going to have to have a chat with those guys if you're still able to blush when we talk about amazing sex. I would have thought you'd be over that by now."

"Why didn't you tell me, Rox?"

"Surely they've popped your anal cherry by now."

Oh, God. "Roxy!"

"What? I'm just saying. Two guys at the same time? It's bound to—"

"Answer my question!"

"No, you answer mine!" Roxy's weak voice cracked. Guilt slammed directly into Jayne's chest when she saw her cringe against a wave of pain. "What are you going to do now?"

"What do you mean?"

"Ah!" Roxy huffed, reaching for the cup sitting on the small table beside her bed. Jayne bolted from her seat and handed the cup of ice chips to her. "You're fucking the boss, right? He going to let you have a few months off to come babysit me?"

"It's not like that and you know it." Was she being intentionally mean? "I can't give them much notice, but I'm sure

238

Devin will understand. And it's not babysitting. I want to take care of you. Whatever you need."

"There," Rox snapped. "That shit right there is the exact reason I didn't tell you."

"What?" Did she think she wouldn't be there for her? "You can't possibly do this alone, Rox. I—"

"I can do whatever the hell I want!" Jayne's argument derailed at the sight of Rox's next grimace.

"This isn't the time to talk about this, Rox. You shouldn't be—"

"Don't," Roxy snapped. "I didn't tell you because I knew you would do this! I don't need you to hover. I don't need you to babysit. I don't need you to give up the chance of your life because of me!"

"It's just a job, Rox."

"I'm not talking about just your job, *goddamn,* this shit hurts!"

Jayne jumped from her chair again, hovering over the only person in the world she had left to call her own. *And Devin and Blake are what exactly?* Jayne ignored the random thought and grabbed the call button. "I'll call a nurse."

"No!"

"What can I do, Rox? Tell me what to do to help you." Roxy's head fell back against the raised bed again, her lips pulling back into a silent cry before she let out a long, strangled breath. Jayne carded her fingers through her tangled hair and tried to sooth her pain.

"Tell me…about…the gigolo twins," Roxy huffed out as the last wave of pain passed. "The doc says one of them pulled some strings to get me in the penthouse suite."

Jayne felt a tug on her heart. She slid a hip onto the edge of Roxy's bed and stared off at nothing in particular as a picture of Devin's handsome face floated through her memories. "That would be Devin, the boss. Well, technically Blake is my boss too, but Devin is the CEO." She fished her cellphone from her purse and showed her some of the latest pictures they took on their trip to the beach. Her entire right side was soaked with seawater from Blake kicking the surf at her. Devin had scooped her up and whisked her off to the dunes into an alcove hidden by the brush. That's where they'd stripped her of her shirt, assuring her that if someone stumbled upon them they would say she was cold and changing into one of theirs. Of course her shirt wasn't the only thing they removed that day. Blake had been crazy with desire, devouring her cries with his kisses as Devin pressed her between them from behind. Her nipples hardened at the memory, sending a shiver down her spine.

"Wow," Roxy sighed. "That good, huh?" Jayne blushed when her eyes snapped down to Rox and found her knowing eyes crinkled at the corners with a Cheshire cat smile staring up at her.

"Yeah," Jayne sighed in response. "That good."

"So?" Rox said.

"So what?"

"Did-they-pop-your—?"

"I—I'm not telling you that!" Jayne heard them talking about it once, or at least she thought that's what they were whispering about. Devin had played with her there. It stung, a little, but those were the orgasms she didn't think she would survive. It shocked her. Who knew that could be an erogenous zone? Each time one of them played or even got close to that spot she wondered what it would feel like to take one of them there. Blake would have to take out his piercing. That thing had a laser aim on her G spot, but she wasn't taking any chances with the back door stuff.

"Fine, then tell me about Devin. Is he the overbearing Alpha, taking charge in the bedroom like he does in the boardroom?"

Jayne giggled. "You've been reading *way* too many romance novels."

"Well, some of us don't have two of *everything* to experiment with."

Jayne shook her head. "He's intense, focused. Maybe a little insecure."

"Insecure? Like a momma's boy?"

"Definitely not! He's vulnerable. I think that's my favorite thing about him." Jayne laughed. "Neither of them is close to their mothers"

"Eh, mommy issues." Roxy wrinkled her nose.

"Do you want to hear this or not?" Jayne teased back. Calmer, Roxy leaned her head back and closed her eyes as Jayne continued. "No mommy issues, but Devin's sister is a candidate for experimental drugs." Jayne told her about the elevator and ladies room episodes. "I mean, it's almost like the twilight zone watching her with Devin. And Devin doesn't see it. Or he doesn't acknowledge it at least. She freaks me out just a bit, Rox."

"What did Blake say about the Bates Motel style intervention in the ladies room?" Roxy's voice had a dreamy quality to it. That's when Jayne noticed the pain med button tucked into her palm which was peeking out from under the sheet. Jayne swiped at a stray tear. Even now, at her weakest and most vulnerable, Rox fought to conceal her pain.

"I didn't tell him," Jayne continued as if she hadn't noticed a thing. "He's caught in the middle, too. I don't think he knows what to do."

"You love him." It wasn't a question. Roxy's odd observation pulled Jayne's glance down to see Rox staring up at her. "I can see him inside you. Hottie-pierced Blake. He's riiiight there." Her hand rose lazily from her side, her finger poking at Jayne's chest. "Devininin is in there somewhere." Roxy's brows furrowed harshly, her hazy eyes staring hard at a spot on her chest. "Or maybe that's a lung." *Definitely on the good stuff.* Jayne thought briefly about calling the nurse to make sure she hadn't pushed the button one too many times. Roxy's lips pressed together in an awkward grin. "You have to stay, Jayne. You have to stay. Let them love you and build the bestest, biggest damn building and let them pop your cherry on top. Hmmm," she hummed. "Blake and Devin heaven."

Tears fell from Jayne's eyes in thin, salty rivulets as Roxy's eyes closed. "Promise me, Jayne. You only get one chance. Don't waste it."

"Go to sleep, Ro—"

"Promise me."

"I…I promise," Jayne said just as Roxy fell to sleep.

Jayne sat in the chair and cried. She sobbed quietly as she watched Roxy breathe. She was right. She loved Blake. She'd been in love with him from the moment he showed up on her doorstep, half drunk and more than a little pathetic. He was a complete, gorgeous mess of a man who had worked his way into her heart and she would want him forever. Devin…Devin terrified her. She'd once read an erotic poem about a lover's caress touching your soul. When it came to sex, these men twisted their fists into her soul's shirt, pushed it against a wall in a dark alley and fucked it until it screamed their names. Devin had the same effect on her heart.

Just thinking about their chemistry made her knees go weak, but he also had this way about him that made her trust him beyond reason. He could completely disarm her with a few simple words or tender caresses. She had never trusted anyone but Roxy that wholeheartedly. Having that kind of trust pulled from your soul against your will was scary as hell. Could she trust him with that kind of power? Would she lose Blake by default if she couldn't?

She didn't know. Rox wanted her to throw everything to the wind and take the chance it wouldn't blow up in her face. She wanted to. She really, really wanted to. Her job was no longer a reason to say no. Roxy was also right about her plans to move back. How could Rox expect her to keep that ludicrous promise? How could she stay in L.A.? Radiation and chemo were brutal. It sucked the life out of the strongest of people. She couldn't imagine leaving Rox to fight that battle alone. And the next surgery? What if Rox didn't wake up at all next time? Knowing what it's like to never see someone you love after they're gone, Jayne wanted every moment she could get with Rox and she wanted them to count.

How could she tell Devin she was leaving? After dealing with those city jerks herself, she knew for a fact they would pull the project if she quit, just like Devin said they would. It was no longer the job of her dreams, but she couldn't just walk away and let Devin pay the price. He hated his job more than she hated hers. He was doing his best to do the right thing by his grandfather's dream and losing this contract would ruin everything. He deserved better than that.

What was she supposed to do? Again, she had no idea. Maybe there was a cancer specialist in California they could try. That afternoon they met with the hospital director, a nice older gentleman whom she'd already forgotten his name. She could never repay Devin for everything he'd done; arranging the private suite and a complete review of Roxy's case with the top rated oncologists and plastic surgeons in the country. Roxy had to approve of course, but he was ensuring she had choices. Maybe one of those choices would be close enough Jayne would be able to stay in L.A.

Tired. She was so tired. She tried to remember the last time she'd had a full night's sleep. Devin and Blake had kept her awake for a solid week before she got the call about Rox. She'd been too upset to sleep on the plane. Early that morning, after spending only a few spare minutes with Roxy when the nurse called her back, Devin and Blake took her home. The smell of the fast food made her stomach churn so Devin cooked them breakfast while Blake tenderly bathed her in hot water and soft kisses in her shower. Naked and exhausted, she was tucked into bed with a tray of scrambled eggs and toast. After forcing herself to eat, the guys stripped down to their underwear and crawled into Roxy's bed with her, one on each side, and snuggled her into a cocoon of warm arms and legs. For a few short hours there was no cancer, no fear, no doubt or confusion. Nothing existed but them. She desperately needed them to make it all disappear again.

Jayne pushed from her seat, standing in awe of her best friend's inner strength for a few quiet moments before she placed a kiss on Roxy's forehead and tucked the sheet in a little more snug. "Love you, Rox," she whispered, and then gathered her purse and left the darkened room.

She held back another sob as she walked alone down the hall towards the elevators. When she reached the family waiting room, Jayne stopped at the door and watched the only two men in the room as they slept. Devin and Blake were sitting side by side, both slumped in the uncomfortable padded seats with their heads lolled to the side and resting on the heel of their hands. They had waited there with her for hours and she knew they would wait hours or even days more if she asked. The thought of leaving either of them made her heart hurt. She didn't want to think about leaving. She didn't want to think about staying. She didn't want to think about anything.

"I like it when you watch me." Her eyes darted over to Blake and his boyish, thin-lipped grin.

"Almost as much as you like watching me." Jayne pushed from the doorjamb and walked over to where they sat. She crawled into Devin's lap and met Blake's lips as he leaned in for a kiss.

"How was your visit?" Devin asked sleepily before he placed a sweet peck on her cheek. "Were you able to speak with her?"

Jayne nodded. "I…" She closed her eyes and rubbed her temples. "It hurts to think." She looked up into Devin's minty eyes, then at Blake. "Can you take me home and make me forget? Just for a little while I want to forget."

~ TWENTY FIVE ~

A violent shove off Orgasm Ridge.

Jayne stood at the mouth of the hallway that led to Roxy's bedroom and stared blankly at the darkened end as if she didn't know what to do next. Blake closed the front door behind them as Devin took her purse. She let it fall from her shoulder and walked in a daze as he guided her further down the hall and into the room.

"Would you like anything to eat?" Blake asked her. A quick shake of her head was her only reply, as it was the last three times one of them asked her.

Devin stood in front of her, Blake at her back as Devin reached for the buttons on her shirt. "What do you need, angel?" Her buttons felt small between his fingers but he managed them well enough, pushing the thin fabric over her shoulders. "Tell us what you need from us," he whispered as Blake took her shirt, pulling it down her arms as he placed an open-mouthed kiss to the top of her bared shoulder.

"I need to forget," she sighed, her head lolling to the side to give Blake's wandering lips better access. "I need you," she breathed, her arms tugging free of her long sleeves. "I need you both to make me forget."

Devin's glance found Blake's. As if they were thirds of the same whole, they moved without words to caress her clothes from her body. Piece after piece floated to the floor until she stood, skin to skin, between them. Devin cradled her face between his palms, trailing his lips along her jawline to her ear. "You're so beautiful." His cock swelled against her soft belly when the sound of her whimper graced his ears. The backs of Blake's hands grazed his chest as he reached around and palmed her breasts, the unexpected touch not distracting him in the least. Silken skin caressed his shaft, his abdomen jumping beneath her fingers as she trailed her nails over his skin down to his cock.

"Will you let him taste you?" Blake asked after her palm wrapped around Devin's cock, giving him several long, slow pulls like he'd showed her he liked. Her eyes opened slowly. Dark and lazy, they held Devin's stare as she sank to her knees in front of him.

"I want to taste him," she said, never breaking their connection. Fire scorched his skin with anticipation as she opened her mouth, watching his every emotion as she guided his cock into her mouth and surrounded him with wet-hot heat.

"Oh, damn," Devin hissed, rolling up onto the balls of his feet as she hollowed her cheeks and slowly pulled back. Fingers twisted viciously into the comforter on the bed beside him, Devin's grip drained his digits of blood. His eyes rolled closed, his head falling back as everything but the feel of his dick in her mouth disappeared. A faint thought snagged him away from the blissful fog. They were supposed to make *her* feel this way.

He reached to pull Jayne to her feet when her high-pitched moan vibrated around him. His head jerked forward, his eyes opened to see her widened eyes staring back at him. One quick glance below her showed him the reason for her sudden cry. Blake had shouldered his way between her spread knees on his back and pulled her smooth pussy against his mouth. Devin's knees nearly buckled as another sharp moan vibrated through his dick and shot straight into his balls. Heavy breath in, long breath out, he breathed through the first wave of spine tingling pleasure. Ready for more, he palmed the back of Jayne's head and nudged her forward then back again, guiding her along his shaft, drawing her in, pushing her out, over and over at a pace that drove him mad with the need to slam into her. Nostrils flared, her breath hissed over his sensitive skin as she panted in time with his thrusts. Her tongue was wild against his head, sending pulsing signals to his balls. His abs flexed hard as his balls answered her call and drew up tight, the heart of his release an imminent detonation.

"I'm almost there, angel." Wanting her to taste him, his fists clenched in her hair a split second before he released her. Neither of them had come in her mouth before and she had never offered, but he wouldn't lie and say he didn't want it. A baser, primal part of him wanted to mark every inch of her, inside and out. The very thought of it violently shoved him right up to the edge. Her palms cupped his ass and pulled him deeper into her mouth, flinging him right over into an orgasmic abyss so deep and hungry he thought his bones would snap from the force of the first spasm.

"Ahhhhh!" Thunder roared in his ears as he emptied his very soul into the woman kneeling at his feet. Spots danced in the air around him as she was pulled from his shaft, the sudden loss of her warmth sobering him as sharply as a cold shower. He looked down to see Blake grip her hips and slide her down his torso and straight onto his condom covered cock.

"Fuck, Jayne. You feel so good!" The sound of Blake's words were drowned out by the echoes of Jayne's cries. The painful bliss stretching across her face told Devin her orgasm was every bit as harsh as his. "That's it, baby. Feel me deep inside you."

"Fu…fu…fuck…ah…ah…ah—ahhhh!" Jayne screamed. Devin hit his knees and captured her scream with his mouth. His tongue darted in then plunged deep, tasting himself just as he tasted her. He knelt behind her, between Blake's extended legs and blanketed her back with his body, his fingers playing along the crack of her ass until he found the place he'd been dying to be.

"Let me inside, angel." His mouth parched, he traced a finger around her entrance, accidentally grazing Blake as he lubed his finger with her release. Blake shot him a warning look, but Devin ignored it. He would be thanking him in a few minutes. With as many women as they'd shared, Blake had never experimented with anal intercourse. They never shared a woman the way they were about to share Jayne and even though he'd just had the orgasm to end all orgasms, he felt his cock rising from the dead.

Devin's finger circled her star, pushing in ever so slightly. Jayne tensed, a breath hissing through her teeth. "Relax," Blake urged, cradling her to his chest as he glared at Devin over her shoulder. "He's only playing."

Instead of relaxing, she pushed against Devin, looking back over her shoulder at him. "I want more."

Holy mother of God he wanted more, too! His cock twitched in time with his finger. A sharp hiss pushed through her teeth again as she clamped down on him. Dammit! He needed some lube. A quick survey of his surroundings found him within arm's reach of both the bed and the nightstand beside it. With only a hope and prayer, he reached out his shaking hand and pulled the top drawer on the night stand open, sending it and all its contents crashing to the floor.

"Holy shit!" Blake said, craning his neck to see the plethora of phallic novelties littering the carpet around them. Roxy was one interesting chick.

Jayne snorted as they found themselves covered in condoms again. Devin swiveled his wrist and scooped up a bouquet of condoms and lube packets from the floor. At least he wasn't wearing a blindfold this time and could roll on his own condom. He fisted a stack of lube packets and ripped the corner off of three or four at the same time. "This will be a little cold, angel. Try to relax, okay?"

Jayne nodded and Blake cradled her to his chest. The look Blake threw him over her shoulder was one of shock mingled with a heavy dose of holy-shit-this-is-really-happening. Wicked excitement pumped through his veins. This was definitely happening. For the first time since Daphne, Devin was about to be a part of something important; something real and good. Only this time he would be an equal part, not just an extra wheel.

~*~**~*~**~*~

Jayne zeroed in on Blake's voice, coaxing her to relax as Devin slowly stretched her. Sharp, biting pain had her gritting her teeth as he added a second finger, letting her adjust for a few minutes before adding another. Seven, ten, maybe even twenty minutes crept by, their bodies writhing in a heap on the floor in a frenzy of moans as Devin's fingers moved in short scissoring thrusts. Slow thrust in, a small twist out; in and out, add more lube. Each time the pain rolled like a hungry flame through her body, burning everything out but the need for more. Blake released her mouth, throwing his head back, baring his teeth in a silent cry as Devin removed his fingers. She clenched against the void he left behind; a hollowness she was desperate to fill.

"Are you ready, angel?" he asked as he caressed her entrance with the tip of his penis in a wicked tease.

"Yes!" she hissed. "Please, Devin, hurry."

"I have to go slow. Just let me know if I hurt you or you want me to stop."

Jayne gave him a jerky nod. Edgy silence dominated the next few seconds until that first small thrust. "Ah!" The burn was sharp and hot. "Oh, God! Devin, wait!"

"Okay, angel," Devin panted. "I'm not going any further."

Any further? "How much more?"

"I'm just inside, Jayne. Once I get past this point it should feel good."

Blake cradled her face and turned her head so that he was the only thing she could see. Open lips kissed open lips, each panted breath mingling with the next. "Watch me, baby. Feel me." One of Blake's hands left her face and pushed between them. Her pelvis bucked against his when his fingers found her clit, pulling Devin off balance and sliding further inside her. "Oh, shit!" Blake's eyes squeezed together then opened wide in panic. "I can feel him!"

Sweat beaded on his forehead and soaked her fingers as she threaded them through his hair and pulled his mouth to hers.

"Mmmm-aaahhh!" Blake's fist curled in her hair, holding her head above his as they panted together through Devin's next thrust. "OhGod-ohGod-ohGod!"

"That's it, angel. That's it," Devin panted. "I'm in, Jayne. Oh my God, woman. I'm not going to last long, angel. So…Sssss-ah-ah-ah! Don't squeeze!"

"I can't…stop!" Full! She felt so full and tight and holy t-minus-orgasm she was dying. And coming. "Oh-my-God!" She was dying and coming, now!

"Look at me, Jayne. Ho…holy fuck you're gorgeous." Blake kissed her forehead, her nose, each of her eyes. "I love you." His arms banded around her back, both his hands now cradling the back of her head. "I love you so fucking much."

"I-love-you-too!" Her entire body vibrated, convulsed. "I love you!" Devin moved out, then back in. Pain was long gone, replaced by a pulsing bliss she rode like a wave.

"Oh, fuck yes!" Blake gripped her hips, hard. He held her as he and Devin convulsed in tandem inside her.

There was no rhythm or beauty to be found in the way their bodies moved together. They loved one another with a raw, visceral abandon she was certain no one would survive. As in, the entire world was in serious danger of eminent destruction. Her world was certainly being tilted on its axis. She would never be the same.

Devin stilled. Her eyelids felt heavy against her efforts to open her eyes. "I've got you, Jaynie girl." Blake's gaze was locked on Devin's as he spoke. "I've got you."

Hot breaths panted against her spine, Devin's breaths, breathing life back into her weary soul. He held himself above her, inside her, his arms shaking with his efforts. "I love you, angel."

She turned her head and he covered her mouth with his own, his kiss slow and deep, his hips pressing one last time against her as if to punctuate his claim on her. Her lungs burned for air before he pulled away, her inner muscles gripping him and Blake as he left her body and crashed to the floor beside them.

"Holy hell," she panted against Blake's chest.

"That was…"

Jayne looked up when Blake didn't finish. "Cataclysmic? Earth-shattering? Life affirming?" she said when neither of them responded to the first two.

"Different," Blake said.

"Different?" Jayne asked. "As in good different?" She looked to Devin for reassurance, but found none; only his questioning glance and a gulf of distance between them despite lying side by side. Her wildly beating heart sunk in her chest. She hadn't said it back. He'd told her again that he loved her and she hadn't said it back. Granted, his kiss hadn't given her a chance to say the words. It was almost as if he were afraid to hear them. Was that because he thought she wasn't ready, or because she was ready but still held them locked inside her despite the truth? She loved him. Why couldn't she say it? She didn't know. Her orgasm was still swimming around in her head mucking up her thoughts.

"Different as in…wow," Blake finally said, his fingers squeezing her butt cheeks as he rolled his hips beneath her. "Different as in…can we do that again?"

"Hmmm, I don't know. I'm not sure it works for me," she teased.

"Liar." Blake gave her butt a playful slap and rolled her towards Devin. The distance she'd seen in Devin's eyes was gone when he propped up onto his elbow and gave her another swift, playful kiss. Maybe she'd imagined it.

"Think we could use the bed next time?" she giggled, glancing up at the bed beside them.

"I seem to remember you begging me to take you on the floor in Vegas," Devin chuckled. "Besides, I didn't want to break tradition."

"Tradition?" Blake asked.

"Yeah," Jayne snorted. "So far none of our firsts have been in a bed." She reached over and ran her fingernails over Devin's nipple and down his abdomen, sending a rippling shockwave through his rigid muscles. "I think you have a thing for floors."

"Hey!" Devin howled. "Stop that!"

"Oh, he's ticklish!"

Devin grabbed her wrists when she reached for his sides, raising his brow in a silent warning. If he and Blake hadn't just screwed her breathless she would have offered more of a fight. Instead she gave in. She'd let them have it one of these days when they hadn't exhausted her.

"Long, hot bath?" Devin offered, threading his fingers with hers.

"And something to snack on?" she asked. She hadn't eaten much in the last few crazy days. Her stomach felt like it had just awoken from a deep hibernation and started eating itself.

"I'll see what I can find," Devin said as he and Blake stood and pulled her up with them.

"I'll get the water in the tub started," Blake kissed her forehead.

An hour later she was sitting between Devin and Blake inside the large garden tub; Blake massaging her feet in his lap as she leaned against Devin at the other end. Only the occasional sounds of the water dripping from one raised limb or the other echoed off the tiled walls as they all soaked in the sudsy water. Occasionally Blake would reach over and add more hot water, the louder sound waking her from an occasional doze.

"I want you to stay," she whispered into the lazy quiet that blanketed the room heavier than the steam from the bath.

"In New York?" Devin asked, his voice tinted with confusion.

"No," Jayne shook her head and peered into the bubbles tickling her palm. A red blush crept up her chest and colored her cheeks. She'd wanted to ask Blake before, but her courage escaped her every time she tried to capture it. Since talking with Roxy, her mind had run on overtime sifting through all the what-if's. She didn't want another day to go by without asking him.

"I want you to stay in Los Angeles," she said, looking up through her lashes to see Blake cock his head in question. "You said when the project was up and running and Devin was back that you would be going back to Vegas."

Blake's grip slid from her foot up to her ankle and tightened like a padded shackle before he pulled her from Devin's arms straight into his lap, draping her legs over his thighs. "Jaynie girl, you are sounding damn silly for such a smart woman." Her hands bracketed his sides. She loved the way these men felt; smooth skin over well-defined ridges, everywhere. His shoulders bowed against her touch when she teased his nipple with her thumbnail, garnering the same chuckle Devin gave when she did that to him. "Get this through your stubborn head, babe. You're stuck with me." The word *forever* hung in the air above the last spoken syllable, remaining unspoken.

"Does that mean you're staying in Los Angeles, too?" Devin asked, sliding to sit behind her, his smooth shaven chin resting on her shoulder. She liked his scruff, but her tender skin, previously untried by so much male attention, was extremely sensitive to the offending stubble. She told him not to shave it for her sake, but he'd done it anyways.

"Yes." She nodded. "I didn't want to—I mean—I did—I do, but—"

"You want to stay here to take care of Roxy," Devin finished for her.

Jayne nodded again, swallowing hard against the knot in her throat that threatened to choke her. "She wants me to stay in L.A. I-I-I still need to stay for a little while. At least until she's home from the hospital and can take care of herself."

"That's totally understandable, angel." Devin kissed the side of her neck, his hands finding hers beneath the bubbles. "Take as long as you need. Blake and I will manage and we'll make sure the city council understands it's only temporary."

But what if it's not? Would Devin ever forgive her if she had to leave and he lost the contract with the city and his grandfather's company? She closed her eyes, her fears remaining only a whispered warning inside her head.

Hours later her eyes opened to a dark room. Instantly aware of Devin's absence, she ran her hand over the empty space only to feel the crisp coolness of the sheets beneath her palm. She raised her head from Blake's chest. Through the moonlit darkness that hovered in the room she could see he was sound asleep. Careful not to wake him, Jayne left the bed, pulled one of their dress shirts over her shoulders with a quick button and padded down the hallway towards the grey-blue glow at the end. Devin sat at Roxy's desk, his laptop opened. The harsh light from the screen splashed across his face and naked chest, casting an ominous shadow around the room. She let the darkness in the hall hide her while she watched him. *Read, type, click. Read, type, click.* Over and over he repeated the motions. He looked so tired sitting there in the dark, squinting against the offensive light. Tired and alone.

Courage drew her from the shadows. Entranced with the promise of forever with this man, she took her first step, and then another. Her bare feet were quiet against the hardwood floor but Devin raised his head, the light from the computer screen reflecting in his eyes as he watched her approach.

When she stood beside him, he leaned against the back of his chair in silent invitation. An invitation she immediately accepted. She slid one knee beside his left thigh, the other beside his right and lowered herself into his lap. His head tilted back as his eyes roamed her face before settling on her lips. Her tongue snaked out, answering another wordless invitation. She felt him harden beneath her, his thin boxers the only barrier between them. Arousal laced through her veins. She watched in awe as his eyes darkened with desire; eyes that were also filled with love.

"You're going to break my heart," she whispered against his lips, her eyes still entranced by his.

"I won't," he answered. His hands remained on the arms of the leather-covered office chair. The muscles in his thighs ticked in rhythm with the muscles in his jaw that now boasted a few hours growth.

"Promise me," Jayne demanded.

"I promise," he said without hesitation.

Jayne's hands betrayed the knot of panic-laced excitement in her stomach as they rose to cradle Devin's face. Her fingers trembled as she threaded them through his hair at his temples. "I love you," she whispered like a secret from her soul to his and watched him absorb the three words like a thirsty drunk.

His hands broke free from the invisible ties that held them from her needy flesh. One gripped the back of her head and pulled her lips against his in a bruising kiss. The other freed his penis from his boxers then gripped her hip, pulling her down as his hips thrust up in time with his invading tongue.

The chair creaked with each inward stroke, counting the seconds of her fast approaching orgasm like a second hand on a ticking time bomb. Flashes of light from his laptop screen behind her reflected off the wall behind him, penetrating her closed eyelids as she was raised and lowered, raised and lowered, over and over until the flashes ran together like an old movie reel. The deeper he went the tighter his grip became. Their mouths pulled apart. His lips were pulled tight over his white teeth, baring them on a silent cry as he squeezed his eyes shut.

The first zing of her orgasm gripped her. Her head lolled back, exposing the long column of her neck to Devin's heated kiss. Her clit throbbed against his circling thumb. Blake's growl of release from the doorway behind her sealed her fate, giving them all a violent shove off of Orgasm Ridge.

~ TWENTY-SIX ~

A line in the sand.

Three weeks, two days and eighteen hours. That's how long it'd been since Blake left Jayne sleeping in Devin's arms at Roxy's house in New York. Thanks to a little maneuvering and political influence, Devin was able to extend Roxy's hospital stay beyond the usual three days. Blake shook his head in disbelief as he circled the lot looking for a spot to park. It was hard to believe someone was sent home only three days after having a major body part removed. He was glad Roxy was given the extra time, but that meant Jayne would be staying in New York that much longer.

While they were there they'd received several calls from the project board and the Mayor's office about some surveys missing from Blake's reports so he and Devin decided it was best that one of them fly back and investigate. Since it was his reports, he volunteered. The spy situation had been relatively quiet for weeks. They never found any clues as to who leaked Jayne's retracted resignation or the Emerald Dream supply lists. He wasn't sure if the missing reports were another attempt at sabotaging their project or the city's incompetence, but with Devin's new pass codes they were easy enough to find and re-send. They were clearly marked with the file codes in the Emerald Dream survey subfolders so he wasn't sure why Devin's temp had such a difficult time finding them. He and Devin both were desperate for Jeanette to come back from maternity leave. If he was staying on at SI he should probably be looking for his own assistant. Lisa, or Lori, or whatever her name was would *not* be in the job pool.

Devin had flown in two weeks after him for the official groundbreaking ceremony and Blake was due to pick Jayne up from LAX at three-twenty-five on the dot. He couldn't fucking wait! He'd come in early, tied up some lose ends then left the office at around ten to get everything ready for their first night together in what felt like an eternity. Honestly? He didn't know why he bothered. She would be lucky to make it out of the airport parking lot without him being inside her one way or another. He was supposed to swing by the office after he picked her up and get Devin after his four o'clock board meeting. What were the odds that they would make it out of his office without taking her on his desk, or against the window again? Or both?

Blake checked his watch for the umpteenth time that hour as he took a seat in the uptown café. Devin's temp had called him. Devin had scrambled a few minutes together and wanted to meet him for a late lunch before he took off for the airport, something about a gift for Jayne. Too worked up for a coffee, he sipped on a glass of water as he watched the door for Devin.

His phone vibrated in his pocket. He reached in and grabbed it, dread knotting in his stomach as he looked at the caller ID. Every time the damn thing rang he expected it to be Mallory. It wasn't. Thank God. It was his landlord in Vegas, probably wanting him to re-up his lease. He silenced the call, made a mental note to call him back later then re-pocketed his phone.

It had been over two weeks since Mallory had called him. His first week home from New York she'd showed up at Devin's apartment in some trashy negligée disguised under a raincoat. A raincoat, in a city that saw less than thirty days of rain a year! He never figured out how she knew he was back, unless she'd been watching the office building. She needed to get a life!

He didn't even let her in the apartment, which set her off like a firecracker. Thank heaven Devin had the forethought to have his and Jayne's names added to his security clearance roster. Devin being in New York and unlikely to answer her calls was a timely convenience, too. He told Mallory he had already told Devin all there was to tell then warned her he had filed for a restraining order against her as the security officer was escorting her from the building. Of course neither was true, yet. He would tell Devin and Jayne their dirty little secrets and be done with her once and for all. If he had to get a restraining order so be it. The bold move seemed to be working.

Ten minutes crept by, then another ten. He couldn't wait any longer or he would miss Jayne. He pushed to his feet, leaving a five on the table for the waitress who brought him the water and headed for the door. Just as he stepped onto the sidewalk someone from inside the restaurant called his name. He turned to see Jack DeVeaux, Danielle DeVeaux's father, rush to the door and spill out onto the sidewalk beside him.

"Mr. Travers! I didn't see you sitting inside. I grabbed us a table over on the other side of the bar." Devin's nemesis reached out his hand. Blake shook it out of sheer politeness and a little bit of shock.

"Excuse me?" What the hell was this guy up to? Blake flipped on his sunglasses and released the man's meaty hand. "I wasn't under the impression I was meeting you here, Jack. Am I missing something?" Why would he meet Jack DeVeaux anywhere?

"Mr. Kirk's office called and told me to meet him here. I thought…" The older man threw his thumb over his shoulder as he caught his breath. "When I saw you I just assumed you were attending the meeting. I've been trying to get him to talk to me for months. I was just so—"

"I am—I mean, I was…supposed to meet him here." Blake looked down at his watch. What the hell was Devin doing planning a lunch meeting with DeVeaux without telling him? And only an hour before Jayne's plane arrived? "I'm sorry I can't join you, Jack. I'm running late for another appointment, but Mr. Kirk should be along shortly." He shook the man's hand and then walked to his car. Maybe Devin was considering his advice to sell out to DeVeaux.

Whatever the hell was going on, God help the man if he caused him to get bumper-locked on the freeway and Jayne had to wait hours for him to pick her up. And she better wait. He didn't want to think about her in a sweaty cab with some old guy creeping on her, staring at her tits in his rearview.

Devin sat in his office shuffling through meaningless stacks of paper, thumbing idly through the contacts on his phone—ignoring the voicemail icon—anything to look busy so he didn't have to go to lunch with Mallory. His mother had already called twice, sounding 'very displeased with him' over his ignoring his sister on her birthday. Both voicemails were deleted without a return call, but apparently she wasn't giving up. The only person he wanted to see or hear from was Jayne. Damn, had it only been a week?

He'd stayed with her until Roxy came home and they had everything squared away with her radiation therapist. He would have stayed longer, but with Jeanette still on maternity leave and the ground breaking ceremony, he had to leave Jayne and fly back earlier than he'd hoped. One of the highlights of the past two weeks besides getting some alone time with Jayne was getting to know Roxy. She truly was one of the most rough around the edges, take no crap people he'd ever met. She hadn't spared him or his ego a single intrusive, foul-mouthed question. She watched his every move with a critical eye, judging him either worthy or unworthy of Jayne's affections. No matter which side of that equation he landed on, he decided she was the best kind of friend he would ever wish for Jayne to have; the kind that only wanted the best for someone they loved. The best was exactly what he was determined to give them both.

Instead of seeing the plastic surgeon who had started her initial reconstruction, Devin managed to convince Roxy to see a plastic surgeon in L.A.; one of the best in the country. While he would admit his motives weren't purely philanthropic, there were definitely perks growing up so close to the Hollywood elite. He planned on using those benefits to his advantage for a change. The sooner Roxy was in L.A., the sooner Jayne could get settled into their home.

Moving in. Just the thought of her living in his space made the corner of Devin's mouth curl up into one of those crazy-in-love, involuntary smiles. Despite their best efforts, going slow wasn't working for them. Every time Blake drew a line in the sand, one of them crossed it within hours. He had a field day busting Blake's balls over the whole asking her to move in conversation. Blake not only begged her, but he'd spent his entire second weekend back in L.A. clearing out her apartment and moving everything into Devin's penthouse by himself. Unaccustomed to the California tremors, Jayne hated living in a high rise so they would have to find other living arrangements soon. He'd already called his realtor. He didn't care where they lived as long as he could come home to her every day.

Giving up his pretenses, Devin tossed his cell onto his desk. Jayne loved him. Another smile tugged at his lips. He'd found himself wearing one goofy smile after another since she'd come back into his life. He'd known she loved him, but the next move had been Jayne's to make. And when she made a move... He reached below the desk and adjusted himself in his slacks. The animated look on Roxy's face when she'd seen the new office chair he'd bought her— and finally put the pieces together—was priceless.

"Devin!" Mallory snapped her pink-tipped fingers in his face. "Are you taking me to lunch for my birthday or not? I know the perfect little café. It's not far." The clutch that matched her nail color, shoes and belt was tucked under her arm as she stood in front of his desk. "Maybe we can invite Blake to join us."

His eyes lingered on his sister for a moment, taking in all the reasons Jayne was so different from the other women in his world. He snapped from his chair, pulling on his suit coat. On the plus side he could take the opportunity to speak to Mallory about her unhealthy preoccupation with Blake. "Blake is running some errands before he picks up Jayne from the airport this afternoon."

"Ms. Simon, you mean?" Mallory asked.

"That's mine," Devin said as he watched her pick up his cell phone and slip it into her purse.

She fished it out, studied it. "So it is," she said, handing it to him. He took it, held out his arm and waited for her to precede him to the elevator. "I never understood your affinity for using the employees' first names. Grandfather hated it, too."

"Uh, yeah, about that," Devin sighed.

Only ten minutes from SI, Devin paid the parking fee, parked the car in the parking garage around the corner from the café and got out, slamming the door with a brutal shove. *Ten minutes.* Ten fucking minutes was all he could stand of his sister's bi-polar thought process. He was crazy for letting his mother bully him into taking her to lunch. Alone. *Crazy!*

"Don't be boorish, Devin. I didn't call her a whore. I just said it's *like* she's a whore." Devin's nerves twitched beneath his skin with every click of her heels against the pavement behind him as she hurried in his footsteps. "You know, the whole Pretty Woman thing. It's kind of cute."

"Three seconds, Mallory," Devin warned. Determined to get the next hour over and done with he kept walking despite his desire to make her choke on her words. The sooner he got her to that restaurant and shoved some arugula down her throat the sooner she would shut the hell up.

"What did I say?" Mallory stumbled clumsily. Devin picked up his pace. Maybe she would give up trying to keep up and he'd lose her. She had her cell phone. *Dammit!* And the first person she'd call would be their mother.

"Why do you say things like that, Mal?" Devin stopped short and whirled around to face her, his voice echoing off the concrete garage walls. "You pretend to be obtuse but you know it's inflammatory. I know you have more class than that." Devin turned to leave but spun on his heels as more words began to spew from the freshly uncapped Mallory super-volcano. "And that's not all! You intentionally stir the pot between me and Mother. You never take responsibility for your own life or make your own decisions. And for Christ's sake, Mal, you have to stop this obsession you have with Blake. It's elementary behavior! You're twenty-four *fucking* years old. It's long past time to let it go." He wasn't ready to tell her about

Blake's part in their relationship. Not until she showed at least one sign of being able to respond with some maturity. He wouldn't subject Blake or Jayne to her brash, lewd conduct.

Instead, Mallory's shoulders bowed into a tight shrug. Her eyes filled with tears.

"Oh, shit." He folded her into his arms and she shook with a series of quiet sobs. Christ, she needed medication, therapy, *something*! "Don't cry, Mal. Let's go get something to eat and just have a nice lunch. Okay?"

Mallory nodded against his chest, pulling away from him as they walked. He dipped his head as she swiped at her eyes and a few seconds later everything appeared to be back to normal. *Medication. Definitely medication.* They rounded the corner of the block and were a dozen yards from the café when Devin looked up from the sidewalk and saw Blake exiting the café. He was just about to call out to him when a familiar looking man followed him outside. Devin froze.

"What's wrong?" Mallory asked, following his hardened gaze as they jerked to a stop. She was in mid-breath, raising her arm to wave when Devin hooked her elbow and pulled it back down.

"No, don't," he snapped. He watched in disbelief as Blake spoke to the man, looking at his watch before he smiled, giving Jack DeVeaux a friendly slap on the back and shaking his hand before they parted ways; Blake walking in the opposite direction than the way he and Mallory came and DeVeaux back into the café. *What the hell just happened?*

"Oh, no. Is that who I think it is?" Mallory squinted against the sun. Her hands tightened on his forearm, but he barely felt it. He took a step towards the café but Mallory held him back. "Devin, don't. He's not worth it. I tried to warn him. I tried to talk him out of it, but he wouldn't listen."

"Talk *who* out of *what*?" What the hell was she talking about now?

"Blake," she said, her head shaking, her lips screwed up into a condescending sneer. "He lost everything, Devin. It's all gone. He was too embarrassed to tell you."

"Gone?" He braced his hands on his knees. His entire world tilted on its axis. "What do you mean, gone?" And what the hell did that have to do with him shaking hands with DeVeaux like they were new best friends?

"Come in." Devin stood behind his desk when his office door swung open. Jayne rushed him, the feel of her in his arms and her lips against his temporarily distracting him from the nightmare that had unraveled in the last three hours.

"I've missed you so...much," Jayne said between kisses, her arms wound tight around his neck, her legs wrapped around his hips like she would never let him go. His heart raced inside his chest as he realized just how much he would miss her if he was wrong about that.

"What's this?" Blake asked, pointing to the four cardboard boxes stacked precisely atop the chair in front of Devin's desk. "You moving out?"

Betrayal. Devin had never felt so betrayed. He should have seen it. All the signs were there. Selling his house, his bike, all the phone calls he ignored and asking for his passcodes. Pushing him to sell out to DeVeaux! That one burned him the deepest.

Confronted with a fresh wave of anger, he took a heavy breath and set Jayne away from him. "No," Devin said, the anger in his bloodstream evolving into adrenaline as he stepped up to Blake, drew back his arm and punched him square in the jaw. "You're moving! Out of this building!" He hit him again. "Out of my penthouse." Another punch to his side. "And out of our lives, you lying-fucking-traitor!"

"Blake!" Jayne fell to her knees on the floor at Blake's side. "Devin, stop!"

Devin grasped her shoulders, drawing her up and away before he punched a stunned Blake in the jaw again. "And that's for getting my sister pregnant, you bastard."

"Mallory is pregnant?" Devin barely heard Jayne's question over the blood pounding in his ears. Devin shook his head. It may have happened years ago, but Mallory's words still carried the sting of a fresh cut.

"Is that what she told you?" The shock in his ex-friend's eyes proved what a skilled liar he'd become. "If Mallory is pregnant it's not mine," he said as he pushed himself from the floor.

Devin wanted to hit him again. "Why, because you haven't raped her lately? Or because you forced her to get another abortion?"

"What?" The question echoed from two different corners of his office.

"No way!" Blake shook his head and wiped at the blood on his chin with the back of his hand.

"You deny it?"

"Of course I deny it!" Blake shouted back. "I knew she would twist what happened, but this? Rape?" Blake shook his head. "Devin, you know me! I would never—"

"Devin, he wouldn't—"

"Oh, I'm just getting started, Jayne. Ask him why he's selling his father's estate?" Devin paced in slow circles, staring at the ceiling as he spoke. "Ask him why he's selling the bike he once loved more than life itself. Why he's 'giving up' his apartment." A part of him still couldn't believe Blake never once asked him for help. He could have paid whatever he owed to whoever had him by the balls in Vegas. If he had a problem, he would have gotten him help. Now? Not now. The minute he'd sent that first email to DeVeaux he'd sealed his fate as a traitor. *Every single leak.* Bile churned in Devin's stomach like ocean waves in a hurricane.

The second he returned to the office he'd called his IT team in and had every one of Blake's emails pulled. He hadn't even tried that hard to hide them, not that he could have. Three historical queries from the SI servers and the IT guys had an entire folder of stuff he'd sent to DeVeaux.

"What does any of that have to do with Mallory lying—"

"Tell her about the emails!" Devin demanded.

"Devin let him finish, ple—"

"I know, you son of bitch!" Devin's fists, thick and damaged, clenched at his sides ready to throw another punch. "Tell her about selling out to DeVeaux to pay off your gambling debts! Tell her about leaking *her* blueprints to the press."

"What?" Blake's head snapped back as he readied his next denial.

"Devin, please. I don't know what's going on, but I'm sure there's a rational explanation. Please," Jayne begged. "Mallory needs help, Devin. I've seen it! I don't know why she would lie about this but she is lying. Blake would never sabotage his own project. *Our* project."

Devin walked to his desk and picked up the legal-sized envelope his head of security gave him less than an hour before. He stared at it for a moment after he picked it up, weighing it in his palms. Eighteen years of history and friendship, hell even love, were reduced to the fifty-two pieces of paper contained within its recycled, fibrous walls. Considering how heavy his heart felt it seemed odd that everything in that envelope should weigh so little.

He tossed it across his desk to Blake, looking his traitorous friend in the eyes as he spoke. He wanted to see the truth in his eyes, even if it was only a flash it would be worth it. "Copies of all your emails to DeVeaux. You can give them to your attorney, or public defender. Either way you're going to need a lawyer."

His office door opened. Two security guards came in and collected the boxes containing the things he'd packed from Blake's office himself. He held Blake's stare, waiting, needing to see something, anything that said he was guilty, sorry, *something*! There was nothing but a false reflection of betrayal. How could someone believe their own lies so absolutely?

"Devin, please. I'm begging you." Jayne tried to step in front of one of the security officers but they stepped around her, ignoring her pleas. "There has to be an explanation."

"Jayne, don't," Blake said, still holding Devin's gaze. "I won't have you begging for me." He looked over at her, his lips curling up into a pathetic, sad smile; a ploy, no doubt, to win her trust. "If he thinks I'm capable of doing…this…" He held out the unopened envelope as if it were some foul, offensive thing. He didn't finish the sentence, just stared at the envelope in his hands.

"Devin—"

"Choose." Devin forced his eyes to Jayne. He felt his heart and his stare soften the moment his eyes landed on her angelic face. He saw his own defeat when he looked into her pleading eyes, but he had to say the words. For him and his family, his grandfather's legacy, there was no choice. "Choose, Jayne. Him or me."

The words sliced through his heart on their way out. Twin streams of tears fell from Jayne's hazel eyes. She stared at him in disbelief. Her eyes slid to Blake's and her hand flew to her mouth, covering her sob. "I can't," she said in a raspy whisper and ran from his office.

Blake tucked the envelope under his arm and followed the last security guard out of Devin's office, taking the time to close the door behind him. Not a single word was spoken in his own defense. Devin wasn't sure which hurt worse, losing his best friend, losing Jayne or losing them.

~ TWENTY-SEVEN ~

Nothing else existed but the air she needed for her next anguished cry.

Jayne knew who it was before she opened the door. Blake's blue eyes were rimmed in red and clouded with pain. The corner of his lower lip was swollen, a bruise already coloring his cheekbone. She could smell the alcohol on his breath when he pulled her from the open doorway of her apartment into his arms and crushed his lips to hers. He swallowed every one of her sobs until she simply couldn't breathe. It hurt to breathe. God, it hurt to breathe. She wanted to crawl up inside him and hide from whatever evil thing had just torn their world apart.

Cradled in his arms he closed her front door and shuffled wordlessly through the empty rooms in her apartment until he reached her bedroom. Her bed was one of the only things he'd left behind after moving her into Devin's penthouse. It was the only place she could think of to go. She had the key to Devin's place, but she couldn't face him. Not yet. Not after what he'd just done. In the span of fifteen minutes he'd taken everything away. The single bag she brought from New York was all she had left and that was still in the trunk of Blake's car.

"Did you drive here like this?" she managed to croak through the knot in her throat.

Blake shook his head. He slid her onto the bare mattress and crawled on beside her. Lying on his side, still silent, his arm constricted around her waist and he hugged her tight against his chest as she drew her knees up into hers. They laid there in the darkness, in the silence, and hurt. It hurt so badly.

She hurt more for Blake than she did for herself. She'd known. Her heart knew from the beginning Devin would make her hurt, but she never dreamed he could wound her so much, so deep. How could anyone know Blake and even think what Devin accused him of was possible? She hadn't seen what was in those emails. She didn't need to. Blake would never do the things Devin and Mallory accused him of doing. Blake's arm tightened around her when another sob broke from her chest. She'd cried all evening, but something snapped free when she felt him against her back, still strong in spite of being ripped to shreds. She knew he was being strong for her and it literally tore her apart. A single sob birthed a flood of tears until she was crying so hard nothing else existed but the air she needed for her next anguished cry.

Hours, maybe five or six later, sunlight filtered through the bare blinds in Jayne's bedroom. Sandpaper. Her eyes felt like they were lined with gritty sandpaper as she blinked them open long enough to see she was alone in the bed. Blake's dress shirt and one of the two I Heart New York sweatshirts she'd bought for Devin and Blake were draped over her arms and legs in a makeshift blanket. The scent of fresh coffee hit her nose and Jayne's stomach lurched into her throat. She threw her legs over the side of the bed and managed to make it to the bathroom sink before she lost its contents. Which wasn't much considering she hadn't had anything to eat since the business card sized bag of peanuts they gave her on the plane the day before.

"Please don't make yourself sick because of me." Jayne startled at Blake's scratchy voice beside her. She looked up at the coffee cup in Blake's hand and immediately heaved into the sink again. She didn't know what was wrong with her. Maybe she caught something on the plane. Everyone was breathing the same recycled air on those things. For hours.

"Get that away from me," she pleaded into the sink. Blake retreated and with him the bitter stench of his coffee. She wasn't much of a coffee drinker, but she couldn't remember hating it more than she did in that moment.

"What time is it?" Jayne asked a few minutes later as she sat on the edge of her mattress, questioning if the coast was clear enough for her to wander any further from the bathroom.

"Just after ten." Blake laid his hand to her forehead as he sunk down onto the mattress beside her. "I picked up some muffins if you think you can eat." The thought of putting food in her stomach made her whole body ache.

"What time did you wake up?" Her fingers curled into the sweatshirt he'd covered her with. She dragged it to her lap, pulled her heels to the edge of the mattress and hugged her knees to her chest as she stared at her single little suitcase he'd set in the corner. Devin bought that bag for her before he'd left her in New York.

"Didn't sleep." Blake's scratchy voice snapped her attention from the memory. Her eyes caressed his weary face. A deep blue swath throbbed behind the silvery-blond stubble that covered his cheek. She reached up to touch the cut on his lip but he jerked his head away.

"What happened, Blake?"

Blake twisted his fist into the palm of his other hand as he shook his head and stared blankly at the empty bedroom walls. *Dammit!* He wished he didn't have to tell her about this part of his life.

"There was this beach party down at Malaga Cove." Ignoring the hangover that still fogged his brain he pushed from the bed and began pacing the room. "Some friend of a friend's beach house. I was a junior in college; young but still old enough to know better." He stopped at the window and stared at the closed blinds as if they were opened to the world outside, seeing only the hazy events of that night so long ago that he didn't bother counting the years anymore. "I didn't care about anything back then, but getting drunk or laid. Well," he huffed. "That and watching other people get drunk and laid." Jayne stared at his back as he stared at the blinds. He could feel her eyes on him demanding the truth.

"I came off the beach where I'd spent most of the evening down at the bonfire, stumbling drunk through the crowd inside the house, looking for a place to crash. I could hear people shouting, see them in a huddle in the center of the room; probably close to fifty of them, all drunk and cheering, chanting different things. I pushed through the ring of people and made it to the center of the room where a group of guys were piled on this one chick. It was the hottest thing I'd ever seen," Blake said, his voice betraying the excitement he felt in his memory. "They rotated from orifice to orifice, one after the other. She was on her back, on the floor. I only got glimpses of her face as different guys…not that I was looking at her face." He shook his head and paced back to the bed, sliding onto the mattress beside Jayne.

"The chick was crying out, the full porn effect with pants and moans, putting on a show. It wasn't the first time I'd seen something like that—I'd been a member of the club scene since I was old enough to sign their membership contracts—but there was something about this particular scene that set me off. My entire body seized with need. I opened my fly right there and started jacking off as one guy after the other gang-banged this girl. It was hot, or I thought it was at the time. Some in the crowd stared cheering me on to finish on her. I was about to come when I saw the girl's hand raise from the floor and point to me, her index finger crooking up and down, calling me to her." His stomach churned as he remembered. "My eyes crossed as they followed the motion. When the room stopped spinning Mallory's face came into focus.

"Oh, Blake," Jayne gasped.

"I didn't touch her," Blake snapped out. "Hell, she was only sixteen years old."

"Was she drunk?"

Blake shrugged. "I don't know, probably." He was so drunk himself he honestly couldn't tell.

"She was raped and you watched?"

"No," Blake immediately denied. "It wasn't like that. She was into it, Jayne. She wasn't passed out or...or saying no. She wanted me to join in for God's sake!"

"But if she was drunk, or-or-or drugged....Blake, how do you know she—"

"Because she said as much when she asked me for money to have an abortion two months later." The words were ground out through his clenched teeth. She'd been flippant about the whole thing; flippant and desperate. "I should have fucking said no." If he'd said no, none of this would have ever happened.

Jayne's head snapped back, her eyes closing in thought. "I don't understand," she said, shaking her head. "Why did she need you to pay for an abortion?"

"Devin's grandfather still controlled her trust fund. She had no access to money of her own." Or at least that's what she'd told him at the time. He was so naïve to her manipulation back then. "She would have had to go to her grandfather or Devin to get the cash and, given the circumstances, that wasn't an option." Blake dug the heels of his hands into his eyes and twisted them repeatedly before he turned and looked at her with regretful eyes.

"I did sleep with her, Jayne. Once." He explained her eighteenth birthday wish and what happened. "I shouldn't have and I swear nothing ever came of it. I was honest and upfront with her. I told her I only wanted sex. She was fine with it and we never touched each other after that day. We flirted and even went clubbing a few times. She was young and sweet, naïve, but she wasn't always like this."

Jayne snorted. "I'm sorry, but I can't imagine her 'sweet' side."

"Something happened a few years ago," Blake shook his head. "That's when she started this creepy stalking shit. At first I played along, taking her out every once in a while, but when I wouldn't sleep with her again she began threatening to tell Devin about the beach party. Only, what she was saying was that she'd lie. Hell, I figured she would say I led her on or lied to her in some way, but rape? I never once thought she'd go this far." He took Jayne's hand and held it to his heart. "I swear to God, Jayne, I never touched her at that party, but I knew Devin wouldn't believe me. You've seen the way he defends her. He doesn't know what she's capable of."

"And what? You slept with her to keep her from crying wolf?"

"No," Blake shook his head. "I was seeing Daphne when she started the threats. I wouldn't have cheated on her." He pushed from the bed and paced to the window again, this time pulling the plastic louvers apart with his fingers and peering through them at the city below. "She stopped all the crazy stuff for a while after Daphne's funeral, but it didn't last. The phone calls started again—day and night she'd call me—and showing up at places when I was out with friends. Once, when I was out with Sydney and her girlfriend, Mallory stormed into the restaurant where we were having dinner, picked up a glass of water from the table, threw it in Sydney's face and stormed out. Her girlfriend came unglued." Blake slid down the wall onto the floor below the window. "It was right after that when I moved to Vegas. She was just one more reason not to stay."

"And now that you're back she's been doing it again?" Jayne left the bed and walked over to the window, sinking to the floor beside him. "All the phone calls you never answer, the night I saw you in the elevator…"

"I wasn't kidding when I said she was unstable, Jayne."

"Oh, I believe you," Jayne said. She told him about Mallory locking her in the ladies room at the French restaurant and Blake felt like such a shit. His stupidity and cowardice had made Jayne a target.

"Jayne." Blake reached out and pulled her into his lap, the feel of her safe in his arms giving him some comfort. "I never thought she'd come after you."

"It wasn't like that," Jayne pushed at his chest and looked up into his eyes. "I mean, she was outrageous for sure, but it was more like she was trying to warn me against you, not away from you."

"What are you saying?" Blake cupped his hands to her cheeks.

Jayne shrugged. "Think about what she said, Blake. *'It was all a game to you.'* That *'you were going to destroy another innocent life.'* It's like she blames you."

"I should have stopped those guys, I know, but—"

"No," Jayne shook her head. Looking up through her lashes she traced his swollen lip with her finger. "It's more than that." She laced her fingers with his and brought his hand to her mouth. "You need to get a restraining order, Blake. I don't know what it is but something is off." He told her about having her thrown out of Devin's building and promised to call his attorney about it.

"What about DeVeaux?" Jayne rubbed her temple. "What's in those emails?"

Blake let his head fall against the wall and he stared up at the spots of sunlight that filtered into the room from between the blind slats. "I can count on one hand the total number of times I've spoken to Jack DeVeaux, all of them in person at some function or another until yesterday. I've never sent an email to the man. Ever."

"Yesterday?" Jayne asked. "What happened yesterday?" Blake told her about running into DeVeaux at the café where he was supposed to meet Devin. "You think Devin saw you?"

"I…he could have. I wasn't exactly trying to hide anything, but that doesn't explain the emails I didn't send."

"No, it doesn't," Jayne sighed. He studied the worried look on her face as she tried to work out what he'd spent all night trying to figure out himself. It was the first time he'd really seen her since New York. Despite his non-plans to jump her the moment he got her in the car, her flight arrived late and took forever to disembark. They were late meeting Devin so he'd settled for a super sexy kiss in the parking garage elevator instead.

She'd changed somehow in the three weeks since he'd seen her. There were worry lines between her brows and her eyes were puffy from crying all night, but something about her was different; more beautiful. "Are you using a new lotion or something?"

"Oh yuck. I probably stink. I need a shower," she pushed from his lap but he pulled her back against him.

"That's not what I meant at all, babe." The cut on his lip stung when he smiled against her lips. "Ow." He winced and pulled away, the tips of his finger pressing against the cut to stop the sting. She giggled and apologized, the feel of her hands on his skin as she searched for a place to touch him that wasn't bruised made his chest hurt. He grunted against the pain in his ribs when he lifted Jayne back to the bare mattress. After three weeks he didn't care about a few bruised ribs or cuts. He needed inside her. He needed to know that despite their world being ripped apart, she was still his in some elemental way.

The pounding on the door could have only been one person. "Ignore him," Blake said, his fingers searching out the hem of Jayne's t-shirt. Her smooth skin felt so good against his palm until her hand clamped over it, stopping him just as his fingers grazed the swell of her breast.

"I can't, Blake." He looked up to see fresh tears streaming from the corners of her eyes. She bit her lip, holding his gaze as Devin unleashed another round of heavy knocks on the door.

"I'll be dammed if I'm going to let him hurt you again." Blake pushed off her and stormed to the front door.

"No," she said, stepping in front of him. "Don't hit him, Blake, please. Let me talk to him." Her palms pressed against his sternum. "Please." He nodded and she turned around, taking a deep breath before she turned the handle and opened the door.

Devin stood at the door, clean shaven, in a crisp new suit. Hovering behind Jayne, Blake glared over top of her as Devin's focus bounced between them before settling on Jayne. "I see you've made your choice."

"You son of a bitch," Blake reached for Devin but backed away when Jayne stepped between them again.

"Blake, please don't." Jayne's pleading voice burned his pride.

"Fuck it," Blake turned and stomped to the kitchen. If Devin was so set on believing he was a rapist bastard then let him believe it. He snatched up the envelope he'd picked up at his bank an hour earlier and stomped back to the front door. To his surprise Devin was still in the hallway when he returned, staring longingly at Jayne in the doorway.

"Devin, you need to hear him out. None of this...whatever Mallory is doing...is what you think."

"Here." Brushing past Jayne he held the envelope out to Devin. "It's my complete financial records for the last three years. I actually made a hell of lot of interest last month for a broke, lying rapist." When Devin wouldn't take it he shoved the evidence at his chest, pushing him away from Jayne's door. "Give that to your lawyer. Save him some time." He snaked an arm around Jayne's waist and pulled her inside. "He'll need it to calculate my defamation settlement," he said just before he slammed the door closed.

~ TWENTY-EIGHT ~

She never asked to see his ID.

Ten weeks. Jayne sat in Blake's car outside the doctor's office. The constant whir from the air blowing through the air conditioner vents somehow calmed the chaos in her mind. How could it have only been ten weeks? Seven of those weeks had been the happiest of her life. Some of them, the last three of those weeks, had been the saddest. Devin hadn't called. No texts or emails. Only silence. There was so much silence.

Blake was hurt. She understood why. She hurt. She hurt for him. Not talking to her about it wasn't helping. Other than a polite *hello* or *good morning* he eventually quit talking to anyone but his lawyers. He trusted no one, not even her.

Her apartment void of everything they needed to live, he'd moved them into a suite at the Millennium Biltmore until they could figure out what to do next. It was a nice room; an apartment really. Still, she felt homeless. Blake had replaced her wardrobe and bought her everything he thought she needed. She needed Devin. Devin was gone from her life altogether; plucked away by the roots like a discarded daisy. Only, some of those roots were still buried inside her, twisted and knotted through the very fibers of her heart. He would never be truly gone.

Blake was there, but not. He spent his time at his lawyer's office, the bar or in the hotel gym. He tried. He'd hold her when she was nauseous and suggest things like going to the movies to get her mind off *things*—aka Devin. It never worked. She spent a lot of time in her empty apartment. She'd take Blake's car and drive for hours and then end up sitting on her bedroom floor, stroking the tie Devin left with her that morning in Vegas. There was a worn spot in the threads; a spot she'd noticed the first night she took it to bed with her and tucked it beneath her pillow. She imagined it was curry sauce from the small Thai restaurant he loved so much, but it could have been anything. It was him. It was all she had left of him that wasn't tainted by betrayal. When the sun began to set she would tuck it back between her bare mattress and box spring and drive back to the empty hotel room. She slept alone most nights. She ate alone—when she ate—and she cried alone. She cried a lot. At least now she knew why.

It was time to go home. She'd done everything she could. She'd spoken to Blake's attorneys. Against their advice she'd even spoken to Jack DeVeaux. Of course he denied ever receiving any emails. He told her about his daughter. Given the new circumstances he was hoping Devin would drop the charges against Danielle. Despite how odd it was to catch two separate people supposedly sending confidential emails to the same address, Devin was never going to believe Blake. Blake didn't deserve to be trapped into raising the child of a man he'd come to hate. That same hate would eventually extend to her baby, if he didn't already harbor those feelings towards her. She still loved Devin, beyond reason. She'd seen the warning in Blake's eyes when she told him as much the last time they'd talked. Without saying the words, he was forcing her to choose. Just like Devin had. She loved them both. That would never change, but she and her baby deserved better.

Her fingers splayed in wonder over her flat belly. It was amazing how quickly everything could change with just a few words and a picture. How clear everything can become. Her heart ached when she thought about the child growing inside her never knowing, never seeing his father. Never knowing how talented he is. Never feeling his arms wrapped around them, making all the bad things in the world disappear. A shiver wracked her shoulders. *I'll never feel him again.* The cold air from the vent chilled the trail of tears that fell against her cheeks. She swiped them away and shook off the thought. This didn't have to be forever. She had time to decide what to do. A few months to figure it all out.

Her hand hovered above the gear shift when a knock on the driver's window startled her. Her head snapped around to see a man standing beside her car holding up a plastic credit card. She squinted to read it but it was too far away. She couldn't hear what the man was saying as he pointed at the card so she flipped the switch on the console and rolled down her window.

"Is this yours?"

He held it closer and she could see her name along the bottom of the card. "Yes, thank you!" She reached for it but he snagged it back.

"Sorry, ma'am. I need to see your ID and I'll also need for you to come inside and sign the release for it. I'm afraid my partner already logged it into our lost and found and well," he wiped the sweat from his brow with the back of his hand. Sweat stains circled his dark t-shirt as though he'd been outside in the hot sun all afternoon. He wasn't dressed in a security uniform, nor had he produced any sort of identification. "I don't want anyone to get in trouble because I didn't follow the rules."

Her cellphone rang. Blake's ringtone blared from her open purse on the passenger seat. She pulled the keys from the ignition and opened her door, reaching for her purse before she followed the man who held her credit card hostage. Blake was at his lawyer's again, going over some of the charges Devin had filed against him. She wanted to be packed and gone by the time he got back to the hotel room or she would have to face making the decision to leave all over again tomorrow. She was such a coward.

"Right this way." Her eyes clouded with tears again as she nodded blindly at the man's directions. Following the sound of his voice, she searched through her purse for her still ringing phone. She didn't notice the van door slide open until it was too late. Wracked with pain, her body crumbled, her muscles seizing the second the Taser's prongs made contact.

~*~**~*~**~*~

Blake's knuckles were raw from the hours he'd spent with the punching bag in the hotel gym. Each pounding blow to Devin's apartment door was felt all the way to his shoulder. "Devin, open the damn door!"

The door swung open, Devin's back already turned to him as he walked back down the hall without sparing him a greeting. "Don't gloat too long. I forgot to remove your name from the security list, a mistake I just remedied. The guards are on their way up."

"I don't give a fuck that you dropped the charges you asshole." He'd gotten the call from his lawyer earlier that afternoon. The IP addresses attached to the emails sent to DeVeaux didn't belong to any of Blake's devices—desktop, laptop or cellphone—but were still registered to SI. That meant any employee with access to a company server could have sent them. Apparently Devin didn't give a shit. "Where's Jayne?"

Devin turned on his heels and Blake saw the toll Devin's asshole moves were taking. Dark halos circled his sunken eyes. He'd lost weight—a lot of weight—and his skin looked as if it had never seen the sun. His eyes were empty. The worried tone in his voice was the only thing that held any life. "What do you mean? I thought she was with you."

Blake choked back his shock at Devin's hollowed appearance. His skin crawled as he took in all the half empty liquor bottles and stacked Thai takeout boxes littering the room. The stench reminded him of the apartment they shared in college. "She took my car this morning, like she does every morning," he said, shaking his head in disbelief. "Except she didn't come back. She's not answering her cellphone."

"I'll call Roxy," Devin said, immediately fishing his phone from his jeans pocket. "She'll know wh—"

"Roxy tried calling you three hours ago. Evidently you changed your number." Blake paced back to the front door.

"Besides, I've already tried that. She hasn't heard from Jayne in days."

"Dammit, I forgot! The security guys took my phone to—where are you going?" Devin followed him down the hall to the elevator.

"I don't know," Blake said, pushing the nickel plated button on the wall. "If she's not here I have to keep looking." He hadn't thought beyond Devin's apartment. He'd been such a dick he was sure she'd changed her mind and gone back to him.

"Let me grab a shirt and I'll drive us over to her apartment." Blake stared at the light above the elevator door, fear of losing her nullifying the hit against his pride taking Devin up on his offer cost him.

They rode in silence towards Jayne's apartment, the roads thankfully void of snarled traffic at the early evening hour. They parked on the street and sprinted up the stairs. Devin had his key out and her door unlocked before he could give it a single knock.

"Jayne!" Devin called out as he rushed through the living room into the kitchen. "Angel?"

Blake sprinted down the hall to the bedroom and switched on the lights. Nothing. The room was as bare as they'd left it weeks ago. He turned back to the hallway, his fingers flipping off the light switch only to flip it right back on as he paused in the doorway. Over his shoulder he saw the tip of something sticking out from between the mattresses. Curious, he turned back and knelt beside the bed, tugging the fine material free. A white plastic wand fell and clicked against the wooden floor as the silver patterned tie draped from his fingertips.

"What's that?" Devin appeared at his side, stooping to pick up whatever had fallen to the floor. "Hey, that's my..." Devin's voice cracked as he grabbed the pointed end and slid the long strip of fabric from Blake's fingers. "That's the tie I wore in Vegas."

"Is that what I think it is?" Blake pointed at the object in Devin's other hand. Devin flipped it over and the tiny digital screen came into view, the word 'pregnant' visible in tiny block letters inside the little square.

"Jayne is pregnant." The corner of Devin's mouth ticked up into a grin that contradicted his stunned tone.

Blake's eyes closed, his head fell back as he looked at the ceiling in disgust of his own stupidity and selfish behavior. *Pregnant. Holy shit.* He wasn't a dick. Dick didn't come close. He was a total asshole shitscum bastard. She was carrying his baby and he'd been a complete bastard to her. He'd been so screwed up and focused on his problems with Devin that he couldn't see what was so obvious and right in front of him!

"We used condoms," Devin said, still staring blankly at the pregnancy test. "A lot of them. And she said she was on birth control."

We. The word bounced around in Blake's head until it crashed violently with a random receptor and its meaning sunk in. Jayne could be carrying Devin's baby. How was it possible to feel happy, sad, fearful and elated all at the same time? He wanted to puke.

"I'll try to call her again." Devin reached into his pocket and pulled out his cell phone. He found her number in his contacts, but the call immediately went to voicemail. It was pointless, but he tried it several more times to no avail. "Where could she be?"

Blake blinked, shook his head. He was seven different kinds of totally screwed up. "I called the hospitals and the airport won't give me any info."

"What about the cops?"

Blake began to pace. "They won't respond unless it's been longer than twenty-four hours."

"We can circle the airport garage. See if your car is parked there anywhere." Blake didn't think Jayne would have left without saying goodbye, but her being pregnant changed everything. He and Devin being asshat jerks changed everything. "Come on," Devin cocked his head towards the front door. "I'll make some calls on our way to see if we can jumpstart the search for your car or something."

Silence reigned supreme once again when they were back inside the confines of Devin's car. Blake's thoughts were anything but silent. They were screaming with such violence he wished he had a way to turn them off.

"I have a bad feeling about this," Blake said, the words churning in his gut so harsh he had to let them out.

"Where was she going that she needed your car?" Devin reached up and picked a cigarette from the pack above his visor, his crutch evidently becoming a vice.

He couldn't judge. He just came off a three day drunk to find Jayne gone and not answering his calls. *And she's pregnant.* The words still didn't feel real. "I don't know," Blake sighed and stared out his passenger window at the lights in the distance just beginning to flicker on as the final rays of the sun faded. "She just drives, I think. She's been sick. I think it helps to clear her head."

"What do you mean, sick?" Both windows rolled down just a crack. Blake sucked in the cool night air as it caressed his overheated skin.

"Throwing up sick," Blake answered. "I can't get her to eat and what she does eat comes right back up. She's…"

"She's what?" Devin asked when Blake didn't finish. Blake's jaw clenched, his teeth popping and snapping under the pressure, but he still couldn't hold back the words.

"What the hell do you mean *what*? All that shit Mallory filled your head with really clogged up your common sense receptors. She's pregnant, asshole! What other kind of sick could I be talking about?"

"I didn't mean…I only wanted to know how she was doing."

"You want a play-by-play?" Blake turned in his seat so he could see Devin's face. He'd had to live with the pain and disappointment that haunted Jayne's eyes for the last three weeks. Devin should know about the pain he'd caused. "She's heartsick you stupid fuck. She goes to sleep crying. She wakes up throwing up and crying. She never smiles. She looks at me with pity instead of love. You promised her the world! You promised *me* the world and I can't deliver that! I can't give her what she wants; what I don't have! All she wants is you!"

"She chose you."

"She didn't choose!" The dashboard in Devin's Mercedes cracked beneath Blake's fist. "How many times does she have to tell you? She didn't choose me. You left!"

Blake's cell phone rang. "What?" He snapped at the property manager of his father's estate after fishing his phone from his front pocket. The last thing he needed was to deal with some BS emergency.

"I'm sorry to bother you, Mr. Travers. I was taking my after-dinner walk, doing my usual grounds check, and on my way back to the house I caught a glimpse of someone walking along the lake. Two people, actually."

Blake pinched the bridge of his nose. He was glad he was selling that place. "Did you call the police?"

"I was going to sir, but it's Mr. Kirk's sister. I didn't want—"

"Mallory is at the lake?" Blake's spine stiffened against the leather seat, his head snapping over to see Devin's face pale against the dashboard lights. "Are you sure it's her?"

"I'm positive, sir. She's driving your car." Blake's heart leapt in his chest, his heartbeat suddenly thrashing against his eardrums. *I'll kill her.* "Or, someone is, sir. It's parked on the access road behind the berm. I'm sorry if I got the wrong idea. I just thought..."

"Call the police and tell them to hurry. We're on our way." Blake dropped his cellphone in his lap, not even bothering to end the call. "Turn the car around. She's at my father's estate."

"Did you need to call the police? The least you could do is let me deal with Mallory after we find Jayne."

"Mallory has Jayne! At-my-fathers-house! Now turn the fucking car around!"

"What do you mean Mallory has Jayne?" Blake reached over and grabbed the steering wheel, pushing it to make them cut across the median. "Dammit! Are you trying to get us killed?"

"I'm trying to keep her from killing Jayne!" Blake held on as Devin's car bounced over the median into the westbound lanes. All the pieces juggled into focus all at once. Like a 3-D puzzle, the picture was so complex, yet so simple.

~ TWENTY-NINE ~

"Why does everyone assume love has anything to do with it?"

Another residual spasm gripped Jayne in the side like a fiery fist clenching and twisting the flesh beneath her ribcage. She gasped for breath as she was pushed along a dark, wooded trail. "Where are you taking me?" All of her questions had gone unanswered. She didn't expect an answer to this one, but she was desperate for a response so she kept asking.

"This way." Jayne stumbled as Mallory pushed her off the trail. It was the only two words she'd spoken since they left the van on the side of a two-lane road. She wasn't sure how far they'd traveled or in which direction. The second she was pulled inside the van Mallory tied her up and pulled a pillowcase over her head. By the time she'd worked her head free enough to see where they were going the van had stopped moving. Mallory got out and left her there alone in the van. She could hear Mallory's voice outside talking with a male she assumed was the man from the parking lot. Then more silence. And heat. The two front windows had been rolled down, but none of the fresh air made its way to the back where she laid tied and gagged on the floor. She'd managed to work her gag free or she probably would have suffocated. She tried once to sit up but her wrists were tied to some sort of cargo hold bolted to the floor of the van. Stretching her neck as far as she could, she'd been able to peer out one of the back windows long enough to see they were parked alongside a country road in the middle of nowhere. Screaming wouldn't accomplish anything.

When twilight came Mallory returned, flinging the side door open and yanking her out after cutting her lose from the floor. The cool night air felt so good against her sweaty skin. Her mouth was so dry. Her head throbbed, probably from dehydration, but that was the least of her problems. The moment her bare feet landed on the gravel Mallory shocked her with the Taser again. Her knees buckled and she hit the ground with a scream. She was going to die. Mallory was going to kill her and her baby. Apparently not before she made her march to her own death. Mallory cut the rope around her ankles then hefted Jayne to her feet, pushing her into the woods with a violent shove.

"Where is the man who was helping you?" They had been walking for what felt like hours when they reached a clearing in the woods. Jayne stumbled to a halt. Moonlight reflected off a small lake that sat in front of a massive mansion at the top of a gentle hill. She could hear the hiss of the water fountain in the middle, spewing twin geysers of water. The sound of frogs and crickets chirping was infinitely louder, drowning out all the other sounds of the woods. Almost drowning out Mallory's condescending taunt.

"Is that what you're worried about? The man who was helping me?" Mallory huffed and gave her another shove. "I liked your other questions better." Her fingers dug into Jayne's tense shoulder, guiding her along the bank. *Why are you doing this? Why did you lie to your brother?* " Her whiney, mocking voice echoed off the water beside them. "Oh, and my favorite one! *If you love Blake so much why are you ruining his life?*" Jayne stumbled over the marshy terrain. Mallory pushed her harder. "Why does everyone assume love has anything to do with it?"

"Doesn't it?" Jayne didn't know if talking to Mallory was a good idea or a bad one. She only knew she couldn't let her baby die without a fight. Her hands were tied behind her back so tight she could no longer feel them. Her shoulders ached beyond her tolerance but somehow she kept going. Even if she managed to get her hands free they would do her no good. For some reason Mallory hadn't replaced her gag. Her words were her only weapon, the only defense she had.

Mallory didn't take the bait. A strained silence fell between them as she pushed them along the bank of the lake until they reached the other side. A long dock came into view, stretching far out over the still water. Jayne refused to look at it. She stared at the mansion instead, its large darkened windows teasing her with hope that someone inside would see them.

"It's empty, in case you're wondering." Jayne couldn't stop the tears from welling in her eyes as she inched closer to hopelessness. "It's been empty since Blake's father died. Nothing but a museum of old paintings and outdated knickknacks."

Jayne's foot sunk into the mud at the edge of the lake just as they approached the mouth of the dock. Hands tethered behind her back, she couldn't stop herself from falling. She landed on her shoulder, her cheek slapping the muddy surface. Pain exploded in her ankle and clawed its way up her leg.

"Get up!"

"I know about the party," she said. It was the only thing she had left.

"Get up!" Mallory shouted again, kicking at her shoulder.

"If he raped you, why didn't you call the police?" Jayne was expecting the shock of the stun gun, but it never came. "You still can, you know? I looked it up. You have until your twenty sixth birthday to file assault charges if you were a minor."

"Shut. The. Hell. Up. You stupid bitch!" Jayne screamed when she wrenched her up from the mud. She struggled away from Mallory but fell again. "All you had to do was go away like any sane woman with a brain would have done by now. I don't want to kill you. I didn't want to kill her! All I want is for you to go away!"

Kill her? Kill who? *Oh no!* "You killed Daphne?"

Mallory snorted a wicked chuckle. "Who the hell else would kill that dimwitted whore?" Jayne couldn't think beyond her shock as Mallory wrenched her up again and shoved her towards the dock.

"I have to say, I had bigger hopes for you. I was sure you were smarter than her."

"Why?" Jayne asked, completely stunned. "If you don't want Blake, why are you doing this? Why would you kill his fiancé? Why are you going to kill me?"

When Mallory didn't answer her right away she thought she might never know until she spun Jayne around to face her. Moonlight reflected against her soulless eyes. Jayne's heart galloped inside her chest as Mallory's lips curled into a scary grin. "Don't you get it?" Jayne bit her lip and gave a nervous shake of her head. "He took everything from me; my inheritance, my happiness, my future."

Maybe she was stupid, or just didn't speak crazy. "B-B-Blake took your inheritance?" She cursed her stutter. Once it started she knew it would only get worse. She'd worked hard to control it, but she was scared and quickly losing her ability to control anything.

"Jesus Christ," Mallory mumbled. "Is there a special-order website for weak and stupid girls? Is that where he found you?" Mallory asked. "You still think this is about Blake?"

Who else?

Stun gun in hand, Mallory gave Jayne's shoulders another violent twist, turning her back towards the dock. "Blake was kind of fun for a while as I was figuring it all out." Jayne glanced over her shoulder to see her shrug carelessly. "Men with huge egos are so easily manipulated, especially those with guilty consciences. They think everything is about them. Blake has a ginormous ego and suicidal tendencies. Unfortunately, my grandfather had neither. No matter what I did to get his attention he never noticed me. He gave it all to Devin. All he cared about was his precious, perfect grandson."

"D-D-Devin?" All of this insanity was about Devin?

"D-D-D-Ding! We have a winner! I mean, don't get me wrong. I didn't want Blake to leave." A twisted giggle chirped from Mallory's lips before she sobered and cleared her throat. "I missed him more than I thought I would when he finally gave up and moved to Las Vegas. He was fun to screw with…both physically and mentally."

"Fun?" Jayne stopped, turning so fast her matted hair left muddy welts across Mallory's cheek. She'd watched the two men she loved most in the world die inside because of this woman's lies and she was having fun? How could she destroy so many lives? "You killed an innocent woman! You've ruined our lives and you c-call it *fun*? You're nothing but a sick, spoiled brat!"

Mallory's hand landed viciously against her cheek. "*That* was fun." Stinging pain blasted through Jayne's cheek and bloomed behind her eye as Mallory mocked her pain with another twisted giggle and pushed her along. "My dear brother sits on his throne at Silverland Industries, ruling mine and Mother's lives like a spoiled king, and he doesn't even want the Silverland name. Tell me. How is that fair?"

Pushing away the dizzying pain, Jayne kept her head down, ignoring Mallory's cruel poke at her stutter as she stepped up onto the mouth of the dock. Her anger fueled a new resolve to survive. "How d-did killing Blake's fiancé make it fair?" None of her psychobabble madness made any sense and Jayne didn't care to figure it out. All she wanted was to escape alive with her baby safe inside her. She didn't know what kind of harm that stun gun was doing to her baby, but it couldn't be good. She didn't know if she could take another zap and be able to walk. Her ankle already throbbed with every step. She forced herself not to panic as a desperate plan began to take shape in the midst of all the chaos. "How does k-k-killing me make it fair?" Jayne stopped walking, making Mallory push her along the boarded path. There was a railing along both sides of the dock. Climbing over it would take a lot with her hands tied, but there was a break in it about two-thirds of the way down that opened up to the water. It would give Jayne her only chance to escape before they reached the end. If she could time it just right...

"You are not listening!" Mallory shouted, giving her another push. "All I wanted was for you to go away, but you kept asking questions!" *Push.* "They always ask questions and never listen." Mallory pushed her again. Jayne lurched further down the dock with each shove. "He took my life away, so I took his! And I'll *keep* taking until *everything* is gone. His friends." *Shove.* "His family."

Shove. "His company, all of it! He doesn't get to be in love. He doesn't deserve to be happy while he's handing down his table scraps to the rest of us!"

Mallory shoved her again, hard, but this time Jayne twisted away. Mallory stumbled, her arms cartwheeling as she tried to grasp the railing. Jayne took a step backward and hip-checked her through the opening in the railing and into the water. She ran. She ran as fast as she could back towards the bank. She heard Mallory's scream of primal rage behind her but she kept running. She ran until she couldn't breathe, then she ran some more until a man stepped out of the darkness with a flashlight and banded his arms around her. She screamed. She screamed and screamed, kicking her feet against anything she could.

"It's okay! The police are on their way!"

She'd believed him before. She wasn't falling for his good guy routine again. If he was going to take her back to Mallory, or kill her himself this time, she was going out kicking and screaming. She hit the ground at the man's feet when he let her go. She kicked at his shins as she screamed louder. Her throat was on fire as she screamed and tried to get to her feet. The man was saying something as he backed away, but she couldn't hear him over her screams. Louder and louder she kept screaming until lights from approaching cars flooded the clearing. The man's unfamiliar face was revealed in the bright light. His hands were held out in a plea for her to understand.

"See? It's okay. The police are here." He held out his hand, taking a step closer as he reached for her.

The first sob broke free of the fear that gripped her chest. Jayne collapsed to the cool ground beneath her and sobbed into the night air. She was crying so hard when the first officer approached all she could say was 'my baby'. Over and over she sobbed the words. The officer cut her hands free. They were so numb when she laid them on her stomach that she couldn't feel anything. Rational thought had left her long ago and she sobbed even harder as she shifted her hands trying to feel something, anything. When the stinging pain came as the blood rushed through her veins she'd never been happier. She cried harder as the officer carried her to his patrol car and wrapped her in a blanket after he summoned an ambulance.

The emergency technicians were about to load her inside when she heard the first of her men call her name. Blake's voice boomed over the clamoring of shouted orders and police radios. A few seconds later his face appeared above her, his eyes darting from place to place like his hands.

"Jayne! I love you. God, Jayne, I love you so much. I'm so sorry. I'm so, so sorry. I love you. I love you."

Jayne slipped her hand from beneath the blanket and pulled him to her. She sobbed against his lips when his arms tunneled beneath her back and he cradled her to him. "I love you too. I love you so much."

He cradled her to his chest and she held him so tight. "Mallory," she sobbed. She tried to tell him what happened but the words wouldn't come out.

"Shh, it's okay. Devin will take care of her."

Devin? "Blake, no!" She clenched his shirt in her fists and tried to pull herself off the gurney but Blake held her wrists. "She wants t-t-to kill him! Blake, you have to stop him! You c-can't let him go near her!"

"I'm okay, angel." The sound of Devin's voice summoned a familiar ache inside her chest. When she turned her head to see Devin standing a few feet away, his hands tucked inside his pockets, the ache flared and spread like wildfire through her body. *He's okay. He's here and he's okay.* It had been nearly a month since she'd seen him. His guilty eyes dropped to the ground, then darted back to her.

"Devin." His name was spoken on another sob she couldn't contain. She reached for him, but he didn't move. She needed to feel his arms around her. She needed to feel him. When he wouldn't come to her she pushed against Blake, throwing her legs over the side of the gurney and twisting against his hold.

"Jayne. Angel, please don't." Devin was suddenly there. She grasped for him, desperately pulling him to her. A violent chill shook her body. She needed his warmth. She needed him. He buried his forehead between her breasts, his body shaking against hers, curling and molding to her as his arms constricted around her. "I'm so sorry, Jayne. So damn sorry," he sobbed, his fists clutched in her shirt at her ribcage.

Jayne palmed the sides of his face and forced him to look at her. She needed to see his face. "I love you," she sobbed. She wanted to be angry with him. She wanted to blame him for everything, for making her choose and for believing Mallory's lies. Mallory manipulated and fooled them all. She couldn't let her win. "I love you so much. Please come back to us."

Devin gathered her hands in his. His eyes held hers, clouding with his own tears. Mallory's voice echoed in the darkness and chaos that surrounded them. A few seconds later Devin and Blake turned to watch as Mallory was escorted to a police car parked at the edge of the road. Her crazed, angry glare sent chills skittering along Jayne's arms and scalp as she passed them. Her haunted eyes shifted from Jayne to Devin, then to Blake before she cast her gaze to the ground and disappeared into the darkness like a ghost.

"We need to get you loaded, ma'am," one of the emergency workers said.

The palm of her hand tingled when the prickly scruff of Devin's beard brushed against it, drawing her attention away from Mallory's disappearing form. She could see the regret in Devin's dark eyes reflecting against the kaleidoscope of flashing emergency lights and her head began to pivot back and forth on its own. He wasn't coming back.

"I have to go," he said, then placed her hand in Blake's. He and Blake shared one of their looks then Devin turned to leave.

"But, wait!" She clamored for Devin's hand, his arm, his shirt, anything she could grab ahold of. "Devin?"

"I'll follow Mallory downtown," Blake said, placing her hand back in Devin's palm. "Jayne needs you."

"I need you t-too!" she said, pleading with them both. She didn't want either of them anywhere near that crazy psycho bitch.

Blake nodded then bent over the gurney, planting a quick kiss on the tip of her nose. "I told you. You're stuck with me, Jaynie girl, even when I'm being an ass." Jayne didn't laugh. She didn't smile. There was no energy left for anything but exhausted worry. Blake's expression sobered. "We'll work it out, babe. I promise, but someone needs to talk to Mallory and find out what happened here."

Mallory is a psychotic serial killer! *That's what happened!* How did she tell them about Daphne? Blake had been right all along.

"This is on me, Blake," Devin said. "She's my sister. I need to go."

"But, Devin, she—" Devin put a hand to Jayne's chest and guided her back down to the gurney when she tried to protest. "Don't worry, angel. I'll come straight to the hospital as soon as I can." His hands were warm, so warm against her cheeks. He kissed her forehead and nose and she wanted to hold him there with her forever. "We need you to take care of our baby, Jayne." Her hands immediately covered her belly. *Their baby.* How did they know?

"Loading you up, Ms. Simon." The woman who'd initially checked her injuries nodded to her partner then shooed Devin and Blake away from the gurney. "Which one of these beefcakes is coming with you?"

"I'll be there as soon as I can, angel." Devin gave her one last kiss, nodded to Blake then stepped away as they lifted her into the ambulance. She held Devin's weary gaze until Blake stepped inside and they closed the doors behind him.

~ THIRTY ~

A clean slate.

Devin stood in the empty boardroom on the top floor of Silverland Industries looking out the picture window at the fast-paced city below. There was only one thing he would miss about SI and that was the view.

He hadn't gone to meet Blake and Jayne at the hospital after he left the Sherriff's office. How could he face them after what he'd learned? How could either of them want him in the same room? Guilt aside, it had been two in the morning before Mallory was processed through booking. He hadn't wanted to disturb Jayne so late when he knew he couldn't stay. He and their family attorney had been ushered in to see Mallory sometime after four o'clock. Hours later he fell face first onto the leather sofa in his mother's den. That was three days ago and he still felt numb. Maybe he was in shock.

The feckless, immature woman he'd always known Mallory to be was a mirage; a complete lie. Devin didn't need a psychology degree to see his sister was a cold, calculating sociopath. He shook his head and stuffed his hands deep into his pockets. He still couldn't wrap his head around it.

Mallory killed Daphne…because he loved her. She'd manipulated Blake until he had turned himself inside out and nearly killed himself and then she tried to kill Jayne. Because he loved them. Mallory was so consumed by hate he barely recognized her as he sat across the table from her inside the small room at the jail.

"One count of attempted murder and two counts murder in the first," her attorney told him before they walked into the room. Officers found a body in the lake they believed to be one of his IT guys. Apparently he was the one who sent the emails to a bogus email account that was somehow mirrored from one of Jack DeVeaux's legit addresses. He didn't understand all the technical stuff, but it was a fake account set up to make Devin believe Danielle and Blake were sending emails to DeVeaux. According to Mallory's confession, he'd also taught her how to tap into his and Blake's cellphones with easy to load spy apps. Mallory could see and hear everything they did or said; anytime. Evidently, when she no longer needed him, Mallory stabbed the guy who'd helped her and weighted him to the bottom of the lake. She hadn't even bothered to deny it.

The D.A. was adding his murder to Daphne's, both of which she'd confessed to. Hell, she'd practically bragged about it. His stomach flip-flopped as he remembered the bitterness in his sister's voice as she told them how she'd waited in the parking lot for Daphne to come out of the gym. Devin couldn't listen to anymore after that. He'd fled the room and raced to the bathroom where he vomited up his soul.

Their mother was in complete denial. She hired a new high-profile criminal attorney. They were already discussing some ludicrous 'affluenza' defense, as if she didn't know right from wrong. Although he could see where he'd been overprotective at times, he never meant to control Mallory's life or take anything from her. He loved his sister, but he would see her spend the rest of her life in a mental health institution or in prison. He would not look the other way like his mother wanted. Oh, the prestigious and always politically correct Mia Silverland would never outright ask it of him, but she expected him to turn a blind eye and ignore the obvious. Mallory was sick, but she knew the difference between right and wrong and now that he could see it he wouldn't pretend otherwise.

One of the large double doors at the head of the conference room opened and Devin turned to greet his invited guests. He stepped around the table and shook Jack DeVeaux's hand, nodding to his understandably cool daughter. "Danielle, thank you for coming." Her lips curled into a calm, friendly grin but her eyes remained cold and unforgiving.

"I'm sorry to hear about your sister," Jack said and ushered his daughter further into the room. Devin nodded again. He hadn't expected the news of Mallory's arrest to travel any slower than the rest of the world's gossip.

"Have a seat," he motioned to the chairs across the table from him as he pulled out his own. Several folders sat open on the table, the pages inside pre-marked and highlighted in all the places that required their signatures. He pushed the one closest to him across the table to Jack. "It's all there, just as we discussed."

Jack perused the top page through his bifocals. His team of attorneys had already reviewed each paged with him on their conference call the day before. Devin was selling him one hundred percent of his shares in SI along with his CFO's he'd bought out the day before, giving DeVeaux a controlling hold in SI's stock. Jack nodded and drew a pen from the breast pocket of his tailored suit coat. Devin held his breath as the tip of the pen hovered over the signature line. He glanced up to see Jack watching him instead of looking at the page.

"Are you sure you want to do this, son? I was never interested in SI. Your grandfather and I were friends."

Devin let the breath he was holding escape slowly through his pursed lips. His grandfather would be so disappointed in him, but this was as close as he could come to saving his dream from complete collapse. "That's why I want you to have it," he said, nodding at the folder in front of him. His heart would never be invested in SI the way his grandfather's was. Jack understood his grandfather's dream in ways he never could.

"I would still like to counter your offer, Devin. SI is worth far more—"

"As I said, Jack," Devin stopped him. He drew is own pen from his pocket and scribbled his signature on the front page inside the second folder. "You'll lose the Emerald Dream." As soon as the city got wind of the buyout they would pull the contract. When they did SI's stock would tank. He wanted to make sure DeVeaux had enough capital to pull it out of a nose dive and not have the employees take the hit in their checks. Some of the board members would probably be forced out but such was the business of business. Thanks to this deal they'd leave well compensated. "If you somehow manage to keep the deal then send me a check." He closed the folder, pushed it across the table to DeVeaux and watched as he signed in all the noted places.

When they were done, Devin walked them down to the elevator. In the lobby the press was gathered in complete ignorance, for once, of what they were about to announce. Before he gave the public apology to Danielle he'd promised as part of their agreement, he stopped her in the hall before they reached the elevator and apologized to her privately. She swiped at a stray tear and gave him a polite kiss on his cheek, graciously accepting his offer before they all descended to the lobby together. As cold as she'd been when they first arrived he truly hadn't expected her to accept his apology. He didn't deserve her forgiveness any more than he deserved Blake and Jayne's.

That evening Devin paced the hall outside his penthouse, afraid to open the door. Earlier that afternoon he sent Blake a text asking him and Jayne to meet him there. He hadn't been home since the night he left with Blake to look for Jayne. The pain in his gut ratcheted up a notch as he remembered the last time he saw her.

He hadn't just screwed them over. He'd twisted the love they found into the ground with the heel of his shoe until it was crushed into dust then spat on what was left. Reacting before he stopped to think had turned into more than an annoying habit. He'd almost gotten Jayne killed. He'd cost Blake months—years—of grief. Blake had been right not to tell him about Mallory's manipulation and games. He never would have believed Mallory being capable of the things she'd done had she not admitted to doing them. He and Blake would have fought and Devin would have cut him out of his life to defend his family. Mallory would have won. It hurt to think it, but it was the truth. He was completely blind to her true nature. Today, however, he'd taken the first steps to make sure that never happened again. All he had to do now was stop being a coward and open that door. He wasn't sure they were even inside. *A text.* He'd sent a lousy text. Dammit, he should have called. He should have gone to the hotel where they were staying and pounded on their door.

Driven by his own disgust, Devin twisted the key in the lock and entered his penthouse. The stench of stale beer and Thai food was gone. Fresh clean air filled his nostrils.

"Blake?" Devin called out as he tossed his keys onto his spotless kitchen counter. "Jayne? Angel? Where are you guys?" He fingered the hand towel that lay perfectly folded next to the sink as he walked through his kitchen to his den. Maybe they were on the balcony.

The balcony was vacant, as was the rest of the apartment. Devin sank to the edge of the leather sofa, carding his fingers through his hair as what was left of his world spun further into chaos. They weren't there. He'd messed up everything, lost it all, and there wasn't a damn thing he could do to get it back.

"Fuuuuuuuuuck!" he shouted into the vast, empty space. Silence quickly swallowed what little relief the outburst had given him. The new silence that now defined his life.

An abundance of long minutes passed as Devin stared out over the balcony railing, feeling like an alien in the world he'd lived in his whole life. He'd always felt it, somehow disconnected from the alternate reality where everyone else around him seemed to live. Now it was official. When he accused Blake of rape and corporate espionage then made Jayne choose between them, he'd cut them both from his life. He could never take that back. When he closed that deal with DeVeaux he'd alienated himself from everyone else in his life. His mother would never speak to him again and every other business contact would see him as a complete failure who'd run one of the most lucrative development companies into the ground. Mallory succeeded. He'd lost everything.

Devin pushed away from the railing, abandoning the darkness of the balcony to retrieve a beer from his fridge. Being so alone was far too sobering. He opened the refrigerator door to find it empty except for four longnecks sitting alone in the middle of the shelf. He was reaching in to snag one when he heard the lock on the front door turn and the sound of Blake's voice call his name. Devin froze. He stood in front of the opened refrigerator doors as the sounds of silence blessedly faded away and Blake stepped in from the foyer.

"Hey," Blake said, stopping at the threshold of the kitchen when he saw Devin.

"Hey," Devin said, blinking a couple of times to make sure he wasn't dreaming. The lonely quiet was filled with an awkward silence. Devin reached in and grabbed another beer. He held it out to Blake but Blake refused it.

"I quit."

Devin stared at him for a second, taking in his bloodshot eyes and haggard features. He tossed the extra bottle back into the fridge and closed the door before grabbing a bottle opener and popping the top on the one he'd taken out for himself. More awkward silence rose between them. What did you say to someone you fucked over? Someone who paid the ultimate price just for being your friend? *'Sorry'* didn't quite seem appropriate.

"When you called and told me about our phones being monitored, I had a security team come in and sweep all the rooms." Blake waved a hand to indicate the space around them.

"Yeah, thanks." Devin took a swig of his beer and looked around the room. "Thanks for cleaning the place up." Blake nodded. More silence. Fuck, he couldn't do this. "Where's Jayne?"

"She's not coming." Those three words struck him like a physical blow to the gut. Ten minutes earlier he'd been resigned to his fate without her. Seeing Blake had given him a sliver of hope he wasn't entitled to have.

He nodded, wishing now more than ever he'd been left alone in his ignorant bliss. The dull ache that had lived in his chest since the day he'd seen Blake talking to Jack DeVeaux suddenly flared to a hungry flame. He pressed on the aching spot with his fist but the pain refused to ease.

"Here," Blake said. A half-eaten roll of antacids rolled across the counter and spun to a stop in front of him. "They help some."

"Thanks." Devin broke off three or four chalky tablets and popped them in his mouth.

"I asked her not to come," Blake said after another long stretch of awkward silence.

Devin's eyes cut back to Blake. What did that mean? Was she okay? Was she still in Los Angeles? All questions he didn't deserve to know the answers to. Was she with Blake now and he was here to warn him away from her?

"Jesus, Devin. Don't look at me like that."

"Like what?" What did Blake want from him?

"Like a starving puppy!" Blake said. Devin *was* starving. He was starving for *her*! Anything! He would take any crumb he could get. "She's okay. The baby's okay, but dammit, she's a mess. What did you expect? It's been three days, man, and you haven't even called!"

"I couldn't." The knot in Devin's chest tightened as it moved up to his throat. "I screwed up, Blake. I screwed up bad."

"Hell, yeah you screwed up." Blake ground the heels of his hands into his eyes. "We both screwed up. I should have told you about Mallory's penchant for evil years ago."

"I wouldn't have believed you." Devin shook his head. He pushed up to sit on top of the island bar, his legs dangling over the side. "None of this was about you anyways. She…she did it all to spite me. Daphne…all of it. You lost her because of me, Blake, and I can never make that right."

"Mallory is sick, Devin. I—we—lost Daphne because of her." Blake left the wall he was leaning against and pushed himself up to sit on the counter beside Devin. "It's not your fault. For as long as I can remember, you've always tried to look out for Mallory. You can't help genetics, bro. Some people just aren't built right."

Devin nodded. He knew what Blake was saying was technically true, but that didn't excuse his own bad decisions. "I didn't have to believe her."

"No," Blake said. "You didn't. You and I will have some work to do on that front, but Jayne needs us, man. She needs us both and I need to know that you're done being an asshat before I let you just walk back into our lives."

"She still wants…" Devin couldn't finish the hopeful thought.

"She's been absolutely sick worrying about you. It's not healthy, for her or the baby." Devin choked on a half sob-half sigh of relief and Blake gave his back a hefty slap.

A baby. The reality of being a father was like trying to grip a mystic fog. No matter how hard he tried he couldn't grasp the full context of the word. "We're going to be fathers."

"Are you ready for that?" Blake asked. "I mean, sharing is no longer an option, Devin. I won't leave her."

Devin was amazed at how excited he was at the thought of having a child with Jayne. Having his best friend share that with him? "I sold SI," he blurted out, needing Blake to know just how serious he was about the part they played in his life.

"I saw that," Blake chuckled. "How the hell did you get DeVeaux to the table in three days?" Devin told him the sale price and Blake choked. "Holy shit."

"I don't care," Devin insisted. "I would have given it to him for a single buck if that's what it would have taken. Running SI was never my thing, man. You knew that. It never will be. Family has always come first," he said, his nerves still raw from all the hateful things Mallory had said to him. "But, my family changed. You and Jayne, and…our baby? You're my family now. And, if you'll still have me, I want different things for our family."

Blake took his time, considering his response carefully before he nodded. "I want different things, too. I want us to start with a clean slate, Dev."

Devin wanted that. He wanted it badly, but was it possible? How did they get from here to there? "Whatever you need. I'll do whatever it takes to get back to what we had."

Blake hopped down from the counter and paced to the other side of the kitchen. Leaning against the cabinets across from him, he unbuttoned his sleeves as he talked. "I didn't rape Mallory," he said, rolling up one sleeve, then another. "But, I did sleep with her."

Devin swallowed hard. "I know." He'd put two and two together during Mallory's initial interview with her lawyers, but he'd tuned out the details. "I'm sorry I believed her about…the other stuff. I should have never listened to her about DeVeaux, either." Devin's mind was still having a difficult time processing Mallory's true conniving nature. "She set up the meeting with DeVeaux. Lori didn't know any better when Mallory told her to call and ask you to meet us at that café."

"She manipulated the timing so you saw me with DeVeaux," Blake said, crossing his arms over his chest.

Devin nodded. "She timed it perfectly." *Happy birthday, Mallory.* She'd even gloated about the look on his face when he saw Blake walk out of that café with DeVeaux, saying it was the best birthday present he'd ever given her.

Blake gave Devin a quick nod. "You also understand there never were any gambling debts?"

Devin took a deep breath and gave Blake another nod. "That was none of my business. Besides," he shrugged, "with the deal I just cut for SI, technically I'll be the broke one soon."

Blake's lips twitched with a mocking smirk. Hands on his hips, Devin watched him push away from the cabinets, taking the two steps necessary to close the few feet of distance between them. "Then I guess there are only three more things left to settle between us."

"Name it," Devin said. He meant it. Whatever Blake needed, he would do. He didn't see Blake's fist before it hit him square in the left eye. Light exploded behind his eyelid, followed by loads of pain and two more punches to his gut. Stunned, Devin was bent over and sucking wind for a good minute before his brain caught up with him. He got it. He would take every blow. Blake owed him that. Arm stretched out, he breathlessly begged Blake for a break. Blake nodded and Devin collapsed against the counter, holding his gut. Holy hell, he couldn't breathe. Once the pain subsided enough for Devin to take a steady breath he gave Blake a nod to continue.

"We're good," Blake said and began rolling down his sleeves.

"Slate clean?" Devin asked, still bracing himself for another hit.

"Squeaky," Blake said and pulled him into a back-slapping hug.

~ THIRTY-ONE ~

One elegant promise of forever.

"Oh my—Devin, what happened?" Jayne cradled Devin's face in her palms and inspected the cut at the corner of his eye. "Blake, you p-promised me you wouldn't fight!"

"We didn't fight, angel." Devin gathered her against his chest. Her feet dangled above the floor as he held her in his arms. Jayne ignored the soreness in her ribs and soaked him in; the feel of his arms around her, the sound of his voice, the scent of his cologne and just…him. She'd missed him so much.

After IV fluids for her dehydration and another ultrasound, Jayne was cleared to go home with a few deep bruises, a clean bill of health and a follow-up appointment with her OB. When Devin didn't come to the hospital before she was discharged later that night, she began to worry. What if Mallory told more lies and Devin believed her? Blake called him, but he never answered. The fifth call went straight to voicemail and Jayne's worry turned to fear. What if Mallory managed to hurt him?

The next day Devin sent Blake a text updating him on Mallory's confession, but nothing to her. No calls, no other texts to either of them for the next two days. As the hours passed, she'd gone through a gauntlet of emotions; fear, sadness, anger. She'd been so angry. Angry at Mallory for…well everything. Angry with Devin for believing Mallory's lies, for making her choose between him and

Blake, for breaking her heart. She was angry with Blake for not being honest with his best friend.

Anger eventually gave way to sadness and more fear. So much had been lost because of Mallory's hate. She couldn't bear to lose Blake, too, but at times it seemed inevitable. At one point she'd resolved to leave again. Blake, who four days earlier couldn't stand to be in her presence, was now stuck to her like superglue. She couldn't even go pee without him hovering around the bathroom door. She talked him into picking up dinner at a diner a few blocks away the night before so she could be the coward she knew she was and sneak out of the hotel without him. She'd already called for a cab to the airport when Blake came back earlier than she expected and caught her leaving him a goodbye note. She broke down in tears and told him her due date. He was just as quick at math as Devin. It didn't take him long to figure out which one of them was the father of her baby.

He was angry at first. Really angry. Not about Devin being the father. No. He didn't understand why everyone kept expecting the worst from him. First Devin believed all those lies about him, now she believed he wouldn't love her anymore because the baby was Devin's. He was right. It was totally unfair to think of leaving him without giving him a chance. It was easier to take the choice away than to have him reject her later when it was too late to protect her baby from the same broken heart she had now. She felt so horribly guilty.

Blake promised her that he'd love her and Devin's baby no matter what happened. She believed him. That may not be true later, but she believed he meant every word he said the moment he said them. She wasn't sure if it was the pregnancy hormones or the stress, but her emotions were all over the map. She'd managed a few moments of happiness in Blake's arms before she was back to being sad.

She'd been on the brink of madness by the time Devin texted Blake asking them to meet him at his apartment tonight. She'd fought Blake at every turn when he'd asked her to stay at the hotel and let him go alone. She needed to see Devin; to look him in the eyes when he said he didn't love her anymore. Make him tell her himself he was never going to hold her again, then beg him to hold her again. Jeez, she was so screwed up. None of it mattered now that she was in his arms, shielded from all the wicked things that could have happened to them.

Blake cleared his throat and Devin loosened his hold. Jayne wasn't ready to let him go. His arms snaked away and she hissed when his fingers gripped her sides. Devin's brows furrowed in confusion before he lifted the hem of her shirt. "Son of a bitch!"

"It's not as bad as it looks," Jane said, pushing at his hands. She grabbed her shirt and tried to pull it back down, but Devin wouldn't let her.

"Not as—what the hell did she do to you?" Devin fell to his knees in front of her and stared at the deep purple splotches on her left side left by the biting sting of the Taser. "I'll kill her. So help me, God, I'll kill her."

Jayne sank to the floor in front of Devin. She moved his hand from her hip to the middle of her chest, splaying his fingers over her heart. "That doesn't hurt near as bad as this."

Devin's shoulders dropped. His eyes closed on a heavy sigh as his chin fell to his chest. "I'm so sorry, Jayne. There's nothing in my life I wish I could take back more than what I've done to you and Blake." Jayne bit her lip to try to stop the quivering sob that threatened to burst from her chest. "I can never—"

Devin's voice began to quiver and Jayne couldn't let him continue. She placed her fingers over his lips. "Do you love me?"

"Angel, please."

"Do. You. Love. Me?" Devin's eyes filled to bursting with love as he nodded silently to her question. There was no doubt in her mind he did. It was all she needed to hear from his lips; the only thing she wanted to know. There was, however, one thing she needed him to hear.

"You promised you would never break my heart, Devin." Devin's eyelids fluttered closed. His chest expanded with a shuddered breath as he nodded his acknowledgement. Her lips began to quiver again when she leaned in, replacing her fingers with her lips. Devin's sad frown parted and he kissed her back, his lips moving desperately over hers. He searched her face when she pulled away. She could see the heavy burden of guilt he harbored. His eyes pleaded for her forgiveness. "Don't ever do it again," she warned. His hand trembled when he cupped the side of her neck and pulled her to him for another kiss. "I mean it, Devin," she pulled away again and reached for Blake's hand, drawing it against her cheek. "I don't know what you expected when you asked for this, but forever is what you got." She turned her head and kissed Blake's palm, then did the same with Devin's. "I'll never choose."

Devin glanced up at Blake then back to her before he reached up and took Blake's offered hand. Blake pulled him to his feet. Devin held tight to Blake's hand when he tried to pull away. Blake's confused furrow smoothed out and his grim expression curled into a gorgeous smile as they shared one of their wordless glances she would never understand to mean anything but trouble. Together they reached for her with their other hands and helped her to her feet. Sandwiched between them, Jayne closed her eyes, leaning her head back against Blake's chest as she looked up at Devin.

"I'll never make you choose again, angel." Devin released her and Blake's hands, drawing his into the small space between their bodies. The backs of his fingers caressed her belly, his eyes momentarily drawn to the place where his baby grew inside her. Blake laced his fingers with hers and pressed her hands around Devin's. She looked down between them and gasped when she saw the opened box cupped in the very center of their joined hands. Inside the box was a single ring. Different shades of diamond bands twisted together in infinite scrolls. Her lips parted in another gasp when Blake reached into the box and plucked out the center band. It wasn't a single ring, but three separate bands that molded seamlessly together into one elegant promise of forever.

"Marry us, Jayne." Blake's whispered request was accompanied by the soft caress of his lips against her ear. She looked up to see Devin's eyes brimming over with fear and love and happiness and the same sense of awe she was sure he could see in her eyes. This was happening. This was real. She, Plain-Jayne Simon, was in love with, was happy with, was going to marry and have babies with two of the most incredible men she'd ever known. And they were in love with her. They weren't perfect. No one was perfect. She was a little scared and a lot excited. Her heart raced as Blake slipped the centerpiece of the ring onto her finger. She hadn't missed the relevance. She was the center of their world. They would always be—

"Jayne?"

"Hmm?" Her eyes darted from the ring on her finger to Devin, then up at Blake.

"You didn't answer us, angel," Devin said, dipping his knees so that he could look into her eyes.

"Oh," Jayne giggled. She held her hand in the air, mesmerized by how the diamonds changed colors. "Yes! Oh yes! But, Devin, I want to wait until Roxy is done with her radiation therapy. I can't get married without my best friend there."

"Really?" Devin stared at her for a stunned second before he cupped her face in his hands and kissed her like a man starving for her taste.

"Whenever you want, babe," Blake said. "Whatever you want, it's yours. As long as we can make it official before the baby is born."

"How long, angel?" Devin asked. His eyes darting to her belly again. "When will we know how long?" Jayne glanced up at Blake and he nodded for her to tell him. "What?" Devin asked, his voice suddenly laden with concern. "Is there something wrong?"

"I'm due in twenty-five weeks." She watched Devin's eyes as he calculated the due date in his head. "Which means I'm about thirteen weeks pregnant." She watched as he counted backward and then added in all the other pieces of her little riddle. His eyes met hers and a tiny sob hiccupped from her chest when he smiled with so much excitement and wonderment glowing in his eyes.

"You knew about this?" Devin asked, his eyes darting up to Blake behind her. Blake nodded silently, his chin rubbing against her shoulder as he wrapped his arms around her waist and drew her closer against him. Devin's smile grew wider. Butterflies fluttered inside her stomach as his hand came to rest over hers, his thumb rubbing gentle circles on her belly. Jayne's breath hitched, shuddering in and out of her parted lips as Devin's eyes brimmed with tears. "Tell me what I'm supposed to say, angel." His breath was hot against her lips. "I don't know the words to describe how I'm feeling."

"There are no words," Blake said, entwining his fingers with hers and Devin's. She tipped her head back to see the corners of his bright blue eyes crinkle with his smile.

"Tell me you love me," Jayne said turning her lips to Blake's. "Always tell me you love me."

EPILOGUE

"You don't have to do this."

Heat crept into Jayne's cheeks despite her determination not to blush. It was silly. They'd seen her give birth, for goodness sake. Well, Devin had. Blake cleaned—everything—after he passed out and the nurses kicked him out of the delivery room.

How could she be so shy about anything after that? Determined to go through with her plan, she ignored Blake's protest and her shy response and focused on getting the knot in Blake's tie to behave. If her last pregnancy was any indication of how the guys would react to this one, tonight would be the only chance she'd get to do this. The second she told them she was pregnant again, her life would be full of *shouldn't do's*, *can't do's* and *are you crazy's*. She wasn't quite ready for that again.

"There," she gave Blake's tie one final jiggle. "You look very…tan," she giggled. The days spent at the building sites in the hot Texas sun had turned his golden-tanned skin to a warm bronze. His white dress shirt practically glowed against his skin. It had been a while since she'd seen him dressed to the nines. Not since their wedding. Now that their offices were in an onsite construction trailer instead of a high rise they often opted for more casual attire. She didn't know how they did it. Two years in Dallas and she still wasn't adjusted to the hot summers. Thank goodness she was due in April. She couldn't imagine spending her last trimester in this stifling heat.

"Jaynie," Blake said, his long fingers circling her wrists. "I want this. I crave it, but only if you're comfortable." She wouldn't say she was comfortable, but she wanted to give Devin and Blake something special for their second anniversary. They'd given her so much; a son, a home near her best friend's new home, a partnership in their new business doing what she loved, not to mention all the perks of being their wife. Her life was so full and she wanted to give them something back.

"Angel, did you send the revised blueprints to the county inspector for the Henderson build?" Devin's voice preceded him into their bedroom.

"Sure did!" She and Blake stepped from their dressing closet just in time to see Roxy snatch Devin's cellphone from his hand. She powered it down and stuffed it into the back pocket of her jeans.

"I was talking to someone," Devin said, his empty hand still poised at his ear as he stared at Rox in disbelief.

"So fire me," Roxy snapped as she bounced little Dillon on her hip. "That's the beauty of owning your own business. You can do whatever the fu—uuuugh," she groaned as she caught Jayne's silent warning glare. Roxy was getting better at censoring herself around Dillon, but a stray word still slipped out here or there.

Jayne's heart swelled as she watched her best friend with her son. *Remission.* It was a word Jayne said every day in her prayers with both hope and gratitude. Jayne reached for her baby boy to say goodnight. Roxy twisted out of her reach.

"Ah-ah. You're late and Auntie Roxy is hungry. The limo is waiting. Get your butts out of here so I can order pizza and trash your house."

"Thank you for watching the little man." Blake ruffled Dillon's hair, scooping up the little Lego construction worker he'd dropped in the hallway. "Those are hard on the bare feet, buddy." Dillon giggled and snapped it from Blake's fingers.

"Wox pway." *Rox play.* Jayne fought the tears that prickled her eyes. He was growing so fast and looking more and more like Devin every second.

"Go!" Roxy said, tossing Jayne a warning glance of her own as she shooed them out of the room. She was privileged to Jayne's little secret and knew how close she was to the emotional train wreck stage of her pregnancy.

"Sweet dreams." Jayne kissed Dillon's forehead, inhaling the scent of his Super Man shampoo before she was ushered out the front door and into the waiting limo. She was sure they had a few naughty plans for the ride home, but Devin and Blake spared no expense when it came to spoiling her.

Neon lights flashed to the heavy bass beat inside the club. Her blood pulsed to the sensual rhythm as Blake and Devin escorted her deeper into the throng of people, some engaged in conversation, some engaged in very public displays of various stages of sexual gratification. All members of the private club they'd joined a few months ago. She and Blake had stumbled upon a couple having sex against their car one night. Jayne had forgotten how powerful watching could be. When Blake got home he'd taken her against their car on their driveway with a very aggressive need she hadn't experienced since before they were married. Jayne began putting together the first pieces of her plan that night. Blake needed this, and she wanted to give him what he needed.

They'd visited the club several times, but always as spectators. There was something about watching a couple make love that was very arousing, almost artful. Tonight she'd be in the thick of things and her stomach was protesting the idea with a riotous flutter.

"Want to dance?" Blake asked, catching her hips as she swayed to the rhythm. She shook her head. She wanted a drink, but that was already on her *couldn't do* list. Devin clasped her hand and her breath caught in her chest. Was it time? They'd just arrived. Maybe she should dance a little while first; loosen up a bit.

"Close your eyes, angel," Devin leaned in and spoke intimately against her ear. Blake pressed up against her back and sandwiched her between their hard bodies. A frantic heartbeat flushed her veins with adrenaline. Her eyelids fell and Devin closed the small space between them. She flinched when she felt his lips touch hers. His tongue forced her lips apart and slid long and hard against hers, his body pressing her firmly against Blake. She could feel Blake's hard length against her lower back. Devin canted his hips against her pelvis. He was as equally aroused as Blake.

"No peeking," Devin said when his lips left hers, his peppermint taste still lingering on her tongue. Something silky was pulled over her eyes, the material cool against her heated skin. She felt a touch to her chin and her head was tilted back against Blake's shoulder. Another set of lips were pressed against hers as Devin's moved to her neck. Blake's hot cinnamon flavor burst over her tongue, mingling with the taste of Devin's kiss. Peppermint fire fueled by lust and love burned away her nervousness.

Blake's hands roamed her body as his mouth consumed hers, but all too soon he pulled away with a tortured growl. "Time to go, Jaynie girl."

Devin took her by the hand and led her away from Blake. He guided her through several twists and turns, starts and stops before she was led up a small flight of stairs. The noise from the club became nothing more than a muted vibration. The sudden quiet brought her nerves back to life. She startled when Devin's hand touched her lower back.

"Easy, angel." His voice echoed in her ears, reminding her they were in a glass box. "Are you still okay with this?" Jayne nodded, her arm stretched out in front of her as Devin guided her farther into the room. Her heels clicked on the floor with each step she took. "We can stop anytime you want."

"N-no. I want to do this." She wasn't backing out now. Blake was out there somewhere, watching and waiting.

Devin stood behind her. The sound of swishing fabric told her he was removing his suit coat and tie. Each breath came harder and harder, hitching in her chest when Devin's lips skimmed along her neck. How was she going to get through this?

"Breathe, angel." She let out a long breath and Devin turned her in his arms. Just like their first night together, his feet shifted in a slow rhythm. Her arms circled his neck as she followed his lead into a slow dance. "No jazz music, but I like the blindfold look on you."

Jayne giggled. The stubble from Devin's scruffy, three day beard tickled her ear as he spoke, sending a delicious shiver skipping down her spine. "T-t-thank you," she said against his broad chest. "For being you."

Devin tilted her chin up. "No, angel. Thank you for loving me," he said before his lips claimed hers. The hot embers that always burned so deep between them flared to life. Everything melted away; the crowd that was watching them, the muted noises, her shyness. All that existed for the next few moments was Devin's wildly beating heart and the feel of his hands on her skin.

Inch by inch her clothes were peeled from her body. Cool air rushed over her exposed skin, sending another shiver to chase the others away. Devin guided her backwards until she felt the cold glass wall at her back. The sudden chill made her gasp and Devin took advantage, invading her mouth with a forceful thrust of his tongue. His hips mimicked the move, rolling hard against her pelvis and sending a flush of excitement through her core.

"I want to taste you, Jayne." Devin lifted her leg, parting her thighs for his touch. "But I need to be inside you more."

"Do it," she hissed as he pressed his fingers inside her. "I need you, too." The sound of his zipper lowering was sharp and quick, followed by the crinkling sound of a condom wrapper. "No," she panted. "I don't want anything between us."

"But, what about—"

"I'm pregnant." She hadn't wanted to tell them; not yet, but it could still be a surprise for Blake. When they'd decided to try for another baby they wanted it to be Blake's. She wasn't keen on the idea of a clinical impregnation of Blake's swimmers to ensure the child was his, so Devin agreed to wear a condom to up the odds in Blake's favor. It worked. And now she was carrying Blake's baby.

"What?"

"I'm pregnant," she giggled again. "I'm having another baby." She felt Devin's body tense against hers. He turned them away from the glass, pressing her back against something warm and solid, and breathing.

"Are you saying what I think you're saying?" Blake's deep voice poured over her like warm honey. Her insides began to shake with excitement. Where had he come from?

"I thought you were watching!"

"I was," he said as he ripped the blindfold from her eyes. Her heart expanded in her chest when she saw the tie dangling from Blake's fingers. Devin had blindfolded her with the tie he'd left with her in Vegas their first night together.

"You remembered," she gasped, rubbing the silky fabric between her fingers.

Blake cradled her face in his big hands and tipped her head back to look at him. "You're going to have a baby?"

"Uh-huh." Her head bobbed up and down in his hands. "Your baby." Blake's stunned expression made her giggle until she noticed the unfamiliar room they were in. "Hey!" Jayne peered around Devin where she'd thought she'd been standing against one of the glass walls of the club's exhibition room. There was nothing but a simple mirror. No windows or glass. "This isn't the right room!"

Devin crowded her against Blake, forcing her to face her other husband. "You didn't think we'd let all those people see our beautiful pregnant wife naked did you?"

"Ah!" Jayne covered her parted lips in surprise. "You knew! How did you know?"

An ache of arousal sparked through her stomach and skittered between her thighs when the backs of Blake's fingers caressed the underside of her tender breasts. "These," Blake whispered, the tip of his tongue snaking out to trace his lips in anticipation.

"We know every inch of your body, angel. Intimately." Devin spoke the words between leisurely placed kisses along the column of her neck. "We see the changes." Her sigh of relief mingled with a little bit of disappointment. She loved that they were so attuned to her and knew her so well, but she wanted so much to surprise them. She also wanted to give Blake what she knew he craved.

"I wanted to give you what you needed," she pouted against Blake's chest.

"I have everything I need right here, Jaynie girl." His sudden possessive grip on her hips made her gasp as he pulled her naked body into his arms and crushed his mouth to hers. God, she loved these men.

Naked. Blake was naked in seconds and dragging her with him onto the bed. His and Devin's hands caressed every inch of her fevered skin. Her hands roamed over their bodies with mirrored excitement, soaking in every ounce of their lusty need.

"Make love to me." The words were no sooner spoken and Devin was inside her. Lying on her side, he pulled her leg over his hip and pushed deep inside her. Blake swallowed her gasp with another forceful kiss, his tongue so hot and strong inside her mouth. Lost in his taste, her body writhed between her men. The quick bite of pain was gone in a breath as Blake pushed inside from behind her. The fullness she'd come to crave overpowered her desire to go slow. She needed them both and she needed them now!

"Jaynie," Blake hissed against her shoulder. "Being inside you is still the most amazing feeling in the world." His hands caged her breasts, offering them up like sacrifices to Devin's wicked mouth.

"Ah," Devin's hips snapped hard. A fierce groan clawed its way from her throat as Devin's fingers dug into her hips, pushing her down as he and Blake pushed up in tandem, filling her to the brink of pain before pushing her over the edge to ecstasy. She exhaled on a long, blissful hum as they pulled out and pushed in again. Over and over they pushed and pulled. Her body was charged with pleasure, strung so…tight.

"That's it, baby. I love you," Blake panted as the first spasms rocked her core.

"I love you, angel," Devin panted. "I'll always love you."

Her body was no longer hers. They were truly one in that very moment; one body, one soul, one fantasy come true.

THE END

D.L. loves to hear from her fans. You can find her as well as all her other Alpha-licious erotic stories at

www.dlroan.com

CPSIA information can be obtained at www.ICGtesting.com
Printed in the USA
LVOW10s0004240715

447468LV00004B/96/P